For Tab, Wilma, Rufus and Sidney.
Thanks for always being my biggest fans.

Bone Saw Serenade

A Novel
Cody J. Thompson

Black Rose Writing | Texas

First printing

ISBN: 978-1-68513-054-1
PUBLISHED BY BLACK ROSE WRITING
www.blackrosewriting.com

Printed in the United States of America
Suggested Retail Price (SRP) $22.95

Bone Saw Serenade is printed in Book Antiqua

*As a planet-friendly publisher, Black Rose Writing does its best to eliminate unnecessary waste to reduce paper usage and energy costs, while never compromising the reading experience. As a result, the final word count vs. page count may not meet common expectations.

DAWN!

THANK YOU SO MUCH!.
I REALLY HOPE YOU ENJOY!

much love,

Bone
Saw
Serenade

SAUL!

THANK you so much! I really hope you enjoy!

1

The city was abuzz on a cold and wet Friday night in Downtown Seattle. The bustling streets overflowed with young men and women as they intermingled, preparing for a night of intoxication, debauchery, or any other number of adventures that awaited. From the group of college boys boasting their significance in cargo shorts, striped polo shirts with the collars popped with enough hair product to keep a submarine hatch locked tight. All the way to the female wannabe socialites in their tight dresses, voluminous hair and heels high enough that there was no way any of them could walk comfortably, and everything in between. Each of them fighting one another for entry into the hottest clubs the city offered. Excitement oozed from their pores at the idea of filling their blood streams with enough legal poison to drop their inhibitions enough to dance the night away and allow themselves to make a few mistakes. But that was a young bucks game. Nothing Eddie VanSant and his co-workers had any intentions of taking part in. Instead, Eddie and a few of his co-workers from the Paramount Theater wrapped up their work week in a dark, dingy dive bar.

Just off the main drag of the crowded Downtown neighborhood sat the Elbow Room. A low lit bar serving potent cocktails and taps pouring a variety of craft beer. A long L-Shaped bar sat to the left of the front door, which creaked and screamed as patrons came and went. Worn out bar stools with chipped silver legs and maroon vinyl seats were shoved underneath. Just behind them sat a couple of high top tables with the same rotting stools. Beyond the high tops sat two pool tables. To the right of the entry door, three booths fashioned with wooden tables. The bench seats were so uncomfortable, patrons fought for standing room. The walls were littered with tin signs and beer logos glowing in bright neon.

Eddie VanSant was a tall, athletic man in his mid 30s. His thick, wavy, neatly styled hair accompanied a well-manicured beard. His wife, Emma, asked him frequently to shave it because, as she says, it covered up his natural good looks. But Eddie thought it made him look handsome, distinguished, yet somehow rugged. Joining Eddie at the table was Johnny Torres, a skinny, creepy guy in his late 30s and Reggie, a portly man with balding black hair. Both worked at the Paramount on the facilities crew. Also joining them was Courtney, a young good-looking girl who recently started working with the IT team. Blonde hair with black streaks had been tied up into a messy bun which burst off her head in all directions. The four co-workers crowded around one of the high top tables as they guzzled down cold pints of IPAs and sucked the marrow out of chewed chicken bones. A graveyard of empty glasses and chewed bones covered the top of the deteriorating table.

"Ah, shit," Johnny said, checking his wristwatch. "It's getting late."

"Maybe for you, old timer," Courtney said, a chicken wing held in both hands as she unabashedly tore away at the minimal meat remaining.

"Keep talking girlie," Johnny said. "I can still out drink any one of you. If I cared to prove a point."

"When do you *not* care about proving a point?" Eddie asked.

"Look at this table top, would you? I think my point *has* been proven," Johnny said with an odd sense of pride.

"What *is* your point, exactly?" Courtney asked.

"Point is, how many of these did *I* drink compared to how many *you* drank?"

"The real question is how many of these glasses did you actually *pay* for?" Eddie asked.

"Now *he* has a point," Courtney said with a cute giggle.

"Whatever," Johnny said, waving off their insults. "I would happily buy another two rounds for each of us."

"*But,*" Eddie, Courtney, and Reggie said in unison. This wasn't any of their first trips to the bar with Johnny. They always knew a "but" was coming.

"*But,*" Johnny said loudly, holding his right index finger in the air as though he was about to make an earth shattering statement. "I need to head out. I'm heading up to New Castle tonight to see my Mom. Any more of these strong beers, shit, I may have to sleep in the weeds."

"Sounds to me like he doesn't *have* the money for two more rounds," Courtney said with a wink towards Eddie. Still searching for any remaining morsel of saucy chicken on the bones.

"And that, is that," Eddie said, putting both hands up like he had just won a game show.

"They have a point, Johnny. Quit lying," Reggie said.

"How do *they* have a point, Reggie? What are you trying to say?" Johnny asked, his patience wearing thin.

"Point is, I make the same money as you," Reggie shot back.

"What does that have to do with anything?"

"On my salary, I wouldn't buy two more rounds either," Reggie fired off.

Everyone shared a quick laugh at Johnny's expense.

"Be that as it may," Johnny said, standing up from his bar stool. "I need to head out. I want to get to New Castle before it gets too awful late."

"I need to head out myself," Reggie said as he stood. "My wife has been home all day with the kids. If I don't relieve her of her duties soon, I may *join* Johnny in the weeds."

"Head out? Are you both kidding?" Eddie barked. "I still have half a beer sitting here. You can't leave a soldier behind."

"Hey, what am I a ghost?" Courtney asked.

"Yeah, you see?" Reggie asked, his hands now on Courtney's shoulders. "Your girl Court will babysit as you nurse your beer."

"Real funny," Eddie said as he lifted his glass to his lips, taking down a large gulp of beer.

"See you guys on Monday." Courtney said. "Stay out of trouble this weekend. Especially Johnny, you degenerate."

"Up yours, Court," Johnny said, lifting his right forearm into the air.

"Take care guys," Eddie said, holding his open right hand into the air as a subtle goodbye.

• • •

They watched as Johnny and Reggie left. Eddie could see through the windows that Johnny had turned left, heading down into the dark alleyway. Reggie had not followed Johnny into the darkness, choosing to make his way to the main street illuminated by street lights and teaming with people who hoped to begin their night of partying as this group retired for the night.

"Let me ask you something," Courtney said. "You and Johnny hate each other, right?"

"Why would you say that?" Eddie asked.

"I heard some things."

"We've had our issues in the past. But I think we have turned a corner on all of that bullshit."

"Didn't he push you up against a wall or something before I started working at the theater?"

"Well, I mean," Eddie said, stumbling over his words. It might have been the beer, or maybe the embarrassment. Maybe a decent mixture of both.

"Don't be so embarrassed," Courtney said with a giggle. "I'm just asking for the facts, not attacking your manhood or anything."

"My manhood?" Eddie laughed. "Yes, he pushed me up against a wall. But that was long ago. We are *very* much past all that."

"Hey, I'm not worried," she confirmed. "If he tried that on *me*? I would end his ability to have children."

"If he did that to you, *I would* end his ability to have children," Eddie said.

Just then, Courtney's cell phone, which was sitting on top of the table mixed in with the empty beer glasses and saliva drenched bones, chimed. She lifted it from the table as her eyes shot open in surprise.

"Ah, shit," she said, flicking her thumb over the screen.

"Everything OK?" Eddie asked, taking another sip of beer.

"Not really," she said. "It looks like the wifi at the theater just dropped. Dammit, I need to head back." She said, tucking her phone into the back pocket of her jeans.

"Can't you just deal with this tomorrow?" Eddie asked.

"That means our camera system dropped, too. I don't want it to be down all night," she said, standing up from her stool. "I guess this is goodbye for me. Are you ready to head out? We can walk back together."

"Nah, you go ahead," Eddie said. "I need to settle up my tab and hit the restroom."

"You sure you don't need any protection as you walk down the scary alley? Just in case *someone else* tries to put you up against a wall?"

"Very funny," Eddie said. "Get the hell outta here. I'll see you on Monday."

"Not if I see you first," Courtney yelled back as she threw the door open and exited the bar.

"I need to close out, please," Eddie said to the bartender.

The bartender retrieved Eddie's credit card and dropped it onto the bar top with a receipt. Eddie scribbled his name before pushing it back across the bar. At the end of the bar in the far back of the room were two doors with an old-fashioned jukebox sitting between them. The right with a "Men's" sign, the left with a "Women's." He entered the restroom to handle his business.

He pushed open the door leading to the alleyway. The alley was cold, dark and the fog in the air made everything damp like a wet, shaggy dog had shaken himself silly. The dampness forced all kinds of unappetizing smells up into the air from past inhabitants and visitors who had called the alley home. He continued down the path, making his way past the back of the Paramount Theater. The alley splintered off in different directions, allowing access to the main street as they cut past the various buildings making up Downtown. When he reached the edge of the theater building, he turned right. This branch of the alley spilled out into the main drag, which led to a parking garage where Eddie's car was parked. The Paramount stood tall in the damp alley, and three open dumpsters sat pushed up against the theater's exterior wall. As Eddie walked, he heard his phone chime in his jeans pocket. He pulled out the phone to see a text message from his wife, Emma. Emma had flown to San Diego that afternoon with their daughter Sophie and the incoming message was a sweet text letting him know they had arrived safely.

Having done this walk many times, he didn't look up from his phone as he walked. He passed the first dumpster, then the second, locked in on the glow of the bright screen. Just then, the enclosed alley echoed with a loud *whack* sound as Eddie's world went completely black. It was inaudible to anyone passing by as the sound was swallowed by the car noise of the busy street, loud music blaring from various clubs and too many young people hooting and hollering as they went about their business, unaware of the vicious attack that had just taken place. He fell to the ground, letting out a throaty gasp as the air flooded from his lungs. His cell phone dropped and bounced away onto the wet asphalt. Standing over Eddie's lifeless body was a man dressed head to toe in black, his face covered by black cloth. In his right hand, he held a hammer. He stepped over Eddie's limp body and picked up the phone, deleting everything Eddie had written to his wife, and tucked it into his back pocket. He then pulled a syringe from his pocket, removed the cap, and sank the needle deep into Eddie's arm. He lifted Eddie from under his arms and dragged him across the wet asphalt, dumping his body between two of the dumpsters before he turned and walked towards the street. There Eddie sat, blood gushing out of his head. He was barely breathing, clinging to the scraps of life left in his body.

2

One Month Earlier.

There's nothing like a warm cup of good coffee on a crisp, chilly Seattle morning. Not burnt to a crisp rubbish marketed en masse to the general naive public on every street corner throughout America. Shopping centers with their drive thru lines filled with gas guzzling SUVs and minivans bursting into the middle of the road. Truly an insult to the modern day coffee aficionado and an abomination on all things coffee. True coffee lovers want real coffee, prepared with care and expertise. The kind only a true coffee *artiste* can appreciate and prepare.

Like so many mornings before, Charlie Claymore, a slender, good-looking man in his mid-30s found himself at the counter of a local coffee shop. With his stylish and trendy hair combed to perfection, he waited patiently for his turn to order. He was new to the Seattle area, and after tedious rounds of research, he landed at Automatic Coffee Roasters. A locally owned shop serving up pastries, rare imported teas, and some of the best small batch roasted coffee in the area. The interior of the small coffee shop, with its stark white tile lined walls was packed with a wide array of clientele. The hipster on his laptop sipping a tiny cup of espresso. The businesswoman feverishly answering emails from the day before. The college English major with her face buried deep into Voltaire. Each patron outfitted with a set of earbuds, transporting them to a world all their own, yet somehow so similar. Clean, polished and upscale, with just a sprinkle of pretension. A coffee lover's dream if there ever was one.

"Are you ready to order?" Asked the tattooed young clerk. The sides of his head shaved real close to the scalp showcasing a big, poofy mohawk. A kid from the local community college possibly working his way through school.

"Yeah," Charlie said in contemplation of the scarce but cautiously curated menu.

Charlie finally landed on his poison for the day. "Let me get a large cold brew with light cream."

"You got it. That will be $5.75," replied the clerk.

When it comes to good coffee, you *have* to pay for it. That's the price of perfection.

"Can I get your name?" The Clerk asked.

"Charlie."

In the nature of the upsell, the Clerk continued, "Any pastries or muffins today?"

"Just the coffee, thanks," replied Charlie. He reached into his front pocket and pulled out his smartphone, which was equipped with a case which holds cash, credit cards, and any other items a minimalist need to get through the day. As he replaced his phone into his front pants pocket, he clicked the tip button. *"The kid is working his way through college,"* Charlie thought to himself. *"That extra 2 bucks will surely go a long way towards his education."*

He stepped to the side of the counter to make way for the growing line of new customers.

Charlie was born and raised in a suburb of San Diego. A quiet guy who didn't often make much of a fuss and had always been content on his own and forging his own path. The path had now led to the outskirts of Seattle, and he was excited for his new life in a new city. Growing up in San Diego, where seasons were all but non-existent, he looked forward to experiencing a real fall and a frigid winter. The constant cold and wet weather excited Charlie, as some of his favorite things were a good book and of course a world class cup of coffee. A perfect accompaniment to the Seattle weather he desired and was thoroughly enjoying. Leaving your hometown, your friends and family can be a daunting experience for most, but this didn't bother him. He was perfectly content resigning himself to a faint blip on the radar of life in a new town where he knew no one. He enjoyed the idea of leaving life's familiarities to become merely another faceless blur as the days moved around him. Friends come and friends go, and Charlie expected in due time, those new friends would surface. But even those content with their place in life can find themselves in surprising circumstances from time to time. Just then, from the back of the line, a strangely familiar voice shouted across the coffee shop.

"Charlie!?" The voice rang out, hitting his ears like the cymbal crash in an orchestra.

As though startled from a daydream, Charlie spun around to see where the voice was coming from. Although the voice had an eerily familiar tone, certainly they must recognize someone else. To his surprise, he recognized the person immediately. Standing in the back of the line was none other than Emma Goodwin. Emma Goodwin was a childhood friend of Charlie's. They had been inseparable all through their middle and high school years. Like most high school friends, Charlie and Emma had lost touch as life sped by, both going their separate ways after graduation. Charlie couldn't believe his eyes. He felt like a child who had been told Santa didn't exist, only to find the jolly fat guy sitting on his couch polishing off a plate of homemade cookies on Christmas morning.

Emma was short and wore a black skirt and matching leggings tucked into a pair of Doc Marten boots. A weathered jean jacket covered her arms and a tan scarf was wrapped loosely around her neck. Her dirty blond hair was pulled into a ponytail, just messy enough to be absolutely perfect. A handbag that had seen better days rested on her shoulder. She juggled a stack of coloring books and a plastic case of magic markers with her right arm, her left, extended towards the ground holding the hand of a little girl. *"Her daughter maybe? Is she a babysitter, or possibly a nanny?"* Charlie's head swirled with assumptions.

"Is that Emma!?" Charlie shouted across the bustling and lively coffee shop.

Charlie, with his arms open, walked to the back of the line of thirsty and dreary customers.

"I can't believe it's you!" He said as they embraced for a friendly hug.

"What are you doing here?" Emma asked.

"You mean the coffee shop or—"

"Yeah, the coffee shop of course. But, what are you doing in Seattle? I thought you were still in San Diego," she said, fighting a losing battle with the heavy handbag.

"Oh, right." Charlie replied, as they both laughed with a slight twinge of excitement that otherwise could be mistaken for nervousness. "I just moved here. I've been here for about two weeks."

"Wow, I had no idea. What a strange and small world we live in."

"Definitely did not expect to run into anyone I actually knew here. Let alone Emma Goodwin of all people. It's great to see you."

Emma shifted her handbag, which continued to slip and make its way to the floor as she held the stack of books and markers. She was fighting a title match against gravity and the championship prize was her bag. Unfortunately, gravity had won rounds 1-6, and 7 could just about call it a wrap.

"Well, it's VanSant now," she said with a sort of shrug and a nervous smile.

"Is that so?" Charlie asked.

"Yep. I did the dang thing. Got myself hitched."

"Hey, congratulations. That's great news," Charlie replied.

The coffee line continued to move forward as each guest put in their orders; A Cafe Americano and a blueberry muffin, a to-go box of hot black coffee and a stack of paper cups for an office building, and too many lattes with those little flowers drawn on top with the foam to count.

"Who do we have here?" Charlie asked with just enough innocence in his voice to capture the child's attention.

"I'm sorry," Emma said. "This is my daughter. Well, *our* daughter, Sophie. Sophie, say hi. This is your mommy's friend from high school."

Charlie knelt down to Sophie's eye level and spoke with continued innocence. Just childlike enough to insult the kid's intelligence. A crime in which all adults are guilty.

"My name's Charlie. Good to meet you!" Charlie stuck out his hand to shake Sophie's. Sophie, unsure about this stranger, grasped Emma's left hand tightly with both of hers, and hid behind Emma's legs, peaking out just enough to have eyes on him.

"It's OK Sophie. He's a friend of mommy's," Emma said. She looked back to Charlie, lowering her voice slightly, "We told her to be careful around strangers. You know, we want her to be as terrified as possible of the world around her."

The two shared a quick laugh at the obvious joking nature towards Emma's parenting.

"Who's the lucky guy who got to marry Emma Goodwin?" Charlie asked.

"His name is Eddie." Emma said with a smile. "We met as we were finishing college and got married not long after when we found out I was pregnant with Sophie, and the rest is history. Oh I have pictures. I am a mom now, of course I have pictures."

Emma frantically dug through her handbag to find her cell phone. "Where is it? UGH! This bag I swear. I am going to throw it out. Watch, I will!"

Charlie, feeling bad about the struggle with the items Emma was carrying, finally reached out, "Can I give you a hand here?"

"Thank you *so* much. I'm losing my mind," Emma said.

Emma handed the coloring books and marker case to Charlie, who promptly hoisted them under his arm for safe keeping. Emma, now with some freedom, had finally won the fight against gravity. An absolute TKO. She reached into her handbag to retrieve her cell phone.

"Here we go. Picture time!" Emma said.

She unlocked her cell phone and started shuffling through photos until she found the right one. She then pointed the screen in Charlie's direction.

"That's my Eddie. Good-looking guy, right? I did well for myself." Emma said with pride.

"Absolutely." Charlie said. "Very good-looking guy. I wish I could pull off facial hair. I don't think I have it in me," he continued.

"Nah, it isn't as good for us as it is for you men." Emma replied, squinching her eyes in disapproval.

"So, what kind of things do you and Eddie get into here in Seattle? What can a guy like me look forward to in this big, beautiful city?"

"I'm probably not the best person to ask, to be perfectly honest," Emma said as she halfway rolled her eyes.

"Oh?" Charlie asked, somewhat surprised.

"Well, you know me. I've always been a sort of, how do I say it kindly," Emma replied, searching her mind for the right word. "Well, kind of a loner, you know?"

"Right," Charlie replied with a nod.

"Besides, I'm such a homebody. I always *have* been. I don't need to be out running around all day looking for things. Especially when I have absolutely *everything* I need at home with me at all times. Isn't that right, sweetie?" Emma said, looking down and rubbing Sophie's shoulder. "With Eddie and Sophie, I mean, what can I say? My life is pretty much perfect."

"You can't complain, and who would listen. Am I right?"

"You got it, Mr. Claymore," Emma said with a bright smile. "And, I'm in contact with my family in San Diego *all* the time. Between them and my little family here, my life is pretty fulfilled."

The coffee line continued to move with Charlie, Emma and Sophie mindlessly moving along with the flow of traffic. When they finally reached the counter, the same tattooed clerk approached.

"Good morning, Ma'am. How can I help you?"

Emma briefly looked towards Charlie, and under her breath repeated, "Ma'am. Hmm." They shared a laugh.

"Can I get a medium iced coffee, no cream and no sugar and a child sized hot chocolate for the little one."

"Absolutely. Can I get your name for the drinks?" Asked the clerk.

"Yeah, it's Emma."

"Drinks will be ready at the opposite end of the counter. Sir, your drink is ready," The Clerk needed to get Charlie's attention, who had been more interested in catching up with Emma than his own drink.

"That will be $8.25, Maam," The Clerk announced.

"Those are on me, of course," Charlie said, whipping out his handy cell phone case from his pocket like Doc Holliday at the OK Corral.

Emma stepped in to stop the gesture, but it was too late. Charlie had swiped his card so quickly, it flashed across the counter in a blur.

"No, Charlie. Stop. I can get my own drinks," Emma said.

"Absolutely not. What are friends for if they can't buy a coffee and a hot chocolate on a cold Wednesday morning? Right? I want to. I'm *happy* to," Charlie insisted.

"Well, we both appreciate it. Don't we Sophie?" Emma said looking downward, almost hoping for Sophie's approval. "Thank you for the coffee," she continued.

"It's my pleasure," Charlie replied.

Holding Sophie by the hand, Emma slowly walked across the coffee shop to the end of the counter. Charlie of course followed along, hoping to continue their conversation.

Charlie jumped in, "Who would have ever thought you and I would be adults, married and having babies?"

"I Know! It's so strange." Emma then caught one subtle thing Charlie said and picked it out of the lineup of words. "What do you mean you *and* I? Charlie, did you go off and get yourself married? Don't tell me they allowed *you* to have a child!" Emma teased.

Charlie rubbed the back of his head and shifted his focus downward. "Not quite. But I *am* engaged, if you can believe it."

Emma was slightly shocked by the news, but more so happy for him, and it showed.

"Well, well, well. Someone went and made an honest man of you?" Emma, with a closed fist, playfully hit Charlie in his left shoulder. "Well, I'm happy for you Charlie. What's her name? Tell me about her."

"Like you, I too am now an avid photo collector of life moments," he told her, removing his phone from his pants pocket.

Charlie opened his cell phone and began flipping through pictures. He showed the screen towards Emma revealing a photo of himself and his Fiance, Gwen on a ski trip. Gwen, a thin, gorgeous woman with features like a model and a body to match, stood next to Charlie in snow gear, thick black hair flowing from under a snow cap. She was holding up her left hand showcasing an engagement band.

"Wow, Charlie. She is gorgeous. How did you two meet? And what did you threaten her with to say yes?" Emma asked.

"She was bartending, making extra money as she went through college. She was working to get her degree in marketing. That's actually what brought us to Seattle, she got offered the job of her dreams, and I picked up and came along."

Charlie continued, "At the time, I was a college lush and she was a bartender. So it was a match made in heaven. And once she realized she could find someone better than me, I had the ring and I popped the question in the snow and here we are. Now we're here, living in Seattle, and somehow, I am standing in a coffee shop talking to Emma Goodwin. I mean, Vansant, I apologize. Could take me a while to get used to that."

Emma waved him off. "Don't be, it's fine. I forget half the time myself."

From behind the counter, another coffee shop clerk yelled out, "Emma! Coffee and hot chocolate ready to go!"

Emma, eyes wide, smiled anxiously at Charlie. "Well, I guess that's me," she said, reaching first for the hot chocolate and handing it to Sophie. She knelt down slightly as Sophie gripped the warm cup.

"Now, be careful with this," Emma insisted. "Last thing I need today, her to spill hot chocolate all over the car. Again!"

Charlie responded nervously, because he didn't quite know any other way. "Right. I totally get that."

"Well Mr Claymore. It was so great seeing you. Congratulations again on your engagement. I am so happy for you," Emma said. "Unfortunately, I need to get going. I need to drop this little monster at school before I get a call from the principal for being late again. Look, why don't I give you my number and we can connect again soon? Maybe get a double date going?"

Charlie retrieved his phone once again before entering Emma's number into his contacts.

"There, I sent you a text. Now you have my number too," Charlie said.

"Great. Now we are text buddies!" Emma said.

"Absolutely. I, for one, could not be more excited. I don't know that I have ever had a text buddy before."

"Well, get ready. I am a *great* text buddy. I send the best memes. Prepare to laugh your ass off, Mr. Claymore," Emma said as she reached her arm out yet again to hit Charlie on the shoulder. "Don't be a stranger, OK? And thanks for the drinks. I owe you one."

"Don't mention it." He said.

"Goodbye, Charlie. It was great seeing you," Emma said before turning to leave the coffee shop.

"See you soon, Emma. See you very soon," Charlie said under his breath.

He reached for his iced coffee, the cup now crying with condensation from sitting unattended. He popped a paper straw inside and took one long sip. He waited a few moments, moved towards the door and stepped into the crisp, Seattle morning air.

3

Charlie waited a week before reaching out to Emma. He hadn't heard from her, but it wasn't as though he expected some magical connection from the chance encounter, and of course he didn't think any flickering flame would automatically flare up again. It had been well over a decade since they had spoken, let alone seen each other. If there ever was a flame burning between them back in high school, it had long been snuffed out. The charred remains of what ifs had been plowed long ago to make way for shopping malls and condominiums. New lives built on top of the burnt and devastated failure of what Charlie once thought could have been. *"Look at yourself,"* Charlie thought. *"She's married, she knows I am engaged."* His mind raced with what ifs and if onlys. Would he seem overly eager if he were to reach out *too* soon? He was a new guy in a new city, which was home to an old friend. It only made sense to reconnect and rekindle a friendship with someone who clearly meant a lot to him. *"I told her about Gwen, and she gushed about Eddie,"* Charlie thought. *"What's the harm? She's an old friend! It would be insane not to see each other again."* He finally psyched himself up enough to reach for his phone.

"Hey, old friend! It's Charlie. How are you? No, that's no good," he thought to himself. He shuffled his phone in his hands for a

few moments, pondering the right words to send. *"What's the big deal?"* He asked himself. *"It's not a date. It's an old friend. Come on Charlie, get it together,"* He thought as a flood of words bounced around in his head.

"Emma, it's Charlie. Hope your week is going well. Wondering if you might want to get together for coffee. Hope to talk soon." He pressed send. It was done. Now, the wait begins.

Enough time had passed allowing Charlie to go about his daily routine and forget all about the text he sent. A light breakfast followed by a short run around his new neighborhood, then a quick shower. He loved running in the mornings in this new town. It was cold and misty and Charlie could wear his long sleeve activewear, something seen as a luxury after the warm and often humid mornings in San Diego. The fresh air and the smell of the trees offered almost a cleansing of the soul each morning. All your sins from the day before could be washed away in the name of exercise. He had just settled in on the couch with a protein shake when he heard his phone vibrate from across the room. He made his way across the dining room to the kitchen counter where his phone had been set to charge. When he picked it up, he saw it was a text from Emma.

"Hey, old friend!" The text started. *"Wow,"* Charlie thought to himself. *"We are more alike than I even remembered."* He went on reading.

"Coffee sounds great. I will talk to Eddie to see what day works. Maybe Saturday, since Eddie won't have to work. I hope Gwen can come. We both want to meet her."

He pondered what to say back for a moment and kept it short and sweet. No need to go to great depths about a cup of coffee on a Saturday morning.

"That sounds great. Saturday is perfect. I'll talk to Gwen. Let me know if Saturday is a go and we will be there." He pressed send.

4

The week had sped by as the sun now rose over Saturday morning. Charlie got up early, as he always did, and followed his morning routine. He was a routine oriented guy who didn't like when things were out of place. Precisely what led Charlie to feeling some anxiety over the upcoming coffee get together - the unknown. He ate a light breakfast of a couple eggs and lightly buttered toast, followed by a brisk morning run through the trees.

Charlie ran longer that morning than days before. He ran faster and harder, pushing himself to the extreme for what purpose, he wasn't sure. He kept running, faster and faster. Breathing heavily, his heart racing in his chest. Running deeper into the trees than he had ever been until he reached a drop off. He barely saw the cliff coming before he dug his heels into the wet dirt, causing him to slide towards an unknown fate. He reached out with his arms, locking on to a tree as he fell backwards onto the cold, wet forest floor. As he sat and caught his breath, he stared blankly out across the cut out of the forest. Down below, a beautiful stream flowed undisturbed. Large, sharp rocks lined the edges of the stream as the water trickled past, bringing sticks, leaves and other debris along with its steady current. He remained there a while, letting the cool morning air wash over him and cleanse his spirit. He laid down on the wet dirt and stared intently up at the tall trees towards the cloudy, gray sky. *"When I die, I would like to die in a place like this,"* he thought. The light, calming sound of a moving stream, birds singing their morning songs harmonizing perfectly with the distant sound of wildlife moving all around him.

Charlie always wondered why we, as people, enjoyed the sound of wildlife. From camping to sleep tapes filled with the sound of wildlife. He found it strange as human beings, we find comfort and a sense of calm in the chaos of nature. The sound of a hawk screeching as it circles in the sky above was a predator stalking its prey, readying for the attack of a helpless, innocent squirrel, field mouse or a cute little bunny rabbit. He understood in the animal kingdom, that is how things worked. He accepted this. But he was never quite sure how humans can find calm within chaos. He knew deep down, he was no different. He wondered the same thing about fishing. So many people find relaxation in catching fish. Dragging a living thing from its natural habitat with a steel hook and laughing, slamming together cans of cheap, piss flavored beer taking snapshots with each other as the fish fought for its life, gasping for air in absolute terror. Charlie found fishing ultimately appalling. He laid on the cold, wet forest floor contemplating the human condition until he was disgusted with himself.

Charlie pulled himself up with the assistance of a nearby tree. He brushed the mud and leaves from his running outfit before taking a deep breath and heading out of the forest. He needed to get ready to meet Emma and Eddie for coffee. He knew there would be plenty of time another day to save the fish and bunny rabbits. After a long, hot shower he began overthinking his wardrobe choices before he gave in and threw on an outfit. Dark gray jeans, fitted nicely to his athletic body, a fresh plain white t-shirt and a jet black bomber jacket wrapped his torso like it was made specifically for him. He threw on a pair of designer work boots and pulled the legs down to cover the tops. He rubbed a little pomade through his black hair styling it just perfect. Once he got to the coffee shop, he would explain to Emma and Eddie why Gwen couldn't make it. He didn't feel the need to let them know ahead of time, out of fear they might cancel. He had psyched himself up for this and wasn't willing to risk it. He was locked in, and couldn't wait to see Emma.

Emma had chosen the location, Cafe Fortuna. A quaint coffee shop and eatery serving specialty coffee drinks, quick and easy to eat breakfast foods and at lunch, a mixed menu of handmade sandwiches and salads. It was a place Eddie frequented with friends for a quick pick me up during the work day when they could escape the office and hold business meetings over lattes and cappuccinos. Charlie parked his car right at the entryway to the cafe. He wanted to scope the place out before he made his big entrance. Cafe Fortuna was just like Emma had described. An old world brick building with a red tile roof showcasing a modern Spanish design. Mismatched couches, old tables and chairs that didn't fit any particular style graced the moderately small interior of the cafe. Large openings stretched floor to ceiling creating makeshift entryways for patrons and employees to walk back and forth between the patio and serving counter. The counter sat to the right just inside, and an old-world register one may assume was only for display was still in use. A repurposed glass display case to the right of the entrance was filled with pastries, cakes and other baked goods. The patio, which was clearly the preferred seating spot for those looking to socialize with its red brick floor, was lined by a small brick wall separating the seating area from the parking lot. Metal chairs had been positioned in circle formations around strategically placed fire pits. Each one was turned on to battle the chilly Seattle morning. In the center of the patio was a large two tier ornate fountain dripping water slowly, calming the spirits of those getting themselves hyped on caffeinated drinks. A yin and yang design tactic, maybe.

There sat Emma in front of the fountain. Her hair pulled back in a loose ponytail just like he had always remembered her. The same worn out denim jacket wrapped her torso atop a dark blue hoodie and the hood was pulled out of the top of the jacket as it fell down from the back of her neck. She sat low in the chair with both feet up on the lip of the trickling fountain as she held her hands to her mouth, blowing into them to keep warm. Charlie entered the patio behind Emma. She hadn't noticed Charlie arrive until he grabbed the back of the chair sitting next to her and pulled it out with a quick motion.

"This seat taken?" Charlie asked.

Emma looked up at him with a large smile. "Hey, stranger. Come here often?" She played along.

It was impossible for him to hide the fact he had come alone. On the flip side, Charlie noticed Emma was alone as well. *"Was Eddie in the bathroom? Was he running late?"* Charlie was endlessly curious, but not to sound overly excited she was in fact alone, he decided not to mention either of their absences.

"Having a good morning so far?" Emma asked.

"Absolutely. I went for a nice run, had a little breakfast. Can't complain," Charlie said.

"Did you save me any?" Emma asked with a slight sniffle in her nose. Clearly the cold weather of Seattle kept her with a lingering head cold. Some people never fully acclimate to cold weather, especially those from sunny San Diego. Notoriously wimpy when it comes to even the most timid of chilly climates.

"If you want some old eggs and hardened toast crust, sure. But how about I get you a coffee and a breakfast sandwich instead?"

"That sounds much better, thank you," Emma replied. "But I think I owe you for the coffee. What would you like?" She stood up to place an order.

Charlie promptly stopped her. "Absolutely not," he insisted. "This is on me."

"You're too sweet, Charlie. Some things never change I guess. You were always such a sweet friend."

"Not even. What would you like?" he asked, standing up and straightening his slick bomber jacket.

Emma pondered the options momentarily.

"I'll have a latte. Too cold this morning for anything iced, I think I want something hot. Oh!" Emma chimed in with excitement. "Get a couple of their spinach and egg white breakfast sandwiches. They're amazing!" Emma gushed over the sandwiches as though they were the best food item in the city. Charlie wasn't the least bit hungry, but in an attempt to not be rude he decided he would eat one.

He made his way into the Cafe passing the glass deli case filled with perfectly crafted pastries, wraps and cookies. He glanced for a moment at the menu board hanging against the wall which was tattered with flyers, stickers and posters promoting concerts from years gone by.

"What can we get for you today?" Asked the Cafe employee. A young girl covered in tattoos with large ear plugs and a nose piercing like a bull.

Wasting no time Charlie placed their order. There was no need to make it difficult or extravagant. "Two lattes and two spinach egg white breakfast sandwiches, please," he recited as he removed his phone from his pocket.

"That will be 16 dollars even," said the Cafe worker.

"Do you accept cards?" Charlie asked.

"Of course," the employee assured him.

"Cool, cool. I saw this old register and wasn't sure," he explained.

"That's original to the building and it still works. So, we figured why not use it? It's a cool piece, right?" The Cafe girl beamed at the idea of a working antique into which she could help breathe new life. "Not everyone appreciates history. This register tells a story, and I enjoy adding new chapters."

"I like that you kept the story going. Unfortunately I won't be adding to that history today. Card payment it is."

The Cafe girl laughed before showing him where to swipe his card for the drinks and sandwiches. He added on a tip to make it an even $20.

"Where are you sitting? I'll bring everything out to you," the Cafe girl assured.

"They are for me and the girl outside, sitting by the fountain."

"OK. It will only be a few minutes."

Charlie thanked her and made his way outside to Emma. He couldn't shake the idea Eddie was not there. She didn't seem concerned either, as she asked for one latte and one sandwich, clearly she wasn't preparing an order for when he might arrive. He wondered if he should inquire about the situation. He didn't want to seem excited at the idea of them being alone, but he didn't want to appear careless either. He would also need to explain why Gwen hadn't come.

"They said sorry, they won't serve you here. I guess you made a bad impression last time you came in," Charlie joked as he took his seat.

Emma without skipping a beat hit back, "Well, then they shouldn't have even allowed you inside the joint."

They shared a laugh together as Charlie fell back into the uncomfortable, metal chair.

"No, they said it will be a few minutes. They'll bring it out to us," he assured.

"Great. I'm in no hurry," Emma said.

They remained silent for a moment, Charlie, hands on his knees staring into the fountain. Emma, still cold, continued to breathe into her hands to keep warm. The silence felt like an eternity. *"Don't be so awkward,"* he told himself. *"This is an old friend, why can't we have a conversation,"* he continued to nag. He decided he better clear the air about both of their significant others not being present. Someone had to address it he thought, might as well be him.

"Will Eddie be joining us?" He asked, caution trembling in his voice.

"No he couldn't make it after all. He got pulled into a meeting super last minute. He said to tell you he was sorry, and he hopes to meet you soon."

A little weight lifted from Charlie's shoulders. Now, he hoped Gwen not being with him wouldn't seem so odd.

"Speaking of, where is your fiance? Gwen?" Emma asked.

"Ah, yes. Gwen." Charlie said with a deep breath. "She got called away on business and had to go out of town."

"That's a bummer. I was looking forward to meeting her," Emma said.

"She was excited to meet you, too." Charlie said. "You know how it is with a new job. She has to take on all the shitty projects. The company she works for has offices all around the country so she got pulled away to Houston. They have a big event happening down there, so it's partly on-the-job training. You know, trial by fire. Run before you walk is their motto."

"Oh well, next time then," Emma said, clearly fine with the fact their party of four was now a party of two.

"So, tell me about Eddie. What's he like, what does he do?" Charlie asked.

"He's a little older than us," Emma said with a quick roll of the eyes. "He's an Events Manager for the Paramount. It's a cool historic Theatre in Seattle. He does a lot of the booking for their concerts and live performances."

"That sounds like a hip job," Charlie said.

"Yeah!" Emma said, sharing the same enthusiasm. "They're working on booking this new hip group from New York who are on their first United States tour, and they had some things that needed to be finalized."

"Who is the band, or group? Anyone I have heard of?" As a music fan, Charlie was legitimately interested in what Eddie might have been doing, and which band he might have been currently wooing at the theater.

"It's some new up-and-coming folk band, The uh, Wolves of West Chester," she said, followed by a slight sick face expression.

"I'll have to check them out," Charlie said.

"I wouldn't," Emma told him. "Unless you are into that sort of, trendy, hipster folk music. You know, the guys who wear a ton of scarves and play ukuleles and sing high school level poetry."

"Sounds like you get to go to a lot of live events because of him. That has to be a big perk."

"Yeah, sometimes," Emma said, with another loud sniffle. Her little nose, red from the cold.

"I'm sorry, would you like to move inside?" Charlie asked.

She shook off his suggestion. "No, I know I look cold but I enjoy it. Anyway, when the coffee comes it will help warm me up. OH!" Emma took her feet off the edge of the fountain, slamming them into the old, cracked red brick floor while pounding both her fists into her thighs with excitement.

"Speaking of cold, does *this* look familiar?" She grabbed the collars of her denim jacket, thrusting them open to reveal the hooded sweatshirt underneath. It was large, too large for a girl of Emma's size.

The dark blue sweater, like her denim jacket, was old and worn. It was well past its prime and had clearly seen better days. The threading for the top right of the pocket pouch had torn away and the remaining flap hung with a sort of sadness in the cold weather. Like a forgotten billboard in the desert sun, remnants of what once was a Blink 182 logo screen printed on the front clung to the fabric, trying with all its might to tell the world it existed.

"Oh my god, is that—" Charlie found himself speechless. His eyes wide open with a mix of surprise, excitement with just a bit of flattery sprinkled in for good measure. "Is that *my* old hoodie?"

Emma's grin stretched a mile wide. She knew wearing this would bring a reaction, good or bad. The former, clearly, being much more preferred. It had worked as Charlie was overjoyed at the revelation.

"It sure is," Emma said with confidence. "You remember? I stole this from you when we were what, 15 years old?" She fell back into her chair with laughter, clapping her hands as she moved.

"I wouldn't say you stole it as much as I let you borrow it, and you decided to never give it back," Charlie reminded her.

"Well, it's more fun for me to think I stole it."

"Whatever gets you by." Charlie went on, "I can't believe you still have it."

"Of course. It's still so comfy and warm. It's my favorite sweater, I wear it all the time," Emma admitted.

This oddly pleased Charlie. To know after all this time, someone that meant so much to him had found comfort in a small piece of him for so many years.

"Well, I am speechless Emma," Charlie gushed.

"Good, I'm glad," Emma told him. "But don't think you are getting it back. I *am* keeping it, you know?"

"I wouldn't even consider asking for it back. It's in its right place."

Finally, the lattes and breakfast sandwiches were on their way out.

"Here we go," the Cafe employee said as she handed each of them their drinks and food from a serving tray. "Is there anything else I can get you?" She handed them each a stack of napkins.

"No, I think we're good. But thank you," Emma assured.

"Okay, enjoy!" The Cafe girl floated away back behind the service counter.

"Take a bite and tell me that isn't the best breakfast sandwich you've ever had," Emma pushed.

Charlie lifted the sandwich to his mouth and took one large bite. He understood why Emma enjoyed the sandwich, but wasn't all too impressed. Still, he played along.

"Wow, that *is* something else. I'll have to remember this place. It's nice to know about good spots in a new town," Charlie said knowing full well he would never forget this day.

The city continued to buzz around them as they sat, ate, sipped and chatted the morning away. One latte turned to 3 as they spoke of the past, discussing their lives since they had last seen each other, gushing about their significant others and sharing laugh after laugh. It was as though no time had passed since they had last seen one another. Everything was different, yet somehow exactly the same.

"I have *always* wondered," Charlie said, looking up at the sky like he was loading a joke shotgun with a punchline bullet. "Are there cows in heaven, and if so, can a guy get a nice pair of leather boots?"

Emma fell forward in her chair, bending over as some of her latte shot out of her mouth to the dark red brick floor.

"Charlie, come on!" Emma shouted through the laughter.

"No really, think about it. If there are cows in heaven, which, I believe there would be. Of course, it only makes sense. Could you buy a suede jacket for a nice dinner? Would God allow that to happen? I say no way!"

Emma was now in a full belly laugh keeled over with her hands on the edge of the fountain. Ecstatic, Charlie found himself locked into the back of his steel mesh chair, laughing hysterically as his face pointed up at the gray, cloudy sky.

"Oh boy, Charlie," Emma said through the laughter and tears. "You've always made me laugh. I missed you."

Charlie was tickled at the admission. The day had melted away as they drank and laughed and told stories. Just then, Emma's phone buzzed in her handbag. She ruffled through, and scrolled to read the incoming message.

"Everything OK?" Charlie asked.

"Oh yeah, of course. It's Eddie. He is asking how coffee went and letting me know he will be home shortly."

Emma typed away on her phone for a moment, pressed send and dropped it back into her messy handbag.

"What time does Eddie normally get home?" Charlie asked.

"He usually comes home around 3 in the afternoon. I am usually not there because I have to pick up Sophie from school. It's no big deal. Normal day for us parents. Speaking of time, I should probably get going. It's already after 2 and I need to pick Sophie up from her friend's house and get her home."

"I understand. I couldn't drink another latte if I tried. Anymore caffeine and I may end up flying home," Charlie joked.

With a big, deep sigh Emma said, "Same here."

They both got up from their seats, Charlie motioned with his right arm to allow her to walk out in front of him, and he followed close behind.

"It was great to see you, Charlie. We should really do this again. Next time, you'll meet Eddie. And I really hope to meet Gwen. When does she come back into town?"

"She should be back in a week," Charlie admitted.

"A full week trip? Wow, that is a long time to be gone."

"They have a lot of work to do. But I'm used to it. Besides, I'm a big boy. I can handle myself alone."

"Yeah, right," Emma mocked.

Not wanting to leave another encounter up to chance, or having to wait for more text exchanges, Charlie thought now would be the wise time to push for another set of plans.

"So, when *can* we do this again?" He asked cautiously.

"I don't know. Let me talk to Eddie, see what we have going on in the next few weeks. How about I text you and we can figure something out?"

His plan had failed, but at least it wasn't completely dead in the water.

Emma leaned in for a friendly hug and after a short moment of embrace, she pulled away, said she would be in contact sometime soon and turned to walk away. And just like that, Emma was gone. Charlie was overjoyed with the meeting, the joking, the catching up and most of all, seeing Emma. He looked forward to not only hearing from her, but seeing her again. Soon, he hoped. Soon, he reassured himself. Soon, he was absolutely certain.

5

Charlie's phone rang early on a Tuesday morning. He took his time walking across the room to answer the call as the chances of it being important were slim. He picked up his cell and glanced at the screen as caller ID showed it was Emma. His reaction time quickly went from zero to sixty, full speed ahead to pick up the call. Her voice sounded rushed and panicked. She spoke as though an unknown fault line residing in her throat had just burst to life, making her words shake and tremble so fiercely that Rome itself would have crumbled from the turbulence.

"What is the matter? Are you OK?" Charlie responded with concern in his voice.

"It's Eddie." She said as though Eddie's name was lodged in her throat and began choking the breath out of her.

Charlie sat down before he spoke again. This conversation sounded heavy and he worried his knees might buckle at the weight of her words.

"Slow down, Emma," He said, trying to calm her cracking nerves. "What's going on?"

"Eddie is missing!" Emma revealed as she burst into tears. "Last Friday he texted me that he was on his way home from work. I left the house to pick up Sophie and we came back home and he wasn't here, so we left for the airport. I was taking Sophie to San Diego to see my parents for the weekend," Emma explained.

"By the time we landed, I called and he didn't answer. I thought very little of it, but Saturday nothing, Sunday nothing. I had cooked up his favorite dish and left it in the refrigerator so he had plenty of dinner for the weekend and when I got home yesterday afternoon, the container had not been touched. I've tried calling him over and over and over again—" Emma was in a downward spiral and her voice was becoming harder and harder to understand. She stopped momentarily to take a long breath. Through the phone Charlie could hear her lungs burst once the air hit them, as the barrage of words blasted through the phone.

She continued, "He hasn't picked up his phone, he hasn't called home, he hasn't *been* home."

"Slow down, Emma," Charlie said, trying to calm her explosive nerves. "When was the last time you spoke to him?"

"It's been days!" Emma shouted.

Charlie's heart sank. He couldn't believe what he was hearing, and couldn't begin to understand how she must be feeling. Terror, shock, the horrible feeling of being alone.

"Did you call the police?" Charlie asked.

"No, not yet. I didn't know what to do. Should I call the police now? My head is spinning and I am just so scared. Charlie, what the fuck is going on!?" Emma was unhinged.

"You *have* to call the police," Charlie urged. "You need to file a missing persons report immediately. You think it's possible he has been missing since Friday?"

Emma was silent. She didn't speak, she continued to weep quietly and breathe into her end of the line.

"Jesus, Emma. I don't even know what to say. Is there anything I can do?"

"I don't know, I just. I don't know." Emma continued to weep.

"You shouldn't be alone right now. Where are you?"

"At home with Sophie. I don't even know *what* to tell her."

"What's your address? When I get there we will call the police and we will get a missing persons report filed. The police need to be involved. This has clearly gone way too far."

They hung up and Emma promptly texted Charlie her address. This short, albeit hectic, phone call reminded Charlie just how flighty Emma could be. After all the time that had passed in their lives, Emma seemed as flighty as ever. Maybe even more so than when they were young. Somehow, to Charlie, this trait added to Emma's charm and sparkle. For one reason or another, her often unstable and shifty behavior sort of excited Charlie. To anyone on the outskirts, it would appear erratic - chaotic even. But when Charlie was close to her, he felt like he was in the eye of the storm. Just enough calm to make the chaos seem right. He couldn't explain it, and if he were honest with himself, he didn't care to try.

Charlie wasted no time in getting himself put together. He jumped into his car, plugged the address into his phone and followed the voice bursting through the speakers as it led the way. Emma and Eddie's home was just over a 15 minute drive from Charlie's. He drove so fast in fact, he made it directly in front of her house in under 10. He didn't want to keep a scared and confused Emma alone in what he could only imagine was a cold, empty house.

He pulled up to a quaint, modern looking ranch style home near the end of Woodson Drive. An upscale neighborhood where all the homes had been remodeled since the days in which they were modestly built. It was obvious even to the untrained eye these homes had been revamped by the same developer as each one was decked out in hip and warm color palettes. Big windows looked out to each home's respective front yards, each one more well-manicured than the next. The homes on Woodson Drive all stuck up like perfectly straightened teeth. As Charlie drove through, he noticed different families minding their business on each property. A man in a bathrobe and house slippers coming out to pick up the morning newspaper, Moms chauffeuring their children weighed down by large backpacks to school, those signs resembling little men in bright neon yellow that said, "Children At Play - Slow Down." Which always screams "family neighborhood". Mess around, and a mama bear might rip your head clean off.

The VanSant home glowed a brilliant sky blue, with light colored wooden tiles sloping downward from the roof and large glass windows wrapping the front of the home. A concrete walkway lined with bright green hedges led from the driveway to the large, decorated front door. After Charlie parked along the curb, he walked up the concrete path to the front door, grabbed the shining silver knocker that was attached and hit it a couple of times. Before he could finish knocking, the door flung open, revealing a shattered Emma. Her hair was a mess, eyes glazed over from hours of crying and she held her cell phone to her left ear. She wore a fluffy white robe loosely tied around her sunken body. She motioned for Charlie to enter as she continued her conversation. He stepped into the front room as Emma shut the door behind him.

"Yeah. No, I know. I'm calling the police right now. My friend, Charlie, just walked in." She dropped the phone slightly, covering the microphone with her right hand. "It's my brother, Billy, in San Diego," She whispered to Charlie before returning the phone to her ear.

"It's Charlie, you remember Charlie. You guys were on the swim team together. Yeah, Claymore. No, don't even worry about me. I'm not alone, Charlie's here. If I need anything or if we find anything out, I'll call you right away, I promise. OK?

Yeah, I love you, too." Emma pressed the end call button and dropped the phone into the pocket of her fluffy robe.

He was filled with a mix of emotions. On one hand, he was slightly shocked to be standing in Emma's home. On the other hand, boy what a reason to be there. Not a situation where someone might bring an appetizer to share. The entrance of the home had beautiful Tiffany Blue tile in a 4 by 4 foot square. Dark, smokey hardwood floors stretched as far as the eye could see through each room and intelligently chosen furniture was placed just perfectly throughout. In the living room just to the left of the entrance sat an expensive white sectional sofa facing a wooden fireplace with modern tiles cascading down either side. A large television hung above the fireplace and mantle which had been adorned with framed family photos. The walls were painted a soft gray and more framed family photos hung throughout the residence. Children's toys, coloring books and garments of clothing were scattered about.

Just past the living room sat the kitchen. White marble countertops paired with dark gray wooden cabinets and stainless steel appliances. A large wooden dining table sat just outside of the kitchen and looked as though it hadn't served a meal in months. Mail, more children's toys and other items sat upon the table turning it into an expensive catchall. Charlie looked to his right down a long, dark hallway leading to the rest of the home. Bedroom and bathroom doors sat open along the corridor. *"This Eddie has done well for himself,"* he thought. Though, he knew it was an inappropriate time for compliments on how they had chosen to live or decorate the space.

"Thank you for coming," Emma said as she wept.

Charlie reached out, grabbed her by the shoulders and pulled her in, holding her tight and close to his chest.

"Everything will be OK. I'm sure Eddie is OK," Charlie said. Mainly because he didn't know what else to say. "First thing we need to do is call the police," he encouraged.

Emma sniffled and tried to catch her breath, "OK. OK." She repeated.

"Where's Sophie? It might be a little too much for a little girl to have the police come and talk about her missing father."

"With the neighbors. They babysit her all the time, so it's perfectly fine for her to be there," Emma said.

They moved to the living room and sat on the large white sofa. Emma on one end facing Charlie, who was sitting opposite of her. She unlocked her phone and dialed 911. Why it took her so long to call, Charlie couldn't quite understand. Maybe speaking with the police and filing an official report would make it all too real. That seemed like the only reason which wouldn't result in pointed fingers.

It wasn't long before the police arrived. Everyone has heard the horror stories of police standing by until a specific time frame has passed. Charlie thought the only upside, if you could find one in this situation, was multiple days *had* passed. Emma had allowed that by default, so the police hopefully *needed* to act. At least Emma had this going for her, even if it might look bad at some moment on the timeline of disappearance. Action would be taken and swiftly. Soon, they heard a knock on the front door. Charlie opened the door and a young beat cop strolled into the house and took a seat on the couch next to Emma. Young, polished and very professional. The name tag on his uniform said "JACKSON." His blue policeman slacks pressed to perfection with a creaseless shirt to match.

"I need you to give me all the information you have about your husband and his whereabouts," said Officer Jackson.

"It was Friday afternoon. Every day when he is about to leave work, he sends me a quick text letting me know. He sent me the text around 3:00 that afternoon. It was right before I left to go pick up our daughter, Sophie, from school. When we got back, he still wasn't home. I thought, maybe, he stopped to have a beer with friends, or maybe traffic had slowed him. Every couple of weeks he goes to a little dive bar downtown with friends, but he usually lets me know. But now it's Tuesday and I haven't heard a thing, he hasn't come home and no one has seen him."

"Why did you wait this long to alert law enforcement?" Office Jackson questioned.

"I was out of town, in San Diego," Emma explained. Her sadness was rapidly turning to anger as that question appeared to set her off.

"I waited out the weekend hoping that he would finally call. Maybe he had lost his phone, or it died. This isn't like him. He's never done anything like this. I trust him so I didn't think I needed to worry."

Officer Jackson shifted his position slightly on the couch, "Now, I know these will be hard questions to answer, and I would like to apologize in advance. Has there been any domestic issues in the home, or has there been any infidelity in the past on his part?"

The sadness in Emma's face had melted away and her expression changed drastically. She wasn't angry, she was furious.

"How dare you!" She shouted to the officer. "Who do you think you are, coming into my home and asking things like this?"

"This is standard procedure. We need to get all the information we can, and often, I'm not saying in *your* situation, but often that happens to be the case. Now, I apologize again. I will say that is clearly *not* the case." Officer Jackson said, both hands up in front of his chest like he was about to block an incoming attack. From here, he softened his approach. "Would he have his cellular phone on him?"

"I would think so, yes. But I truly don't know," Emma answered. "I really don't have any more information."

"I'll head back to the station and contact the phone company to see where his phone last checked in on a cellular tower,"

Officer Jackson said. "It could give us some answers if he skipped town, or if he is hiding out somewhere or, in the worst-case scenario, if something has happened to him. But I assure you Mrs. VanSant, we are here to work with you and we will do everything in our power to bring your husband home safely."

Emma recited Eddie's cell phone number for the officer. He again assured her they would do everything within their power to assist in finding him. She wasn't left with much confidence. She felt she would have a better chance at a positive outcome if she found herself in a desolate desert, her feet buried deep within quicksand, and the only rope to pull herself out had been tied to a block of ice left to melt in the blazing sun. For now, his assurance was all she had to go on and she knew deep down she had to sink or stay afloat on those empty promises alone. Words that flutter through the air like butterflies made of dust and just as you reach for them, they dissipate quicker than they had materialized. Emma thanked the officer and Charlie walked him to the door and kindly let him out. He slowly walked back across the house towards the living room and took a seat next to Emma on the couch and put his arm around her shoulder.

"Everything will be OK. I promise," Charlie whispered with fading confidence.

She looked Charlie dead in the eye, tears forming again in her glazed and exhausted eyes.

"How can you promise anything?" Emma asked as she became inconsolable.

"I can't *promise*, I guess. But the police will find Eddie and I'm sure he is OK. And anything, *anything* that you need, I'm right here," He said as confidently as he could, with a generous mix of white lies that could masquerade as assertion.

Emma leaned into Charlie's chest and wrapped her right arm around his stomach, embracing his body with full force. Almost instantly, her expression changed and she sat right back up, scooting herself a few inches away from him, as she began rubbing her thighs nervously.

"Where's Gwen?" Emma asked, wiping away the tears from her right eye.

"Still out of town for work," Charlie said, rolling his eyes in frustration. "I called her on the way here and told her what's going on. That reminds me, I should call her and give her an update, I know she's worried for you."

"When does she come home?" Emma asked, continuing to rub the water dripping from her eyes like a rusted faucet.

"Saturday. I'll pick her up that evening."

"So, you'll be home alone tonight?" Emma asked, coyly batting her eyelashes in his direction.

"Yeah. Bachelor pad week," He joked.

"Would you stay here?" Emma asked shyly. She tried to change her tone so as not to sound like she was making more out of the situation. "We have a guest room, I don't mean. Well, you understand right? I just don't want to be alone."

Charlie thought for a moment about her proposition. He did say he would be there for her, and staying with Emma for an evening wasn't only something he felt right about doing, it was something that oddly excited him. The rush of the unknown aside, he hated the idea of leaving her and Sophie alone in that house. The house felt dark, empty and cold like it was covered by a weighted blanket.

"Sure, Emma," He said with a friendly smile. He outstretched his right hand and placed it on her left thigh. "Don't worry. I won't leave alone."

"Thank you," she said, grabbing his right hand with her left and squeezing it tightly.

"I just need to run home for a bit. I have a couple things to take care of," Charlie said, looking away from her.

6

Emma was overjoyed at Charlie's speedy return, which was noticeable by her expression when she opened the door after a few light knocks. Emma had clearly continued to cry and unravel while she was alone.

"I'm happy to see you," she said as the door opened, her voice cracking as she spoke.

"I said I would get back as soon as I could," Charlie said as he entered. "And look, I come bearing gifts," He continued, holding up two slightly chilled bottles of pinot grigio. The bottles wept as tears of condensation rolled down the thick, clear glass bottles.

"My favorite," Emma said as a faint smile almost broke out on her face. "Thank you. I could probably *use* a drink or two, if I'm being honest."

"Some nice white wine is just what the doctor ordered," Charlie said. "We should let these bad boys chill a little. We have plenty of time to search for answers at the bottom of these bottles."

"Sounds good to me," Emma said with a slight child-like giggle.

Charlie's heart fluttered at the sight and sound of laughter, as light as it may be. Like most of his life, he wanted to chase that feeling. They spent the entire day filling every inch of real estate on Emma's sectional sofa in various positions. From Emma and Charlie sitting across from one another while Emma enthusiastically shared story after story about her beloved husband, to her folded into herself like a wet beach towel across Charlie's lap while she cried softly and everything in between. For a good while, Emma slept on Charlie's shoulder as he sat in absolute silence hoping not to disturb her so her body and mind could recharge. He imagined she hadn't slept, and feared the Sandman would soon become a stranger to her. Sleep is a luxury taken for granted by the light hearted. It brought him immense joy to listen to Emma breathe sweetly while she slept. It wasn't long before his eyes grew heavy at the sweet sounds of her deep breaths. Charlie's head drifted backwards as though it had been weighed down and soon, the quiet home was filled with the sounds of simultaneous snores. The day had retired and the moon had come out to play as Emma finally woke. With her hands on his chest she pushed herself so she could sit upright. She let out a long yawn as she rubbed the sleep from her eyes and began surveying the room. Her last memory of the day was a home filled with beautiful sunlight, now the home grew darker by the minute as the sun dipped behind the horizon. Charlie lifted his head from the back of the couch, as the pressure of her weight shook him just enough to break him from the unscheduled rest.

"Oh, hi," she said, her voice cracking and slightly strained. "I didn't mean to sleep the day away. I'm sorry about that."

"Don't be," Charlie said as he made small circles with his head to stretch his neck. "You probably needed a good rest."

"You're right. I didn't sleep a wink last night."

"Wow, the day really got away from us, huh?" Charlie said as he looked around the dark room.

"That's OK. We still have all night together," she said with a bright smile, sending shockwaves through Charlie's body.

"Speaking of the rest of the night," Charlie said, clapping his hands together. "How about we break into some of that wine?"

"Sounds great, but I need to go get Sophie first. She's spent all day with our neighbors. They're probably going to kill me."

Emma stood and walked across the living room towards the kitchen to retrieve her cell phone. She picked it up and clicked into her contacts and called the neighbor.

"Charlotte? It's Emma," she said, holding the cell to her right ear. "I know. I'm *so sorry*. I fell asleep on the couch. I don't even know how it happened but I feel terrible. Is it a good time to come by and get Sophie? Thank you and again, I'm terribly sorry I left her there so late. I'm walking out the door right now."

• • •

She dropped her cell phone back on top of the dining room table, pulled her robe tightly around her body as she walked towards the front door.

"Sorry but I need to go get Sophie," she said.

"Oh, that's OK," Charlie assured. "Don't let me get in your way, do whatever you need to. Hey, do you want me to come with you?"

"Uh, no," Emma said, her eyes closed tightly. "I don't think that's a good look."

"What do you mean?"

"How would it look if I went to pick up my daughter with a strange *man* the *same day* I reported my husband missing?"

"Point taken," Charlie said.

Emma rushed out the front door. From the couch through the front windows, Charlie watched as she walked at double speed across the street. He continued to watch as she shuffled up the walkway to the front door and kept a close eye as she walked back towards him, her hand tightly clenching Sophie's as they safely crossed the street. Charlie turned to look over the couch as they both entered. First Sophie, followed closely by Emma.

"Oh, Sophie," Emma said as she shut the door. "You remember meeting mommie's friend? This is Charlie. He's going to hang out here for a while in case we need anything, ok hun?"

"Good to see you again, Sophie," Charlie said, his left hand held high in the air with a minimal wave.

Sophie stared at Charlie emotionless, then looked up at her mother with a slight judging glance.

"OK then," Emma said, catching all the vibes from Sophie. "Come on, let's get ready for bed."

Emma, with her left hand planted on Sophie's back, ushered her down the hall towards her bedroom. As they walked, Emma bent and turned back to Charlie. She began motioning as though she was drinking from a large bottle and pointed towards the kitchen. Message received loud and clear. It was wine time.

Sitting on the dining room table was a large silver bucket, perfect for icing down a bottle of adult grape juice. Charlie retrieved the bucket and entered the kitchen. Luckily, Emma and Eddie had a fridge with an ice dispenser attached. He pushed on the lever and held the bucket to catch ice cubes as they shot out, banging, clanging and echoing throughout the silent home. He opened the fridge and pulled out the two bottles of white wine, shoving one deep into the bucket of ice to stay cold. He opened a couple of cabinets until he landed on some wine glasses and a silver and black corkscrew. He put one bottle under his left arm, gripped the wine glasses and corkscrew in his right hand and carefully carried the bucket into the living room, setting them down onto the coffee table. He set the corkscrew on top of the first bottle of wine and began spinning the top until the metal screw dug deep into the cork. In one quick motion he pulled the cork out resulting in an audible popping noise. He set the opened bottle down onto the table and continued to wait patiently for Emma to return. Emma finally resurfaced from the darkness that had engulfed the hallway. She approached the couch and sat down hard next to Charlie.

"Alright, where were we?" Emma said with a smile, her eyes sparkling in the minimal light remaining.

"I have us all set up," Charlie said, waving both of his hands over the wine, glasses and ice as though he was a magician.

"Perfect timing," Emma said.

Charlie lifted one wine glass, and the opened bottle of pinot grigio. As he tilted the glass to pour, Emma reached over and with one hand lifted the second bottle out of the bucket of ice and grabbed the corkscrew with the other. Without skipping a beat she dug the corkscrew deep into the cork and ripped it out of the bottle. She dropped the corkscrew, still clinging to the cork, onto the coffee table as she rested back into the couch. Charlie sat for a moment in shock. He had figured that they might go glass for glass with one another, but Emma clearly had different plans. *"Who am I to argue?"* He thought. He set the wine glass down, lifted the full bottle to his mouth and sat back on the couch.

"Let's see if this wine is any good, shall we?" She asked as she raised the full bottle to her lips, tilted it back and took a big mouthful. "Oh yeah, this is good stuff. Thank you for bringing wine. Lord knows I could use a drink tonight."

"I was happy to," he said.

The room continued to grow darker as the sun completely disappeared, making room for the moon to take over the night sky. The dull moonlight broke through the front windows, dimly illuminating the VanSant living room. He didn't know if this was normal behavior for Emma and Eddie. Maybe they enjoyed the darkness? Maybe they wanted to save energy? He didn't know but he continued to grow uncomfortable.

"So," he finally broke. "Should I turn on a light or something?" He asked with a shy quality.

"You know what we should do?" Emma asked as she shot up like a bottle rocket from the couch. "We should start a fire! What do you say?"

"I say let's do it," Charlie said with a big, goofy smile.

Emma jumped up and off the couch full of enthusiasm. On the mantle sat a long candle lighter. She knelt down and began turning a steel key which stuck out of the beautiful blue tile lining the fireplace and without looking, reached up for the lighter. Clearly this was not her first time.

"Can I help you with that?" Charlie asked.

"Nope," Emma answered matter-of-factly. "It's a gas fireplace, it's easy to light."

In the silent home they could both hear as the gas flooded into the fireplace. Inside sat a large iron grate and fake fire safe "logs" on top. Emma reached her left hand deep under those fake logs, flicked the lighter and with a soft boom, the fireplace engulfed with a low roaring fire that illuminated the room. Gorgeous oranges, yellows and reds danced and intertwined on the walls throughout the room, giving off the perfect ambiance for an evening between friends over wine. *A lot* of wine.

"Grab that blanket, would you?" Emma asked, pointing to the back of the couch.

Draped over the back of the couch was a Mexican serape. White, pink and blue stripes stretched across the hand woven threads. Charlie lifted it and walked to Emma who was sitting back on her ankles in front of the fire.

"Lay it down right here," she said, pointing at the hardwood in front of her.

Charlie fluffed the blanket up into the air and allowed it to float to the floor below, landing in a perfect rectangle. Emma raised from her knees and scooted herself onto the blanket. Then, with her open left hand, she patted the floor offering an invitation for Charlie to join her. He stretched his legs out towards the fireplace. Emma followed along, both allowing the fire to warm their feet. With her right hand she lifted the wine bottle and held it up in front of her face as she admired the flames as they danced through the liquid inside.

"To friendship, huh Charlie? Thank you for being here," Emma said as she extended the bottle towards him.

He lifted his bottle with his left hand and tapped it into hers, resulting in a dull clinking sound. They both leaned their heads back, tilted their respective bottles and took a long drink. The rest of the evening was spent with Emma and Charlie drinking and talking, talking and drinking. One bottle each soon turned to 2 bottles as they were forced to break into some of Emma's own bottles of decadent red wine. It wasn't long before they both felt the creeping force of drunkenness possess their bodies and minds. Charlie watched closely as Emma loosened up with every swig of wine.

"I-I don't usually drink t-this much wine," Emma said with a slight and charming laugh.

"I don't think many people drink as much wine as we have tonight," Charlie said, sharing a laugh.

"Eddie doesn't like to drink a lot," she said, scrunching her face a bit. "Well, h-he *likes* to drink. But, you know, I mean, like, not *this* much."

"Well shit, who does? Tomorrow is going to be rough," He said.

"Eh, who cares?" Emma asked as she tilted the bottle back for a long drink. "What have I got to do tomorrow? Sit on the c-couch, wait for my h-husband to come home?"

"Emma, don't say that," Charlie said.

"I'm just scared. What are we going to do if he never comes home? If they never find him?"

"Don't think that way," He said as he reached his right arm out, wrapping it around her shoulders. "Everything will be fine."

"Yeah?" She asked, her voice soft and sweet as it hit his ears. "You think so?"

"I *know* so," He assured, looking down as their eyes met.

Fireworks began shooting inside of his guts as her eyes met his. Her bright blue eyes sparkled like two perfect diamonds in the glow of the fire. Charlie felt lost as she continued to look up at him and he noticed she had a smile on her face. She looked comfortable. She looked content. For the first time in a while, she was calm. She turned her face and watched the flames dance away to a song they couldn't hear. They sat for a moment in silence, his arm around her as she rested her head into his chest.

"Did you know when we were kids," Charlie said, breaking the long silence. "I had such a crush on you. I don't think I have ever had the guts to say that."

Emma didn't respond. Not a word, not a movement, nothing. He looked down at her to see her eyes were shut as she had fallen asleep under his arm. He looked back at the fire and smiled. Maybe it was better she didn't hear what he said. Maybe it was the wine talking. He shook her softly, just enough to wake her.

"Hey," he said. "I think it's time to go to bed."

She said nothing, just nodded her head slowly.

"Come on, you," Charlie said, standing up, grabbing her by the forearms and pulling her to her feet. He could tell she was wobbly from the wine.

"Let's get you into bed," He said as he ushered her out of the living room.

He assisted her down the long, dark hallway to her bedroom. He pulled the unkept covers down on her and Eddie's bed, helped her crawl in and pulled the covers up to her chin. She stared up at him with a big smile, her eyes unable to focus on him as he stood over her.

"Are you going to lay down with me?" She asked.

"Oh no," Charlie said. "I'm sleeping on the couch. Don't you worry about me."

"N-no, d-don't do that," she stuttered. "Eddie. Eddie's office. There is a pull out bed if you want to s-sleep there."

"Then I shall sleep in the office," He said as he turned to leave the room.

"Charlie w-wait," she said. She didn't sit up or open her eyes as she spoke. "D-don't forget the f-fire."

"You got it, Emma," He said. As he pulled the door shut quietly, he stuck his head back into the dark room. "Goodnight, Emma. Sleep tight."

7

The next morning was one of those rare occasions when the clouds broke and allowed the sun to come out to play. Charlie awoke to the sun beaming through the shutters, beating down onto his tired and hungover face. His eyes felt drier than a sun cracked river bed, and his mouth envied the feeling. He smacked and licked his lips as he reached aimlessly for a sippy cup of water on the table next to the pull out bed. He lifted it to his cracked lips, tipped the cup upside down and let the lukewarm liquid fill his mouth and drip to the back of his throat as he guzzled it in record time. He took a deep breath, held it for a moment and let it all out in one quick rush as he tossed the sippy cup to the floor. It crashed onto the hardwood floor and scattered away as it bounced loudly across the room. The guest room was painted the same gray as the rest of the house with framed posters and newspaper clippings of Eddie's favorite sports teams adorning the walls. The Seahawks and the Mariners were clearly his favorites. "*Root Root for the home team, Eddie,*" Charlie thought. A large, vintage wooden executive desk sat in the corner with a new iMac sitting on top. A couch that looked like it should have been retired in the 1980s sat against the center of the far wall. This was Charlie's bed for the night.

An old pullout bed, not comfortable in the slightest, but adequate enough when your only other option is a hardwood floor or outside in the weeds with the spiders and mosquitos.

Charlie rolled over and dropped his feet to the cold, hardwood floor. He sat up, rubbed his eyes and took a deep breath. He reached for his cell phone and checked the time. 7:23am. He stood up and reached for a small duffle bag filled with some daily essentials; A toothbrush, assorted toiletries and some scattered clothing. Charlie changed into his athletic running gear and slipped on his running shoes. Just the mere thought of a morning run whilst hungover would make even the most hardened drinkers cringe. Charlie didn't care. He needed to run. The cold, breezy air mixed with the damp smell of fresh morning dew revitalized him. Charlie never missed an opportunity for the ultimate circle of life. Detox just to retox. Rinse, repeat. Quietly he opened the door and made his way down the hallway to the front door, hoping not to wake Emma. The house was cold, dark and lifeless. He went to the kitchen and on the fridge sat a small dry erase board with a marker attached at the top. He scribbled on the dry erase board "WENT FOR A RUN. BE BACK SOON!" And signed his name underneath. He made his way to the front door, and he was off, starting at a slow, balanced pace before taking off into a full sprint.

He had no trouble navigating his way through Emma's neighborhood. It was much different running through the perfect facade of suburbia compared to running through the woods, but Charlie enjoyed the change of scenery. He wanted to soak in how the other half lived. He ran down to the end of Emma's street and stopped at the corner. He glanced to the left, and then to the right, noticing a few blocks down what appeared to be a city maintained trail. A perfectly safe place for a brisk morning jog. When he reached the trail, he didn't break stride and took off with a burst of energy, charging at full speed. Soon he noticed something out of place in the distance. He slowed down to a walking pace and continued down the path for a closer look. The running trail cut through the suburban area and was lined by chain link fencing on either side, keeping it safe from cars, stray dogs or anything else that could find its way onto the trail. About 30 yards down, Charlie stopped and stared at the scene through the fence. Across the road, a couple of police cars were stopped and had surrounded a silver Toyota. The car was parked like any other vehicle along the curb in front of a large grass field leading to a public park. The driver's side door was open, and from where he stood, Charlie could see inside. He didn't notice anything out of sorts, although what did Charlie know? What does anyone expect to see when they stop at a crime scene or any other crash? It's as though for one quick moment we all fade from humanity and somewhere in our brains we hope to see something shocking. We all become blood thirsty wolves in the blink of an eye.

The police stood outside of their vehicles, appearing to be in no hurry as they all moved in their own respective directions, taking photographs and talking to one another. A large, middle aged man in black slacks, tan blazer with a black tie stood to the side. He was a balding man with a black mustache and a large middle aged belly was fighting its way through the buttons of his dress shirt. Charlie thought he must be a man of importance, as he noticed each of the uniformed officers seemed to be not only answering to him, but as details did emerge, they reported to him.

Charlie stood holding on to the fence and watching the police activity for a suspicious length of time. Another middle aged man also dressed nicer than your typical beat cop noticed him standing and staring, which quickly sparked their attention. He began pointing in Charlie's direction. The large, balding man in the tan blazer turned towards the trail and their eyes met. Charlie was immediately snapped from his curious daze and stepped back from the fence. He nodded at the police officers, turned and ran back down the trail in the direction he had originally come. Once he was out of view from the officers, he picked up his pace and went from a light jog back to a full sprint. He headed back to Emma's house, hoping he would arrive before she woke up. When he returned he jumped over the hedges, flung open the front door and slammed it shut behind him. The door banged the jamb with so much force, it let out a loud thud that probably could have awakened the dead. He cringed, hoping he hadn't woken Emma and Sophie, when from behind him he heard a voice.

"What's going on?" It was Emma.

Charlie turned to find her leaning around the corner of the kitchen to see what all the commotion was. There she stood, rocking some mean bed head, fluffy white robe and sipping a cup of fresh hot coffee.

"I just went on a short run," Charlie said. "I didn't wake you, did I?"

"No. A phone call woke me up," she said. "Some detective just called."

"What did he say?" Charlie asked, walking across the large living room to meet her.

"He said they have some information they want to share with me, they're heading over now."

Just then, the doorbell rang.

8

The alarm clock rang snapping Angus Pratt out of a deep slumber. In one motion he rolled over and slapped the top of the bedside clock to shut off the piercing sound shooting throughout the room. *"6:00am always comes too soon,"* he thought as he rubbed his face. He took in a long deep breath as he stood up, the breath acting both like a brutal wake up call and a burst of energy to give him the strength to do so. He made his way to the bathroom at the far end of his bedroom and turned on the faucet, filling his hands with cold water and splashing his face. The cold water filled his hands again and again as he plunged his face into his palms. Refreshing yet awful.

Angus Pratt was a veteran Detective for the Seattle Police Department of 25 years. A large man, reaching close to 6 and a half feet tall. A decent sized belly pushed his sleep t-shirt out over his boxer shorts and a shiny scalp served as a graveyard to what once was a magnificent head of hair. Thick strands of salt and pepper remained on the sides of his head matching the thick mustache above his lip. His wife Laura was still asleep as he prepared for his morning shower. He tried his best to not disturb her, although she had grown accustomed to his morning movements. He shut the bathroom door lightly before he opened the old-fashioned glass shower door that hadn't been updated since it was installed, reaching into the shower, flicking on the hot water. He stood back, letting the hot water wash over him as the room filled with steam. A few minutes of bliss with nothing but the white noise of water encapsulating all of his senses.

Laura was a middle aged woman of tremendous beauty. Blonde hair flowed like a waterfall on a postcard and rested gently onto her shoulders. She entered the kitchen of their home wearing a soft pink bathrobe which wrapped her thin frame and matching slippers. The Pratt children sat at the dining room table in their modest kitchen. Their home looked as though it had been plucked right out of historic Palm Springs. Mid Century modern paradise was their design aesthetic. Large pink and blue tiles wrapped the walls just above the counter tops, with appliances that looked as though they were sold from a 1970s Sears catalog, yet brand new and clean as a whistle. Angus Junior, their son of 8 years old, was a thin boy, wearing blue jeans and a Seattle Seahawks t-shirt with a mop of messy brown hair atop his head. Karen, their daughter had just become a teenager. She was the spitting image of their mother with long flowing blonde hair pulled back into a tight ponytail, wearing a freshly pressed school issued uniform; blue slacks, white button-down shirt, blue blazer with an embroidered school emblem on the chest. She held a pencil in her right hand as she went over her homework.

"What do you guys want for breakfast?" Laura asked.

"Bacon and toast," Karen said.

"Cake!" Yelled Junior.

"You can't have cake for breakfast, you know that. Don't be such a wise ass. And bacon and toast is not a full breakfast. You're growing children, you need a balanced breakfast. And *that* is why," Laura said, as she began mimicking a drum roll with her two index fingers on the counter top, "*This* is on the menu!"

Laura reached into the top cupboard and removed two cereal bowls. She turned around with the bowls in one hand and a box of Special K Red Berries in the other.

"Cereal? That's it?" Karen asked, disappointed as she dropped the pencil onto the table and sat back in her chair, crossing her arms.

"That's right!" Laura said as she moved across the kitchen setting the bowls and cereal on the table.

"Eww, it has fruit in it!" Junior said, squinching his face in playful disgust. "Where are the spoons, what are we supposed to do, eat this with our *hands*?"

Laura, now at the counter pouring two cups of hot coffee, shot around at Junior's remark.

"What did I say about being a wise ass? You have hands and feet, get up and get them," Laura said. "I shouldn't have to remind you of this stuff."

Karen stood up from the table and made her way across the kitchen, retrieving two spoons. As she made her way back to the table, Laura stopped her.

"Hey, hey! Grab the milk while you're at it."

"So much for full service," Karen remarked.

"Ha, Ha," Laura shot out.

Each of the children took their turns filling their bowls with the cereal and milk before nose diving their respective spoons in.

From the hallway Angus Sr. entered the kitchen, dressed nicely for his day of work. Black slacks, bright white button-down shirt with a black tie stretching down his body. The tip of the tie would have landed perfectly on the buckle of his belt, had it not been for the belly pushing it out away from it's landing spot.

"Good morning family," Angus said as he entered.

"Good Morning Dad!" The children said in unison as though it was a rehearsed routine.

Angus made his way across the kitchen to Laura, putting his arm around her shoulder and kissing her gently on the side of her head.

"Good Morning, honey," Laura said, handing him a cup of fresh, hot coffee.

"Thank you, sweetheart," Angus said as he lifted the cup to his lips to take the inaugural sip.

"Dad, what's a wise ass?" Asked Junior.

Angus continued with another large gulp of his morning coffee before lowering his cup, "You are," He said.

"Real funny," Junior replied as the rest of the family laughed along.

"Ha, wise ass," said Karen.

"Hey, don't you start," said Laura. "Long day ahead, honey?"

"Don't know yet," he replied, taking another large sip of coffee. "We'll have to wait and see."

"If you're going to be late, can you please call and give me a heads up?"

"Of course, don't I always?"

Angus polished off his cup of coffee like it was his mission in life, dropping the empty cup into the kitchen sink.

"Where is my thermos, hun?" Asked Angus.

"It's, uh, in the dishwasher I think."

"Great. I want to make the next one a double for the road."

Angus opened the dishwasher and removed a large, green thermos. He grabbed the coffee pot, pouring every last drop, filling the thermos.

"Well, I'm off," Angus said as he set the thermos onto the dining room table before reaching for a coat rack that sat in the corner. He pulled a tan blazer from the rack and threw it on. He then walked back across the kitchen to plant a goodbye kiss on his wife.

"Goodbye honey, enjoy your day," he told her.

"You too. Be safe, OK?"

"Of course. See you tonight kids, have a good day at school," he said as he exited the kitchen. He opened the front door and stepped out into the cold morning air. Before he could shut the door behind him, Laura called out.

"Hey, don't forget your coffee!"

Without needing to come back inside, he bent around the door frame and with his long reach he grabbed the thermos from the table.

"Thank you, my love," he said. "And Junior, don't be a wise ass today. Love you guys!" He slammed the door shut behind him.

Laura turned back to the coffee pot to get herself a refill when she noticed Angus had polished it off and the pot was bone dry.

"You couldn't at least save me one cup?" She yelled.

A moment of silence fell over the home as Laura began refilling the coffee maker for a fresh pot.

"What a wise ass," Junior said.

She couldn't be mad at Junior for cursing this time. Although maybe not the best use or timing for the insult, she agreed Angus had in fact acted like a wise ass.

Angus walked across the front lawn towards his car. A big tank of a Buick, the black paint shining in the morning sunlight. As he took his seat inside the vehicle, his cell phone rang.

"Detective Pratt," he answered.

"Angus, it's Frank," the voice on the other end said.

"Hey, Frank, give me some good news, what do you say? What's going on?"

"We've got a situation over here."

"Damn, that quick huh?"

"What do you mean by that?"

"I just got in the car and you already need me? I haven't even had my second *or* third cups of coffee yet."

"Job security, right?"

"You got that right. OK, where am I headed?"

"The park on Pine Avenue. You know the place?"

"Yeah, I know the place, it isn't too far from here."

"North end, right across from the Broken Trail. A few patrol cars are parked there, you can't miss them."

"See you soon."

9

Angus rolled up the large public park on Pine Avenue. A lush field of brilliant green grass stretched deep and the park was adorned with tall, beautiful trees. A playground area for children sat off to the far right of the park with a massive jungle gym embedded into wood chips. To the left was a clubhouse for locals to have birthday parties and gatherings. A crisp blue pool sat just inside the fencing on the other side of the club house, the water serene and calm before the disruption of children with their cannonballs with their endless splashing and water aerobics classes. He parked behind one of the three patrol cars surrounding a silver Toyota parked along the curb. The front door of the vehicle sat wide open as uniformed officers took pictures and collected items from the interior. He walked up to the scene and was stopped by his partner, Detective Frank Mckenna. Frank was shorter than Angus, but at 6 foot 5 who wouldn't be. Frank had curly black hair that was cut close to the scalp, was clean-shaven and wearing blue slacks, a matching blazer and a white button-down shirt with a matching blue tie.

"Good Morning, Angus," Frank said, catching his partner's attention, reaching out for a hand shake.

"Good Morning Frank. So, break it down for me. What have we got here?"

Frank pulled a notepad from the inside pocket of his blazer, flipped it open, and began to fill Angus in on what they had gathered thus far.

"We had a woman file a missing person's report yesterday for her husband, Eddie VanSant. Says he has been missing since Friday evening."

"And she just reported this yesterday?" Angus cut him off.

"She said she had been out of town, in San Diego. She had been trying to reach him through the weekend and waited to see if something changed. Anyway, he had sent her a text message saying he was on his way home from the office on Friday, and it appears he never made it."

"And how did we end up here at the park this early in the morning? I assume we won't be doing any laps in the pool, huh Franky?"

"Not today," Frank said, shaking his head with a sly grin. "She provided her husband's cell number to an officer who contacted the phone company and had them run a check on the phone. You know, check to see if it had pinged any cell towers in the area, see if we could track it by the GPS. And, luckily for us the phone still had some battery left and we were able to track it," Frank said, turning around and pointing at the silver Toyota. "To this exact location."

"And can I safely assume this is *his* vehicle?"

"You nailed it. It appears to have been abandoned here and his cell phone was sitting on the floor of the passenger side. If you think that sounds strange, the keys were still in the ignition as well."

"Interesting, interesting," Angus said, rubbing his chin.

"There are no signs of a struggle inside the vehicle, but this definitely screams foul play. I don't know anyone who would leave their car like *this*. Doesn't look like a runaway situation to me. If he was off with another woman or something, I mean, I would think he would at least have his cell with him."

"Doubtful he would disappear for three whole days without a whisper to his wife either. Have you provided this information to her yet?"

"Not yet, I wanted to give you the breakdown first."

"Do you have her information on you? I want to speak with her."

In an instant, Frank's expression changed as he glanced around Angus' large body. On the other side of the street sat a heavily trafficked path used for biking, walking and other forms of exercise.

"Who's this guy?" Frank asked.

Angus turned around and looked toward the trail. Looking through the chain link fence stood a man in running gear, staring intently on the officers as they went through the abandoned vehicle.

"What's this guy's deal?" Frank asked again.

"This whole town is full of looky loos. They can't get enough of police activity. They always want to stick their noses where they don't belong. All it takes is a little acknowledgement and they usually go away," Angus shared.

Frank pointed in his direction and cocked his head backwards at the man. His body jerked away from the fence like it had just been charged with a burst of electricity. He turned and took off down the trail running at a decent pace.

"See what I mean?" Angus asked with a sly smirk.

"Yeah, move along, jackass." Frank muttered.

Angus returned a couple of giggles at Frank's jab.

"Alright Frank, let's dust for prints, and I mean all over this car. Door handles, steering wheel, seat belt, the whole thing."

"We're on it. They're finishing that up now."

"Did they bag and tag everything? And I mean *everything* in that car."

"Still working on it. Don't worry, we will strip this thing down if we have to."

"I want every bit of data on that cell phone dissected. Text messages, phone calls, emails. Dates and times for each. Have the guys at the station make a couple hard copies of all of it. I want it on my desk as soon as possible."

"You got it."

"Let's get in touch with the city about these red light cameras. Let's see if we can get any video of the car as it made its way to this spot. And make sure they really do a deep dusting on this thing. If we can get a quality print, I have a hunch we will find the missing husband."

"You got it," Frank assured.

"What is the wife's name?"

Frank looked back at his notepad, "Her name is Emma. Emma VanSant. I have her address here, too."

Angus glanced over the scribbled words on Frank's pad.

"I think she lives right around here," Angus said, as he began looking around him for street signs. "I'm going to call her myself to see if I can stop by. Maybe she remembered something else and can shed some more light on all of this."

Angus paused for a moment thinking of his next move.

"I don't know, Frank. There's something fishy about this. And it's not the Fish Market."

10

Charlie and Emma found themselves back on the couch together, but this time, wine had been replaced by much needed coffee. Both of their heads rang as they sipped the hot, black and bitter beverage. They sat mostly silent, aware at any moment a detective would interrupt their conversation. Eventually, someone had to break the silence. The sound of silence can become a piercing ring once the awkwardness sets in. Luckily for Charlie, it was Emma who spoke.

"Do you want a refill?" She asked, almost in a whisper. "I know I can use one."

"Sure," Charlie replied, handing her his empty cup.

Emma stood up without saying another word. Charlie didn't like seeing her in pain, from the unknown surrounding Eddie's whereabouts or the hangover. He felt bad for thinking it, but he hoped with all his heart that the pain she was suffering now was thanks to the cabernet and pinot they had polished off only a few hours prior, and not from the loneliness filling her heart. He resigned to the fact it was probably 50/50. Just then, a couple of remarkably loud bangs on the door pulled them from their collective stupor.

"Do you mind answering that?" Emma asked Charlie.

Charlie obliged. He opened the front door to find a large detective standing on the front step.

"Good Morning, I'm Detective Pratt. I just called a short time ago. I'm here to speak with Mrs. VanSant." Angus said.

"Of course, of course," replied Charlie. "Please, come in."

"And who might you be?"

"My name's Charlie," He said before a short pause. "I'm a family friend."

"Gotcha. It's always nice to have a good friend around during times like these."

"It sure is," Charlie said.

Emma entered the room still in her fluffy white robe although now she had tightened it and had fixed her hair up into a cleaner ponytail. She walked in with a serving tray holding 3 coffee mugs, a small silver dispenser of milk, a mason jar with assorted sugar packets and a fresh pot of steaming coffee. The way she nonchalantly carried that tray made Charlie wonder if she had worked in a diner or something in the past. A true pro move, if he had ever seen one.

"You must be Mrs. VanSant. I'm Detective Angus Pratt, you can call me Angus," He said, stretching his massive hand to Emma with a mile wide smile. He was charismatic, something that must go a long way when dealing with vicious criminals and distraught spouses.

"I'm sorry," Emma said, both of her hands still tied up with the tray of mugs and coffee. Emma sat the tray, mugs, accessories in the middle of her coffee table. She wiped her hands on her robe before shaking Angus' hand.

"You can call me Emma," she said, her petite hand disappearing inside his massive grasp.

"Nice to meet you," Angus said with a smile. "I wish it were under better circumstances of course. May I sit?"

"Yes, of course. And I have a fresh pot of coffee if you would like a cup?"

"Even better!" Angus said with a clap of his giant hands.

Charlie sat down at the far end of the sofa directly across from Angus. Emma positioned herself right in the middle of the couch between the two men.

"Charlie, would you like a cup?" Emma asked.

"Yes, thank you," Charlie said. "Why don't you let me pour those. Would anyone like milk or sugar?"

"I like mine straight up," Said Angus.

"Splash of milk and a Sweet n Low, Please," Emma instructed.

Charlie filled each cup and tore open a Sweet n Low emptying the contents of the packet into one mug, topping it off with a splash of milk. The coffee turned a deep caramel color as the contents swirled together. He handed the mixed cup to Emma, followed by a mug to Angus. He took his own cup and sat back sinking deep into the thick cushions.

"Thank you, Charlie. Boy do I love a fresh hot cup of coffee," Angus said, lifting the mug to his lips taking a large gulp. Almost as though the heat didn't bother him one bit. "OK. *Now* we can talk," he said, along with another loud clap of his hands followed by him rubbing them together like he was rolling invisible dough.

"OK," Angus said, drawing in one deep breath into his massive chest. "You gave the reporting officer your husband's cell phone number. My partner, Detective Frank McKenna, tracked his cell phone through GPS."

Emma let out a loud gasp, covering her mouth with both hands. Almost as though she was keeping her jaw from hitting the hardwood floor. Through her shock and amazement, Angus moved on spilling the details as though it was a normal reaction.

"That GPS location led officers to the park over on Pine Avenue," Angus said, pointing towards the front window in the park's direction. "The officers located Eddie's vehicle, which had been abandoned. His cellular phone was found on the floor of the passenger side of the vehicle."

Emma dipped her face into her hands, drawing fast, panicked breaths.

"Was he in the car? Did you find him?" Emma was spiraling.

"Ah, no," Angus assured. "There were no *immediate* signs of struggle inside the vehicle. And, this could be good news. No obvious blood or weapons were found. The officers are having the car towed to the station for further review. We will have that car dusted for prints, checked for blood. We will tear that thing apart to get answers if we have to."

Charlie sat silent, sipping his coffee and counting the knots in the wood making up the flooring throughout the home. He didn't feel as though it was his place to jump in with questions or commentary. He didn't want to say or ask the wrong thing, which could upset Emma worse. If there were any relevant questions, he figured Emma would ask them on her own. He felt his place was best used as a source of comfort, not a disruption. Angus noticed the silence and his staring at the floor and felt Charlie was being eerily calm. Angus had been around the block in his time as a detective. He had seen everything that even the scariest and most twisted human mind could dream up, and knew it wasn't his place to call Charlie's behavior into question. But he knew deep in his mind, he would break out the big gun questions when he had to. Angus glanced towards Charlie long enough for him to notice. He straightened up, gripping his coffee mug tightly and began paying more attention to the conversation. Angus then turned his attention back to Emma.

"We are lucky his phone was somehow still powered on," Angus continued.

Emma's eyes opened wide, shocked it was still turned on knowing it could have been sitting there for days undisturbed. Angus noticed her shock.

"Yeah, my thoughts exactly. It was close to shutting itself off when we found it, so we got lucky. My partner is on his way back to the station to do a deep dive into that thing. We should be able to track his whereabouts, see who, if anyone, he had any contact with through email, text messages, phone calls, voicemails. You name it, we'll have it, and I mean soon."

"Thank you Detective."

Angus put his hand up to stop her. "Please, call me Angus. No need for the formalities. Is there anything else, anything at all that you haven't already told us? Any outstanding arguments in the home? Any sort of fighting that has occurred? Anyone you can think of that might want to harm him in any way, or anyone he might have run off with?"

"No, no not at all. I mean, like every marriage, the typical arguments, I guess. But even then, we are a happy married couple." Emma said, sniffling. "Uhm, he texted me he was on his way home from work, like he does most days. I left here Friday to pick up our daughter, Sophie, from school. We headed to the airport not long after we got back."

Angus stopped her, "So you left town the day he went missing?"

Emma looked at Charlie confused, then back to Angus.

"What exactly are you implying?"

Angus put his big baseball mitt hands in the air in defense mode. "No implications here, trust me. I just want to get every bit of information possible. Now, where did you go, and what were you doing out of town?"

"I was uh," Emma wiped her eyes, "Taking Sophie to see my parents. In San Diego. It's such a short flight we go as often as we can."

Angus' eyes lit up and he looked at Charlie, "San Diego, huh? Nice place. I love the beach. I can't get enough of the beach," he said, rocking back in his seat with a childlike grin.

Charlie pressed his lips together and widened his eyes in uncomfortable agreement. The room went silent for a moment, almost too long.

"We, uh, we're both from San Diego," Charlie said pointing at Emma.

"That's great. I love San Diego. I get so sick of this cold and the rain, you know?" Angus said, staring at Charlie. He then fixed his stare back onto Emma.

"And when did you come home?" Angus asked.

"Yesterday. I tried calling, texting, everything to get a hold of Eddie. I didn't know what to do while I was so far away, honestly."

"You said you have a daughter. Where is she now?"

"She's over at the neighbors. I dropped her off before you got here," Emma said, the cuffs of her robe swallowing her tiny hands. She reached up to her face and wiped her nose with her right hand.

"I suggested it might be best for her to not be here with the police, you know, asking questions about her dad," Charlie interjected.

Angus's stare fixed dead on Charlie. It was so intense, he felt like a hole was being burned right through his chest.

"That's good thinking, Charlie," Angus said with a deadpan smile.

He looked back at Emma, "Did you notice anything out of place in the home when you returned? Clothes missing? Anything disrupted, broken, sign of entry?"

"Nothing at all," Emma said. "I had prepared his favorite dish, lasagna with meat sauce, and left it in the fridge. You know, to surprise him for dinner. I wanted him to have something of substance in the house while I was gone. But the container is still in the fridge, completely untouched with my note still stuck on top. That's why I think he never made it home."

"Right," Angus said. "Well, I know I couldn't pass up a good home-cooked meal."

Angus allowed another long pause to cover the room before speaking again.

"Anything else we need to know?" He asked.

"No, I said all I know to you and the officer yesterday," Emma said.

"OK then," Angus said as he smacked his knees with his hands, rocking back in his seat to get the momentum to stand up. "Well I'll get out of your hair. Thank you for the coffee, it was delightful, I do appreciate it. As soon as we know anything, we will be in touch."

Emma and Charlie both stood up with him, as Angus made his way to the front door, they followed closely behind.

Angus turned back to Emma and Charlie. "If you think of anything else that may help us, we would definitely appreciate it."

"Absolutely, thank you Angus," Emma said.

"Don't thank me yet," he said, "But trust me, we will do everything we can, and we *will* find your husband. For now, try your best to go on with your life. Now, I know that's hard to hear, heck, it's even hard for me to say. But it is especially important for your daughter, what did you say her name was?" He asked.

"Sophie," Emma said.

"Yes, especially for Sophie. I know this is hard and I know this is painful, but for the sake of Sophie, try to keep things routine. It's going to hurt like hell, but put on a happy, strong face for Sophie. It will make a world of difference."

Emma nodded softly as a bottomless pit of despair had replaced the spot where her heart once lived. She couldn't allow Sophie to feel this alone, this lost, this cold.

Angus reached for the knob of the front door, opening it to allow the sunlight and fresh air to sneak its way into the house. He turned around again.

"So, how do you two know each other, exactly?"

Charlie straightened up as Emma looked over her left shoulder at him.

"We," Charlie stuttered with nervousness. "We went to school together. High school. We were high school friends."

"Uh huh," Angus said. "And now you both live here in Seattle huh? Small world."

"I actually just moved here with my Fiance, Gwen. I didn't know Emma lived here. Now I just want to be here for her. It won't be easy going through something like this without a good friend."

"It's true, I appreciate having someone here for me," Emma said, smiling up at Charlie.

"Well, a good friend is worth his weight in gold. And you are no small boy Charlie, so that must really be worth something," Angus said, reaching out and grabbing Charlie by the shoulder. His big hand gripped so tightly, Charlie recoiled in pain.

"OK then," Angus said. "Thank you again for the coffee, and I *will* be in touch. Good day to the both of you."

When he got to his car, he opened the door and stared back at the front window of the VanSant home. He was partially shocked to see Charlie staring out at him. When their eyes met, Charlie smiled and waved. Angus returned the gesture before taking a seat in his boat of a Buick.

11

It was Friday morning, and a few days had passed since Detective Angus stopped by the VanSant home. She had taken his advice and done everything in her power to keep their family routines intact, even with Eddie not a part of them. She had thought about pulling Sophie from school and keeping her at home for the time being, but knew that would go against not only Angus' advice, but her own better judgment as a Mother.

"Come on, Soph. We can't be late for school, *again*," Emma shouted down the long hallway.

"OK, Mom!" Sophie shouted from down the hall, still in her room putting the finishing touches on her outfit.

Sophie emerged from her bedroom dressed like most little girls her age; Pink, sparkly sneakers with cute unicorns printed on them, pink denim jeans, a white zip up hooded sweatshirt with red polka dots. Her bright yellow blonde hair pulled up in two perfect pigtails.

"Take your backpack," Emma told her.

Sophie threw her purple and pink backpack over her shoulders, putting it on one arm at a time.

"Come on, we've got to go. Where are my *keys!*" Emma said, letting out a short grunt, feeling the pockets of her denim jacket.

"Look, they're on the counter!" Sophie yelled.

"Thank you, Sophie. I would lose my head if it weren't for you, kiddo," Emma said as she jetted to the counter to retrieve the keyring.

"Mom, where is my lunchbox?"

Emma had just made it to the front door when she was reminded, Sophie should probably eat that day. Most kids Emma knew needed to eat every day. And her little princess was growing daily not only in height, but also in appetite.

"Right, right. Lunch. A kid *has* to eat."

Emma turned back and ran to the kitchen again, picking up Sophie's lunchbox from the dining room table. The lunchbox was sparkly, covered in glitter, different tones of pinks and purple and little cartoon characters most folks older than 22 would never recognize.

"What would I do without you, kid?" Emma asked, leaning over and kissing her right on top of her head.

"Mom, gross!" Sophie shouted.

"Hey, I'm your mom. If I want to give you a kiss, I can," Emma shouted back. "OK, come on, let's go," Emma said as she opened the door and escorted Sophie outside.

They walked hand in hand down the path to the driveway. Emma latched Sophie into a car seat in the back of her dark blue Toyota Prius. Safety and saves money - a Win Win to any consumer. Emma jumped into the driver's seat and in a rush, backed out of the driveway.

Just as the tires hit the pavement, her phone began to ring, sending shrill ringing sounds that pumped through the car speakers. She recoiled a bit before glancing at the touch screen console of her Prius. It was her brother, Billy. She reached for the screen to accept the incoming call.

"Hello there, brother," Emma said in a long, drawn out tone.

"Hey sis," Billy said, his voice shooting through the speakers. "I'm just calling to check on you and Sophie. Are you doing OK?"

"Oh yeah, we're great. Isn't that right, Sophie?" Emma asked, looking over her right shoulder towards her daughter. Sophie didn't reply.

"Are you sure you don't want me to fly up there and stay with you for a few days? Help take some of the burden off? I don't know, just be around?"

"Thank you, but really, all things considered, we're doing OK. Besides, Charlie has been a huge help and he's so close in town. Anything we need, he's right here."

"Yeah, I know. You've said that before. I just, I don't know, Emma."

"What don't you know?"

"I feel like maybe you need family right now more than anything."

'Charlie *is* like family, you know that. He was basically our third sibling growing up. Besides, if you come here, who will be there for your own family? Kelly and the kids? They need you, too."

"I think they can manage for a few days, Emma," Billy said after a short pause.

"And I can manage, too. Trust me, we'll be OK. If anything changes, you'll be the first to know. If you came here, what could you do? Really? The police are doing everything they can."

"Emma, I really think —"

"Billy, please," Emma pleaded. "I'm a big girl. I can handle myself. If I need anything, I can call Charlie. And like usual, you and I will be in touch regularly. So if anything changes, I'll tell you."

"OK, Emma," Billy said, finally backing down. "Please don't feel that you need to do this alone. If you need me, you know where I am."

"I know brother bear. I know," Emma said with a relaxing sigh. "Look, I need to drop Sophie at school. I'll call you later."

"Sounds good, sis," Billy said. "I love you, Emma. Stay in touch, please."

"I always do," She said. "Love you, talk soon." She reached and pressed the button on the console screen ending the call.

Drop off was never a fun experience for Emma. Parents were required to walk their kids into the school and line up for the teachers, perform a flag salute and then wave as the students marched off to a day of learning. Emma saw it as nothing more than an opportunity for moms and dads with nothing better to do than stand around, gossip and make trouble. Because of the gossip, Emma, unfortunately, knew way too much about these parents, their friends and families. She had heard all about how Silvia Leonard's sister had an affair with the pool guy. She got the full breakdown of how Rick Epsosito's oldest son had been arrested for suspected DUI. And of course, the week-long gossip-a-thon around Dave and Shelly and their unpaid taxes and ongoing battle with the IRS. All of this she deemed a massive waste of her time, and no one's business. Most mornings Emma bit her tongue as the other moms and dads complained and told stories. Every day the urge to yell "Why can't you useless idiots just shut up already!" grew stronger.

She was also well aware word had gotten around about Eddie's disappearance, and she fully expected the flames of gossip to pick up with the wind and burn right in her direction. If there was anything that could make drop off even less appealing, that was it. She had hoped they would mind their own business, but if history proved anything, she had a better chance of hitting the lottery, being struck by lightning and finding a four-leaf clover all at the exact same moment. Emma pulled into the parking lot and found a spot close to the side gate where parents would enter the school for morning assembly. On the walk, she felt like a dead girl walking. Hopefully her favorite meal awaited her at the end of the path.

"Good Morning, Emma!" Yelled Silvia.

"Hey, Silvia. How are you?"

"Couldn't complain, and who would listen anyway?" Silva said with a long, annoying fake laugh.

"*I know I wouldn't,*" Emma thought to herself.

All the children gathered in the quad at the center of the large campus. The school had multiple buildings all separated by large concrete slab walkways, and unmanicured trees dumped leaves as though they were in mourning. At the edge of the quad sat a modest wooden stage. A middle aged woman with somewhat disheveled brunette hair, black-rimmed glasses with a floral skirt and a dark blue cardigan wrapping her body stood patiently at a microphone stand.

"Good Morning, families," The teacher shouted as the speakers shot feedback throughout the large outdoor area.

Everyone, including Emma, shut their eyes and covered their ears at the ungodly sound.

"Today one of our 4th graders, Noah Bennington will recite the pledge of allegiance. Everyone, please place your hands on your heart and say the pledge along with Noah," The teacher urged.

A little boy in blue jeans and a vintage Ken Griffey Jr t-shirt took the microphone and began reciting the pledge of allegiance. The entire crowd followed along, staring at the American Flag whipping in the wind at the far end of the quad. Emma stood, hand on her heart but her mouth never opened. She didn't feel the need to weigh in, but thought it appropriate enough to play along. The teacher took back the microphone and went into the typical, boring morning announcements. Useless proclamations that if they had been given during a meeting, some smart ass would say on the way out, "This could have been an email."

"Have a great day at school, Sophie. I'll see you this afternoon. Mommy loves you," she said as she kissed Sophie on the top of her head again.

"Come on, Mom," Sophie said.

"I can kiss you as much as I want, get that into your little head, kid. Now go on to class, you little monster you."

"I love you mommy," Sophie shouted as she ran off to catch up with her classmates.

"Love you too, kiddo," Emma shouted back. She knew Sophie didn't hear her, but that didn't matter.

Emma exited the campus through the same side gate when she spotted a couple of the parents standing in a circle, conversation formation. As she approached, she could hear their conversation, and what she feared most had come true.

"You know her husband is *missing*?" Asked Silvia.

"Oh my God, poor thing. I can't even imagine what I would do if I were in her shoes," another parent added.

"You know," said another parent. It was Shelly, a real pain in the ass award recipient. Almost a unanimous decision by the judges many years in a row, if the contest were a real thing. "*I* heard there was another woman. He ran off with her, and won't be coming back." She said, rolling her eyes in gossip glee.

"You did not hear that, did you?" Asked Silvia.

"Can you blame him? He's such a sweet, good-looking guy. You know she wasn't keeping him happy. I have a friend, who knows someone, who saw him over in Bellevue last weekend at a little cafe with a young girl. But you didn't hear it from me," Shelly said, putting her index finger over her lips, like she was bottling a secret.

Emma had heard enough.

"Oh really, Shelly? Is *that* what you heard?" Emma asked, with enough cut in her words to shape a diamond.

All the parents turned, eyes wide open like they had encountered a ghost.

"Oh, uh," Silvia said with a harsh stutter. "We're not talking about *you*. We're talking about uh, someone else."

"Yeah," Shelly agreed. "My friend's daughter's boyfriend. That is who we were talking about." She tried assuring Emma.

"You know what I think? I think you are all full of shit, and can all go to hell." Emma shouted, storming off to her car.

"Emma, you got this all wrong!" Silva shouted.

"You know what, Silvia? You can fuck yourself," Emma shouted back with a ferocious tone. "As a matter of fact, why don't you go fuck your pool boy again. I know you think that's *so in* right now." Emma slammed the door to her car, backed out recklessly and sped out of the parking lot.

Silva, Shelly and the other parents stood silent for a moment, unsure of how to proceed after being told off by someone they otherwise liked, even if their conversation didn't show it. Silva broke the silence,

"For the record, my *sister* fucked the pool boy. *Not* me."

12

Angus arrived at the police station around 9:00am each morning, barring any field work necessary regarding ongoing investigations. His office, on the second floor of the police station, was situated at the far end in the back of a large room. The office space was kept dark, which is how Angus preferred it. The office was slightly old-fashioned and out of date. Cream painted walls were crying out for a new coat and new color, and dark wooden desks with scratched steel legs that should have been dismantled years ago, made the dark office seem all that much darker with just the right amount of dingy, vintage charm. Just beyond the rows of the old desks were two offices. One belonged to Angus, and the other to his partner Frank McKenna. Thick, heavy wooden doors separated the main room from the offices, paint slightly peeling in different spots on each, with large glass windows that allowed the detectives to see the main room. Angus entered through the door at the opposite end of the room, and made the long, slow walk to his office. Although Angus was no longer a uniformed officer, he arrived every morning in what could only be described as his own uniform. The same black slacks, white button-down shirt with a black tie and his signature tan blazer. He couldn't get to his office without walking past a couple of officers who were sitting at their respective desks. One of which was on the phone, the other typing away on his keyboard, switching his view furiously between the bright monitor and a stack of paperwork on his desk.

"Stan, what's good my man?" Asked Angus.

"Typing up reports to get them into the system. Another beautiful morning at the department," Officer Stan said sarcastically.

"You're changing the world one key press at a time, Stan," Angus said. He tapped his hand on his desk a few times, "Don't work too hard, alright?"

"You got it, Detective." Stan went back to pounding away on his keyboard.

He cracked the door to his office open which resulted in a loud squeal from the continuously warping wood and cracking door jamb. Angus worked in a modest office without many frills or decorations. An old wooden desk sat in the middle of the room with a low riding desk chair pushed underneath and a few framed photos sat on top of the desk of his family. The most vibrant decor in the entire office was a felt Seahawks pennant hanging just above the couch, across from his vintage desk. He removed his tan blazer, tossed it around the back of the chair, and sat down, letting out a deep sigh as he relaxed. On his desk sat a manilla folder with some papers inside. He stared at it momentarily wondering where it may have come from. He opened the folder and began flipping through the pages within. Just then, the door to the office next to his flung open, and seconds later Frank appeared in his doorway.

"Oh good, you are already hard at work, I see," Frank said.

"Frank," Angus said with a twinge of annoyance in his voice, "I had a feeling *this* had something to do with you," he said pointing at the mess of papers.

"Of course," Frank said as he entered the office and promptly took a seat on the couch. "That right there is all the information we pulled from Eddie VanSant's phone. Just like you asked."

"Good, good," Angus said, nodding his head in approval. "Tell me, do I need to read all of this or can you give me the abridged version?"

"I think you better go through it," Frank urged.

Angus slammed the folder and pushed it away from him on the desk.

"I haven't even had my third cup of coffee yet, Frank. You know the deal."

"I had a feeling you might say that. That's why I'm one step ahead of you."

"Oh yeah?" Angus asked, rubbing his face. It was just after 9:00am and Angus was already exhausted from the day. "How's that, exactly?"

"I've got a fresh pot brewing as we speak."

"You see, Frank. You're a smart guy. Why you decided *not* to lead with that information, well, that's an investigation even *I* don't want to oversee."

"I'll crack the case for you, my friend," Frank said as he stood up from the couch. "I just want to keep you happy and caffeinated."

"Smart man," Angus said with a smile.

Frank left the room to retrieve the coffee Angus desperately needed. Not only did Angus need it, but Frank wanted him to be the determined bulldog detective he knew he could be. When you are partners long enough, you learn the tricks to get the other person going. Frank had studied Angus for years, and could write a doctorate paper on his wants, needs and of course his many quirks. Three cups appeared to be the lucky number for Angus. He checked his watch and tapped his fingers on the desk as he waited impatiently for his coffee to arrive. Even a few minutes seemed like years to Angus. Soon, Frank entered the room again, this time holding two coffee cups, steam shooting from the mouth of both. He set one on Angus' desk and he lit up like a Christmas tree.

"Ah, Frank. A king amongst men. You do know that's how I describe you to my friends and neighbors, right?"

"You mean, I've graduated from being the village asshole?"

"Oh, long ago," Angus said, sinking deep into his chair with his cup of black gold. He took a long sip followed by a deep and clearly antagonizing *AHHHH*. He sat back and let the hot coffee run down his throat as he began to burst to life. He sat up straight, set down his mug and slapped the top of his desk. "OK, *now* we can get to work. What have we got here, huh? Phone records, GPS coordinates. Good, good. Anything sticking out to you, Frankie?"

Frank leaned forward on the couch, "Well did she or did she not say she had called him, what, *countless* times over the weekend? If you flip to the next page, you will see those calls. Unless my eyes deceive me, I see about 6 phone calls from Emma's phone to Eddie's stretching from Friday evening through the time she contacted police. Now, I don't know about you, but I've never categorized 6 of *anything* as countless, have you?"

"No, I haven't," Angus said, his tone becoming more serious.

"And only two of those phone calls resorted to voicemails being left. I know if my wife were missing, I think I would have called much more than 6 times."

"What was the nature of the voicemails? Did she sound concerned in any way, or was she nonchalant about the whole thing?"

"Oh no, she definitely sounded concerned. Much more concerned in the text messages to him, which you can see if you flip a couple pages back."

"Uh huh," Angus said, skimming the text messages Frank had printed out for him to review. "Let me see here." Angus read some of the text messages aloud.

"About to take off, will text when we land XOXO."

"Landed in San Diego safe and sound. Love you."

"Brother is already drunk at parents house, god he is so annoying. Wish you were here XOXO."

"What is this XOXO I keep seeing in these messages?" Asked Angus.

"That is a text message shorthand for hugs and kisses," Frank said with a laugh.

"Well, *that* I don't understand," Angus said. "Every year these kids and their *slang*. Why can't anyone just *talk* to someone?"

Angus continued skimming the text message exchanges aloud.

"Haven't heard from you, is everything OK?"

"You didn't lose your phone again, did you? CALL ME!"

"I am getting worried, where are you?"

"There's a lot of that type of content in there, and a lot of other mindless chatter mixed in. Messages from friends about baseball. Not much to go on," said Angus.

"I felt the same. We have to wait until we get the video back. Although there was some aggressive back and forth with some guy named Johnny. Could be worth checking out."

"Any word on when we can see the footage?"

"Well, well. Speak of the devil here he is," Frank said looking out Angus' office window as another detective approached.

"Good Morning, gentlemen," Said the detective.

"Good Morning, Ted," Said Angus. "Give me some good news, would you?"

Ted was another veteran detective on the force. He was tall, slim with perfectly combed silver hair. He wore an all black suit, white button-down shirt with a thin black necktie. Clearly a detective who had seen a few too many episodes of X Files.

"Can I assume that is your *third* cup, Angus?" Asked Ted.

"Don't worry, Ted. I greased the wheels," said Frank. "For all of our sake."

"Really funny," Angus said. "Have we got anything to see or what?"

"Yep, I have some footage ready."

"Great news!" Angus shouted as he rose from his chair, threw on his tan jacket and made his way out of the office. Frank stood up and followed closely behind.

● ● ●

The door opened to a small video room which was kept pitch black aside from a wall of surveillance screens. There was a small desk in the room equipped with video recording equipment, computers, hard drives and more screens. At the desk sat an audio visual technician for the department. Ted held the door open for Angus and Frank to enter.

"Come on down, boys," Said Ted, playing like a television game show host.

"Good Morning, Detectives," Said the technician.

The technician was Kelly, a young tech savvy woman with short brown hair tied up into a messy bun. She didn't dress like someone who worked for law enforcement, and she didn't need to.

"You mind shutting the door all the way?" Asked Kelly.

"You need a bigger work space, Kelly," Said Frank.

"Yeah. I make do. Here, take a look."

Kelly began clicking around with her mouse, retrieving the pre-selected videos.

"The first is from the day Mr. VanSant went missing. This was picked up that morning, sometime after 8:30. As you can see, we picked up his Silver Toyota driving through an intersection. I was able to zoom in to verify the plates on the front with what Detective McKenna provided. And if we zoom in a little closer and pan up, well, who do *you* guys see?"

Frank and Angus looked at each other uncomfortably, and each took in a deep breath in unison.

"Oh boy," said Angus.

It was Emma, clear as day. She had driven Eddie's car the day he went missing.

"Did she tell us she had his car at *any* time that day?" Asked Frank.

"No, no she didn't," Angus said, rubbing the top of his head.

"If you boys enjoyed that, I think you will like this one even more," Kelly said looking over her shoulder with a sort of devilish grin.

She clicked her mouse a few more times to bring up the second video.

"Same day, but much later in the evening. We got the manager to give us the footage from the Pool Center at the park on Pine Avenue," Kelly told them.

From the pool center, about 50 yards down the street, they could see Pine Avenue. The video played for a short time when from the far left of the video, Eddie's silver Toyota came into view, slowed down and parked along the curb in perfect sight of the camera set atop the clubhouse. Even from 50 yards back, the detectives could see what appeared to be a man sitting in the driver's seat. The mystery man exited the vehicle and calmly walked down Pine Avenue towards the intersection at the end of the street. The man was wearing black pants, black shoes, a black sweatshirt and a black ski mask.

"You can clearly see, whoever this is, abandoning the vehicle right there on Pine Avenue. If we switch to this camera view," said Kelly, clicking away at her computer. "This camera was facing the opposite end of the street, so we can see him walk down Pine and turn left on Cedar Street. But unfortunately, that is where we lose eyes on him." Kelly said as she clicked away from the videos.

"What do you make of it, Angus?" Asked Frank.

"Well, that's our guy, there's no question about it. But," he says, biting his bottom lip and sucking in air slowly. "Emma driving the car. It raises a *big* flag. Even more so, the direction this guy is going is the route I took from the park to the VanSant home. The VanSant's live off of Cedar, on Woodson."

"So you're thinking—" Frank started but was cut off by Angus.

"I'm thinking alright. Maybe it isn't just one person behind this."

"So, is Emma now a suspect?"

Angus stared intently at the glowing wall of screens for a moment.

"Everyone is a suspect." Angus said.

13

Emma was in her kitchen tidying up that morning when she heard a knock on her front door. The kitchen sink faucet was on as she did dishes. She turned the water off, dried her hands and threw the towel over her left shoulder. Today she wore a light gray oversized sweatshirt and yoga pants with her hair in what was clearly her signature slightly messy ponytail. She made her way across the living room and opened the front door. Standing on her porch was Charlie.

"Come on in," Emma said, using her right arm to lead the way.

Emma swung the door shut behind him as he made his way to the living room couch and took a seat.

"Don't mind me, I'm an *absolute* mess today," Emma joked, her hands clenched into fists and pressed against her hips.

"Oh stop it, not even. You look great," Charlie said with a mile wide grin.

"You're too sweet," Emma said. "Sorry I'm running a little late, I still need to shower. Feel free to turn on the TV and watch something, I won't be too awfully long."

She had made her way back into the kitchen to finish the last couple of dishes in need of cleaning.

"No problem," Charlie said, sitting back in full relaxation on the sofa. "Say, where's my little friend this morning?"

"She's in her room, on her iPad, like usual," Emma shouted from the kitchen. "These kids, I tell you what, you can't break them away from those screens no matter how hard you try."

"That's what today is all about. Breaking away from the screens, unplugging, getting out into the fresh air and getting some beautiful sun on our skin," Charlie shouted back.

Charlie had offered to take Emma and Sophie to the Woodland Park Zoo. Nothing like some lions, tigers and bears to take a kid's mind off of her missing father. It wasn't a cure all, but Charlie hoped maybe it would help at least a little.

"You have a prayer, Mr. Claymore," Emma said as she entered the living room, drying her hands on the hand towel.

He stood up from the couch and met her at the entrance to the kitchen.

"What can I say? I have high hopes for today. Besides, who doesn't love seeing a tiger, live in the flesh."

Just then, he put his hands up like an attacking animal and playfully made cat noises and poked at Emma's stomach. She immediately stepped back, pushing his hands away from her.

"OK, weirdo. That isn't creepy, like, *at* all," she said with an annoyed tone to her voice.

"I'm sorry, I was just playing around." Charlie said.

She stared at him with confusion in her eyes for a moment before deciding maybe it wasn't that big of a deal.

"No, it's fine. It's just, you know, might not be appropriate."

"I totally get it. I sincerely apologize. I was just trying to have a little fun."

"Maybe let's just keep our hands to ourselves today, though? That work?"

"Loud and clear," Charlie said with a mock salute to Emma.

"Put on some TV, read a book. Do *something*. I'm going to shower and get ready and then we can get going."

Charlie promptly sat back down, sinking into the soft sofa, kicking his feet up on the coffee table and clicking on the TV. He clicked through some channels for a short time when he heard a loud, forceful knock at the front door. Charlie shot up at the sound. It was no typical neighbor knocking. That knock had purpose, it had meaning behind it. He walked to the front door and jerked it open. Standing on the front porch was Detectives Angus and Frank with two uniformed police officers behind them.

"Hey, Hey, Uh Hi," Charlie said, clearly nervous.

"Good Morning Mr. Claymore. Do you remember me? I'm Detective Angus Pratt. This is my partner, Detective Frank McKenna. Is Mrs. VanSant home?" Angus and Frank both flashed their badges before putting them back into their respective jacket pockets.

"Yeah, of course. She just went to get into the shower," Charlie said. He shifted his stance and scrunched his face in confusion. "Is something wrong? Is there something I can help you with? Wait, did you find Eddie?" Charlie shot up straight with momentary excitement.

"We need to speak with Mrs. VanSant. Please, go get her," Angus said.

Upon hearing the unrecognizable voices echoing through her home, Emma emerged from the hallway. She was just as confused as Charlie about this clear show of force. Four police officers banging on the front door to your home could put anyone into a panic.

"Good Morning, Detectives. What can I do for you?" She looked at Charlie like he had done something wrong. "You didn't invite them in? Come on in guys, I can get some coffee going. I know Angus *loves* his coffee."

Angus interrupted her as she walked towards the kitchen.

"Uh, no, thank you Mrs. VanSant," Angus said sternly.

"Mrs. VanSant," Emma questioned. "Why so formal all of a sudden?"

"Look, Mrs. VanSant. We have reason to believe you may have more knowledge about the whereabouts of your husband than you have let on. You're going to need to come with us," Angus said with a tone of seriousness in his voice.

Emma and Charlie's eyes met, both in complete shock. They both stuttered words for a moment attempting to buy time for their brains to catch up with what their ears just heard.

"Whoa, hold on a second," Charlie said, stepping between the officers and Emma. "What are you trying to say here? What the hell is going on? She didn't do anything."

"Mr. Claymore, please get out of the way. Don't make this harder than it needs to be," Angus urged.

The two uniformed officers pushed their way past the detectives and stopped at the doorway. Charlie, fists now clenched tightly, could feel his blood beginning to boil. He glared at the officers from the top of his eyes, his face taking on an expression as though he was an entirely different person. Possessed by the demon of protection in the name of Emma.

"You guys are making a *big* mistake," Charlie growled, standing his ground.

"Mr. Claymore," Angus said, staring up at the sky showing he had very little patience left in this exchange of words. "Remove yourself from the doorway immediately. Mrs. VanSant you're going to need to come with us. We can do this the easy way, or we can make this a very unpleasant situation for all of us, and I am in no mood for unpleasantries."

"It's OK Charlie," Emma said, pushing him softly out of her way, now in tears. "I'll go."

One of the uniformed officers reached for Emma, grabbing her by the arm and pulling her out of the door into the cold morning air.

"I said I will go!" Emma shouted at the officers, attempting to shake their hands off of her.

"Get your fucking hands off of her!" Charlie shouted at the officers, as he began pushing towards them.

Angus moved between Charlie and the policeman. He now stood chest to chest with an enraged Charlie.

"You can calm down, Mr. Claymore or you'll be coming with us, too. Don't think we aren't keeping an eye on you."

Charlie and Angus stood their ground, glaring into each other's eyes as though either one of them could have reached in and tore out the other's soul. Charlie was breathing fast and furious, his heart beating through his chest like the idling engine of a muscle car. Angus, calm and composed, had been face to face with much worse than the likes of Charlie Claymore, and he was composed and confident.

"Watch your step, Mr. Claymore. One more move and I'll cuff you *and* her and drag your asses out of this house. You got it? Stand down," Angus instructed.

"Detective Pratt," one of the officers shouted into the house, "Do you want us to cuff her?"

"No, that's not necessary," Angus said, not breaking his intense stare into Charlie's furious, almost possessed eyes. "I don't think we will have a problem with her, will we?"

Something inside Charlie clicked and he relaxed his position, breaking his stare and taking a few steps back away from Angus.

"I didn't think so," Angus said with a slight smirk. He continued to keep his eye on Charlie, "Emma, you are under arrest for the disappearance of one, Eddie VanSant," he shouted loudly. He continued to recite her rights. Once he wrapped up the spiel, he nodded at Charlie and turned to leave.

The two uniformed officers escorted Emma down the long walkway, past the driveway to the street and into a black and white police car, its lights spiraling out of control filling the neighborhood with flashes of blue and red.

"Charlie, watch Sophie, please!" Emma pleaded. "Please, stay with her!"

Angus stopped as he made his way down the long concrete walkway and turned back to Charlie, who remained in the doorway. He continued watching as they arrested Emma for the disappearance of her own husband. A crime Charlie knew she had no part in.

"Looks like you're on babysitting duty, old friend," Angus said. "While we're talking, I should suggest that if I were you, I wouldn't leave town. Got it?"

Charlie didn't respond, he just shot daggers through Angus' body with his eyes. For a moment he imagined daggers piercing through his torso, splattering the driveway, yard and trees with blood. In such an inconsolable rage, he imagined a hammer dropping onto that big, shiny bald head. Less messy, much more violent.

"Thanks for your cooperation Mr. Claymore. We'll be in touch. Have a great day."

As Emma was escorted to the police vehicle, she glanced around the neighborhood and was immediately filled with shame and embarrassment. All of her neighbors - Moms, Dads, their children, people she considered friends, all watched in shock as she was taken away by police. The idea that Emma could have had anything to do with Eddie's disappearance would send a shockwave through not only this neighborhood, but the entire community. Emma feared her life would never be the same.

14

Emma sat in a sterile interrogation room equipped with a light so bright, she felt as though her skin was burning like a Thanksgiving turkey left in an oven. She sat at a small metal table, with a large mirror covering the wall in front of her. She stared at it for a moment, but realized she couldn't stomach the sight of it. Partially because she knew some faceless detective was behind that mirror analyzing her. Also, because she couldn't stand the sight of herself. She couldn't believe where she found herself. Stuck in a nightmare that just wouldn't end. She began pinching her left forearm just to be certain she was awake. And realized, this was all too real. She was sick with sadness, embarrassment and filled with enough rage to power a large city. She sat alone for what seemed like an eternity. Trapped like a rat, at the mercy of police officers who she thought were there to help. She couldn't imagine why they thought she had anything to do with Eddie's disappearance, and knew they couldn't have any concrete evidence. She thought they were on their way to becoming friends, now all but certain they saw her as the enemy. A criminal. A woman who would harm her own husband and the father of her child. She was a hurricane of emotions, thoughts swirling around inside her skull and nothing she could do would help her find safety or security in this moment. The door shot open as Angus entered. He set a bottle of water down in front of Emma, which she picked up and held tightly in her small hands, nervously crinkling the plastic.

"Alright Mrs. VanSant, let's not waste any time here," Angus said, staring into the mirror.

"Emma," she said.

"Excuse me?" Angus asked, turning around to look at her.

"It's Emma," she responded, clearing her throat nervously. "My name is Emma."

"Right," Angus said. He pulled out the chair opposite Emma and took a seat, slapping a manilla folder onto the table. "Well, let's get right into it, Emma. I asked you on day one if there was anything else you might want to share with me. I think you made a bit of an error. I'm giving you the opportunity right now to fix that error."

"What do you mean?" Emma asked.

"Are you certain you didn't leave *anything* out of your story? Anything at all?"

"I can't think of anything I missed."

"OK," Angus said, nodding his head. He opened the manilla folder, pulling out a printed photo of Emma driving Eddie's car.

"What can you tell me about this photo? And, by the way, pay *very* close attention to the date and time on this."

He slowly slid the photo across the table for her to examine. She picked it up and her eyes went wide for a second and she let out a small laugh before setting the picture back down on the table.

"What, this?" Emma mocked. "This is why you arrested me? Because I drove my husband's car?"

"Emma, this isn't a joke," Angus said.

"Come on. You can't think I had anything to do with Eddie's disappearance. You really think that? Based on what, one photo?"

"Well, explain it," Angus urged.

"What, this one photo of me driving my husband's car?" Emma said with a giggle.

"If I have created such a comedic situation, please, fill me in on the details. Don't keep me in suspense Mrs," He stopped himself. "I mean, Emma. Let me in on the joke, please."

"OK," Emma said, straightening her posture and placing her arms down on the table. "It's quite simple, really. Eddie had to work that Friday. Just like I told you. That morning, I took his car to drop Sophie off at School. Once she was safely in class, I drove home. At that point, he took his car and drove to work. Are you satisfied?"

"No, Emma. I am *not* satisfied," He replied.

"I'm sorry," she said, shaking her head. "I don't know what to tell you. Because that is the cold hard truth. Take it or leave it."

"You need to get serious," He urged. " Why did you choose to drive *his* car instead of yours that morning?"

Emma sat silent, staring at Angus as a sly smile washed over her face. In her mind, Angus was playing checkers while she played chess. And she felt as though she had just locked in on the move of the century.

"Come on Emma," Angus said seriously, leaning back in his chair and rolling his eyes. His patience was evaporating faster than drops of water on the blacktop in July.

After a few moments Emma finally sat forward and spoke.

"Our neighbor's had their gardeners show up early that morning and they were trimming some trees in their backyard. The trailer was hooked to their truck, you know, to haul all that junk away? It was blocking our driveway. My car was blocked, and his car was not. Sophie needed to get to school, so I took his car. Is that a good enough answer for you? Does that, I don't know, crack the case?" Emma sat back in the chair with a smug look on her face. Check mate.

"OK then," Angus said, sitting forward, shaking his head and crossing his arms on top of the cold, metal table. "What we don't know is why you conveniently left that detail out of your statement. Seems to me like a big piece of information, you driving your missing husband's abandoned car the day of his disappearance."

"It must have slipped my mind. My husband had disappeared, and, for the record, is still missing. Instead of searching for him you want to arrest me? Please, Detective." Emma sat back in her chair, shaking her head.

"So," Angus pushed.

"So, what?"

"So your story can be verified by your neighbors? And by the gardeners?"

"Call them up. Please," she said with confidence. "Check my phone, check my GPS. I was home the rest of the day until I went to pick up Sophie from school."

"We will *definitely* be taking your phone. That I can assure you."

Emma pulled her cell phone from the pocket of her yoga pants and tossed it across the table.

"Take it, be my guest," she said with a smug look on her face.

Angus realized this may have been a mistake. He stuck the cell phone in the chest pocket of his white button-down shirt. "Thank you," He said with some attitude.

"Before I take this over to get checked, what can you tell me about this photo?" Angus removed another photo from the folder. It showed the masked stranger exiting Eddie's vehicle at the park on Pine Avenue. "Look familiar to you?"

Emma's eyes widened and all the smug attitude was wiped right out of her expression as it switched to shock.

"Oh my god," she said, putting her hand over her mouth. "Is that? Is that the person who took Eddie?" Her eyes began to fill with tears.

"We think so, yes," Angus said. "Here's another set of photos."

Angus showed her the opposite angle from the pool building, which showed the masked stranger heading down Pine Avenue and taking a left on Cedar, which led to her home.

"Whoever this is, abandoned Eddie's vehicle at the park before leaving on foot. He went down Pine, took a left on Cedar, which, correct me if I am wrong, doesn't that lead right to your home? Do you recognize this person?"

Emma shook her head, the hurricane in her head had strengthened. The air in the room was thickening, and it was getting harder for her to breathe.

"No, I don't know who that could be."

"No idea whatsoever? This doesn't remind you of anyone you might know, or someone who might know Eddie and want to hurt him?"

Emma picked up the picture and looked closer.

"I could be wrong. In fact I am certain I'm wrong. I *must* be," she said to herself out loud.

"It clearly rang a bell, so, out with it. Who is it in this picture?"

She took a long deep breath, "It looks like Eddie's co-worker, John."

Angus pulled a pen from his shirt pocket and flipped open a small notepad sitting on the table. He started writing onto the pad feverishly. "John who? What is his last name?"

"John Torres, they call him Johnny. They've worked together for years. Eddie and Johnny were both up for this promotion at work, and Eddie was chosen over him. I know he was angry about it at first, but that was close to a year ago. Eddie said they were on much better terms. They even go get beers after work sometimes. You know, in a group with coworkers? Oh my *god*."

"Emma, we don't know for certain who this is, Johnny or otherwise. Are you close with Johnny? Do you consider him a friend? When was the last time you specifically spoke with Johnny?"

This was now the second time Johnny Torres' name had been mentioned, once by Frank in the text messages found on Eddie's phone, and now from Emma. Angus knew this was someone worth looking into.

"I never speak to him unless we happen to be in the same place at the same time. I don't know him or consider him much of *anything*," Emma nervously held the water bottle in her hands, crinkling it over and over.

"Is there anything else you haven't told us? I can't stress this enough, Emma. Now is your absolute *last* chance to tell us anything."

"No," Emma said, shaking her head, "That's all I know. I swear."

"Stay here. I'm going to have our technician go through your phone and verify your gardener story. I really hope for your sake that you are telling me the truth."

"I am telling you the goddamn truth," Emma said, completely out of patience.

"I sure hope so," Angus said, reaching for the door knob to leave the room. Just before he opened the door he stopped and turned back to Emma, "What about your friend, Charlie?"

"What about him?" Emma asked, a confused look washing over her face.

"We got a tip that someone saw you with Charlie before Eddie disappeared. Just you and him at a cafe. You two sat together for a few hours, did you not?"

"What does that have to do with *any* of this?" Emma asked.

"Maybe nothing, I don't know. If there was anything to tell, I would hope you would open up about it."

"There's nothing to say," Emma said, sniffling and rubbing her nose. "He's an old friend that I met for coffee. He's a good friend and nothing more."

"I'll take your word for it," Angus said, turning back to the door. "Don't you go anywhere, now."

Angus smiled and winked as he left the interrogation room. Emma stared at herself in the mirror for a short time. Angry at herself, at Eddie, at the police and the entire world. She took hold of that water bottle, cocked her arm back and threw it with all of her might into the mirror. The bottle cracked open, sending water splashing all over the room.

Angus verified Emma's story about the gardeners, just the way she told it. He also had the police technician dig through her phone as though it were a gold rush excavation. Nothing jumped out linking Emma to Eddie's disappearance. No phone calls, text messages or any other communications between her and Johnny Torres. In fact, Johnny's number wasn't even in her phone as a contact. Dead end. All they found were the same text messages and outgoing calls to Eddie they had already seen, with nothing from him whatsoever in return. Another dead end. The only thing that stuck out to Angus was the text messages back and forth between Emma and Charlie. They were in contact often, more so after Eddie's disappearance had been reported to the police. Although, almost as to confuse Angus even further, a lot of the messages from Charlie were about this mystery fiance of his, Gwen. Angus decided Charlie really must be one hell of a friend, albeit overbearing and demanding. All the digging led to nothing but dead end after dead end, and Emma would be sent home. He found himself relieved by this. He liked Emma, he felt for her. And the thought of her doing anything to harm Eddie, in the end, even he found it hard to believe. The door to the interrogation room swung open again as Angus filled the doorway. He looked at Emma with a smile and motioned for her to stand up.

"Are you taking me to jail?" Emma asked.

"No, you're free to go. Here's your phone," Angus said.

"So, what? Everything checked out? Can you *finally* get back to looking for my fucking husband?"

"Emma, please," Angus said, putting his hands in front of his large body to calm the situation, "I know you're angry at me and I apologize. Please understand where our heads are. We have to check under every rock and around every corner to get answers."

Angus put out his big hand to shake Emma's. She returned the favor, shaking his hand and cracking a faint smile.

"Come on," Angus said, motioning to the open door, "I'll have an officer give you a lift home."

Emma made the long walk through the brick lined corridor of the police station with Angus following closely behind. They reached a large steel door at the end of the cold hallway. He removed a key card from his pocket, swiped it along the card reader which let out a loud buzzing sound. He then swung the door open leading to a lobby of the police station. To Angus' absolute shock, the first person he saw sitting there was none other than Charlie Claymore. Sitting and gripping the arms of the chair so tightly that his knuckles were white. The way he was feverishly biting the inside of his mouth, if he wasn't careful, he could have bit clear through his bottom lip.

"Well, well, look who it is. How did I not guess you would be here?" Angus asked.

Charlie ignored him as though he was a ghost. He grabbed Emma gently by both of her arms and spoke close to her, "Are you OK? What the hell happened in there?"

"Everything is fine. I'm fine, it was a big misunderstanding," Emma said.

"Just tying up some loose ends, Mr. Claymore," Angus said without making eye contact. Still unsure if he trusted Charlie, he wasn't prepared to respect him.

Charlie glared up at the large detective before he turned his attention back to Emma.

"Come on, let's get you home," Charlie said, putting his arm around her shoulder leading her to the exit. As they reached the automatic doors, Charlie turned and looked over his shoulder, shooting a glare in Angus' direction.

Angus smiled and waved as the doors slammed shut behind them. Just then, Frank came rushing up the hallway, his face was flush and he appeared out of breath. He was rushing his words trying to speak.

"A-A-Angus," Frank rushed out. "We, we've got to go!"

"Whoa there, calm down," Angus said, resting his large hand on Frank's right shoulder. "What's going on, buddy? You look like you've seen a ghost."

"We've got to go," Frank urged. "We've got a homicide at 8135 Woodson Drive."

"Woodson Drive!?" Angus shouted, much louder than he probably should have in a police station. "Isn't that —"

"The same street where the VanSant's live," Frank cut him off.

They turned and ran towards the back exit of the station. Just when they thought things couldn't get more interesting, all hell began to break loose.

15

Emma sat low in the passenger seat of Charlie's car as he escorted her home. Charlie was noticeably angry about the entire situation. First her husband had been kidnapped and if that weren't bad enough, the detectives who should be out finding both Eddie *and* the kidnapper decide to arrest *the wife*. This was one of his closest friends, and he was taking every bit of it too personally.

"That guy's an asshole," Charlie said.

"Yeah," Emma said, staring at her hands, cupped together in her lap. "He's just doing what he thinks is right."

"How can you say that? He *arrested* you for the kidnapping of your *own* husband!"

"You think I don't understand that, Charlie? I think I get it more than you do."

Emma turned and stared out the window, she didn't want to look at or be around anyone, including Charlie. He looked at her, back to the road and then back to her, realizing he needed to soften his tone. She was right. If anyone had the right to be upset, it was her. Charlie was just getting in the way with his attitude. Two storms can not materialize at once. That would be pure chaos. He needed to be the yin to her yang. The calming force to the storm brewing inside both her chest and skull.

"Emma, look," Charlie said. "I apologize. It's just," he rested his left elbow on the car door and placed his head against his open palm. "I want to help, I want to take care of you and be here for you. So yes, *I am* taking it personally because I care about you. But that's it. I don't want to create more trouble for you. Please forgive me."

Emma turned to Charlie and smiled. She reached across the car and grabbed his right hand and squeezed it, "I know, Charlie. Thank you."

"By the way, I hate to ask," Emma's voice served as a warning of what was to come, "But, I know I asked you to watch Sophie."

"Oh, yes. Don't worry," Charlie said, cutting her off. "I dropped her at the neighbors house, they said they can keep her as long as you need. As soon as I get you home I will go over and get her and bring her home. I even made lunch for her."

"Wow, look at you," Emma said, impressed. "What was on the menu today, chef?"

"Oh you know, just a little blue box action. Some of my famous mac and cheese. Nothing crazy, but *never* boring either. My blue box blues have been known to be legendary."

They both shared a laugh. Charlie was ecstatic that his presence seemed to calm Emma's nerves and help take her mind off of the awful situation in which she and Sophie had been forced into. As Charlie's car drove down Cedar, they passed by Pine Avenue. Emma looked out the window to her left and stared down the road towards the park. Her vision locked as her head spun around staring out the back window.

"You OK?"

"Yeah, I just," Emma shook her head. "I don't think I can ever visit that park again. They showed me pictures from the day his car was abandoned. They have video of the car being parked, and some guy wearing all black and a ski mask got out. He walked down the street, and then walked down this *exact road* towards our home. I mean, what the *fuck?*"

Charlie's face washed over with concern, "Did you recognize whoever it was? I mean, that has to be the guy who took Eddie, right?" He said, followed by a large gulp.

"I think so. But no, I didn't recognize him. It's just so eerie that he probably knows where we live. I mean, what if he came to the house after he dropped off the car? What if Eddie was actually home?"

Just when Emma didn't think the deep end could get much deeper, the edge of the pool dropped and what seemed like a never ending waterfall had appeared, pouring misery right into the deepest caverns of Emma's soul, pulling her deeper and deeper into her own personal hell. Charlie slowed his car, flicked on the turn signal and turned left onto Emma's street. Before he had straightened the steering wheel back into position, they both knew life on that street was about to get much more complicated.

"You have *got* to be fucking kidding me," Charlie said, frustration boiling over from within.

"Oh shit!" Emma shouted, sitting straight up in her seat. "What the *fuck* is going on now?"

Stretching all the way down Woodson Drive, the otherwise quiet and safe neighborhood was now lined with police cars. Their bright red and blue lights flashing and illuminating everything as far as the eye could see. Uniformed officers had taken over the neighborhood and had surrounded a home close to the end of the road.

"Who lives there, Emma?" Charlie asked.

"That's Mrs. Hart's home," Emma said, covering her mouth with her right hand. "Oh no. I hope everything is OK."

16

Angus and Frank pulled up to the house on Woodson Drive, across the street and a few houses down from the VanSant's. The street was overrun with black and white cop cars, parked all over the road blocking any and all traffic in and out of the neighborhood. The lights flashing on many of the cars sent brilliant reds and blues bouncing off the other homes. Angus and Frank jumped out of the big Buick and rushed to the scene, making their way onto the front lawn of the home. The house was a trendy looking ranch style with large mid century modern windows stretching floor to ceiling. The home was less updated than some of the others on the street, say, the VanSant home. The two detectives were met by a uniformed officer who had been waiting on the front grass. A clean cut, bulky officer by the name of Steven Williams.

"Officer Williams," Angus shouted as they approached. "First, let's get this street locked down tighter than this, huh? We don't need people coming in and out of here. Frank?"

"I am on it, boss," Frank assured. Frank turned and called out to two more uniformed officers who were standing on the driveway. "Hey, you two, get the tape and let's lock this entire street down."

"Alright Williams, tell me what's going on here," Angus said.

"The victim is Mary Hart, she lived here alone," Officer Williams said. "A neighbor called in for a wellness check. The neighbor, one Donald Pritchard, claims Mrs. Hart is outside with her garden almost every morning. He said he hadn't seen her recently and has been banging on the door each day to no answer. He became concerned, as she is an older lady. Responding Officer Davis knocked to no answer and began walking around the house. The back window on the master bathroom was open, and when he looked inside he saw the resident deceased in the shower."

"No chance of natural causes?" Angus asked, sure of his assessment.

"Well," Williams started before clamming up. "Come with me and you'll see. But I would suggest you prepare yourself, it isn't pretty."

"Where are we with evidence? Shoe prints, fingerprints or any DNA that has been recovered?" Angus asked.

"We're still working on it," said Williams. "From our initial inspection, it looks like whoever did this knew what they were doing. They were careful and methodical. We might be fucked on this one, Angus."

Officer Williams escorted Angus through the home. The closer they got to the bedroom, the more obvious it became there was a dead body in the house. The wretched stench of death had claimed this house as its own and taken over the air all throughout the residence. An obvious struggle had taken place. The bedroom door had been smashed and splintered to bits, sending shards of wood all over the room. The inside of the door had blood spatter and smears that had long since dried up, leaving stains of dark crimson that had become almost black. There were apparent blood droplets along the carpet as well. The bed was in shambles, glass shattered on one side of the bed and a broken picture frame laid on the carpet. The bed was situated in the middle of the room with a nightstand on either side, and a big vintage dresser sat pressed against the wall opposite the bed. Just past the dresser was a doorway which led to the master bathroom. The blood droplets led a path directly into the bathroom. Angus stepped carefully through the bedroom to not disturb the evidence still being collected. He stepped across the floor and stopped in front of the bathroom door.

"She in here?" Angus asked, holding a handkerchief up to his mouth and nose.

"Sure is, sir," Williams said, also holding a piece of cloth to his face. "You're going to want to be careful, sir. On the dresser there, we have covers for your shoes."

Angus reached into the box pulling out two rubber sole covers. He carefully slipped them over his brown dress shoes before entering the bathroom. Inside, to the left was a countertop with an old-fashioned sink and faucet and two windows above. To the direct right was a toilet, and past that was a large glass-enclosed shower. The glass shower door had been smashed to pieces, and on the floor of the shower was Mary Hart, stiff, lifeless and covered head to toe in her own blood. On the sink, two bloody hand prints were present, surrounded by a blood spatter and droplets that looked like they had burst out of her body from an apparent blow to the head. As she lay in the shower, Angus could clearly see the cause of death - blunt force trauma to the face and head, as her skull, or what was left of it, had been caved in. She had suffered a very violent death. Hunched over the body of Mary Hart was a photographer, wrapped in a sterile bodysuit with a mask covering his face.

"What have we got here?" Angus asked the photographer.

"Looks like somebody really wanted her gone, huh?" The photographer asked.

"Sure appears that way," Angus replied as he surveyed the bathroom. "We've got forced entry through this window?"

Angus nodded his head towards one of the two windows above the sink. The window to the right had the screen only attached halfway, and the window was wide open. Outside, he could see and hear more officers cataloging evidence, taking pictures, the whole deal.

"I would say so," The photographer said. "Although the smashed door appears to be from the inside of the room. Seems pretty curious to me. Glad I have my job and not yours in times like these," The photographer said with a slight giggle, as he hunched down to take another snapshot of what remained of Mary Hart.

"Has the coroner been in yet?" Angus asked.

"Yeah, he's out front if you want to speak to him," The photographer confirmed.

"Thanks," Angus said. "Keep up the good work, son."

"Will do, sir." The photographer replied as another bright flash illuminated the violent scene.

Angus emerged from the house and made his way down the front lawn. Sitting in the back of a large transportation vehicle was the coroner, with Frank standing outside speaking with him.

"How did it look in there?" Frank asked as Angus approached.

"Not the sunshine and fairies we hope to see. Real ugly scene," Angus said.

"Well, well, well, if it isn't Angus Pratt," The Coroner said, looking up from a legal notepad in which he was vigorously writing. "It's been a while, old friend."

The Coroner was Harry Donovan, an old man who had been doing this work for decades. He was small with ice in his veins when it came to death, and his golf game. With his clean-shaven face and silver, curly hair, he wore a hazmat suit pulled down to his waist revealing a neatly pressed purple polo shirt.

"There he is," Angus shouted, extending his hand for a handshake. "They haven't kicked you out of this job yet?"

"You can't fix what isn't broken, Angus. You should know that. And I'm the best at what I do," Harry said, shaking Angus' hand with a strong, old school grip.

"So, any initial thoughts?" Angus asked.

"I was just getting the information from Harry," Said Frank. "Definitely an intruder overnight. Assumption is the intruder came in through the back window which leads to a bathroom."

"Yeah, I was just in there. It isn't pleasant. Whoever did this wanted her gone and to be absolutely certain of it. Blunt force trauma to the head by what appears to be a hammer of some sort," Harry said without looking up from his pad of paper. "Multiple strikes to the head and face, caved in the skull in a few different locations. Whoever it was, they wanted it to be as violent as possible. This is one of the most violent acts I have covered in as long as I can remember."

"Jesus," Frank said, shaking his head and placing it in his palm.

"Did she have any family or anything close by? Any known enemies?" Angus asked.

"Two sons, one older 20s, one in their 30s. They don't live here so I assume you can rule them out but per usual, you two should get statements from each of them," said Harry.

"All the neighbors say she was a sweet old lady and didn't ruffle any feathers. Mostly just kept to herself," Frank assured.

"Send me that report once you have it ready, would you, Harry?"

"Don't worry, I know the drill. I have been doing this since you were pissing in your overalls, kiddo. You don't have to tell me how to do my job," Harry said back in a half-joking tone.

"You're always the charmer, Harry."

"That's why everyone loves me so much," Harry said, looking up at Angus and giving a slight wink.

"Good to see you Harry," Angus said as he turned to walk away. He twisted around to yell back, "You got a tee time I can jump in on soon?"

"Don't be a deadbeat, Angus," Harry joked. "If you want to tee off, you know it will cost you."

The two veterans shared a laugh as Angus turned and walked towards the front lawn of the Hart home. Frank followed behind him.

"What do you think?" Frank asked.

"What do I think about what, exactly?"

"Do you think this is somehow linked to the VanSant disappearance?"

"I don't know yet," Angus said, as he sucked his teeth in, making a whistling sound. "One, we have a body violently attacked with what appears no motive whatsoever. On the other hand, we have a missing person and for all intents and purposes, we have to assume is still alive somewhere. Until we see evidence proving otherwise, I can't link them. But I will tell you this Frank, our lives just got a bit more interesting."

Just then, Charlie's car arrived at the scene, blocked out from the sea of police vehicles.

"Why does it seem that anytime chaos arrives, those two are not far behind?" Angus asked, a sense of frustration growing in his voice.

"Well, she lives here," Frank said. "It looks like he is just driving her home."

"It's just very peculiar," Angus said, his frustration growing.

A uniformed officer moved one of the police vehicles just enough for Charlie to pull through the chaos so they could reach Emma's home. They drove by slowly watching the home of Mary Hart, wondering what could have happened. When they finally reached Emma's home, she immediately took off running towards Angus and Frank. Charlie raced to try to stop her, but his efforts were meaningless.

"Emma!" Charlie shouted at her. "Come back!"

Emma raced in full sprint, but was stopped by an officer standing at the curb.

"Whoa, Ma'am. Slow down," The officer said. "You can't go in there."

"What the fuck happened in there!?" Emma shouted, her voice cracking as she shouted.

"It's OK, let her go," Angus shouted as he walked down the lawn towards the street. "Mrs. VanSant, you know I can't let you in there. You need to go home. We have got this completely under control."

"Bullshit," Emma shouted back. "If you have it under control, why are there so many cops here? Why are *you two* here? What happened to Mrs. Hart?"

"She was murdered, Mrs. VanSant," Angus said through a deep and long sigh. "That's all I can tell you. Now please, head home and try to calm down."

"Calm down?" Emma said as her patience, already at an all-time low, unraveled even deeper. "First my husband goes missing and now Mrs. Hart is murdered? Are you kidding me?"

"There's nothing you can do here, Emma. Please, just go home."

"How was she murdered?"

"I can't tell you that," Angus said, shaking his head.

Charlie had appeared on the curb and wasted no time grabbing Emma from behind, holding on to her tightly with his hands on her shoulders.

"What happened here?" Charlie asked.

"It doesn't concern you, Mr. Claymore," Angus said. "Please take her home."

"She was a family friend, I demand to know what happened in there!" Emma shouted.

"When the time comes, I will gladly share any information with you and the rest of your neighbors. Until then, please go home."

"Come on, Emma," Charlie said, pulling her towards the street.

"This is bullshit, Angus. And you know it," Emma said, tears now flowing down her pretty face.

"Thank you for that, Mrs. VanSant," Angus said as he turned away.

Charlie ushered Emma across the street, leering back towards Angus the entire way. Angus stood on the front lawn of the Hart home, never breaking eye contact on Charlie as they walked.

"Definitely something peculiar about those two," Angus said. "Alright, let's see what other information we can gather around here and head back to the station. We've got a lot of work to do."

"Double pot of coffee, sir?" Frank asked.

"Make it a triple," Angus said, patting Frank on the top of his back.

In marathon pace, Charlie shoved the key into the front door and pushed it open, gently leading Emma inside. Charlie slammed the door so hard the windows shook, and for a second, he thought maybe he had shattered one by force alone. Emma stood in the living room, hands up to her face walking in quick, panicked circles. She was crying so hard she could barely get words out. Charlie rushed to her side, wrapping his arms tightly around her small body.

"Shhh," Charlie whispered. "Everything will be OK. I got you. I got you." He continued to hold her in his arms as she wept, her face planted deep into his chest.

"Charlie," Emma said through cries. "What am I going to do?"

"I don't know, kid." Charlie whispered. He placed his chin on top of her head, allowing her to rest her forehead into his throat. "All I know is you will get through this. And I'll be right here, by your side, through it all."

She stayed there for a moment, feeling his pounding heartbeat on her face before placing her palms against his chest and pushing her body away from his. Not all the way, just enough to look into his eyes.

"Kid?" She asked with a light sniffle. "Wow, I don't think anyone has called me that, in *decades*."

"You remember, huh?" Charlie asked with a smile.

"Of course," she said with a quick wipe of her nose. "You used to call me kid back in high school. I always loved that. It made me feel so, I don't know. *Cute*."

She fell back into Charlie's chest, allowing him to wrap his arms around her. He loved hearing that his words made her feel cute. Charlie always thought Emma was cute, in fact he always had feelings for her. He realized at that moment some things never change. Just then, Charlie's phone vibrated in his pocket. Emma softly pushed her body away from his as he pulled out the phone. He looked at the screen; it was Gwen calling.

"I should," Charlie said with a shrug. "I should probably take this."

"Yeah, I think you should."

17

On a cold, foggy night, an old light post sat in a dark parking lot of an apartment complex, it's bulb flickering on life support, dancing like a busted strobe light on the glassy, wet asphalt. An old, light blue Chevy pickup that could have reasonably been used for parts in 1992 rolled it's way into the lot, finding its resting place for the evening in a numbered parking spot. The truck was so loud it could have woken the dead. The engine turned off, followed by its beaming headlights. The front door opened and out stepped Johnny Torres. A thin man, almost *too* thin, with messy jet black hair resembling someone who has just rolled out of bed. Resting on his face was not so much of a 5 o'clock, but more of an 8 o'clock shadow. Absolutely not intentional, just a lack of care that showed all too clearly. He wore dark blue jeans that sat tight on his legs and waist, and a plaid button-down shirt with a dark blue jacket on top one might guess he stole from a forgotten gas station on the side of a dusty old highway. In his hand he held a bag from a drive-thru filled with greasy, poorly made fast-food, and a newspaper folded under his arm. He shut the door of his truck and made his way across the dark parking lot, the broken street light bumping along with his footsteps as though he was walking along to a silent soundtrack.

The apartment complex sat next to a sprawling field of green grass, butted up to a greenbelt filled with large pine trees that stretched deep into the darkness of night.

The complex consisted of a few numbered two-story buildings. From the outside, the complex itself appeared to be neatly maintained. Nice wood siding, the paint wasn't chipping and well-manicured landscaping. Each bottom floor apartment had a decent sized patio, the top level apartments, a balcony for BBQs or reading a book with your evening tea. Stairs cut through each of the buildings leading the way to the top level units and at the top of each set of stairs sat two doors, each leading to their respective living quarters. Johnny reached the steps connected to one of the apartment buildings and jogged up the stairs. At the top he turned to his left, inserted his key into the deadbolt before stepping inside. He flicked the light switch illuminating a scarcely decorated, filthy apartment. The unit was a one bedroom, one bathroom but an unknowing visitor would have no clue, let alone think someone actually called this place home. To the right of the front door was the kitchen which hadn't been remodeled since it was originally built God knows when, and definitely hadn't been cleaned in what appeared to be the same time frame. To the left sat what would otherwise be a living room. Cutting between the two was a short hallway which ended at the master bedroom. Most folks like to turn their living quarters into a home. They decorate, make it their own, turn it into a haven for relaxation, comfort, spreading and giving love. Johnny was cut from a different cloth. The place was a wreck, as though a typhoon had hit every single fast-food joint in town and finished its reign of terror inside of Johnny's apartment, creating a mess of debris from wrappers, hamburger buns and milkshake containers. On the living room floor was a mattress, unmade, no sheets, just a large comforter and a couple of tattered and misshapen pillows strewn about. Against the wall just in front of the mattress sat an old, discolored cooler with a television on top. A small wooden table sat next to the mattress, much like the kitchen, was decorated with food containers everywhere accompanied by old clothes, newspapers and various trinkets.

Johnny shut the door to the apartment, moved across the living room and sat down on the mattress. He reached over to the wooden table to grab a remote and clicked on the television. Reaching into the bag of food he removed a hamburger and some french fries, placing the burger on his lap and the fries directly onto the carpet. Johnny unwrapped the hamburger and took a large bite. As he chewed away at the rubbery, greasy food, he picked up the newspaper, straightening it to see the news of the day. On the front page of the local paper was an article about a missing person. His eyes were fixated on this article as though it held the secret to life within its writing. The article detailed the disappearance of Eddie VanSant, Johnny's long-time co-worker. He reached for his hamburger, taking another large bite, and before he could finish chewing, he grabbed a handful of french fries and threw them into his mouth. A classy way of eating for a classy guy. Feverishly, he read through the article about Eddie to see what, if any, were the latest developments. He dropped the paper to his lap and stared up at the ceiling as he continued to chew the fast-food, finally swallowing it down with one large gulp. He crumpled the newspaper in his hands, rolled it into a ball and threw it across the room where it found its new home for the foreseeable future.

"You got what you deserved, you son of a bitch," Johnny said out loud. He reached to the wooden table and picked up a drink container that had been sitting and rotting for some time, and took a long drink. "You got what you *fucking* deserved."

18

Angus sat at the desk in his cold, dark office clicking away at a laptop computer, a warm cup of hot coffee sitting to his left shooting steam into the air. He was interrupted by Frank entering the office, carrying a manilla folder.

"Is that cup number 3 or should I come back?" Frank joked.

"I've honestly lost count," Angus said looking up with frustration in his eyes. "What can I do for you?"

Frank dropped the manilla folder on Angus' desk before taking a seat on the office couch.

"We got the forensics back on Mr. VanSant's vehicle, thought you might want to take a look."

"Oh, perfect, thank you," Angus said with a smile. "Any stand outs here? Break it down for me, what am I looking at?"

"Found a couple of prints on the steering wheel, didn't ring any bells when we ran them through the system. The car was exceptionally clean to be honest. But," Frank said, sitting up and leaning forward, "If you flip to the photographs, you will see we may have found something slightly interesting."

Angus flipped through some of the pages to the printed photographs. He held one up to Frank, "This picture?"

"Yep, that's the one," Frank said. "In the trunk, we found some fibers stuck to the upholstery. The lab checked them out and they are definitely some type of rope. And I mean a *thick*, strong rope."

"Well now that *is* something," Angus said with excitement.

"I stopped by the theater where Eddie worked and we cut some samples from the rigging they use, and I will let you take one guess as to what we found."

"They were a match?" Angus asked.

"You nailed it. It matches the rope used at the theater exactly. But, what could it mean? Could it mean anything, *really*? Maybe he transported some of the rope, or some equipment and it left some of the fibers behind."

Angus scratched his head while he considered the possibilities.

"In those text messages on Eddie's phone. We read some interesting back and forth between Eddie and another employee, Johnny Torres. Remember those?"

"Of course."

"Emma mentioned the man in the video surveillance had a similar build and look to this Torres guy. I think it might be time to shine the lights on him and see what we find."

Angus sat back deep in his chair for a moment considering all the options in moving forward with investigating, as, like in an old video game, a new challenger had entered the fight. Angus wanted to dig in deep to see not only if he had any answers, but if he was in any way involved. At that moment, if he shook a magic 8 ball, all signs would definitely point to yes.

Snapping out of his moment of contemplation, Angus spoke. "Grab your coat. Let's stop in at the theater and have a chat with whomever is in charge. I want to know exactly how these two interacted. If we can get some information or documentation from their boss, or Human Resources, we can turn that over along with the rope fibers to a judge and get a warrant."

"I'm one step ahead of you," Frank said as he stood up. "I already put in a call, and they are expecting us at 10:00am."

"10:00am," Angus muttered as he checked his wrist watch. "Perfect. Let's get going. You know Frank, you're always one step ahead of me, if I didn't know any better I would think you were after my job."

Angus stood up and threw on his tan sport coat before walking towards the door.

"I don't want your job," Frank said with a smile. "How about I keep doing the actual work and you deal with the politics and bullshit from upstairs."

"As long as I can keep the bullshit paycheck, we've got a deal," Angus said as he passed Frank in the doorway, slapping him on the shoulder a couple of times.

"Yep, that's what I figured," Frank said, shaking his head.

• • •

Angus and Frank pulled into the parking garage just down the road from the Paramount Theater. It was an old theater with a vintage neon sign hanging downward from the roof dropping to the entryway. Brilliant, bright red neon shot out from the sign. The beautiful blue and red marquee wrapped around the front of the brick building and the white board on the sign beamed with upcoming concerts and performances. Just below the marquee was the entrance with an old world box office, lined with gold trim and glass separating the ticket sellers from the incoming crowds. Small round cut outs allowed for bright gold speakers to fit into the glass so outsiders could purchase and pick up tickets. To the right of the theater, cutting between the buildings stretched a long and dark alleyway. It was lined with dumpsters and it reeked up the neighborhood from its intoxicating melange of trash, piss and stale stagnant water. The detectives exited the car and walked out of the parking garage and down the street leading to the entrance of the Paramount.

"So this fucking guy, he tries to tell me Barry *freakin* Bonds was better than Ken Griffey Jr. Can you believe that?" Frank said in disbelief.

"Well, Barry Bonds was a monster hitter in his day, I'll give him that. But better than Griffey? Please," Angus said, shaking his head and waving his hand through the air as though he was swatting a bee.

"Hey, look," Frank said, "I told him, I'll give Bonds the credit he deserves. He was a monster at the plate. But he was *not* Griffey. Give me a break."

"Well how many of those home runs were doctored, huh? If he had that career without shooting himself full of juice, maybe I could see it."

"Same here. I agree. Imagine if Griffey juiced," Frank said.

"You watch your mouth, Frank," Warned Angus. "You're liable to be shot in Seattle for saying something like that. Shit, I might shoot you myself!"

Both men laughed at the joke of Angus putting a bullet in Frank for disrespecting the Kid. He was a hero in not only Seattle, but all of baseball. A living legend.

"Of course The Kid didn't juice. But imagine if he had? He would have hit over 1000 home runs in his career. Bonds and Griffey, it's no contest."

"OK," Angus said as they reached the box office. "Who are we meeting here? He's expecting us, correct?"

"Absolutely," Frank said, removing a notepad from the inside pocket of his sport coat. "His name is Darryl Gray. He manages operations here at the Paramount."

Frank knocked on the glass doors and the men waited for someone to allow them inside. Soon, a middle aged man wearing dark blue slacks and a polyester polo shirt with a Paramount logo embroidered on the chest appeared.

"Good Morning, you must be the detectives," Said Darryl.

Darryl was a good-looking man with short well styled hair, although the front hairline appeared to be retreating from a fight like a battered infantry unit. Clean-shaven face, and in good, athletic shape.

"And you're Darryl?" Asked Frank.

"That's me," Darryl said, reaching to shake their hands.

"I spoke with you on the phone, I am Detective Frank McKenna, this is my partner Detective Angus Pratt. We wanted to talk to you about two of your employees Johnny Torres and Eddie VanSant."

"Come on in, we can go back to my office and talk," Darryl said, shaking both of their hands.

A door to a small office, just to the side of the main stage, was opened by Darryl as he ushered the detectives inside. It was unfinished, it's walls plastered with performance and event posters from years past. A small but respectable wooden desk sat towards the back of the room, and in front of the desk sat two wooden chairs lined with worn out brown leather on both of the arms and the seats.

"Make yourselves at home. Can I get you guys anything?" Darryl asked, holding the door for the detectives.

"No, thank you," said Angus, who, if he were being honest, would have loved a fresh hot cup of coffee. He imagined a theater that sold concessions must make a hell of a cup, or people wouldn't buy it. "We shouldn't take up too much of your time."

"What can I do for you guys?" Darryl said, taking a seat behind the desk.

"As I'm sure you are aware one of your employees has been missing. We have reason to believe another employee of the theater may either have information or may have been involved."

"Eddie and Johnny," Darryl said, shaking his head, and running his hands through what was left of his hair. "It's a real shame about Eddie, he's a good guy. A good employee. You think there's any chance he will be found?"

"We don't like to speculate," said Frank. "What we need now is information that may *lead* to us finding him. That's the priority."

"Well," Darryl said, opening a small personnel file on his desk. "Johnny and Eddie have never really been friends, they don't really get along. Honestly, never have. Although I know sometimes they go out for beers with a group of other folks from the theater. You know, there are always those people in your life that just don't quite fit or mesh?"

"Yeah, I understand," Angus said.

"Well, that's Johnny and Eddie. They were both up for the same promotion, and I chose Eddie. He's a hard worker, we work well together and Johnny wasn't happy about it."

"Why was Johnny passed up? Aside from the things you mentioned of course. Anything else you can tell us? Is he a loose cannon, is he a bad employee?" asked Frank.

"No, he's a fine employee. I didn't see him as a good fit for management is all. You know, dealing with performers and artists and agents. It takes a special person, someone with patience and understanding. Those are *not* two of Johnny's strengths."

"So what does Johnny do here?" Asked Angus.

"He works on the stage production team. Building the sets for performances. Lights, sound, rigging."

That word rang in Angus and Frank's heads like a cymbal crash in an orchestra. *Rigging.* They glanced at each other for a moment, but didn't remain there for long. This was a poker game and they didn't want to show Darryl their hand.

"What were some of the issues the two have had?" Asked Angus, hoping to get back to the conversation at hand.

"I have a couple of HR reports Johnny turned in on Eddie," He said, handing over the pieces of paper from Johnny's personal file.

"It's nothing too out of this world. Just stupid complaints about Eddie being over bearing, being pushy, those kinds of things. But Johnny takes everything so personally. He's hard to reason with. I never made a big deal about these complaints, because it was almost like in his own words, he was justifying why Eddie got promoted."

"No actual incidents that may lead you to believe Johnny would be out to get Eddie? Any altercations?" Asked Frank.

"Well," Darryl said, with his eyes wide open, removing another report from the file. "A month before Eddie went missing, this event occurred. Essentially, Eddie had asked the crew to rig up some lighting for a rehearsal. The director of a play didn't like the lighting and wanted to test some color changes. Eddie had asked them to do it, and it never happened. Johnny claimed the request, which was via email, had never been sent to him. Long story short, Eddie got his ass chewed out when they went to a scene change and the stage lit up yellow instead of red. Eddie, doing his job, questioned why the lights hadn't been changed. Eddie was pissed, which led to Johnny pushing Eddie up against the back wall behind the stage."

"Yikes, sounds like a bad incident," said Frank.

"It wasn't pretty. Luckily a couple of the other crew members were around and broke them up, and they went their separate ways. I spoke to them both, they shook hands, said no hard feelings yadda yadda, we went on with our business."

"Thank you Darryl. We appreciate everything you have provided for us." Angus said.

"Any chance we can keep these documents? They may come in handy." Asked Frank.

"No, I need to keep those. But I'm happy to make you a couple copies on our way out."

"Perfect, that's much appreciated," Angus said. "One other thing. You mentioned these two would go out for beers sometimes with other employees? Do you know the last time that might have happened or where they may have gone?"

"Unfortunately no, I don't know when they last went. But I could almost guarantee they went to the Elbow Room."

"What's the Elbow Room?" Frank asked.

"It's some shitty dive bar behind the theater. Down at the end of the alley. It's a shit hole, but it's close and cheap. A lot of folks from the theater drink there."

"Any idea who might have been with them at the time? Or who usually goes along?"

"Probably Courtney," Darryl said. "She's in charge of IT here."

"Any chance she's here today? It would be great to speak with her. Just in case she may have some information we haven't heard yet."

"Oh yeah, of course," Darryl obliged. "Let me call her. She's been pretty broken up about all of this and I'm sure she would be happy to help."

It wasn't long before Courtney appeared in the doorway to Darryl's office, her hair again tied up in a messy bun, strands of blond and black shooting off in all directions.

"Hey, Darryl, you wanted to see me?" Courtney asked sweetly as she leaned into the door.

"Yeah, come on in," Darryl said. "This is Detective Pratt and Detective McKenna. They wanted to talk to you about Eddie."

"Oh," Courtney said, standing straight up with excitement. "Did you find him? Is Eddie OK?"

"Ah," Angus said, rubbing the back of his head. "Unfortunately, he's still missing. We just have a couple of questions for you."

"Sure, anything I can do to help," she obliged.

"Darryl tells us you and Eddie often go to the Elbow Room after work?" Angus asked.

"Yeah, sometimes," she said.

"Can you tell us the last time you went out with him?" Angus asked as he snapped his fingers in Frank's direction.

Frank reached into his jacket pocket retrieving a pad and a pen to dictate her story.

"The last time was a few days before his wife reported him missing," she told them. "Friday night we went out and had a couple of beers together."

"So he was reported missing on Tuesday, September 5th. So this would have been Friday, the 1st?" Frank asked.

"Yeah, I think that's correct," she said.

"Detail the night for us. Who was there? Did everyone leave together? How intoxicated was everyone? Everything you can remember," Angus said.

"It was Eddie, myself, Reggie and Johnny."

"Who's Reggie?" Asked Frank.

"He's another guy that works here. Same department as Johnny," Darryl said.

"Yeah, he's a good guy," Courtney said. "The four of us went down to the Elbow Room, probably a little after 4:00pm. We each had a couple of beers, shared some chicken wings. Nothing too out of the ordinary."

"No altercations between Eddie and Reggie or Johnny?" Frank asked.

"Altercations?" She asked. "No, nothing. At least that I noticed."

"So, something may have happened outside of your knowledge?" Angus asked.

"I can't really say. We were together the whole time until we all headed home."

"What time did you all leave?" Frank asked as he wrote feverishly.

"We left at different times," she confirmed. "Johnny and Reggie left first and Eddie and I stayed behind. I don't know how long he stayed. Not long I don't think."

"OK," Angus said. "Do you know where they each headed once you left the bar?"

"Reggie always parks on the street. I don't know why, I think he has a fear of parking garages or something. So he left and went out to the main road. Johnny, Eddie and myself always park in the garage around the corner," she said.

"So the three of you walk down that alley when you leave, do I have this correct?" Frank asked.

"Pretty much," she confirmed.

"Do you have any camera feeds that we can view? Maybe we can see if something happened to Eddie after he left the bar?" Angus asked.

"See, that's the thing," Courtney said, rubbing the back of her head nervously. "I left the bar when I did because I got an alert on my phone. Somehow the internet had cut out here at the theater, which killed my camera system. So unfortunately, we don't have any footage from that night between 8:00pm and about 10:00pm, when I finally got everything up and running again. Maybe the Elbow Room has some cameras you can look at?"

"Not a bad idea," Frank said. "Thank you Courtney. If you think of anything else at all, please call me," Frank handed her his business card.

"Will do," she said, putting the card in her back jeans pocket. "I really hope you can find some answers soon. Eddie is a good guy. I pray wherever he is, that he's OK."

"Thank you, as do we," Angus said.

Frank and Angus stood up, reached across the desk and each shook Darryl's hand and all three of them exited the office together. Darryl escorted the men to the side exit of the theater which led into the alley. Darryl pushed the double doors open which allowed the foul aroma to pour into the building.

"If you two want to check out the Elbow Room, head to the end of the alley and hang a left. It's just up the way on the right, you can't miss it." Darryl said.

"Thank you, Darryl," Angus said, shaking his hand once again. "We'll be in touch."

Frank and Angus made their way down the damp path towards the bar. This was one time the detectives hoped they really could find an answer at the bottom of a bottle.

19

Frank held the door open to the Elbow Room for Angus to enter. Inside they were hit by the smell of stale beer, and the air was thick from old grease bubbling away in the fryer. Everything was sticky from the mix of spilt beer, cocktails and grease. Darryl's categorization as a "shit hole" was generous in both of their opinions.

"Don't touch anything, Frank," Angus urged. "I don't want to add tetanus shots to today's agenda."

"Not a problem, sir," Frank said, an unimpressed look gracing his face.

Behind the bar was a large man in the way of girth, not so much height. Slicked back gray hair covered the top of his head, and a matching color beard covered his splotchy face. He wore a tattered Hawaiian shirt and tan shorts. He was rubbing down the top of the bar as though a little elbow grease might clean up the Elbow Room. The detective felt his attempts were wasted, as the grime that had built up had become all too permanent.

"Can I help you gentlemen?" The bartender asked.

"Well, I hope that you can," Angus said, taking in a deep breath, which he soon regretted.

He reached into his tan jacket and pulled out a photograph of Eddie VanSant.

"Do you know this man? And if so, when was the last time you saw him?" Angus asked, holding the picture over the bar for the man to see.

"Oh yeah, that's Eddie. Good guy. It's a shame what happened to him," The bartender said.

"What do you mean by that?" Frank asked.

"Well, the dude is missing, isn't he?"

"That's correct," Frank confirmed.

"That's what I mean. It's a shame."

"When was the last time you saw him?" Angus asked.

"He was here a week or so ago. It was a Friday, I think."

"Friday the 1st?"

"Yeah, sounds about right," He confirmed. "He was in here with some of his work buddies. They come in here a couple times a month."

"Did you notice if he left with anyone? Or did he leave alone?" Angus asked as Frank took notes.

"Nah, he left alone," He confirmed. "He walked out by himself after his buddies took off. I know he walks down the alley towards the garage. Same as that Johnny creep."

Frank and Angus' ears perked up.

"What do you mean by saying 'that Johnny creep'?" Frank asked.

"Johnny was in here, too," He confirmed. "He's an asshole. I don't like him coming in here. He's always up to something, trying to get one over on whoever he can. I don't know why they even waste their time on him."

"Got it," Angus said, again, not wanting to expose his hand in what seemed like a never ending card game. "Silly question, but you wouldn't happen to have any cameras in this place, would you?"

"Look around you," the bartender said. "You think we would splurge on a camera system?"

"Didn't think so," Angus said. "Well, thank you for your help."

"Anytime," he said back.

Frank and Angus made their way to the door, hoping to get out of that stinky bar as soon as they could. As they stepped out into the alley, the bartender called back to them.

"You know, if I were you guys," He said, continuing to wipe down the bar top. "I would look into Johnny. That dude is sketchy. I wouldn't trust him."

"Thanks again," Angus said. "You have been more than helpful."

The two detectives stepped out of the bar and turned right as they intended to take the long way back to the parking garage. They had dealt with enough unpleasant odors and atmosphere the alley provided.

"Take those documents, along with the text messages and rope fiber findings from Eddie's trunk and get a warrant to search Torres' home," said Angus, a sense of urgency in his voice. "If we find one trace of evidence in his apartment and I mean a rope or fibers that match, blood or anything else, I want him cuffed and brought in, you hear me?"

20

Johnny woke to the sound of a violent barrage of knocking at the front door. He rolled over and slowly rubbed his eyes as he waited for his body to catch up with his brain. The pounding was so intense, it was like his entire apartment was shaking. Once his brain realized what was happening, he noticed the pounding was accompanied by shouting.

"Seattle Police, open the door now!" The voice shouted.

"What the *fuck*," Johnny whispered to himself as he stood up and slowly made his way to the front door, stumbling over trash, food containers and more debris.

Johnny, wearing a white tank top and blue boxer shorts opened his front door to find Detective Frank McKenna and a couple of uniformed police officers standing on his porch.

"Mr. Torres," Said Frank, "I'm Detective Frank McKenna and we have a warrant to search your home and vehicle."

The two uniformed officers pushed past Johnny, making their way into the filthy and cluttered apartment.

"Wait, what are you," Johnny stuttered. "What the hell is going on? You can't just come in here like this!"

"Actually, we can," Frank said back, shoving the warrant into his chest with enough force to push Johnny back a step or two. "It's all right there in this warrant. We need to search your apartment and we need to get into your vehicle. The more you cooperate the easier this will be on all of us."

"What the fuck is this even about?" Johnny said, his voice raising and growing angrier by the second.

"Don't worry what it's about, it's all in that document from the Judge. Read it if you want. Otherwise, stay out of our way and let the officers do their jobs," Frank said. "We will also need to get inside of your vehicle. Now, you can either give me the keys so I can open it, or one of my officers can bust in. Your call."

Johnny rubbed his eyes and walked into his messy kitchen. The entire place reeked like a fast-food restaurant that had been abandoned for years. He grabbed his truck keys and threw them underhand to Frank.

"Thank you for cooperating," Frank said with a nod. "Now gentleman, make sure you check everything. And I mean *everything*. If you have to open his ass and take a peek, go for it."

Frank looked at Johnny, who was horrified by the instructions given to police officers who were in full destruction mode. The officers began tearing the place apart, more so than Johnny had done himself. One of them lifted his stained mattress, tossing it over against the wall so it stood upright. The other used a baton to poke around the trash and debris that was scattered all about, hitting cups, plates and rotting food off the counters and tabletops onto the floor below.

"I'm kidding, Johnny. We won't actually check inside your ass. That's what they do after booking. Don't act like this is your first time!" Frank said with a giggle and a wink. "By the way, I love what you have done with the place. Real nice decorating. I especially think the food wrappers really bring out the stains in the carpet."

Frank turned and headed back down the stairs to the parking lot. He walked towards the big Chevy truck and tossed the keys to a uniformed officer.

"Hey, Wilkins," Frank yelled. "Do your worst."

"You got it, sir." The officer shouted back.

Standing at the edge of the parking lot was Angus. He stood where the asphalt met with the large grass field, staring out at the deep forest of pine trees. Frank walked over to meet him and give him a breakdown of how the interaction went.

"Well, not only was he surprised but now he is thoroughly pissed off, too," said Frank.

"Good," Angus said, nodding in approval. "That's what we want. If he's unhinged, let's see where he takes it."

"What are you looking at out there?"

"I don't know about you," Angus said pointing out at the trees. "If I were Torres, I would think that massive, untouched area of trees could be a pretty good dumping spot."

Frank stared with his partner for a moment, contemplating what may lay hidden out in the vast forest.

"Good thinking, Sir," Frank agreed. "Maybe let's not get ahead of ourselves. Let's see what these guys find first."

"Right," Angus said, nodding. "OK Gentlemen, leave no stone, seat or anything else unturned. If this son of a bitch has a stick of gum hidden away, I want to find it and I want you to chew it in front of him."

A loud chorus of "Yes Sirs" rang through the air.

Now, the intensity has turned up. The detectives finally had a possible suspect and motive right in their hands. It was so close, Angus could taste it. He was salivating. Angus always got himself fired up in these situations. He was cool, calm, collected and respectful and he felt those were important qualities for a successful detective. But when the heat was on, he could turn from a rabbit to a tiger. And today, he was hungry.

"Sir," Yelled Wilkins, the uniformed officer going through the old Chevy. "I think we found something."

Angus and Frank rushed to the truck. Like a predator on their prey, their noses filled with the scent of blood.

"What have you got, Wilkins?" Asked Angus.

"I don't know if there is any significance, but check this out," Wilkins said. He was sitting inside the bed of the truck, and pushed far underneath a tool chest was a large spool of rope which had visible traces of dirt and dried mud clinging to the fibers. The officer had pulled it out from under the white tool chest stretching across the bed, similar to tool chests found on maintenance trucks.

"Well, well, well," Angus said as he stared over at Frank. "Does that look familiar to you, Franky?"

"Sure does. That looks identical to the rope used at the Paramount. Which means—"

"Same as the fibers found in Eddie's trunk," Angus said.

"Bag it and tag it, Wilkins," Frank instructed.

The officers continued to search Johnny's apartment for some time. Johnny stood, arms crossed, leaning against his kitchen counter through it all. It wasn't like he could run out for a paper and to grab a coffee. He was a prisoner in his own apartment. Innocent until proven guilty, but this wasn't looking good for Johnny. The police finally made their way outside carrying bags of various items they had found they thought could be evidence. The most notable from inside the home was a pair of old black work boots. The soles of the boots were caked in mud with forest debris clinging to the bottoms. All in all a good day for Frank and Angus, as the rope, muddy boots along with the Paramount Theater reports and text messages between the two was plenty for Angus to bring Johnny in for questioning, and possibly arrest.

Frank and Angus made their way up the stairs to find Johnny still standing in his kitchen. His face was twitching with anger.

"You assholes had enough fun yet? Look what these guys did to my place," Johnny said.

"I saw it before they walked in, they did you a favor," Frank joked.

"Mr. Torres," Angus said as he removed a pair of handcuffs from his back pocket. "You are under arrest for the kidnapping of Eddie VanSant." He continued to read him his rights as he slapped the cuffs on his wrists, he escorted him out of the apartment and put him in the back of a police cruiser.

"Wilkins, take him to the station and book him," Angus said. "Then put him in interrogation room 2 and wait for my arrival."

"Right away, sir," Wilkins said with a nod.

Angus and Frank stood shoulder to shoulder, watching as the police cruiser left the parking lot with their new suspect.

"Do you really think this is our guy?" Asked Frank.

"I don't know Frank," Angus said, scratching his head. "It all lines up. A history of hate between the two and getting passed for a job promotion, that's the motive. The rope and muddy boots, seems all too perfect and suspicious. I told you the forest would be a good place for a dump site."

"The muddy boots and dirt all over that rope, we might be on the right path."

"Let's get back to the station and question this guy. And as soon as we can, I want a full team out here to comb that forest. If this is going where I fear it is, Eddie might be out there right now."

21

Emma heard a knock at the door as finished preparing Sophie's lunch for the day. Like most days she was running late heading out the door, but who could blame her? She was attempting to juggle both roles as a parent. Not to mention Sophie's dance recital was fast approaching, and though she had definitely considered canceling the event, she knew in her heart it would devastate Sophie. And by no means would she allow that to happen. She was having a hard enough time dealing with life, and the chance of disappointing Sophie wasn't a chance she was willing to take.

"One second," Emma shouted from the kitchen, hands caked in peanut butter and jelly. She grabbed the kitchen towel hanging on the handle of the oven, wiped her hands and threw the towel over her left shoulder. She opened the front door to find Detective Angus standing on her porch.

"Angus," Emma said, letting out a loud sigh and staring at her feet before connecting with his eyes. "How can I help you this morning?"

"May I come in?" Angus asked with a friendly nod.

"I'm actually in a bit of a hurry. I'm running late getting Sophie to class."

"Right," Angus said, looking down and scratching the back of his neck nervously.

"What can I do for you?" Emma asked, her patience gauge inching closer and closer to empty.

"Well," Angus said, letting out a deep sigh. "I just wanted to let you know we just picked up Johnny Torres for involvement in Eddie's disappearance."

Emma struggled to catch her breath at the bombshell he had just detonated at her feet.

"Oh my god," she said as she choked on a mix of words and air.

"Now, it may not *mean* anything," Angus assured, putting both hands in the air, both as a calming measure and to catch Emma if she were to faint. At that moment, Angus imagined a fifty-fifty chance of either occurring. "I just wanted to tell you first. Face to face, and let you know *all* the information we have."

Emma cupped her mouth with her left hand and nodded, her eyes glassy, like a lake on the first snow of Winter.

"OK, OK," she said through deep breaths.

"We found rope fibers in Eddie's trunk. They matched the rope fibers from the Paramount Theatre that have been used for some sort of stage rigging. We matched those fibers with rope found in the bed of Johnny's truck. The rope that was confiscated for evidence had traces of mud and dried dirt within the fibers. An officer also removed a pair of muddy work boots from his apartment. Those things, along with their history at work and Johnny's well documented disdain for Eddie, we think we might be on the right path."

"So, what do we do now? Did he say anything?" Emma asked, a sense of urgency growing inside her.

"Johnny is on the way to the station now so we can question him. We'll check his cell phone for everything. Same as we did with," Angus cut himself off, knowing his words could infect some very open wounds. "I just wanted to stop by here first to let you know where we are. As soon as we know *anything* more, I *will* come see you, Emma. We *will* find Eddie."

Emma thanked Angus for the courtesy house call. It eased some of the tension she had building towards him. She knew deep down he was only trying to help her. If she were in his shoes, she would drag the spouse in on day one. As embarrassed and angry as she was, she knew he only meant well and was tying up every loose end he could.

"I also need you to know we will be combing the forest outside of Johnny's apartment complex tonight. Detective McKenna is compiling the team, and we'll be searching every inch of those damn woods. If Eddie is out there, we *will* find him. I'm only telling you this as a courtesy, I would highly suggest you stay away from the area. Stay home, be with Sophie, watch a movie or play a game. Anything to keep your mind off of those woods. As soon as we know anything at all, I'll come see you."

Emma stood with her glossy gaze locked on absolutely nothing at all, as though she was staring into another dimension. The foundation of her life cracking under the pressure and weight of everything she had piled upon her shoulders. Angus tried to snap her out of her stress induced stupor.

"Promise me you won't go near those woods tonight," Angus said with force in his voice.

"Yeah, Yeah, I promise," Emma said with a whisper, nodding her head.

Before Angus could say goodbye, a car had pulled into Emma's driveway. It was Charlie, arriving bright and early with a couple of coffees. Charlie walked up the concrete path towards the front door when he noticed Angus towering over and filling the space that otherwise would be the entryway to Emma's home.

"Good Morning, Emma," Charlie said with a big, bright smile. "Angus," he muttered as he passed by him, entering the house.

"Look who it is. Bright and early. With coffee to boot! What a guy. You have one of those in your car for me?" Angus said, playfully.

"Sorry, Angus," Charlie said with a shrug. "I didn't know you would be here. By the look of it, Emma probably didn't know either. But you can have mine if you'd like? I got chamomile tea."

"No thank you," Angus said, shaking off the offer. "Not really a tea guy."

"More for me then," Charlie said as he took one long gulp of his drink, he and Angus' eyes locked in a dead stare. The tension between the two had grown so thick, one might need fins and a snorkel to maneuver through.

"Are you almost ready to go?" Charlie asked, looking at Emma as he handed her the hot cup of coffee.

"Yeah, just about. I just need to finish a couple of things."

"So you're driving her around and taking her daughter to school, huh?" Angus asked with a little roll of the eye and a smug smirk.

"Yes, I am. She needs a friend right now. Is that a crime? Do you want to drag me off in front of the neighbors next?" Charlie said, stretching his arms outward, his wrists touching together offering himself to be handcuffed.

Charlie's anger was growing. Unlike Emma, his patience gauge wasn't dwindling, he arrived with his running on pure fumes that were ready to ignite. It was like Charlie arrived looking for a fight.

"Hey, come on," Emma urged, positioning herself between the two men.

"Take it easy, Mr. Claymore. I'm not here to start trouble. Emma, I'll be in touch. You two have a lovely day," Angus said with a friendly nod and a smile. A few paces down the walkway he turned around, "Oh and Charlie. Enjoy that tea."

Emma shut the door behind Charlie as he swung around half way through the living room.

"What the hell was that all about?"

"He was letting me know some new information about Eddie."

"What did he say? Did they find anything?"

"He said they arrested Johnny Torres. The creepy, asshole co-worker that is always starting trouble."

"So they think Johnny had something to do with this?"

"They don't know yet. They took him in this morning. He said he's on the way to question him right now and they'll let me know as soon as they know anything."

"Wow," Charlie said, shocked. He wasn't sure if Angus could be trusted but felt an overwhelming sense of ease roll over him. "Well that's good news, right?"

"Maybe," Emma said as she took a sip of her coffee, and let out a deep sigh. "They said a team is going to search the woods by his apartment tonight and told me to stay away."

"Why do you need to stay away? It's your husband. Shouldn't you be there?"

"I guess not," Emma said with a shrug. "He said to stay home with Sophie and they will let me know what happens."

"Maybe it's for the best," Charlie said in agreement.

"Sophie!" Emma yelled down the long hallway. "Hurry up, we are going to be late for school."

Emma went back to fixing Sophie's lunch, set her coffee on the counter and paused. She planted her palms on the counter and dropped her head, allowing her wispy blonde hair to fall over her face. With her right hand she pushed the strands behind her ear, looking Charlie dead in the eyes,

"You ordered chamomile tea?"

They both let out a deep laugh.

22

Johnny Torres sat in the same cold room that once held Emma, surrounded by lightly painted concrete walls. A paper cup of terrible coffee sat on the table in front of him as he puffed on a cigarette. He felt as though an eternity had passed since they pushed him into that room and instructed him to sit and wait. As the paper on his cigarette burnt down and the coffee turned lukewarm, the heavy security door to the interrogation room finally opened. In walked Detectives Pratt and McKenna. Angus holding a manilla folder in his hands.

"So," Johnny said as he took one last drag from the cigarette, dropping it to the floor and stomping it out. "Are we going to get this party started or what?"

"The party's started, my friend," Angus said with his large, deep voice bouncing off the cold, concrete walls. "You're the guest of honor."

"I sure feel honored. You really rolled out the red carpet. With the piss poor coffee and cheap cigarettes. A man really feels special here. Not to mention how you smashed up my apartment and tore apart my truck."

Angus and Frank both pulled out steel chairs that had been pushed under the table. They took their seats, Angus to the left and Frank to the right.

"I think we may have done you a favor on the matter of your apartment. I don't know that I have ever seen someone living in such squalor. Really, how do you live like that?" Frank asked with a coy smile.

Johnny laughed to himself, sat way back in his steel chair, leaned to his left and spit onto the floor. "I live just fine, thanks."

"You know, Johnny," Angus started in, his tone deep and severe, making it well known he was not going to put up with any nonsense. "You're a real classy guy, aren't you?"

"What can I say?" Johnny said, putting his hands in the air as though he was proud of himself. "So, what's this all about, gentlemen? Can we get on with it?"

Angus, not breaking his stare deep into Johnny's eyes, opened the manilla folder and began shuffling through the mess of papers inside.

"Tell me about you and Eddie VanSant."

"Eddie VanSant?" Johnny said laughing.

"I assume you're well aware he has been missing for quite some time?" Frank asked.

"Yeah, I'm aware. All I have to say is good riddance."

"You see Johnny," Angus replied. "You seem to be the only one happy with him out of the picture. Now, why is that?"

"He's an asshole, that's why."

"Johnny, this is a serious situation. A man is missing. A husband, a father," Frank started before being interrupted by Johnny.

"Yeah, yeah, I know all about Eddie. You don't need to sell me on Eddie. Everyone *loves* Eddie!" Johnny said, throwing his hands in the air. "I am aware of good ol' Saint Eddie."

"Saint Eddie?" Asked Frank.

"Yeah, that's what I like to call him. Because everyone thinks he's such a good guy. He *is* such a *good* guy, isn't he?"

"You aren't really helping yourself here," Frank urged. "I suggest you take this a little more seriously."

"Take what seriously?" Johnny asked as he realized the situation he was in. He had an attitude for days, but his brain was a little slow on the uptake. "You guys really think I had something to do with this?" Johnny let out a deep belly laugh.

Angus began shuffling through a few more pieces of paper.

"We have extensive documentation of your constant negative interactions with Mr. VanSant. Here, tell us about some of these. You've had it out for Mr. VanSant for quite some time."

Johnny pulled another cigarette out of the crushed soft pack sitting on the table, flicked the lighter and took in a deep, long drag.

"We've had it out a few times. It doesn't mean I killed the guy, does it?"

"How do you know he's dead?" Asked Frank.

"I don't!" Johnny shouted. "I don't know where the guy is. I don't really fucking care, either. If he's gone, he's out of my hair. So no harm no foul if you ask me. Wherever he is, he's better off. We are *all* better off."

"We can pin a motive on you, Johnny. So maybe cut the shit and get serious." Frank urged, hitting his closed fist on the table just loud enough to send a slight shockwave through Johnny's body.

"What motive? When did it become illegal to not like a guy?"

"Did you or did you not pin him against a wall at work?" Asked Frank.

"So you went by the Paramount I see," Johnny said, nodding his head with a thoughtful smirk.

"We did," Angus confirmed. "And it seems as though you've had it out for him for what appears to be years."

"Nah," Johnny said, shaking his head, flicking the ash from his cigarette onto the floor. "I just don't like the guy."

Angus rolled his eyes and took in a long, deep breath. He flipped to a few photos from inside the folder, pulled them out and slid them across the table to Johnny.

"Explain these to us then, wise ass," Angus said, sending daggers from his eyes through Johnny's soul.

Johnny shifted in his seat, sat up to look at the printed pictures.

"A rope and some boots, so what?"

"Explain them to us," Frank urged.

"I own boots and I had a rope in my truck."

"The rope we found in your truck matched rope fibers we found inside Mr. VanSant's trunk. Explain it." Angus said, growing angry and impatient.

"We work at the same theater, man. What can I say? It *really* isn't uncommon for him or I to have rigging rope in our cars."

"Why was the rope found in your truck covered in mud? And why are your boots covered in mud?" Asked Frank.

"My disabled mother lives in New Castle and her house gets cold. I head out into the woods, you know, right by the apartment complex and I drag out firewood for her a couple times a week so she can keep a fire going at night. Is that a crime now? To save a few bucks on firewood? I mean, the shit is just *out* there, it's *free*."

Angus and Frank looked at each other, fearing they may have hit a wall with Johnny Torres. There was definitely still something fishy in the air, and Angus would sniff it out one way or another.

"Tell us about this other photo," Angus pushed it towards Johnny.

"What about it?"

"Does that guy look familiar to you?" Asked Frank, pointing at a photo of the masked man leaving Eddie's car at the park.

Johnny lifted the photo and sat back in his chair as he looked it over. His eyes squinched as though he was really digging in deep to see who this mystery man might be.

"I don't recognize whoever this is," Johnny said, dropping the photo back on the table. "Where is that, the park over on Pine?"

"You tell us," Angus said.

"I don't know for sure, but it looks like the park over on Pine," Johnny said with a shrug. "Is that the guy who took Saint Eddie?"

Both detectives sat quietly, waiting for Johnny to spill his guts. Angus could feel something building, and was waiting, hoping for him to crack. The fault lines were activating, now it was time for the cracks to grow and expose what may lay underneath the surface. Johnny finally broke the silence of the room, but not in the fashion in which Angus had hoped.

"When was this even taken?" Johnny asked.

"It shows the date and time right there in the corner," Frank said, pointing at the lower right edge of the photo. "It was taken two Fridays ago, right before midnight."

"Well then," Johnny said, sitting back in his chair, allowing himself to get more comfortable. "I'm good. You see, every Friday I head to my Mom's in New Castle. I bring her firewood and help her out around the house most weekends. So, I wasn't even in town when this occurred."

Angus dropped his head in disappointment. He would need to verify the story before he could rule anything out completely. Angus knew he would try to hit them with an alibi, and he was determined to find a crack in the armor.

"You savvy gentlemen clearly have the ability to find things out about me, what with having my personal file and all. I'm sure you can easily verify I was there. Or *was* I?" Johnny said with a wink.

Angus grabbed the papers from the table and aggressively shoved them back into the folder, slammed it shut and stood up so ferociously the table pushed back towards Johnny, forcing him to jump out of his chair to get out of its path.

"Get your fucking head on straight, pal," Angus shouted, pointing his long, beefy index finger in his face. "Tonight, we're searching every goddamn inch of those woods. And if we find any trace of that poor husband and father out there, I will *personally* come back here and put your head through that damn door."

Angus slammed his chair against the table, forcing Johnny to jump back even further, as the force pushed the table almost completely across the room.

"Frank, hold this son of a bitch until we check those woods. I don't want this guy anywhere near another human being until we know what is out there."

"You got it, boss," Frank said as he stood up from the table.

Angus reached for the door knob, pulling the heavy door open. He stopped for a moment, took a deep breath and flipped through the manilla folder. He removed a photo and slammed it down onto the table top so hard, he may have pushed the table legs a few inches into the concrete floor.

"I want you to look at that while you sit here and wait," Angus snorted like a raging bull. "You can sit here and think about them while we search out in the cold and the mud for Eddie."

He leaned down, pressed his palms hard onto the cold, steel table top positioning his face nice and close to Johnny's.

"And when I get back, if we find *anything* out there, I promise you, I will shove my foot so far up your ass you will taste the grass I walked in this morning."

Angus shoved the table towards Johnny before leaving the room, slamming the heavy door behind him resulting in a deafening thud.

Johnny gathered himself, made sure he didn't soil his pants and looked at the photograph Angus had left behind. It was a photo of Eddie, Emma and Sophie. Together, from happier times, smiling without a care in the world.

23

Emma found herself yet again waist deep in double parenting duties. When a parent within a functioning partnership is left alone, it isn't only the family that suffers a loss. Chores suffer, daily activities suffer, the house suffers and much more, love suffers. Sadly, the VanSant's home had revealed stress fractures from the pressure and some things had to give. When push came to shove, laundry and clutter won the battle and had occupied the once neat and organized household. But Emma was determined to not let these things win the overall war, and tonight was the night to stand up, fight and fix it. She had plowed her way through three loads of laundry, reorganized the once vibrant living room, that today, appeared like it could have been featured on a television show about learning how to reorganize one's life but as the "before" example. After climbing the mountain of clutter, it was time to work with Sophie on some homework. It was easy material for any adult like simple addition and childish journal entries about kittens and cloud shapes, but for Emma, she might as well have been swimming across the Pacific Ocean with a cinder block tied to her waist. All bandwidth she may otherwise have had dissipated under the stress and anxiety of her new and foreign daily life. Not to mention, she still had dishes to do.

Emma fought exhaustion, scrubbing away at more than a day's worth of dishes. As she scrubbed away, she heard a knock at the door. She let out a deep sigh followed by an overly dramatic eye roll. *"Oh god, what now?"* She thought to herself as she shut off the faucet, dried her hands the best she could and threw the wet, dirty dish towel over her left shoulder. She rushed to the front door, hoping whomever it may be could be sent back to wherever they had come from post haste.

She opened the door to find Charlie standing on her porch wearing dark jeans and a big puffy winter jacket. He was holding a white take-out bag, the plastic handles tied into a neat little bow. He held it up to Emma with a large, goofy smile.

"Charlie," Emma said with excitement, trying to hide her exhaustion by lifting her voice high with enough energy she thought maybe she could trick him into thinking everything was fine. "What are you doing here? What's all this?"

"Special delivery," Charlie said as he shook the bag slightly, drawing Emma's eyes to the take-out food. "I know you have a lot on your plate, and I can't even imagine trying to go through everything on your own. So I thought I would deliver dinner."

"Come in, come in," Emma said, stepping out of the door frame allowing him to enter. "You didn't have to do that. We can take care of ourselves."

Without thinking, Charlie's eyes looked Emma up and down. It didn't take a Detective Pratt level investigation to see Emma was falling apart.

"What, all this?" Emma said, catching Charlie looking her up and down. She motioned down her body with her right hand like some sort of disheveled showgirl at a car show, displaying her discolored gray robe covering a pair of oversized pajama pants and a t-shirt that was so big on her small body, it must have been Eddie's. "This is just, well, it's comfortable. Not that I am out of clean clothes or anything."

Emma took the towel off of her left shoulder and threw it across the room. She buried her face in her hands and rubbed her eyes with her palms. Charlie could tell she was approaching a breaking point. He reached out and wrapped his arms around her, pulling her into his chest, refusing to let go.

"Hey, it's OK," He said with a soft and subtle shush sound.

"I know, I'm sorry. I don't mean to take any of this out on you."

"Come on," Charlie said, finally releasing Emma from his comforting arms. "I brought dinner for you and Sophie. I assumed you could at least use some help in the dinner department."

"You're a lifesaver," Emma said, grabbing the bag of take-out food from Charlie and heading into the kitchen. "It smells good, what is it?"

"There's this new Chinese food place by my house. I eat there now and then. The food is great, I sort of just guessed on what you both might like," Charlie said.

Emma set the bag on the freshly clean countertop and ripped it open in a savage fashion, bypassing the neatly tied knot as though she had not eaten in days. And truly, who knew if she had. She removed a couple of white box containers, opened one and promptly grabbed a piece of orange chicken with her fingers and shoved it into her mouth. She closed her eyes as she chewed, letting out a satisfying *"mmm."*

"Someone must have been hungry," Charlie joked.

Emma, her mouth full of the fried chicken, continued to chew and responded to Charlie only with an exaggerated nod. She began opening the rest of the containers to examine the contents.

"This is a lot of food. What did you get?"

"Well the orange chicken you already found, clearly," Charlie said with a laugh.

"I also brought a container of their house beef. It's grilled beef with grilled onions, peppers, baby corn and broccoli. There are also a couple containers of rice, of course, and for good measure I picked up a couple orders of cream cheese wontons and an order of their house specialty chow mein."

"Wow," Emma said in surprise, still opening the many containers. "Is this all for us to share?"

"Oh, no. I brought all of this for just you and Sophie. I actually can't stay tonight."

"Aww, why not?" Emma said, shooting sad, bunny rabbit eyes at Charlie as she took a bite of the house special beef. Again, using just her fingers. She was clearly starving and this was no time to be proper.

"I'm meeting Gwen in about 20 minutes. We have tickets to a," Charlie stuttered. "I don't even know honestly, something she wanted to see. I'm trying to be a good fiance and go along with it." Charlie followed this with a long exaggerated shrug.

"Well that sucks," Emma said. "I was excited to take a break from this mountain of chores and have dinner with you."

"Will you take a rain check?"

"For you, anything."

"Cool, it's a date," Charlie said with a large smile. "Well, I really need to get going. Enjoy the food. There should be enough for you both to have some leftovers."

"Thanks Charlie. This is such a sweet gesture," Emma said as she took another piece of the orange chicken with her fingers.

"Watching you go to town on that food is all the thanks I need."

Charlie walked into the kitchen, opened a drawer, then another. He walked back to the counter and stood behind Emma, who was admiring all the beautiful food she was about to devour. He stood over Emma, pushed real close into her back and reached around her with his right arm. Emma, in a bit of a shock, froze momentarily, unsure of Charlie's intention.

"You may want to try one of these," Charlie said in a low whisper as he shoved a fork deep into the container, removing a large, slathered piece of chicken and raising it to her eye level. "It makes eating much, *much* easier."

Emma gently took the fork out of Charlie's hand and held it for a second. She turned around and found herself face to face with him. She gazed up as he stared intently down into her eyes. Their eyes remained locked for what felt like forever, as though they were stuck in space and time, lost in tractor beams from each other's eyes.

"Thank you," Emma finally whispered.

The two continued gazing into each other's eyes. And then, Emma brought the fork to her mouth and snatched the piece of chicken off of its metal prongs.

"What a great *idea* you had," Emma said sarcastically. "I didn't even know these magical devices existed. *Phew.* What an absolute life changing *invention* you have discovered."

"OK, OK," Charlie said, taking a few steps back and rubbing his head.

"I'm serious," Emma said, taking another large bite. "I had no idea eating could be so easy. And so much less *messy.*"

"Are you having fun?" Charlie joked.

"What, you don't like me eating with my hands?" Emma asked, reaching for Charlie's face with her fingers, thoroughly covered in sauce.

"OK, You made your point."

Emma fell onto the counter laughing.

"Well, enjoy your dinner," Charlie said with a goodbye bow. "I'll go ahead and let myself out."

"Oh Charlie, I'm just playing around."

"I know," Charlie said with a smile. "I'll call you tomorrow."

"Sounds good," Emma said, not taking her eyes off of the food.

Charlie walked across the house and reached for the door handle. As he was about to leave, he was stopped.

"Charlie," Emma shouted from the kitchen.

Charlie turned around to see Emma, looking around the corner.

"Thank you, again. Not *just* for the food. But, I don't know. For everything."

"You got it," Charlie said with a sly smile. "Have a good night."

Charlie shut the door behind him and walked down the path to his car parked in the driveway. He removed his cell phone from his pocket and started flipping through his apps to the one which provided directions.

In the "Destination" field, he searched for the Pinewood Apartment Complex. The directions popped up on his screen as he backed out of Emma's driveway and like steam from a boiling pot, he was gone.

24

As the sun began to set, Angus arrived at Pinewood Apartments. The tenant parking area, an otherwise quiet and slow moving lot, had been transformed in a matter of hours. Tents had been erected, police cars lined the perimeter on all sides, spotlights were being set up both on tripods in the large grass field along with makeshift poles with bright white beams illuminating as far as the eye could see. As Angus pulled his car into the lot, he was pleasantly surprised by the amount of people who had come to make up tonight's search team. He knew an evening search through a dense forest was not ideal, but on such short notice this would have to do. Angus parked his boat of a vehicle right at the edge of the grass. Frank, who was standing a few yards into the field when Angus arrived, turned from what appeared to be a deep conversation to greet Angus, holding a large bullhorn. If this were a zoo, Frank would have looked like the ringleader.

"Frank," Angus shouted as he exited his car, slamming the door behind him. "How are we looking?"

"We're just about set to head in," Frank replied.

"Look at all these people, good turnout. Good news, huh Frank? We could really use some good news."

"Yup," Frank said as he surveyed the area. "We should be able to get eyes on every inch of that forest. If Eddie, or anyone else, is out there we'll find them."

Angus began surveying the landscape and taking in as much as he could in a short amount of time. He was snapped out of his gaze by Frank.

"Speaking of a good turnout. Look who we have over here," Frank said, pointing towards the far end of the lot.

Angus turned and focused through the remaining sunlight to see what Frank was pointing out. His eyes burst wide open as he noticed that parked at the entrance to the apartment complex was a black BMW. And sitting in the driver's seat was none other than Charlie Claymore.

"Well, well, well. Mr. Claymore. What are you doing here?" Angus asked out loud.

"I noticed him pull in. He's been there for about 30 minutes. He hasn't got out or spoken to anyone. I don't know what he's doing."

"Don't worry about him," Angus said. Just then, Angus' eyes shot wide open again. This time, he was certain his jaw had unhinged from his skull and dropped straight onto the asphalt. He half expected Frank to step on his tongue.

"Are you OK? What is it?" Frank asked with concern.

"No, no, it's nothing," Angus said as he stared into what Frank could only assume was another dimension.

It was then, standing at that distance, Angus was reminded of the morning they had found Eddie's car at the park on Pine Avenue. Frank had pointed out a looky loo at the park, standing just beyond the chain link fence on a running trail. The final puzzle piece had snapped into place which allowed Angus to remember exactly how and why he recognized Charlie.

"You sure you're OK? We have a coffee station here," Frank said, reaching out with his left hand grabbing onto Angus's right shoulder.

"No, I'm fine. Thanks," Angus said, shaking off the memory of Charlie and trying to regain his composure. "Did you lay out the details for everyone?"

"Nope, I was waiting for the boss," Frank said, handing Angus the bullhorn.

"I had a feeling you would say that," Angus said with a roll of the eyes, reaching out and ripping the bullhorn from Frank's hands.

Angus set off into the grass field that led to the entry of the forest. He would deal with Charlie in due time, for now, the search must go on as planned. The forest butted right up to the grass, with a long line of beautiful pine trees serving as a makeshift border between the land of the grass and the land of the pines. He stomped his way through the low cut green grass where an unfinished wooden stage was now sitting right in the middle of the spacious field. Sitting on an easel next to the stage was a blown-up photograph of Emma, Eddie and Sophie. Angus took a deep breath as he stepped onto the wooden deck. He looked around for a moment, taking in everything going on around him. A buzz was in the air, a mix of excitement and nervousness. Fear and anxiety of the unknown awaiting them in this dark, lonely forest. Angus lifted the bullhorn to his face to address the crowd.

"Gather around, let's go. We have some daylight left and I want to use it. Come on, let's go," Angus shouted.

Angus was more animated in this moment than at any time he, or anyone else on the force could remember. The large crowd gathered around and every person hung on every syllable from Angus' deep and commanding voice. Passion, rage and desperation swirled together, forming an intoxicating mix in the evening air.

"We've all gathered here today to search these woods. A husband, a father, a son, a friend and a member of your own community is missing and we have reason to believe he might be out there. Alone, cold and scared. Waiting for us, *for you*, to find him and bring him home. Look at that photo. Look at this loving family. A wife and young daughter are sitting home *right now*, alone, praying with every single fiber of their being that this man comes home safe. That's where each one of you comes in. Every single one of *us*. Think of your own families. How would your family continue if you were gone in a blink of an eye? And how could you get out of bed every single day knowing one of your loved ones might be out there in the cold, in the dark, in the mud, thirsty, starving, *terrified*. Freezing every second with no hope in sight? *We* are that hope. *You* are that hope. We will find Eddie VanSant. If we have to rip every tree out by their goddamn roots, overturn every single boulder, if we have to drain every river or stream. We will find Eddie VanSant. It's a time like this we learn the true meaning of community. It's a time like this when we find the true meaning of love. So, I ask everyone of you, are you with us?"

The entire crowd burst into a raucous cheer. If they had any doubt about the long night ahead, each one of them now were willing to run full steam ahead through a brick wall for Angus.

"Now, remember. It's going to be a long and cold night. Stay warm, stay safe and stay in sight. Each of you was given a headlamp to battle the darkness. If you get lost or find yourself in danger, flash your headlamp three times and scream for help. If you find something or *someone*, flash your headlamp three times and scream for help. That will alert an officer to come find you. Each of you has been broken up into a unit represented by the colorful vest you were given. Find your unit leaders and follow their lead."

Angus dropped the bullhorn on the stage and jumped off into the grass. The crowd cheered as he walked through them like the hero of the day, burning a path through the dense crowd like he had just split an ocean in two. Standing at the far back of the crowd was Frank, shaking his head and in the middle of a slow clap like he just witnessed a hole in one at the Masters.

"Great speech, sir. Very inspirational," Frank said with a wink and making an OK sign with his right hand.

"Shut up, Frank."

Frank let out a hearty laugh as he patted Angus on the back. The two stood together quietly as each of the units gathered at the entrance to the forest which was growing colder and darker by the minute. Six units in total gathered, each adorned in different neon vests and bright headlamps. The crew members lined up shoulder to shoulder as they awaited word to head inside and begin their search. The spotlights shined brightly onto the search party, sending streaks of light dancing around the grass field as the light bounced off of the reflective material on the vests. The headlamps, all flicked on one by one and illuminated the entrance to the vast empty space. It was as though Angus and Frank were witnessing the beginning of a sold out drum and bass concert. All the lights were in place, the only thing missing was the fun. A large uniformed police officer stood on top of the stage looking out upon the search party. He lifted the bullhorn to his face.

"Unit Leaders. Stay together, stay safe and leave no stone unturned. You are cleared to head in."

In the blink of an eye, the search party disappeared into the darkness. The loud, indistinct chatter had dissipated and now all the men could hear were the crickets, the wind and their own hearts beating deep within their chests.

"I guess we just cross our fingers and wait," Said Frank.

Angus turned and looked over his left shoulder, noticing neither Charlie's car nor Charlie had moved an inch.

"Stay here, keep an eye on things."

"You got it, boss," Frank obliged.

Angus turned and made his way into the parking lot, but decided to head in the opposite direction of Charlie's vehicle.

Like a true detective, he figured it would be best to sneak up on Charlie. He didn't want to scare him away, and if he saw Angus coming, he might dart off into the night to avoid confrontation. Charlie sat silent, intently watching all the action. Not knowing how long this search could take, he had outfitted himself with a thermos of hot tea and a small cooler sitting on the passenger seat. He reached over and opened the cooler, removing a homemade turkey and cheese sandwich. It was wrapped neatly in a sandwich baggy, which he crumbled up and dropped back into the cooler. He took a big bite and washed it down with a loud gulp of his hot tea. With a mouthful of tea and turkey, he was startled out of his distant viewing location by a loud knock on his window. He jolted forward in his seat, thrusting his right hand over his mouth in hopes of not spitting food and tea all over the inside of his clean, luxury car.

"Mr. Claymore," A loud voice boomed. "You mind rolling down the window?"

Angus had snuck around the back of the parking lot, making it nearly impossible for Charlie to see him coming. Charlie rolled his window down and looked up at him.

"Good evening, Detective," Charlie said with just the right amount of smug attitude.

"Enjoying your evening, Mr. Claymore?" Angus asked, noticing his cooler stocked with food, snacks and a thermos. "Preparing for a long night?"

"You know how it is," Charlie said, examining the scene in which he had been caught red handed. "We all have to eat, right?"

"Right," Angus said, boasting a large and condescending smile. "Are you planning on joining a search unit? I can get you a beautiful neon vest. You would look great in one."

"No, I think I'm just fine here in the car."

Angus had knelt down low enough to rest his forearms on the driver's side door. He knew he had minimal time, and wanted to search his vehicle as much as he could. It was still a poker game, and Angus' poker face was impressive. He glanced for a moment until his eyes landed on something dangling from the rear-view mirror. A small white piece of plastic resembling a door hanger in a hotel room. In red print it clearly said City Star Parking with a small barcode.

"What uh, what have you got there?" Angus asked.

"My parking pass?" Charlie asked.

"What's it for?"

"One would assume it's for pain free parking, but I guess you want to make it as painful as possible?"

"What lot is that for?"

"I don't know. I think it's for a few different lots around downtown. Is that a crime now too? To park easily in a busy city?" Charlie barked.

"Well, who's pass is it? Last I heard you didn't have a job. Why do you need a parking permit?"

"Not that I even need to answer that question," Charlie said, rolling his eyes all along the way. "It's my fiance's. She lets me use it when she's out of town."

"Is that right?" Angus said, not breaking his smile which could melt ice. "What the hell are you doing here, Charlie?"

"I wanted to monitor the search and see if you guys find anything," Charlie said, staring straight out the front window, almost refusing to look at Angus. He was getting nervous, and he knew no answer would really make his appearance seem acceptable.

"I thought maybe I could let Emma know," Charlie said, stuttering through his nervousness. "If you found something, maybe I could, I don't know, let Emma know."

"If we find something? You mean if we find Eddie. Her husband. You remember her husband, right, Mr. Claymore?"

"Yes, of course I remember."

Angus put both of his hands on top of Charlie's car and he turned his view towards the forest.

"If we find, *something*, we will let her know, Mr. Claymore. You're not a part of this investigation and unless you plan on checking in and joining a search party, you have no reason to be here."

"I didn't realize you had jurisdiction over this parking lot," Charlie said, shooting attitude.

"I have jurisdiction everywhere," Angus said, staring dead into Charlie's eyes. He straightened up, rested his hands on both of his hips and took a few steps back from the car. "Why don't you step out of the car?"

"Am I under arrest for something? What's the charge? Eating turkey and cheddar in a parking lot?"

"No, you're not under arrest. But why don't you step out and let's have a chat, huh? What do you say?"

"I think I'm going to decline."

"OK, Charlie, here's the deal," Angus said, kneeling down and putting his face into the window. "If you make one mistake, if you get in the way of anything we have going on out here. I will personally make your life an absolute living hell. You got me? You have no reason to be here and I don't appreciate you sitting here with your, whatever the hell that is, a lunchbox full of snacks. This isn't a midnight double feature for your enjoyment. So why don't you get the hell out of here?"

"I don't have to do shit, Angus. If I want to sit here and enjoy a sandwich, I have every right to do so."

Angus was growing furious. It seemed as though anytime he turned around during this investigation, Charlie was there. If he went to talk to Emma, Charlie. He found Eddie's missing car, Charlie. He arranges one of the largest search units in recent memory and who does he find? Charlie.

"OK," Angus said, nodding his head. "How about this? I *do* arrest you. How do you like that?"

"On what charge?"

"Obstruction of justice. You're interfering with an official investigation."

"That would never hold up and you know it," Charlie said, letting out a slight laugh.

"Try me," Angus said, not breaking his stare deep into Charlie's eyes.

He straightened back up and looked over across the parking lot to Frank. He raised his left arm, snapping his fingers to wave him over.

"OK, I'll leave," Charlie said, now fearing he may spend the night in jail. He turned the key in the ignition, kick starting the engine.

"I just wanted to see what happened with the search. Believe it or not, my only interest is helping Emma. I don't want to interfere."

"If you want to be a good friend to Emma," Angus said, kneeling down and positioning his face close to Charlie's. "Then stay the *fuck* out of our way."

Charlie nodded and didn't say a word. He rolled up the window, put the car into drive and circled around the parking lot before heading towards the street. Angus stood with his hands on his hips and didn't move an inch until Charlie's car was completely out of sight.

"What the hell was that all about?" Frank asked.

"Charlie *fucking* Claymore," Angus said, shaking his head.

"Did he say what he was doing here?"

"No. But I don't trust him," Angus said, his body noticeably tense. "Assign a couple units to watch over the VanSant home and Mr. Claymore. I want to know what these two are up to."

"I'll put out a bulletin and make sure we have eyes on them," Frank assured.

"Oh, and Frank," Angus continued. "It might be nothing, but look into City Star parking."

"What the hell is City Star parking?" Frank asked.

"I'm not sure yet," Angus said, not relieving any of Frank's confusion. "Charlie had a parking permit for City Star parking on his rear-view. It might be nothing, but, make a note and look into it. See if we can nail down a name from a checked out parking pass."

25

Emma stood in her living room for what felt like hours. Her
fingertips barely touching the soft linen blinds that hung over
the windows to the outside world, her face hidden to the side as
she squinted at a mysterious car parked across the street. She
could see two men sitting inside. She kept the lights off in the
house, hoping whoever sat in the car couldn't see her staring out
at them. Her mind raced between good and bad outcomes, and
nothing she could tell herself would persuade her from
assuming the worst. It was late, the clock on the mantle had just
struck 9:00pm, so Sophie was sound asleep, but the safety of the
VanSant home was in question. Emma didn't have the bravery
to leave the house to ask the men what they wanted or who they
were. The continuous feeling of the walls closing in on her gave
her a sense of safety, plus, she thought, as long as she could see
the two men they wouldn't be able to surprise her. She couldn't
take the assumptions and the spiraling of her own thoughts any
longer. She reached into the back pocket of her jogger pants and
pulled out her cell phone. Without breaking her stare on the
vehicle, she dialed Charlie.

"Why hello there, Emma," Charlie's voice rang from the
phone.

"I need you to get over here," Emma said, a sense of dread in her voice.

"What's wrong, Kid?"

"I, I don't know," Emma said with a nervous stutter. "There's this car outside. It's been there for hours. I can see two men sitting inside, I don't know what the hell they want."

"Stay inside. You didn't go talk to them, did you?"

"Of course not," Emma barked back. "Just, get over here. I'm *so* scared."

"I'm on my way. Keep your eyes on them and if either of them makes any movement, call me."

"OK, just hurry." Emma clicked the phone, ending the call abruptly. She continued to duck down and kept her eyes glued on that car.

A few moments later, Emma noticed headlights as they illuminated the street. Charlie had arrived. *"Thank god,"* she thought to herself. She heard a soft knock on the front door.

"Charlie?" She shouted, "Come in, come in."

Charlie flew in like he had been shot out of a circus cannon. He quietly shut the door behind him before meeting Emma at the front window.

"What the hell is going on?" Charlie asked in a low whisper.

"Shhhh," she shushed him aggressively, grabbing him by the shoulder and forcing him into a kneeling position. "Stay down. Look, they're right there."

"I saw as I pulled in. I thought maybe I would scare them away."

"Could it be the people who took Eddie casing the joint? What if they're after Sophie and me next?"

Emma was a wreck. Her hair was an absolute mess, like a bird with one good eye had made a nest atop her neck. Her big fluffy robe was tattered and wrinkled and her eyes looked as though she hadn't slept in days.

"I think it's a couple of cops," Charlie whispered.

"Why would the cops sit outside *my* house? I didn't do anything."

"Maybe they're here to make you feel safe. If you knew cops were right outside, maybe it would put you at ease."

There was a long pause where neither of them spoke. Charlie then stood from his kneeling position.

"I'm gonna go ask who they are and what they want," Charlie said, this time at normal speaking volume.

"No, you can't," Emma shouted through whispers. "And keep your voice down!"

"Why?" Charlie asked. "They're outside, they can't hear us. You're being too paranoid."

"What do you expect from me, Charlie? I have weirdos sitting outside my home *clearly* watching me. How would you expect me to act?"

"Look, Emma," Charlie said, softly grabbing her by her shoulders, forcing her to look him in the eye. "I'm gonna go out and ask what they want. As I approach, they'll either allow me to talk to them, or they'll bail. At least if I go out there we'll know what they want."

"I can't let something happen to you too."

"I'll be fine. Watch the car. If anything happens, call Angus. You need to calm down and rest. This shit isn't helping."

"What do you mean by that?" Emma asked, feeling challenged by Charlie's words.

"You're spinning out like a top. You need to slow down and you *need* sleep. I'm gonna go and see what they want. And afterwards, I'm staying the night here with you and Sophie. You need a good night's rest. Your mind is gonna turn to mush if you don't get some real, quality sleep. I don't care if I have to sleep on the floor right next to your bed, whatever it takes for you to feel safe tonight and get some rest, I'm doing it."

Emma sank into Charlie's chest, wrapping her arms tightly around his neck. She let out a long sigh that in any other situation would make a man's knees buckle. The sound of contentment, the sound of safety, both of which Charlie had been fighting for all along.

"Thank you," Emma whispered. The tone in her voice changed from terror to comfort. "I always knew I could count on you."

"I'll always be here for you," Charlie said, his arms now wrapped tightly around her waist.

Charlie and Emma broke their hold on each other as he made his way to the front door.

"Just, watch that car," Charlie said. "If they do anything, I don't know, *weird*, call Angus immediately."

Charlie opened the front door and stepped out onto the porch. He wasn't a tough guy or even a brave guy. But tonight was not the night to cave to cowardice. He needed to be brave for Emma. He may have to take an ass whooping in the middle of the dark street for her, but he was willing to. He stood for a second in the dark, considering the options before him. Should he be polite to the men and lead with a *"Good evening gentlemen!"* Or should he go out like Clint Eastwood, guns blazing and tell them to hit the road before or he would go high noon on them both? He took a deep breath, let it out slowly and proceeded Clint Eastwood style. With his chest puffed and fists clenched so tight the blood was cut off from his fingertips, he took off in a power walk. He thought maybe this approach would intimidate the men and they would leave. By the time his loud, pounding footsteps made it to the middle of the road, he realized he was wrong. For a split second he considered maybe, just maybe, this approach would result in him receiving that ass whooping after all, as the men didn't move an inch. As he got closer, he noticed the driver's side window began to roll down.

"Good evening, Mr. Claymore," an unfamiliar voice rang out from the window.

Charlie broke out of his Eastwood power stance and began relaxing his body one muscle at a time.

"Can I help you gentlemen?" Charlie asked with what he hoped was an assertive tone. His heart was beating so hard and fast, he figured the men must have thought they had entered a Looney Tunes bit, watching a cartoon heart protrude through his shirt.

"Everything's fine, Mr. Claymore," The voice from the driver's side assured. "We're just keeping an eye on Mrs. VanSant's home. All is well, sir."

"Who the hell are you guys? You're scaring the daylights out of her."

"I'm Detective Collins," The man in the driver seat said. "And this is my partner Detective Williams. We were put on duty to watch over Mrs. VanSant."

"Who told you to do that?" Charlie asked, a touch of attitude behind his voice.

"Not that it is any business of yours, but because I know you will report back to Mrs. VanSant, Detective McKenna put in the order."

"Detective McKenna?" Charlie asked, confused. "What's the meaning of this? Why do you need to watch her? You understand she's the *victim* here?"

"We understand Mr. Claymore," Detective Collins assured, making it abundantly clear he had no patience whatsoever for Charlie's questions. "Don't worry yourself about the why, we'll be staying put on Detective McKenna's orders. If Mrs. VanSant has any question, she can call him."

Detective Collins' hand stretched out of the window, holding up a business card.

"What the hell's this?" Charlie asked.

"Detective McKenna's card. If she has any questions or concerns, she can call him at any time. He will be more than happy to explain our intentions."

"Come on, guys. Why don't you get the hell out of here?" Charlie said, putting the business card in the back pocket of his jeans.

"No can do, partner," Detective Collins said. "If she has any questions or concerns, she can call McKenna. Until then, if you don't mind, please step away from the vehicle and head back inside."

"This is horseshit, you guys know that? You're continuing to make the victim feel like a suspect."

"Good night, Mr. Claymore," Detective Collins shouted as the driver's side window began to roll up.

"Fucking snakes," Charlie whispered to himself as he turned and made his way back across the street. He opened the front door and slammed it shut, visibly angry at the encounter.

"What did they say?" Emma asked.

"It's a couple of cops. Here, take this," Charlie said, removing the business card from his back pocket. "Detective McKenna put them on the job. They said if you have any questions to call him."

"Maybe that *is* a good thing," Emma said, a slight glimmer of hope in her voice. "Maybe they're watching the house to *protect* Sophie and me. It actually puts me at ease a little."

"If you feel good, that's all that matters, I guess," Charlie said, scratching the back of his head. "Don't worry about them. What you need to worry about is getting some sleep. You look exhausted."

"I *am* exhausted," Emma said, running her left hand through her messy hair, her right hand covering her mouth as she let out a deep yawn. "Will you really stay the night?"

"Absolutely," Charlie assured her.

"Wait, what about Gwen? Is she going to be all weirded out that you are staying here again?"

"Don't worry about her," Charlie said, shaking Emma's worry off as though it was a burst of smoke in the air. "Trust me, she gets it."

"OK," Emma said with a smile. Her bright yet exhausted eyes cut straight through Charlie. "I can't wait to meet her."

"Why's that?"

"I don't know," Emma said, shrugging the question away. "She's been so understanding, she seems like she could be a great friend."

"She's an outstanding person. One of these days the four of us will get together."

"Four of us?"

"Yeah. You and me, Gwen and Eddie. When he comes home, of course."

"Oh, right," Emma said, rubbing the back of her head. "I look forward to that."

Emma yawned again, she was clearly about to keel over right where she stood and Charlie knew he needed to get her to bed.

"OK, it's bedtime," Charlie said, clapping his hands together. "Should I tuck you in?"

"No," Emma said, shaking her head softly. "Let's sleep out here."

"On the couch?" Charlie asked, surprised.

"Yeah, is that OK?"

"Of course. If you're comfortable out here, I'm good with it. I just want you to be happy and comfortable."

"Well that will make me happy *and* comfortable."

Charlie took a seat right in the middle of the large sectional, kicked off his shoes and put his feet up on her coffee table. Emma sat with her legs up on the couch curled underneath her body.

"Well, you made yourself comfortable, didn't you?" Emma joked.

"What?" Charlie asked, pointing at his feet, crossed on top of her coffee table.

"Typically I would tell you to get your damn feet off my table," Emma said as she snuggled her head onto Charlie's right shoulder. "But I'll allow it tonight because your shoulder is just way too comfortable to care."

She reached for a blanket that hung on the edge of the couch and pulled it over her body, snuggling it right up to her chin as she shuffled and settled deeper into Charlie's shoulder. Charlie looked around and saw the television remote on the couch. He clicked the set on and began flipping through some channels before landing on ESPN.

"Oh, are you a sports fan?" Emma asked.

"Of course," Charlie said. "I love baseball. I want to catch up on the scores."

"Eddie's a big Mariners fan. This is *definitely* a baseball household."

"Ah, yes. The Mariners," Charlie said sort of sarcastically.

"You don't like the Mariners?"

"No, of course I do," Charlie said. "How could I not? Root for the *home* team, right?"

"Is there a team you follow or like more than the Mariners?"

"Don't worry about that," Charlie said. "Just relax, close your eyes and get some sleep. I'll be right here keeping you safe."

"You promise?" Emma asked, digging her head deeper into his shoulder.

"I promise."

Charlie sat deep into the sofa, his right arm around Emma as she drifted softly to sleep. Her head rested on his shoulder, slipping ever so slightly onto his chest. He sat deeper into the couch hoping to allow her maximum comfort, and he rested his head on the back of the couch. As she snuggled closer and closer into his body, he could feel her heart beating softly against his chest. He couldn't help but smile as he drifted into a comforting sleep. At this moment, Charlie was content. He was happy. He knew deep within himself what they were doing was wrong, but he couldn't help but think at the same time, nothing had ever felt so right. At that moment, Charlie's world was perfect.

26

The next morning came quicker than either of them wanted. The bright light of a new day poured into the front windows and washed over their bodies. Charlie was awakened by the sound of morning cartoons. His eyes shot open as he straightened his neck to see what had disturbed his perfect slumber. Sitting on the couch was Sophie, snuggled up in her pink and white unicorn pajamas, perfectly imperfect bedhead flipped all over the top of her head as her little legs dangled off the edge of the couch. Charlie rubbed his face for a moment and focused his dreary eyes on her.

"Sophie," Charlie said with a bit of surprise.

"Good morning, Charlie," Sophie said, not looking away from the cartoons.

"When did you wake up?"

"I don't know," Sophie said.

"Someone is clearly not much of a morning person", Charlie thought. He looked down at Emma, still asleep on his lap, completely unbothered by the blaring cartoons. He gently rubbed her shoulders and leaned in closely.

"Sophie's here. You should wake up," he whispered.

"Hmm," Emma muttered as she pushed herself up with her left arm, her right hand rubbing the sleep from her eyes. She let out a long, deep yawn as though it came all the way from her toes. "What was that?"

"Mommy," Sophie shouted. "Can I have cereal for breakfast?"

"Oh shit," Emma blurted out, as she jumped from Charlie's lap. "Good morning, sweetie. When did you get up?"

"Earlier," Sophie said. A trace of agitation in her voice. "Can I have cereal, *please*?"

Emma stood and walked around the coffee table to Sophie, leaning over to give her a kiss on the forehead.

"Give Mommy a minute and she'll get you some cereal, OK?"

From the couch, Charlie and Sophie could hear the clanking noise of bowls being moved about, silverware falling onto the counter and a cupboard being rummaged through.

"What's your favorite cereal of *all-time*?" Charlie asked playfully.

"Mmmm," Sophie thought for a moment. "I don't know."

"Nice talking to you, Sophie."

Charlie slapped his knees and stood and adjusted his pants and shirt, now wrinkled beyond belief. He looked around the room, took in a nice long deep breath and made his way into the kitchen.

"Are you doing OK?" Charlie asked, showing genuine concern.

"Oh yeah, I'm fine."

"I'm just asking because," Charlie stopped himself, unsure how to proceed. He wanted to address how they had slept cuddled on the couch. But naturally, there was no easy way to broach the subject.

"Because we slept on the couch together, Charlie? Is that what you're getting at?" Emma asked, not with anger in her voice, but definitely not without it either.

"Well, yeah. I mean, it just sort of happened organically."

Emma opened a box of kids cereal. Loaded with sugar and marshmallows and fun characters dancing about on the box. She poured two bowls almost completely full with the sugary bits.

"It's perfectly fine," Emma said, briefly looking up from the breakfast as she spoke. "I appreciate you. I hope you know that. I really needed you last night. I just," she stopped herself.

"You just what?" Charlie prodded.

"I just don't want you to get the wrong idea," Emma said.

"Absolutely not. Trust me. I'm trying to be a good friend and that's it."

"I know," Emma said, nodding her head but continuing to look down. "I just hope you know I appreciate you. You really mean a lot to me. Everything you've done to help me and help with Sophie. Just, thank you."

Emma and Charlie's eyes met, and Emma let out a cute half smile.

"You're welcome, Kid," Charlie said, smiling back.

"There it is again. Kid, you called me kid."

"Yeah, so? Is that OK?"

"No, I mean, yeah. Yes," Emma looked down and laughed. "Let me start *that* sentence again, oh boy." Emma took in a deep breath as though she needed to steady herself. "Yes, it's perfectly OK. I liked it in high school. I still like it now."

Their eyes met again and locked in place as though the rest of the world was in ruins and there was nothing worth looking at but each other. They smiled and remained locked in that moment. Right then, either one of them would have traded their left hand to stay in that comfort for eternity.

"Well, get used to it, Kid," Charlie said, smiling brightly.

Charlie thought Emma was blushing as she brushed her hair behind her right ear.

"Do you want some cereal?" Emma asked.

"No, I'm good. In fact I should probably get going."

"So soon?"

"I promised Gwen I would meet her this morning. She wants to go searching for a new dining set."

"That sounds like an absolute *blast*," Emma said sarcastically.

"You know how it is. Engaged *or* married, what else are Saturdays for? Looking for overpriced furniture no one needs and no one can afford."

They both laughed, knowing there was way too much truth behind his statement.

"What are your plans tonight?" Emma asked.

Charlie thought for a moment, looking around the room as though he was trying to find the perfect answer floating through the air.

"Nothing that I can think of. Do you need something?"

"Well," Emma said, again brushing her unwashed and tangled hair behind her ear.

"What is it, Emma? Out with it, kid."

"Tonight's Sophie's big recital. I know she is absolutely heartbroken that Eddie can't be there. I know it doesn't appear so *now*," Emma said, her eyes wandering around the room, searching for the confidence to ask Charlie a favor.

"I was going to ask if you and Gwen could come with me? It's hard to sit out there in the crowd alone, everyone looking at me wondering about Eddie. Looking at the poor lonely wife all alone at her child's recital. I don't know if I can do it. But I don't have the heart to pull her out of the thing. I *have* to suck it up and go. It might be nice to have some reinforcements."

Charlie looked down and nodded. He wasn't sure how to answer. He knew she needed him. But the recital could be an incredibly awkward moment for the both of them. After a few moments he thought, *"Fuck all of those people. They can't judge us."*

"Of course, Kid," He said confidently. "We'll be there. Maybe we can pick you guys up and ride together and make a night of it? We can all go out to eat afterwards."

"That would be amazing!" Emma beamed at the suggestion and was clearly ecstatic at the acceptance of her invitation. "Sophie needs to be there by 5:00pm, does that work?"

"It absolutely works."

"And I can finally meet Gwen," Emma said, with a playful bounce. "I have been looking forward to this."

From the living room, Sophie had grown restless waiting for her cereal, and she was about to shatter from her own impatience.

"Mommy, where's my cereal?" Sophie's voice shouted from the couch.

"Time to get the princess her cereal," Emma said, rolling her eyes.

"I should get out of here anyway," Charlie said as he checked his pockets for all of his things.

Charlie walked through the living room to the front door, opened it and allowed the gorgeous sunlight and fresh morning air to pour into the home. As he exited, he turned and leaned around the door frame.

"See you at 4:00 tonight. Sophie, enjoy your cereal.".

Emma entered the living room holding two large bowls filled with sugary cereal and milk, each adorned with a silver spoon. She handed one to Sophie who immediately began devouring the sugary bits like she hadn't eaten in weeks. Emma sat next to her, pulled a blanket over her legs and began eating.

"There you go, cereal for my princess."

"Mommy," Sophie said, her mouth half way full of cereal and milk. "Why did Charlie sleep over?"

Emma wasn't sure how to answer her daughter's question, but knew she had to say something to keep the curious brain inside her child's head from spinning out of control with hypotheticals.

"Well Honey, Charlie's a good friend. And he stayed the night to help us out."

"Does Daddy know he slept over?" She asked as the shiny spoon approached her mouth, overflowing with cereal and dripping of milk.

"Yes honey," Emma said. She hated herself for lying to her daughter. "Daddy knows all about it. Now, eat your cereal before it gets too mushy."

The sun sat low, shooting laser beams through the old, dusty blinds of Angus' office. The rays illuminated his exhausted body as he leaned over the desk as though he had been pulled from a cement mixer. He tapped his left index finger on the desk in no particular beat. A broken record skipping to its own tune by an open wound of a man festering an infection of anger, anxiety and impatience. The finger tapping grew from a soft pitter patter to more reminiscent of a hammer being dropped on the decaying desk. Before his hand balled into a fist, which could have easily escalated to Angus smashing right through the wood, Frank entered the room.

"You look happy today. Can I sit?" Frank asked, filling the doorway, holding a folder in his right hand.

Angus motioned for him to sit. He knew what Frank was going to say, and as much as he needed to hear it, he didn't want to.

"So," Frank said, letting out a deep breath of discontentment. "We had to let Johnny Torres go." Frank rolled his eyes and threw his hands into the air with a slight shrug.

"I figured as much," Angus said, dropping his head into his hands.

"His story checked out. There was nothing we could do. We held him as long as we legally could."

"So you spoke to his mother?"

"Yeah," Frank assured him. "I took a drive up to New Castle. He delivers firewood to her every week, just like he said. Those days, he almost always stays the night."

"And you're absolutely *certain* he was there on this particular day?"

Frank closed his eyes and nodded in affirmation. Frank was just as unhappy as Angus about this news.

"Not only did his mother confirm the story, we checked with a gas station in New Castle. Here, check these out," Frank said, tossing the folder to Angus.

Angus pulled out the contents, dropping them onto his desk. Inside were three printed black and white photos of Johnny at a gas station.

"I checked with a gas station near his Mother's place. There's one of him on the road into New Castle and one on the road out the following afternoon. I figured if he was in the area, that spot would catch a glimpse of him. And boy did it ever," Frank said, rubbing his forehead. "Check the timestamps, Angus."

Angus held the photographs up to examine them better. He dropped them back onto the desk and began rubbing his eyes, as though he thought he could reach his brain and tear it out through his eye sockets.

"Same exact fucking time Eddie's car was abandoned at the park," Angus grumbled.

"Not only that, but they found jack *shit* in that forest. Angus, we had no choice."

"So we're back at square one?" Angus asked, the distinct sound of failure trembling in his voice.

"Unfortunately," Frank said carefully, hoping not to light the fuse that was Angus.

"Fuck!" Angus yelled, as he ran his large arm across the top of his desk, scattering the contents across the room. "And we have units watching Mrs. VanSant and that fucking Charlie Claymore?"

"Yeah, Angus. Let's not overreact. They're on the job."

"They know something. They *have* to know something," Angus said as he paced the floor. "Hey, you have your notepad on you?"

"Of course," Frank said, reaching into his jacket pocket.

"You have Charlie's information from when you spoke to him, right? His address?"

"It's all right here," Frank assured, as he began flipping through the pages.

"Let me see it, let me see it," Angus said, snapping his fingers at Frank.

Frank tossed the small pad to Angus.

"Perfect," Angus said as a curious smile covered his face. He grabbed the small slip of paper with Charlie's information scribbled upon it, and tore it from the small pad. "I'm taking this."

"Whatever you want to do, Sir," Frank said. Angus was in no place to be reasoned or argued with. "What the hell are you going to do, Angus?"

"I think I'm going to pay a little visit to my friend Charlie," Angus said as he tucked the slip of paper into his back pocket. "There's nothing like a surprise visit from a detective. I want to see what this son of a bitch is up to."

28

Charlie arrived at Emma's a little before 4:00pm. He wasn't worried about being early, he knew he needed a few extra minutes with Emma before they left for the recital. He would have to explain to Emma why Gwen was not with him, yet again. Emma believed tonight would be the big night when the two most important girls in Charlie's life would meet. But like before, he had not delivered, and Gwen was nowhere to be found. As Charlie parked, he noticed the copper colored Buick across the street. The same two detectives sat keeping watch on everything happening at the VanSant home. Charlie exited his car and looked towards the detectives giving a friendly nod. The detectives made it perfectly clear they saw Charlie, but didn't make any motion in return. Charlie didn't care. He wasn't concerned with them or what they thought about him, about Emma - about *anything*.

He stood at the front door for a moment and straightened his clothes. He wore nice, jet black jeans flowing perfectly over a pair of shiny designer black boots, a blank black t-shirt with a two tone black and grey bomber jacket. His hair was combed perfectly with the slightest little wave in the front crashing over the back of his head. When the door opened, there stood Emma, dressed like she was headed for the red carpet. A total transformation from the last few days. She wore black leggings that went all the way down and wrapped her feet. The leggings were pulled tightly and made it impossible not to follow them down her legs with your eyes to see sexy closed toed suede high heel boots. A beautiful emerald green dress wrapped her small frame as though it was tailored precisely to her specifications. Her hair was done up, the back which usually fell downwards in a half done ponytail now shot upward into a beautifully done bun. Two strings of flowing blonde hair fell on either side of her face, framing it so elegantly it could take your breath away.

"You're early," Emma said, walking away from the door back into the house.

"I like to be early rather than late. I don't mind waiting."

"I just need to finish some makeup," Emma said as she walked down the hallway to her bedroom. Suddenly she stopped and turned back to Charlie as a concerned look washed over her face. "Wait a minute, don't tell me," she stopped herself.

"Yeah, yeah. I know," Charlie said with a big exaggerated shrug.

"Gwen couldn't make it, *again*?" Emma asked.

"I know, it's incredibly frustrating. But believe it or not, I'm getting used to it."

"What happened? Where is she?" Emma asked as she played with her right ear ring.

"Her company is working on some big event and she got called away for a meeting."

"On a Saturday?" Emma asked.

"Some big wig from New York is in town and tonight was the only night he would meet with her entire team. Her hands were tied. She's very sorry, and sends her love, of course."

"Next time, I guess," Emma said as she entered her bedroom. "Just make yourself at home."

Charlie took a seat on the couch, patted his knees and blew out a deep breath. He continued to look around the house for what seemed like ages. The clock struck a quarter past 4:00 when Emma finally emerged from the hallway.

"Sophie, we need to get going sweetheart," Emma shouted back down the hallway. She was moving a mile a minute, wrangling Sophie, putting on a different pair of earrings without looking and collecting costume materials.

"Can I give you a hand with all of this?" Charlie offered.

"Grab all of this stuff and throw it into a bag," Emma said, handing Charlie a pink duffle bag.

Emma turned to walk out of the kitchen, but stopped suddenly and looked Charlie up and down.

"Wait, is *that* what you are wearing?"

"Yeah, why?" Charlie asked, his hands outstretched in confusion, looking at his outfit. "What's wrong with this?"

"Nothing, nothing at all," Emma said, continuing to stare. "You know, most parents and attendees will be, how do I say this, a little more *dressed up* tonight."

"These are $200 jeans," Charlie shot back. "This jacket alone costs more than most of those father's suits."

"Be that as it may, they're still jeans, Charlie."

"I guess I just really don't see it as an issue."

"Come with me," Emma grabbed Charlie by his right wrist and led him down the long hallway into her and Eddie's bedroom.

Charlie stood in the doorway for a moment, unsure of how to act. He was standing inside Emma and Eddie's bedroom. He felt significantly uncomfortable. To the right in the room sat a King sized bed, loaded with enormous colorful pillows, and a thick duvet had been tossed, turned and remained unmade. On either side of the bed sat nightstands, both with matching lamps. On the right table, a black alarm clock flashed red, digital numbers next to a framed photo of the VanSant family. On the left table, a stack of books sat underneath the golden lamp. On the wall above the bed hung a framed and matted photo of the VanSant family overlooking the room, each of them smiling. The floor was covered in dirty clothes thrown all over without care. Charlie wasn't concerned about the shape of the room, he knew Emma had more important things to worry about than untucked sheets and scattered clothing. Emma had opened the doors to the closet which sat just to the left inside the bedroom. She flipped through articles of clothing that hung neatly in a row. She stopped and pulled out a dark gray suit.

"Here we go, this will do," Emma said, turning to Charlie holding out the suit.

"What is all this?" Charlie asked.

"It's a suit. You *have* seen a suit before, right?" Emma laughed.

"Of course I've seen a suit. I *own* suits. I just, well I haven't fully unpacked from the move yet."

"Don't worry about it, throw this on. You're about the same size as Eddie, maybe a bit thicker."

"Oh, that's nice," Charlie said, slightly offended.

"I don't mean like that, calm down," Emma said. "I mean you're a little more *built* than he is. But this should fit like a glove. Go into the bathroom and throw it on. And make it quick, we need to get out of here."

"I don't know if I'm comfortable wearing this," Charlie said as he grabbed the hanger.

"Just throw it on. Eddie won't mind. People will be looking at me enough as it is, I don't need them thinking I brought a slob to the recital."

"Slob?" Charlie said, now he was officially offended. "Did I tell you how much this outfit cost?"

"No one cares about that. Come on," Emma stood behind Charlie and pushed him, her hands pressed into his lower back, into the master bathroom. "Get your ass in there and change. Come on, do it for me."

That was an argument Charlie could never win. So naturally, he gave in. He went into the bathroom and threw on the suit. He stood there, draped in Eddie's clothes and stared at himself in the bathroom mirror. He couldn't help but think about the mornings Eddie and Emma got ready for the day together in that bathroom. All the evenings before bed, going on and on about every boring, mundane detail of their days. As uncomfortable as he was, he didn't want to let Emma down. Seeing her happy meant everything to him. So again, he said *"fuck it,"* and went along with what Emma had requested. Charlie opened the bathroom door and slowly walked into the bedroom.

"Let me take a look at you," Emma said, grabbing the lapels of the sports coat and adjusting them slightly. "There we go, see? You look great. You look just like Eddie."

"Great," Charlie said sarcastically. He sat on the edge of the bed and began putting on his slick, black boots. "Are these shoes OK, at least?"

Emma stared for a moment at the shoes, evaluating the entire look. "Yep, those will do," she said as she exited the bedroom like a tornado that had come and gone.

He slipped on his boots and made his way into the hall towards the living room. Emma stood at the entrance to the kitchen to see what would be his grand entrance. Dark gray, tailored slacks, a fitted dark gray sport coat, black button-up shirt and an emerald green tie to match Emma's outfit.

"Ah, a masterpiece," Emma said, as she playfully clapped at him.

"OK, OK," Charlie said, waving Emma off. "That's enough."

"You look good, what can I say?"

"I look like Eddie," Charlie muttered.

"Like I said, you look good. Eddie *always* looked good."

"Well, when he comes home maybe he can give me some tips."

"I'm sure he would be happy to," Emma said, checking the bright gold watch on her left wrist. "Sophie, we really need to go."

Sophie ran full charge down the hallway. Red, glittery dance shoes on her feet, black leggings stretched down her little legs from underneath a large puffy jacket that wrapped around her.

"Mommy, can I wear my costume now?" Sophie asked eagerly.

"No, honey," Emma said. "We don't want it to get messed up before the recital. You can put it on when we get there."

"OK," Sophie said, picking up the pink duffle bag and throwing it over her tiny shoulder.

"So, we're all set?" Charlie asked, clapping and rubbing his hands together.

"I think so, you have everything Sophie?"

"Sure do, Mommy."

"Alright, we're all set," Emma said.

Charlie opened the front door allowing the two ladies to exit before him. Once out on the porch, he shut the door as Emma inserted her key to lock up.

"We need to take my car, because I have her car seat," Emma said.

"Fine by me. Want me to drive?"

"Sure, that would be great," Emma said, handing Charlie her set of keys.

Once they got to the driveway, Charlie clicked the button to unlock the doors. He opened the back door to allow Sophie to climb in, and Emma strapped her into the seat. He then opened the passenger side door, holding it for Emma to enter.

"Why thank you, good sir," Emma said.

"My pleasure, Maam," Charlie said back playfully.

He walked around the front of Emma's car and looked across the street at the two detectives. Again, he nodded in their direction, and this time, the detective in the driver's seat, Detective Collins, lifted a radio to his mouth and began speaking. Charlie couldn't hear a word he said, but he was certain they reported that Emma was on the move. This made Charlie's blood boil, but he couldn't show it. Now was not the time to overreact, or react at all. Tonight wasn't about him, it was about Sophie. He opened the car door and got in without incident, kicking the ignition over and backing out of the driveway. The sun had begun to set as they arrived at the community theater and Charlie found a spot as close to the entrance of the building as he could. This theater, The Gaslamp Theater, was very old-fashioned. A large marquee wrapped the building illuminating the entire street. Large gas-style lamps lined the small downtown area as though it was plucked right out of a time forgotten. A beautifully ornate sign shot straight up into the night sky with the word "GASLAMP" shining bright in blue neon, with more neon tubes running down the sign, framing the wording. Bright light bulbs wrapped the sign outside of the neon, twinkling both simultaneously and freely from one another. A small box office sat under the marquee where guests could purchase their tickets. He turned off the car, jumped out and ran around to the passenger side to open the door for Emma. Once out, Emma leaned in the back to unlatch Sophie and helped her onto the sidewalk. Sophie jumped out, landed on her feet and immediately burst with excitement and began jumping up and down on the sidewalk. Her happiness could not be contained, and seeing this made Emma melt with adoration. It had been so long, Emma almost couldn't remember seeing her little girl act this way. Pure childlike enthusiasm and completely carefree. Emma's heart could have burst from the scene.

"You have your bag and costume?"

"Yup," Sophie said, a smile beaming ear to ear.

"Then let's do this, kiddo," Emma said, putting her hand up for a high five.

Sophie obliged, cocking her right arm back as far as she could, and flinging herself forward to deliver the ultimate high five.

"Give Charlie one," Emma encouraged.

Again, Sophie cocked her arm back like she was about to put Nolan Ryan to shame. Charlie knelt down and lifted his right hand, as Sophie slapped him with a perfect high five. Direct contact.

"Great high five, kid," Charlie said.

"Alright, let's go. We're going to be late," Emma said.

Sophie took off running down the sidewalk to the theater where she had seen a couple of her school friends who were also dressed in costume for the performance. Emma crossed her arms tightly against her body in a sad attempt to battle the cold as the two walked side by side.

"Do you need my Jacket," He cut himself off. "Or, uh, I mean. Do you want *this* jacket?"

"I'll be OK. We won't be outside for long," she said as she looked up at him with an adorable smile. "But thank you."

The neon lights danced within Emma's eyes as she looked up at Charlie. He felt like his chest housed a thousand butterflies as his heart fluttered inside of him. He couldn't break his stare as the flickering neon looked like fireworks going off in her eyes. He was mesmerized. But there was no time for this and he needed to snap out of it as they reached the entrance of the theater and were met by Sophie's dance instructor, Mrs. Wallace. She was an older woman in great shape. Dark skin, long flowing black hair and absolutely stunning.

"Hi, Mrs. Wallace," Emma said, reaching out to shake her hand.

"Mrs. VanSant, it's so great to see you. How are you?"

"Doing the best I can," Emma said with a smile.

"I'm so glad Sophie could take part in the recital. I can't imagine what you must be going through. Have you heard any news about Eddie?"

"No, nothing new," Emma said with a sniffle, as the cold continued to bother her.

"Oh honey," Mrs. Wallace said, reaching in and grabbing Emma for a hug. "If you need anything at all, please call me."

Emma finally broke away from the long hug, as Mrs. Wallace studied Charlie.

"And who might this be?" She asked.

"Oh, I'm sorry," Emma said, turning to Charlie. "This is an old friend of mine, Charlie Claymore. He just moved to town and he has been helping out *a lot*."

"Well, it's great to meet you Charlie."

"You as well, Mrs?" Charlie asked. "I'm sorry, I didn't catch your name."

"Mrs. Wallace, I'm the girls dance instructor."

"Great," Charlie beamed. "I'm really looking forward to the show tonight."

"Well, it means a lot to the kids. You don't need to stand out here in the cold, honey," Mrs. Wallace told Emma. "You're family, you can head in and take your seats."

"That's great," Emma said. "Sophie, come over here, kiddo."

Sophie ran back to Emma as she knelt down to look her daughter in the eye.

"You'll be great. I will be in the audience watching and cheering you on."

"OK, Mommy," Sophie said.

"Give me a hug," Emma said as she pulled Sophie in. "Give your mommy a kiss."

"Mommy, come on," Sophie said, pulling away. She pushed off of Emma and ran back to her friends.

"Love you, Sophie," Emma shouted to no response. "Kids, right?"

"I have 3 myself." Mrs. Wallace said. "They grow up so fast. They need you and need you, and then one day, like a lightning strike, they think they know better than us."

"Right," Emma said, looking up at Charlie. "Well, we should probably head inside."

"Of course, dear," Mrs. Wallace said. "Enjoy the show. It was great to meet you, Charlie. Thanks for taking care of these sweet girls for us."

"Great meeting you, Mrs. Wallace. And I'll do what I can."

Charlie and Emma took a few steps toward the entrance to the theater before he put his right arm out, stopping her from moving another inch.

"I just realized something," Charlie said, a puzzled look washing over his face. "You call Sophie kiddo quite often."

"Yep," Emma said, pulling his right arm down to her side, wrapping both of her arms around it. "Where do you think I got it from?"

Charlie's stomach buzzed like a beehive that had been kicked. He looked down at Emma and their eyes met. The neon lights continued to dance in her eyes and Charlie again was lost.

"Come on, you," Emma said, squeezing his right arm tightly.

Emma walked into the theater followed by Charlie. Inside, there sat an old snack counter selling bottled waters, sodas and snacks. On either side of the snack counter were large entryways with dark burgundy curtains cutting off the lobby from the main theater. They turned right as they entered and walked across the lobby. Charlie pulled the curtains out of the way so Emma could walk through. The Gaslamp wasn't a large theater, it was mostly used for community events, plays and small dance recitals. Three sections of seats divided by long walkways led to a small stage in front of the room. The theater was mostly empty, aside from a few of the families that had arrived.

"Where do you want to sit?" Charlie asked.

"Definitely *not* over there," Emma said, pointing to the left side of the room.

Taking up a good portion of seats in the left section were the parents from Sophie's school that Emma had hoped to avoid. They were standing up and mingling with one another, and Emma wanted no part of the gossip they would be spewing.

"Let's sit right up front," Emma said, pointing at the dead center of the room where the seats were still wide open.

"Lead the way," Charlie said, motioning with his right hand for Emma to head down.

They took their seats right in front of the stage, 3 rows back. Luckily, they found two seats in the center of the aisle, a perfect viewing spot. They sat together and reminisced on their past, talking about their time in high school, discussing Eddie and Gwen in great detail and cracking jokes. For a short time, Emma forgot about the troubles waiting to side swipe her outside of the theater. For one evening, the Gaslamp Theater would be her safe zone.

"Do you remember all the plays we went to see in high school?" Emma asked, laughing as she finished the sentence.

"Oh yeah, I remember," Charlie said, joining in with laughter.

"I remember one in particular, you asked if I wanted to go with you and when we got there, you thought we were on a date." Emma let out a loud laugh.

"Well, that's one I would *kind of* like to forget, if you don't mind."

"Oh, that's sad. Why?"

"It's awkward when one person thinks it's a date, and the other one absolutely does *not* see it that way," Charlie said, letting out another giggle.

"Well, that's all in the past now."

"Right, all in the past. Let's just uh, let's leave that story where it is," He said, nervously wiping his sweaty palms on Eddie's suit pants.

The lights went down in the theater and the recital was underway. Group after group of children of all age groups showcased their best talents on that stage. One group of young boys did a breakdance routine, a high school aged girl did a Betty Boop-esque dance number, which left the entire crowd in a confused state of bewilderment. And more tap dance routines than one could even pretend to remember. Then, Mrs. Wallace took the stage followed by a huge applause from the audience.

"Good evening ladies and gentlemen. My name is Debra Wallace and I'm the dance instructor for the Gaslamp Children's Dance Troupe. Tonight my youngest dancers will be performing for you a medley of popular dance routines throughout modern pop music. The kids have worked tirelessly to learn this routine and I think you will be pleased. Now, without further ado, I present to you, the Gaslamp Children's Dance Troupe."

Mrs. Wallace exited the stage as the kids took their places. Sophie stood right up front so Emma and Charlie could see her without obstruction. They both erupted into loud cheers, as did most of the audience.

"You got this, Sophie!" Emma shouted from her seat. But Sophie was so locked in to the performance, she didn't hear her.

From the side of the stage, Mrs. Wallace's voice could be heard counting down for the performance to begin, followed by pop music beginning to play loudly through the house speakers. The kids first went into a well choreographed, but not so perfectly executed version of a Paula Abdul dance, followed by the ever popular Floss dance that is such a phenomenon with kids these days and many other popular dances mixed in throughout.

"Oh my god, how good is she?" Emma blurted out.

"She's nailing it, she's the best on the stage." Charlie added.

"I know, right?" Emma exclaimed. "Ugh, I'm just so proud of her. My little girl is dancing her little heart out."

Emma was beaming. So much so, Charlie thought if she opened her mouth for too long, actual beams of light may shoot out of her throat and be mistaken for a spotlight. Emma was getting so caught up in the moment of excitement and pride, she began clapping along with the music. A parent sitting in front of her turned around and shot a dirty look.

"Sorry," Emma whispered to the parent, putting her hands together in her lap.

"Don't apologize to them. You're allowed to enjoy this as much as you like. Want me to tell him to kick rocks?"

"Oh, stop it," Emma said, swatting Charlie's left knee. "I'm just excited."

Charlie was sitting with his hands on his legs in a relaxed fashion when he felt something move underneath his left arm. He shot his hand up off of his knee and looked down to see Emma's right hand, moving underneath his arm as she locked her hand inside his. He rested his hand back down onto his leg, when Emma reached her left hand across her body and held on to the top of their interlocked hands and moved in closer to his body. Charlie looked at her confused, but she didn't take her eyes off the stage. He thought maybe it was the excitement of the recital and thought it best to not to make any more of it. The performance ended and the girls all took a bow before exiting the stage. Emma, Charlie and many other parents gave a standing ovation. Charlie knew then that the hand holding was only out of her unbridled excitement. They clapped and whistled in support before returning to their seats. As soon as they sat back down, Emma returned her hand to Charlie's without hesitation. He knew it was wrong, but he didn't care. Nothing had ever felt more right than her hand inside of his.

When the performance ended, Charlie and Emma stood in the lobby with the other parents waiting for their children to arrive. Sophie came out like a bolt of lightning running through the lobby. Emma knelt down and pulled Sophie in for a hug.

"Oh honey, you did so great. I'm so proud of you. You killed it up there."

"Great job, Sophie," Charlie added. "You were the best one up there."

"Are you ready to head home? We'll have a big bowl of ice cream to celebrate how well you did."

Emma let go of Sophie, stood up and took her by the hand as the three of them made their way out of the theater. As they turned down the long sidewalk, Emma walked past some of the parents from Sophie's school. She gave a friendly nod, and they returned the gesture. That was as much as she wanted to give. When they reached the car, Charlie unlocked the doors, first opening the back to let Sophie climb into her child's seat. Emma leaned in and locked her in tight.

"I'm so proud of you, honey. You did so great."

"Thanks, Mommy," Sophie said, a smile that could light a ballroom on her little face.

Emma shut the door and stood in front of Charlie, studying his face. Charlie was having a hard time making eye contact with her and she clearly noticed his awkwardness.

"What's your deal?" She asked.

"I don't have a deal? Do I have a deal?"

"You seem, I don't know, uncomfortable."

"Not at all."

"This was a good night. Let's keep it that way."

"Absolutely," Charlie said, opening the passenger door to let Emma in.

"Emma," Charlie said as she was about to enter the car. "I hate to ask, but the hand holding. What was that?"

She stood with her back to the car, staring into Charlie's eyes with burning intensity.

"Was that wrong?"

"I don't know how to answer that, Emma."

"At the moment it felt right. Why should I deny what feels right? Why should *either* of us deny something if it feels right? You're a good guy, Charlie. You make me happy and comfortable. So, I don't know. I guess I can't really explain it. We're *friends*. I wanted to, so I did."

"You don't have to explain anything. Forget I asked," Charlie said, motioning for her to enter the car.

"When things feel right, they just feel, I don't know, right," Emma said, looking around the street to see who was around and who might have eyes on them.

Charlie's eyes lit like two roman candles shooting fire into the night. He felt that a door had been opened for him, and he was more than prepared to step inside. Charlie wrapped his right arm around Emma's waist, pulling her tightly against his body. He bent down, planting an open mouth kiss on Emma's lips. To his pleasant surprise, she didn't immediately pull away. For those few seconds, if he didn't know any better, he might think fireworks were shooting off above them like the 4th of July. She then planted her open, right hand on his chest and softly pushed his body away from hers. She stared into his eyes with an adorable smile. As her eyes caught his, every muscle, joint and fiber of his being started to shake like a rattlesnake's tail.

"Come on, you," Emma said, patting his chest a couple times, signaling the moment had come to an end.

Emma got into the car as Charlie shut the door softly behind her. He stood on the sidewalk for a moment trying to calibrate himself. He felt himself staring off into space when across the street, he was brought back to the reality of planet earth. His heart raced, this time with much more anger than excitement. Across the street, standing on the sidewalk with a paper cup of coffee was Angus, leaning against a brick wall beside a small cafe. Charlie sent bolts of invisible lightning in his direction. Angus caught them and shot them right back. The two kept their eyes locked onto each other, as though they may be forced into a duel. Angus finally loosened and let out a big toothy smile and waved at Charlie.

"Good Evening, Mr. Claymore," Angus shouted. "Lovely evening, wouldn't you say?"

Charlie said nothing as he walked around the car and opened the door.

"Drive safe, Mr. Claymore. I *will* see you soon," Angus shouted, with a big boisterous wave.

Charlie slammed the door and pulled the car out away from the curb. As he drove down the empty street, Angus had moved to the edge of the sidewalk and waved as the car passed by. All the excitement rushed out of Charlie's body. *"What did he see?"* Charlie thought to himself. *"And why was he watching us?"* Charlie was determined to find answers.

•   •   •

Charlie set the car in park but left it running in the driveway. It was early, and Charlie wanted nothing more than to spend more time with Emma. He wasn't sure how to broach the subject and figured he could test the waters. *"You miss 100 percent of the shots you never take,"* he thought to himself. They were old friends after all, so what could go wrong?

"So," Charlie said, patting his knees with his open palms. "It's early. Do you feel like, I don't know. Do you want to hang out for a while?"

Emma sat silent, staring intently through the windshield of the car. She nodded softly, as though she was hearing the most beautiful song playing inside of her head.

"Can you stay out here for a moment?" Emma asked quietly, like she was spilling a secret. "I want to take Sophie inside."

"Yeah, of course," Charlie said.

Emma exited the car and opened the back, unlocking the car seat straps which held Sophie safely in place and lifted her out, allowing her little feet to land on the driveway.

"I'll be right back," Emma said through the open back door.

Charlie watched as Emma, Sophie's little hand in hers, walked up the long concrete walkway. Soon, they disappeared into the front door, as he noticed lights in the order of which the rooms were set each pop on. He continued to sit in the running car. *"Why couldn't I go in with her,"* he wondered to himself. *"Had I done something wrong?"* He thought back to the kiss, as anxiety flooded over his entire body like a sea of fire. He was burning with emotion, his mind hosting a stock car race for the ages inside of his skull. Buzzing and speeding through his mind were so many thoughts he didn't want to confront. He just hoped in the long run, he wouldn't crash out. Before his emotions reached a fever pitch, he saw Emma exit wearing a new outfit. Loose fitting sweat pants, a large cardigan draped around her body and a pair of house slippers. Charlie was deflated. He turned the car off, opened the door and stepped out. Emma met him on the driveway, holding the cardigan closed around her to keep warm.

"I guess I should be going," Charlie said, looking down and scratching the back of his head.

"Is that OK?"

"Of course," Charlie said with a smile. "It's been a long night for both of you. It's probably best to turn in."

"It isn't that I don't *want* to spend time with you. It's just—" Emma stopped herself.

"What is it? You can tell me anything."

"I don't know. Maybe I need to slow everything down."

Charlie was taken aback, as though her words had literal weight behind them, and had pushed him against the car. An action Emma fully acknowledged.

"I don't mean it like that," Emma assured. "It's just. My *husband* is missing. And now you kissed me. It's just very confusing and I'm worried it's becoming too much. I think I just got caught up in the moment."

"I get it. Truly, I understand. And I am very sorry if I went over the line," Charlie said.

"Maybe we just need to, I don't know, pump the breaks a tad. I still want to see you, Charlie. Please don't think I'm saying otherwise."

"Absolutely, and you *are* right. I don't want to create any tension or make things any harder on you."

"I know," Emma said, putting her hand on Charlie's chest. "Hey, what do you say we have dinner one night this week? Just a nice, *friendly* dinner. You can come over, I will cook something. What do you say?"

"I say that sounds like your best idea yet. I can't wait."

"Great. It's a date. Well, a *friend* date," Emma said with a cute giggle.

"It's a date," Charlie said, blinking his eyes awkwardly.

Emma wrapped her arms around Charlie's shoulders, leaning in for a hug. Charlie reached down around her waist and pulled her in to return the gesture.

"Thank you, Charlie," Emma said, not letting go of him. "For everything. You don't know how much of a help you have been."

"I'm glad to hear it. Everything from tonight aside, all I want is to be here for you."

Emma finally released her arms and stepped away from Charlie, motioning in no uncertain terms their time together that evening was coming to a close.

"So, dinner this week. Count on it, sir," Emma said, pointing at Charlie as she walked backwards down the concrete path to her front door.

"Dinner this week, you're on," Charlie said, pointing back.

"And Charlie, you can hold on to the suit. It looks good on you."

Emma took a few more steps backwards before turning around to her front door. She bit her bottom lip, concealing a big smile in Charlie's direction. Charlie walked to his car and stood outside watching her every move until the door shut. He looked up, marveling at the starry sky for a moment, before turning his vision and focusing on the unmarked police car across the street. The same car was in its now permanent position, also watching every move Emma made. His emotions immediately switched from intense glee to unmeasurable rage.

"Haven't you seen enough?," Charlie shouted at the officers, before lowering his voice and muttering to himself. "Stupid fuckers."

He opened his driver's side door, climbed in, turned over the engine and sped off down the road. His night had ended. But boy, what a night it was.

29

Charlie wasn't on the road long before he noticed something suspicious behind him. As he passed by the park on Pine, he passed a car that had been parked alongside the curb. Charlie only noticed this, because as he passed the beam lights popped on, pulled away from the curb and began driving behind him. As he continued down Pine, the bright lights shined, illuminating the inside of his own vehicle. When he turned right onto Mirror Pond Place, the lights followed. When he took a left onto Hathorne Avenue, a street which drivers need to yield to oncoming traffic, the following car had clearly run right through the red light and continued behind him. When he decided to u-turn at the intersection of Prospect and Warren, the car behind him also pulled a u-turn. He knew he was being followed, and closely. At the time, he figured the person or people trailing him were probably the same people who had been keeping an eye on Emma, or maybe some other useless paper pushers who had been put on his tail. He figured, *"what the hell does it matter?"* They already knew who he was and where he lived. So he continued home like normal. If they wanted to find him, they could and there was nothing he could do to stop it. He continued driving a short time before turning left onto the dark road to his house on Lochwood. The road was old and in need of repaving and the lack of street lights made for a spooky atmosphere. Street lights wouldn't do much anyway, with the large overgrown trees sitting on either side of the broken road adding to the element of fear. The only things lighting up the road were the dim lights hanging from the old homes and the beaming lights of his car, and of course the car intent on following him.

Charlie's house sat at the end of the road, where the asphalt met a thick, vast forest. A steep driveway led to the home which was surrounded by pine trees, a dirt lot and a path which cut through the forest. He turned into his driveway, sped up momentarily and then slammed the brakes, causing a loud screeching noise as his car came to a halt. He jumped out of the car but left the engine running. He stood outside the car on his driveway staring out at the dark, barren road as he saw the car that had been following him pass by, stop at the end of the road, and began turning around. Charlie ran towards the end of the driveway as the car began speeding up, rushing out of the neighborhood. Charlie reached the edge of the driveway right as the car sped by. It was moving much too fast for Charlie to try to stop it, and he knew that. He slammed his feet into the concrete at the last second, the force causing him to jolt forward a few extra steps before he gathered his footing. As the car passed, the driver turned and looked right at Charlie, their eyes locking. A moment that was gone in a snap, but also felt as though time had dropped into slow motion. Their eyes stayed, fixated on each other as the car sped by towards the end of the street, shooting through a stop sign, turning right and leaving the neighborhood. And like a flash of light, it was gone as quick as they both had arrived.

"You son of a bitch," Shouted Charlie. "What the hell do you want from me, Angus?"

30

The steel framed glass door to the Sunnyside Cafe opened as Angus and Frank walked into the old, musky restaurant. Frank, wearing gray slacks, a white button-down shirt with a matching gray sport coat and Angus in his patented black slacks and tan jacket over a white shirt. The restaurant was very old-fashioned, not only for the area but in general. For someone who was not aware of the Cafe, they would think the entire world continued to spin, moving from year to year with progress, technology and science, all the while Sunnyside Cafe stayed right in the same spot in history from when it was opened. Locals liked it this way. It added to the charm.

"Just the two of you today?" An older woman asked, greeting them.

The employees didn't wear uniforms and they were not done up with sashes, buttons or colorful attire. They clearly rolled into work in whatever clothes they might wear to run errands. The only uniformed items were the name tags pinned to their tops. This woman's name tag read "Rose." Rose was in her late 50s if one had to guess, hair done up in a perfect perm.

"Yes Ma'am," Replied Frank.

"Would you like a booth, or would you like to sit at the counter?" Rose asked as she pulled two menus from the side of the hostess stand.

"Booth if you have one, please," Frank said.

Frank and Angus followed Rose to their booth. The Sunnyside Cafe had wall to wall wood paneling and the restaurant was wrapped by large booths with dark red vinyl benches and formica tables. At the front of the restaurant sat an old-fashioned lunch counter, with barstools topped by the same dark crimson vinyl and worn out wood flooring stretched the length of the space. All over the walls were old time photos of Seattle, the owners, guests from years long past and knickknacks even thrift stores would decline to accept.

"Here you go, boys," Rose said, motioning to a booth in the far back corner of the cafe.

"Thank you, Rose," Frank said.

Angus sat in the booth facing the rest of the restaurant, Frank across from him.

"Can I start you boys off with something to drink?" Rose asked.

"Coffee, please. Black," Angus said, opening his menu, not looking up.

"Coffee for me too, Rose. Thank you."

Rose took off to retrieve two cups of coffee. They both began flipping through the menu to decide what to have for breakfast.

"Have you had the house made donuts from this joint?" Frank asked.

"*Donuts?*" Angus asked, confused. "No, I can't say that I have."

"Well, if it means anything to you, I recommend them. They make them fresh daily and they're good enough to change your life."

"Frank," Angus said, shutting his menu and folding his hands on top of the table. "Let me tell you something. I refuse to be an old cop who comes into a cafe and orders coffee and donuts."

"Oh come on. That's such a bullshit stereotype."

"Be that as it may, I will not take part in perpetuating it."

"You won't at least *try* a donut?"

"No, I will not try a donut," Angus said, as he lifted his menu and began studying each offering.

"Not even if I, your closest friend *and partner*, recommend it to you? If I tell you it will *change* your life, you won't try *one* donut?"

"No, Frank. I will not be trying a donut this morning. But I thank you for the recommendation. Consider it noted."

"I don't get you sometimes," Frank said, deflated and sitting back in his vinyl bench seat, like a child who was told he couldn't get a new toy.

"You don't have to get me, Frank. We just have to work together."

"Yeah, yeah. I get it," Frank said, looking over his right shoulder towards the opposite side of the dining room. "Look, when she comes back, order me a bear claw and a side of bacon. OK?"

"A bear claw and a side of bacon? Geez, Frank. It's 8:37am. That's all cake, fat and salt."

"I like cake, fat and salt, alright? Those three with coffee are what I consider a perfectly balanced breakfast."

"If you say so."

"Just order it for me, OK? I need to hit the restroom."

Frank stood up from the table and walked to the front of the Cafe, where two saloon style doors sat fixed on the wall to the left of the counter. Angus broke from his menu to look across the room when he noticed in a booth two spaces away sat a man with a dark blue hat, facing the opposite way. Angus couldn't see his face, and he returned to his menu. Just then, the man stood up from his booth and made his way over.

"Charlie, how did I know that was you?" Angus asked, not surprised by his sudden appearance.

Charlie sat down across from Angus, pushed Frank's menu to the side of the table closest to the wall and crossed his arms on top of the worn out formica.

"Why did you follow me home last night?" Charlie asked, defensive and shaking with anger.

"I'm a detective, Mr. Claymore. Following people around happens to be a small part of the job." Angus, showing no respect to Charlie's presence, continued to look over the menu refusing to look at him.

"First you arrest Emma, then put police outside of her home. You *scare her* half to death, not knowing who the hell they are—" He stopped as Angus cut him off.

"Emma is perfectly fine, Mr. Claymore. Those officers are there for her protection." Angus said, closing the menu and setting it onto the table.

"Don't you think it would have been nice to tell her? She was scared shitless. Her husband is missing, there is some psycho coworker of his out there running around. She doesn't know what the fuck going on."

"She has my card and my partners, if she has any questions she can call us."

"What gives you the fucking right to follow us around town? The other night at the recital? Following me to my *home*?" Charlie asked, pounding his right fist onto the table top.

"First of all, calm down," Angus said, trying to avoid causing a panic to the other guests. "Second, it isn't my job to inform you of a damn thing. My job is to find Mr. VanSant. Period. It begins and ends with him. If that means we have to look into some things, that's exactly what we're going to do. Get used to it."

"Leave Emma the fuck alone," Charlie said, staring deep into his eyes.

Angus didn't break his own stare back. He assumed he had been face to face with people scarier and tougher than Charlie Claymore.

"You're very fond of that girl, aren't you?" Angus asked, sitting back in the booth.

"*That* girl? Her name is Emma. And what business is that of yours?"

"Everything is my fucking business," Angus snapped, leaning forward as he pounded his closed fists into the table. "The way I see it, you have two choices. Either stop seeing Mrs. VanSant immediately, or fall in line with the process. Because we are not going away. You can take that to the bank."

The two men continued to stare and shoot hellfire at each other, rage boiling up inside both of their souls. Charlie was the first to break. He tapped his fingers on the table a couple of times, looked around and got up.

"Just, leave her alone Angus. And find her damn husband already," Charlie barked as he turned and headed towards the exit.

"Have a great day, Mr. Claymore. I'm sure I will see you *very* soon," Angus shouted back, with a smile and a wave.

Charlie didn't turn back around as he rushed out of the Cafe, pushing the glass door so hard, he could have ripped it off its hinges. Angus noticed Frank, standing outside the saloon doors who had seen the whole thing. Once Charlie disappeared he rushed back to the table.

"What the hell was that all about?" Frank asked.

"Don't worry about it. I have it under control," Angus said. "I've decided to make your day, Frank."

"Is that so?"

"That is so," Angus said, closing the menu and pushing it to the edge of the table.

Just then, Rose reappeared, pad of paper and a pencil in hand.

"Is everything OK, gentlemen?" She asked sweetly.

"Of course, Ma'am. Just an old friend," Angus said with a smile.

"So what can I get you boys?"

"My friend here will have a bear claw and a side of bacon," Angus said, pointing at Frank. "And I will have a donut, loaded with rainbow sprinkles please."

"You got it," Rose said, departing from the table.

"A donut, huh? Well, color me surprised," Frank said.

"I figure, what the hell?" Angus said. "Besides, you are paying so what do I care? But I'll tell you this, Frank. This donut better be amazing."

31

Charlie was confused for days after the recital. The hand holding, the goodnight kiss, her explanation of it just *"feeling right."* What did it all mean? Where was he headed? Where were *they* headed? He knew deep down these feelings couldn't be real, at least not in her heart. *"She is in a state of grief,"* he kept telling himself. But what if it *was* more than that? What if after all these years the tiny flame they once had in high school could ignite into something bigger? Something powerful that could engulf their hearts and lives, finally fusing their souls together once and for all? If Eddie came home, then what? He thought about this until his brain began to do somersaults within his skull. All this confusion created a pit inside of Charlie's stomach. He was confused, he was restless, he was sick over it. Not to mention it had now been days since he had heard from Emma. All these thoughts and beating himself up over their actions left Charlie with one lasting thought he couldn't break - Sometimes the flames you hold the closest burn the worst.

He couldn't take it anymore and he finally reached out to check on dinner plans. It had taken most of the week to psyche himself up enough to reach out, and they had set the date for Friday evening, 6:00pm, and after so many restless nights and skipped meals Friday had finally arrived. Charlie tossed clothes around his bedroom, looking for what could be the best dinner outfit. *"It's just dinner at Emma's place. Dinner with a friend,"* he kept telling himself. *"It shouldn't be this big of a deal!"* Finally, he landed on what he considered a perfect outfit. Funny enough, it wasn't much different than his typical attire. Black, slim fit jeans pulled over dark boots. Plain black t-shirt with a dark blue bomber jacket. His hair slicked back with just the slightest cut to the left side. Very old-fashioned and debonair he thought of himself. As he continued to put the final touches on his evening look, he heard a loud pounding at his front door. He slowly turned away from his bathroom mirror, throwing a curious glance over his left shoulder. He stomped down the stairs and bounced over to the front door. He knelt down slightly and glanced through the peephole. Within an instant, the excitement of the upcoming evening escaped like a helium-filled balloon if it were to cuddle with a razor blade. Happiness transformed into anger, a feeling he had become quite familiar with. Standing on his front porch was the one person he didn't want to, or need to see. He unlocked the deadbolt and opened the door.

"Angus," Charlie said with a twinge of frustration in his voice. "What can I do for you?"

"Good evening, Mr. Claymore," Angus said, letting out a deep sigh. "I hope I'm not disturbing you. May I come in?"

"Would you care if I said you *were* disturbing me?"

"Not particularly," Angus said with a large smile. "So, can I come in?"

"What's this about?"

"I just want to talk to you for a moment."

"Yeah, sure. Why not?" Charlie replied, stepping out of the doorway making room for Angus to enter.

Angus stepped into Charlie's home and began searching the house with curious eyes. Soaking in the layout, burning images into his memory. Charlie shut the door loudly behind him. He didn't even know why. A show of power? Trying to intimidate him? Or to just make it perfectly clear this visit was not a welcomed one.

"Quite a place you have here, Mr. Claymore," Angus said with surprise in his voice. "You live in this big old place all by yourself?"

"No, my fiance Gwen lives here, too," Charlie said, stuttering his words just slightly. "She isn't home right now."

"Fiance, huh?" Angus replied pretending to be shocked.

"Yes. Her name is Gwen," Charlie said, pointing at a framed photo on the wall by the front door.

"Wow. She is very pretty, Charlie. How long have you guys been an item?"

"An item? What year is it?"

"Just asking a question, you know. Making conversation."

"You came all the way out here to make conversation?"

"Is that a problem, Mr. Claymore?"

"Cut the shit, Angus."

Angus paused for a moment, staring down at the hardwood floor beneath his feet. He knew he needed to navigate this situation carefully and not entice Charlie to ask him to leave. Besides, at this moment he was an invited guest. Charlie had allowed him to enter. This was an unofficial visit. The ball was in Charlie's court and Angus knew it.

"I wanted to see what you're all about. There's something funny about you. Something I can't quite nail down."

"Is that so?"

"Yes, I think so. You may have Emma tricked, and your little fiance there. But you can't fool me."

"Fool you? OK. What the hell do you want? I have somewhere to be."

"Big plans huh? I should have known, you're all dressed up. Big date with your fiance tonight?"

"No, I am having dinner with Emma," Charlie said, scratching his right cheek and staring at the floor. "I don't owe you an explanation."

"Emma?" Angus said, letting out a little laugh.

"Yes, Emma. What's so funny about that?"

"You see, that's what I find funny about you. This woman's husband has been missing for weeks. Yet every time we speak to her, or see her, you always seem to be around. Why is that, Mr. Claymore?"

"We're friends. I don't know how many times that needs to be explained. If one doesn't need a good friend after their spouse goes missing, when would you need a friend? Explain that to me." Charlie's anger grew like a fire that was out of control.

"That's the problem. I can't quite explain it. But I *will* find out."

Angus, knowing full well he was inside the house without official jurisdiction, walked around the first floor of the home. He turned to his left and walked towards the dining room. The dining room sat directly to the right inside the front door. Just past the dining room to the left was the kitchen, with modest white tile counters and old, wooden cabinets. Hardwood floors lined the entire bottom floor of the home, and a rustic looking dining table sat completely clean and empty. Against the wall of the dining room sat a rustic wooden desk with a computer sitting on top. As he entered the dining room, he began looking around the table, somewhat frantically. He moved the head chair and looked around towards the wall. He set the chair back down with force, bumping the table loudly.

"Hey, what the fuck do you think you're doing? You can't search my fucking house," Charlie said as he followed closely behind.

Angus didn't respond, he had become a man blinded. Blinded by rage, by purpose - he didn't care which. He rushed into the kitchen and began opening drawers, cabinets, looking around the counter for something, *anything*, that might give him a clue as to what Charlie might be up to. He couldn't for the life of him believe Charlie had no ulterior motive with Emma. And the fact Emma and Charlie continuously told him *"We are just old friends"* made the fire in his heart burn stronger and stronger with each release of those words that he was beginning to hate.

"Angus, I need you to leave. You can't do this!" Charlie shouted.

Charlie stood outside the kitchen as Angus continued his rampage. Charlie knew this wasn't legal, and he had seen more than enough.

"Fuck it, I'm calling the police," Charlie said, as he turned from the kitchen.

"I *AM* the fucking police!" Angus shouted at him, still rummaging through each and every drawer and cabinet as though the secret of life was hidden underneath a cereal bowl. He only stopped when he could hear Charlie barking from the other room.

"Frank," Charlie shouted. "Get over here and get this psycho out of my fucking house!"

Charlie had called Frank. *"Shit,"* Angus thought. *"Frank must have given him his business card."* Angus pulled himself out of the maniacal search and rushed to the front door. Both hands and arms up in the air as he tried to shush Charlie. His huge body made it from the kitchen to the front door in what seemed like 2 steps. He gently grabbed Charlie by the wrist that was holding his cell phone and whispered. Trying with every fiber of his being to calm Charlie and stop him from reporting this activity.

"No, No, OK. OK," Angus whispered, holding his right index finger to his lips. "Just, put the phone down. I'll leave." He pleaded.

Charlie was only interested in removing Angus from his home, as he was late for his dinner plans. He didn't want to even *speak* to Frank. He gave in to the pleading and removed the phone from his ear and clicked the 'End Call' button.

"OK?" Charlie asked. "You all good?"

"Yeah. I apologize," Angus said, rubbing the back of his head. "You have to see where I'm coming from. This case has just got me, I don't know, just so worked up."

"I'm glad you are taking it seriously. But for the last time, you are looking at the wrong person. My only interest is taking care of Emma. She needs someone to be there for her. That person is me, so get used to it. Now, if you don't mind."

"Alright, alright," Angus said.

He began walking towards the front door when his eyes glanced to his right, noticing a door directly across from the entryway of the home. Right in the middle of the wall, to the right of the staircase leading upstairs was a closed door. The door had a steel latch which was clamped shut with a thick, bulky padlock. Angus couldn't help but notice, and it made his already curious mind go haywire. Knowing Charlie wanted him gone, and that it could land him in some seriously hot water, still, he inquired.

"Say, Charlie. Where does that lead?"

"I don't know," Charlie said with a shrug. "I think it's the basement."

"You mean you've never opened that door? How is that possible?" He asked with a curious yet friendly smile.

"We're renting this house. The landlord told us she keeps a bunch of cleaning supplies down there and uses it for her own personal storage. It doesn't bother us, because we don't need the space."

Charlie had opened the front door to not only encourage, but force Angus to leave. Angus refused to walk outside, as he was now fixated on that locked door.

"Do you mind if I take a look? Just for curiosity's sake?" Angus asked with a friendly laugh.

"I can't even open the door," Charlie said matter-of-factly. "Even if I wanted to take you down there, we don't have a key."

"Hmm," Angus mouthed out loud. "Well. Enjoy your evening and again, I hope no hard feelings. I'm just on edge over this case. I feel like I'm up to my eyes in quicksand here."

"No hard feelings at all. But please don't come back here like this. Not only is it nuts, it's also pretty uncool."

"Again, my sincerest apologies."

"Don't mention it, Angus," Charlie said as he shut the door behind him.

32

Regardless of Angus' outburst Charlie still arrived at Emma's early. He had stopped at a local market to pick up some fresh flowers. He picked out a nice spring mix for Emma - Pink tulips and yellow lilies loaded with greenery and the useless accoutrement that always comes along with bouquets. He had also found a smaller bouquet of pink daisies to surprise Sophie. Impressing her daughter could only lead to impressing Emma, an easy win-win. When he arrived, he rang the doorbell and instantly Emma opened the door. A smile was already present on her lovely face, which grew brighter as she saw flowers in Charlie's hands. She was wearing a perfectly fitted blue button-down shirt, tucked into black capri pants, and a large puffy navy blue scarf adorned her neck and shoulders. Her hair was done up in a bun, with strings of wispy hair again framing her face perfectly.

"Aww, Charlie," she said with a coy smile. "On time *and* you brought flowers?"

"Hey, what's dinner without some flowers?"

He entered the home as Emma shut the door behind him.

"Here you go, Ma'am," Charlie said, handing Emma the larger of the two bouquets.

"These are beautiful. Thank you. That's so thoughtful."

"You are so welcome. Now, where is my little buddy?"

"Sophie is staying with a classmate tonight. I guess it will have to be dinner for two. I thought that would be better anyway."

Charlie's chest was a buzz as his heart fluttered. He took in a deep breath as he tried to regain any sense of composure he had when he arrived, doing his best to not show his hand to his opponent.

"Well, these are for her. Maybe you can show them to her tomorrow?"

"That's *so* sweet," Emma said, leaning in with a kiss on the cheek. "She will absolutely love them. Let's go into the kitchen. I'll put these into a couple of vases."

Emma reached up into the cabinets above her stove and removed two glass vases. Large for her flowers, and a smaller one for Sophie's.

"These will do the trick," she said, her voice bright and upbeat.

She drew some water from the faucet, filling the vases just enough to allow the stems of the flowers to drink. First, she dropped her flowers into the larger vase. She fluffed them to make them look just perfect.

"Voila," she said, holding her hands outward towards the bouquet, like she had just completed a magic trick.

Next, she dropped Sophie's daisies into the smaller of the two vases.

"There we go, perfect," she said loudly, admiring both. "Stay here, I'll put Sophie's on her night stand. She will *flip out* when she sees them. Would you mind putting this vase on the dinner table?"

Emma disappeared down the dark hallway with Sophie's brightly colored bouquet, as he placed the larger of the two vases in the middle of the dining table. The table had already been prepared with two bright white dinner plates, navy blue cloth napkins and serving ware. He noticed a bottle of white wine in an ice bucket and two long stem wine glasses next to each plate. He picked up one of the forks that had been placed ever so perfectly within the folded cloth napkin and looked it over. At the end of the fork's handle was an engraved logo showcasing the letters "VS."

"VanSant," He whispered to himself, with a light nod.

He heard footsteps coming towards the kitchen. Before Emma could make it back, he wrapped the fork in his palm and shoved the personalized item into the inside pocket of his bomber jacket. When she walked in, she stopped for a second and stared at him with confusion. He trembled, thinking maybe she had noticed his sticky finger activity.

"Well, something smells great," he said loudly, hoping to distract her and change the subject.

"Why thank you, sir," Emma said.

She walked past him and entered the kitchen and continued preparing dinner. Charlie let out a light sigh, hoping he had fooled her.

"I hope you came hungry," Emma said. "I made my signature dish, the one I am most famous for."

"Is that so? Famous dish, huh?" Charlie joked.

"Hey, don't knock it until you have at *least* tried it, smart ass."

"I'm not knocking anything. Honestly it smells amazing. So, what's on the menu?"

"My famous homemade lasagna with meat sauce, all cooked from scratch," Emma said proudly. "It was Eddie's favorite dinner. Well, I mean, *it is* Eddie's favorite dinner. It makes me feel better cooking something with him in mind. It's almost like he isn't missing."

Charlie wasn't a big eater, especially with filling meals like lasagna. But for this special occasion, he would let go of his health food obsession and properly gorge himself on whatever

Emma had prepared. He didn't care if it was mutton chops covered in butter with baked beans slathered in lard and bacon. He would eat as much as it took to see a smile on her face.

"Sounds absolutely wonderful," Charlie said with a smile. "I sure am hungry. I don't think I have eaten for *three full days* in preparation for this meal."

"Oh get out of here," Emma played back.

"I'm serious, I am absolutely famished. *Feed me!*" He joked.

"It isn't done yet," Emma said, checking the oven timer. "Say, why don't you grab that bottle of wine from the table. I've had it chilling all evening."

Charlie grabbed the bottle of chilled white wine from the ice bucket with one hand, and the wine glasses with the other. Emma opened a drawer on the island in the kitchen and removed a corkscrew. She handed it across the counter to Charlie.

"Would you do the honors?"

"It would be my pleasure," Charlie said.

He twisted and turned the corkscrew all the way down, pulling upwards as the opener sat on the lip of the bottle. He pulled and pulled until the cork released, letting out a satisfying POP sound.

"Don't you just love the sound of a wine bottle popping open? It just instantly transforms my day," Emma said, filled with glee.

Charlie filled the glasses one after the other half way full. Large pours before dinner but Charlie didn't care. He lifted one for himself and handed the other to Emma.

"To friendship," Charlie said, holding his wine glass towards Emma.

"To a great, long *lasting* friendship," she replied.

They clinked their glasses together and each took long sips of the decadent white wine. It exploded in Charlie's mouth of white grape, berries and a slight oak character. Charlie let out a long lasting, "*Mmmm*" as he swished and swallowed down the wine.

"It's good, isn't it?" Emma asked.

"Very. Where did you get it?"

"I don't even know. To be quite honest, it was already here. So I pulled it out and said, why not?"

"You picked very well."

"Thank you, sir."

They clinked their glasses again before they each took another long sip.

"So," Emma said, before pausing a second. She looked long and deep at Charlie. "Where has Gwen been? What's she up to?"

Charlie's eyes shot open as he attempted to take another sip from his wine glass. He swallowed the delicious liquid, wiped his mouth, and nodded softly.

"You know Charlie," Emma said in a more serious tone. "We've been spending a lot of time together. I mean, *a lot* of time. And she's never around. What gives?"

"She's a busy person. What with this new job and all. I told you she's been traveling a lot. It's hard to pin her down."

"It seems odd is all."

"What do you mean?"

"How is she *never* home? I know if Eddie were here and was spending this much time with an old friend who happened to be a girl, I might start asking questions."

"She's *very* understanding."

"She must be."

"What do you mean by that?"

"Oh, nothing," Emma said, with a slight roll of the eyes.

"No, tell me."

"Well I mean," Emma paused for a second. "It's starting to feel like maybe she doesn't even exist. I mean, I've asked you to invite her over *here*, to *coffee*, to the *recital*."

"Honestly, the recital might have been a bit awkward for her."

"Why would the recital have been awkward for her?" Emma asked, her tone much more serious.

"Well," Charlie said, taking another sip of wine. "The hand holding? The good night kiss?"

"I told you, we're friends. That's why I held your hand. It didn't mean anything. And *you* kissed *me*, remember?" Emma asked with a condescending shrug.

"Yeah, no. I mean, I remember," Charlie said, nervously sipping the wine.

"Charlie, come on," Emma said, setting down her wine glass. "You really think any of that would have happened in front of Gwen? Give me some credit for fucks sake."

"Well, no. I don't think so. But now that we are on the subject, what *did* the hand holding mean?"

"Uh uh, I don't think so Charlie Claymore. Don't try to change the subject. Where's this mystery girl? Is she even real? Be honest."

Just then, Charlie's phone buzzed in his pocket. He glanced at the screen and then held it up for Emma to see. The screen clearly showed the incoming call was from Gwen.

"Ah ha!" Charlie shouted, "Speak of the devil. What do you think of that?"

"OK. OK. I stand corrected," Emma said, throwing her hands in the air, feeling she had just lost the game.

Charlie flicked his finger across the screen of his phone in a magnificent, exaggerated fashion as he lifted it to his ear.

"Hey, you," Charlie said loudly into the phone. "Yeah, I'm at Emma's having a glass of wine. We are about to eat dinner. How are you doing?" He said, staring at Emma with squinched eyes.

Charlie then covered the microphone of his phone and turned to Emma.

"I'm going to step out front to take this," He whispered.

"Of course, do what you need to. But don't be long, dinner is almost ready," she whispered back. She then raised her own phone to her ear, mimicking him, "Tell her I said hello!"

"Yeah, Emma says hello," Charlie said into the phone. "She says hi back," he said to Emma as he walked towards the front door.

It wasn't long before Charlie reentered the home. Emma had already removed the lasagna from the oven and was cutting into the large dish of baked noodles and meat sauce.

"Everything OK with Gwen?" Emma asked as she continued to cut their dinner into portions for serving.

"Yep, all is well. She was just checking in."

"Where is she tonight?"

"Working late, as usual. They really run a tight ship over there. I told her I wouldn't be home too late."

"Well, how about I send some of this home with you for her? After a long day of stressful work, I imagine a home-cooked meal would do her just right."

"That's very sweet of you. She would love it, thanks."

"Go sit down at the table. It is *finally* time to eat," Emma said.

Charlie took a seat at the table, carrying his glass and the bottle of wine with him. Emma, wearing large oven mitts carried the dish over to the table and set it down between the two plates.

"Wait a second," Emma said. "I could have sworn I put two forks on the table," she let out a loud grunt of annoyance as she walked back into the kitchen. She opened a drawer and removed an extra fork. When she got back to the table, she set it down next to the bright white plate that sat in front of Charlie.

"I'm so sorry about that. My brain is just all over the place."

"Don't beat yourself up about it," Charlie said. He knew she didn't forget the fork, but he continued to let her believe she had.

"Hey, fill me up, good sir," Emma said, holding her wine glass across the table.

Charlie refilled both of their glasses, starting with Emma's. He set the wine back inside the bucket of ice to stay chilled during dinner. He held his glass up and over the table towards Emma.

"To Eddie," Charlie said. "May he come home safe and as soon as humanly possible."

"To Eddie," Emma said loudly.

They clinked their glasses one more time, and took deep sips of the wine.

"Thank you for that, Charlie," Emma said with a sweet smile, staring deep into his eyes. "And thank you for being here. You truly are a good friend."

"That's what friends are for, my dear," Charlie said with a large smile. "Now, let's see how famous this lasagna is, shall we?"

33

Charlie arrived home later than expected that evening. Wining, dining, laughing and reminiscing of days past, mapping out hopeful plans for the future and of course, lending a shoulder for Emma to cry on as she lamented about Eddie. Emma continued to put on a strong face, but Charlie could see through the veil she was hiding under and knew she was crumbling. The cracks in her foundation were being exposed faster than she could try to cover them as the pillars of her life were toppling. The best he could do was to be anywhere she needed him. Dinners, recitals, phone calls, it didn't matter. If she wanted him to walk on the Moon, he would find a way to get there. Through lying, cheating, stealing or even killing, he would find a rocket so they could watch the sunrise over Earth together.

The door of the home opened as Charlie reached inside to flip on the light switch. In his hand, he held a grocery bag with the plastic handles tied into a perfect knot. He moved to the dining room and flicked on the light switch before setting the bag down and removing the contents onto the table. Inside was a takeaway container of leftovers Emma had sent with him for Gwen. Charlie had led Emma to believe Gwen was forced to work late, and she knew as well as anyone that after many late nights, dinner can become a distant stranger - a lost luxury. He placed the container of food on his empty dining table. Just beyond the table sat a couple of black heavy duty travel cases filled with photography equipment, a large stand up light and a thick white drape. He began rummaging through the equipment placing specific pieces on the table. First, he fashioned a stand out of some metal rods, to those rods, he attached the thick white drape. The drape sat perfectly flat on the table top and ran cleanly up the metal rods, creating a crisp backdrop stretching up towards the ceiling. Just to the right of the drape, he set up a tripod. At the top of the tripod sat a wide, circular lamp. When he clicked it on it illuminated the space with bright, fresh light. He then picked up the container of food, removed the lid and set it directly in the middle of the thick white cloth. Next, with a loud grunt, he hoisted the heavy duty black case onto the table. Inside sat 3 professional cameras that had been shoved safely into protective foam. Lining the right side of the case sat 6 lenses, each pushed into the foam for safe keeping. He removed the middle camera and picked up a lens, snapping it onto the body.

Charlie knelt down low beside the table as he took a few pictures of the food, moved to his left and stood up higher snapping a few more. He continued to maneuver around the table snapping photos of the now room temperature lasagna. After each series of photos he reviewed them on the camera's small preview screen. After he felt he had got the right angle of the food, he switched off the photo light. He then moved over to the desk which sat against the wall just beyond the dining table and sat down in an office chair. On the desk sat an iMac computer, a wireless mouse, wireless keyboard and a collection of random cables and wires. He picked up a cable and plugged it into the camera. On the screen popped up a window showcasing all the photos he had snapped. He began scrolling through them before clicking on and dragging a specific picture to the desktop. He clearly had found a picture of the lasagna that was to his liking. Perfect lighting, nice angle. He could work with that. Charlie sat back in the office chair for a moment, using his feet to twist back and forth. An odd smile came across his face as he stared straight ahead deep in thought. He continued this for a while, as though he was pumping himself up. His face transformed as his eyes became sunken, his smile slightly devilish. Just then he lifted both of his arms, slapping them onto his thighs, jumping out of the chair.

"Let's do this," he said to himself out loud.

He picked up the container of lasagna and walked across the hardwood floor with what appeared to be intentional stomps creating loud thuds underneath his boots. It sounded like a bull was making his way across the room, all the rage within it's bones had flooded to the surface of his body and was pouring out of his skin, filling the room with a warm, terrifying aura. He reached the doorway leading to the basement and removed a single keyring from his back pocket. The keyring was fashioned with one golden key. He pushed it into the padlock and with a quick turn, the padlock snapped open. He lifted it and shot the latch over from its resting place, and replaced the open padlock on the now opened latch. He reached down and grabbed hold of the door knob pulling the door open. The house was so silent you could hear each screw bend and all the mechanics of the knob twist and turn. Charlie stood outside the now open doorway, staring into a dark oblivion. A set of raw wooden stairs sat just inside the door. At the bottom of the stairs, a faint light peeked from around the unfinished wall which lined either side of the staircase. Old, out of code wiring rained down the wooden studs, lifeless and forgotten. The walls of the basement were built with cinder blocks that had become stained and moldy after years of abandonment. The concrete floor was cold and damp, cracked and chipping like the floor of a sun drenched desert. Charlie began slowly walking down the stairs, using each step to make a statement, stomping loudly with intention. With each step his boots sounded louder than the last, sending echoing booms throughout the lower level of the home. Once he got to the bottom of the stairs, he continued to stare straight ahead at the bricks in front of him. He took in a deep breath and let it out slowly with an *"Ahh"* sound.

The room itself was quite spacious, though this basement had not been used or taken care of in what seemed like years. To the far corner sat many old boxes, wet, moldy and disintegrating. The contents of which now sprawled out like lifeless bodies after 10 car pile up. To the far right underneath the staircase sat a workbench. Rusty tools that hadn't been used or appreciated in a lifetime were scattered about with no organization. The room was dead silent. If you listened closely, you could hear flies buzzing about and spiders as they crawled through their webs. He turned his head slowly to the right, looking over the dark concrete room. He reached for the wall and flicked a light switch. Hanging from the ceiling of the basement was one solitary exposed lightbulb. It flickered as light danced off the walls until the bulb finally steadied and illuminated the room giving it a perfectly terrifying essence.

"I thought you might like something to eat," he said in a deep, devilish tone.

There, across the room sat Eddie. Chained to a chair, his mouth duct taped shut. Eddie was wearing a plain white t-shirt, covered in filth and torn. Tattered and stained blue jeans wrapped his legs down to his bare feet. His hair was a mess and the top of his head was caked in dried blood that at one time had poured down his forehead, over his face and stained the right shoulder of the shirt. Memories left behind of a terrible head wound. He began to squirm in the chair, his wrists and ankles chained to the arms and legs, another chain wrapped around his chest, holding his body down tightly. Charlie walked slowly and calculated across the concrete allowing each foot step to ring out and echo through the room. For now, intimidation was the name of his game. Once he got to Eddie, he knelt down. The predator and his prey, sitting eye to eye. Charlie reached up and grabbed one side of the duct tape and painfully tore it off of Eddie's face causing a loud tearing sound. Even though Eddie couldn't move, he pushed back violently, trying to put as much distance between himself and this monster as he could. The chains that wrapped his beaten body were locked on so tight, it almost cut off circulation where they landed. He began stretching the muscles in his cheeks and face, rotating his jaw up and down, while rapidly opening and closing his mouth over and over and licking his dry, cracked lips before straightening up and staring Charlie dead in the eyes.

"Fuck, you," Eddie said as he gasped for air.

Charlie, kneeling down to Eddie's level, laughed maniacally in his face. So much so, he almost fell backwards onto the cold concrete floor.

"Fuck *me*," Charlie asked. "Is that any way to talk to someone who brought you a nice treat? Now come on, I *know* you are hungry. And look, I brought you a *very* special surprise. Don't you want to know what it is?"

"Go fuck yourself," Eddie said, his teeth clinched tightly. His eyes didn't unlock from Charlie's as he spoke.

"Come on. You haven't eaten in days. I wanted you to be plenty hungry for tonight," Charlie said, holding the food container up and pushing it into his dirty, bloody face.

"Look familiar? Now I *heard* this is someone's favorite dinner," Charlie said. He lowered his voice to a whisper, "Yours. It's yours."

"No. It can't be," Eddie said, his voice breaking as he spoke.

"That's right. I knew you would recognize it. This is Emma's famous lasagna you love so very much. I bet you haven't had *this* for awhile."

"Stay away from my fucking wife!" Eddie screamed, spit and sweat splashing over Charlie's face as he shouted.

"Shut the fuck up and eat," Charlie said, showing no reaction to the screams.

"Let me fucking go!" Eddie screamed as loud as his weak body would allow, shaking the chair violently, so much that Charlie had to stand up and step back.

"Hey!" Charlie shouted.

Eddie didn't care, he continued to shake the chair so violently. Charlie thought maybe he would break the damn thing.

"Someone, anyone! Help me!" Eddie continued to shout.

"I said shut the fuck *up*," Charlie shouted, swinging his right hand with all his might, punching Eddie right across his left cheek.

Charlie wrapped his right hand around Eddie's throat and pushed him against the back of the chair, making it almost impossible for Eddie to breathe. Charlie came in close, so close the tips of their noses touched.

"If I tell you to shut the fuck up," Charlie said quietly. He then screamed into Eddie's face, "Then you shut the fuck up!"

Charlie finally let go of Eddie's throat. As he released his hand, Eddie gasped, filling his lungs with moldy, musky air.

"I do something nice for you and this is the thanks I get? Eddie, be a fucking gentleman, would you?"

"Just," Eddie stopped himself as his throat swelled and his eyes pooled with tears. "Please. Let me go. What the fuck do you *want* from me?"

"You know exactly what I want," Charlie said matter-of-factly. "But that's besides the point. We will get to that later. Right now, I want you to eat this."

Charlie again shoved the container into Eddie's face, pushing the lasagna so hard, it smeared sauce and cheese onto his nose and cheeks.

"Oh my god, where's my head?" Charlie said with a laugh. "I almost forgot, I have a second surprise for you."

Charlie reached into his jacket pocket, removing the VanSant fork. The silver fork was so bright and shiny that the minimal light in the basement bounced off of the handle so much you could almost hear a *"BING"* sound echo faintly through the room. The bold monogrammed VS on the handle sparkled as he twirled it in his fingers.

"Now you *must* recognize this," Charlie said.

"Where did you get that?" Eddie asked, every muscle fiber in his body shaking uncontrollably.

"I had dinner at your house tonight. Well, Emma's house now. I don't know that you will ever live there again," Charlie said as he started to laugh. "I don't know if you will ever live, *anywhere*, again!"

Charlie shoved the fork into the lasagna, lifting out a large portion of noodles. He shoved it into his mouth as he chewed rudely, his mouth wide open between bites, smacking his lips loudly.

"Why are you doing this?" Eddie shouted, his crying had grown in intensity. The pain and anguish became too much to bear.

"It isn't really anything you need to worry about, pal," Charlie said as he continued to chew. "I really think you should try some of this before I eat it all. Quit trying to be a tough guy, you won't win."

Charlie again knelt down to Eddie's eye level. He stuck the fork into the container and dug out another bite of lasagna.

"Now come on, take a bite. Don't be such a bitch," Charlie said.

Eddie refused to open his mouth, clasping it so tight, the jaws of life might buckle at the effort. Charlie didn't care, he pressed the fork and lasagna into his face, rubbing it all over his cheeks, lips and chin. Eddie finally opened his mouth, bit the lasagna off the fork, and spit it right into Charlie's face.

"Go fuck yourself," Eddie said, breathing heavily, writhing in the chair.

Charlie didn't move. He stayed there, knelt down and stared directly into Eddie's scared, trembling eyes. As he held the fork in his right hand, he cocked his arm backwards, swinging it around his body, stabbing Eddie in the ribs with the sharp prongs of the fork. He held it there for a moment, then twisted the fork towards himself before pulling it out of his skin. Eddie belted out a horrific yelp, as blood poured out of the fresh wound, flooding down his body. A crimson stain grew on his shirt as blood began dripping onto the floor.

"You, are a fucking, monster," Eddie said through deep breaths. "You, are fucking, mad!"

Charlie stared directly into his eyes and broke into a creepy giggle. He dug the bloody fork into the container and dug out another bite of lasagna. He shoved the fork into his mouth, lasagna and blood smeared the sides of his mouth and lips as he chewed.

"Aren't we all?" Charlie asked, continuing to chew the food. Eddie's blood now smeared across his mouth and lips.

Charlie took the container of food and dumped it onto the concrete floor.

"There, if you want it, it's yours. Eat it like the pig you are," Charlie said.

Charlie walked to the work bench and grabbed a large roll of duct tape. He tore off a long piece and stuck it over his mouth. Eddie shook the chair violently as though he imagined he could somehow escape. Charlie moved behind the chair, reached towards the ground, and lifted a large black pipe. Without warning he swung it down onto the back of Eddie's head. Eddie immediately stopped moving as his head fell forward causing his chin to bounce off of his chest, before his head dipped and didn't lift again.

"Sleep tight, asshole," Charlie muttered as he dropped the pipe to the concrete floor, where it clanged for a while before rolling across the room. He walked back to the stairs, picking up his pace and jogging to the top. He shut the door behind him, shut the latch, closing the padlock in place. He took a seat at his desk in the dining room and again started going through the photographs. He clicked through a folder on the desktop of his computer titled *"Gwen."* He shot through a few photos of her until he found the one he felt was right. The picture showed Gwen, sitting at a table as she prepared for lunch. She was wearing a black hooded sweatshirt, holding a fork in her hand, clearly excited about a big salad on the table in front of her.

"That should do the trick," he said out loud.

He then opened Photoshop and began editing three photographs together. The picture of Gwen and her salad, Emma's lasagna, and a photo of himself. He began altering the 3 photos, replacing the salad in Gwen's photo with Emma's lasagna, and then spliced in the photo of himself, making it appear as though he was sitting at the table *with* Gwen. Charlie was good at this, and to the untrained eye, when finished, it looked like an authentic photo of two people enjoying a meal. Just then, his cell phone rang. On the screen it showed "Gwen". He lifted the phone, swiped across the screen and answered the incoming call.

"Hey, Mom, how is it going?" Charlie said. There was a pause as the person on the other end spoke.

"I got home late. I was out with a friend. I told you earlier, remember? I was having dinner with Emma."

"Yes, Emma is a *female* friend. What boy would be named Emma?"

"Things are going really well, actually. We are spending a lot of time together, getting to know each other better. It's been great. I, I really like her."

He opened up the "Messages" app on his computer so he could send a text. He found the message thread between himself and Emma, and inserted the photoshopped picture. He then typed under the photo *"Gwen says 'Thank You' for the lasagna. She loved it! Talk to you soon. Goodnight!"* and pressed send.

"Hey Mom," Charlie said, stopping her from telling a long drawn out story. "I need to get going. I'll call you in the morning, OK? I love you."

Little did Emma know, the monster was under her nose the entire time. He was in her home, in her and her child's life and unbeknownst to her, she had invited him into her otherwise picture perfect world happily and willingly. And now, there was no turning back.

34

3 Months Prior.

It was a chilly Summer morning in Seattle, when a taxi cab slowly pulled up to a home nestled against the forest on the outskirts of town. The taxi crawled down the road and stopped in front of 825 Lochwood Place, a two-story home with a large front yard and a clean, brand new jet black BMW sitting in the driveway.

"Is this the place?" The cab driver asked as he rested his right arm across the passenger seat, looking towards the back.

"Sure is," Charlie said as he reached into his back pocket for his wallet. "What's the damage?"

"22 bucks even," The cab driver said.

Charlie flipped through loose bills inside his worn out, brown wallet. He removed a $20 and a $10, handing them to the driver. "Keep the change."

"You need me to wait for you to take you back into town? I've got nowhere to be," The driver said.

"No thanks," Charlie said, fighting with the wallet as he forced it into the back pocket of his blue jeans. "I'll be here for a while."

Charlie stepped out onto the gravel road which clashed unrestrictedly into the home's front yard. Dirt with yellow patches of grass and weeds decorated the front yard looking like an abstract painting. Charlie stood in that spot, admiring the home from the road as the taxi turned around. Charlie looked over his right shoulder towards the cab as it left, and once it turned and was out of view, he made the walk up the driveway. As he passed the black BMW, he stopped to admire the crisp set of wheels. It was a dream car for some, unattainable to many, including Charlie. He knelt down and looked through the windows so he could admire the interior, the dash, the beautiful craftsmanship. "*Now that's a car,*" Charlie thought. He made his way to the front porch as he brushed his wrinkled clothes. He had on an old pair of blue jeans, a white t-shirt with a black raggedy old zip up hoodie that he wore wide open and a Yankees ball cap. He reached up and knocked on the front door. When the door opened, a good-looking older woman stood in the entryway. Shoulder-length blonde hair, styled professionally, big blue eyes and wearing clothes one might wear while gardening - Light blue jeans and a white tank top, both of which had been decorated with soil.

"Can I help you?" The woman asked.

"Are you Margaret?" Charlie asked nervously. "My name's Charlie Claymore. I called about your ad in the paper for the house for rent."

"Oh yes, Charlie," Margaret replied. "Uhm, what are you doing here exactly? I don't remember us finalizing, well, *anything.*"

"No we didn't," Charlie said. "I was just in the neighborhood and thought I would stop by and introduce myself and maybe I could look around. If that isn't too much trouble."

"No, of course not. I'm sorry, where are my manners? Come on in."

The woman held the door open as Charlie entered. He took a few steps inside and stopped a few feet from the wall opposite the front door, standing directly in front of another doorway that had been left wide open. Charlie stared into this dark doorway, seeing a set of stairs leading down to a basement.

"Can I offer you anything to drink?" Margaret asked.

"No, I'm good. Thanks," Charlie replied as he turned around to face Margaret.

"Come on let me show you around," Margaret said as she motioned with her right hand towards the kitchen. "Sorry I'm such a mess today, my husband and I have been working in the garden."

"I should thank you for allowing me into your home without notice."

"It's no problem," Margaret said. "As I told you on the phone, we're not officially moving to our new home for a while. We're still waiting on word from our financial advisor and need to put pen to paper. I want to make sure you know the house isn't really ready to be rented yet."

"I understand," Charlie said, nodding his head with a smile. "I just like to be prepared and have all my ducks in a row."

"I just wanted to make sure we are on the same page," Margaret said. "So, as you can see, this is the kitchen and dining room. Could use some updating, but you know how life is. It's like, something *always* gets in the way."

"I think it's perfect. It's a gorgeous home. I would be lucky to live here."

"Well thank you. I appreciate that. We've done the best we can, when time permits of course. Stay here, let me get my husband."

At the far end of the kitchen sat a white door with glass panel inlays in the wood. The door sat wide open, allowing a chilly air to fill the home. The smell of earth and forest accompanied the brisk air as it flowed into the kitchen, making the house seem damp. Margaret rushed out the door and down a small flight of stairs to the backyard. Charlie stayed behind to take a look around, admiring the different items on the kitchen counter, knickknacks of a lived in home and framed photos on the walls. A large wood dining room table sat covered in miscellaneous items. A purse laid on its side, its contents spilling onto the tabletop, some dirty plates and half full cups of coffee from a now forgotten breakfast. He noticed a gorgeous black fitted jacket draped over the back of one of the chairs. For a moment he wondered if it was his size. It wasn't long before Margaret made her way back into the kitchen accompanied by her husband.

"This is my husband Jerry. Jerry, meet Charlie," Margaret stopped herself. "I'm sorry, what was your last name again?"

"Claymore," Charlie said, reaching out his right hand. "Great to meet you Jerry."

"Great to meet you too," Jerry said, reaching out and shaking Charlie's hand.

Charlie was right, the jacket on the chair probably would fit him. He noticed right away Jerry and him were almost identical in size.

"Margaret tells me you are interested in renting the place?" Jerry asked.

"I sure am, this is a beautiful home. Anyone would be lucky to live here," Charlie said with a smile.

"It's a big house," Jerry said with a nervous laugh. "Will you be able to keep up on everything?"

"Not a problem, I'm a pretty handy guy. I can fix things myself. You probably won't hear much from me regarding things like that."

"Well that would be a blessing, right honey?" Jerry said with a laugh. "Did Margaret show you around?"

"She did," Charlie said, rubbing the back of his head and looking around the room. "By the way, a basement, huh? Boy, I have always wanted to live in a house with a basement," Charlie said, hoping to change the subject.

"It isn't finished, it's more of a work area for me. When I actually have time for projects."

Margaret rolled her eyes and let out a playful laugh.

"You see how she treats me?" Jerry asked.

All three of them shared a quick laugh.

"Would you like to see the basement?"

"Absolutely, if you don't mind?" Charlie asked, looking down, his eyes sheepish with a nervous smile to match.

"Not at all," Jerry said. "Come on, I'll show you around. Margaret, why don't you grab a couple of cold drinks? We can sit at the table and iron out some details when we come back. Does that sound like a plan?"

"Sounds like a plan to me," Charlie agreed.

Charlie followed Jerry down the narrow wooden staircase. It was cold and had a damp feeling all throughout. So much so, you could almost feel the dampness of the air settle onto your skin. A musty smell permeated the air of the basement, not quite moldy, but absolutely mold adjacent. On the way down the stairs, the unfinished drywall stopped about halfway down so you could see straight through the framed studs into the large room. At the bottom of the staircase, a sharp right turn opened into the main area. Cinder Block walls lined the basement, and across the room underneath the staircase sat a workbench with a handheld light hanging on an old screw. To the right of the workbench was a small storage closet housing old paint cans, tools and other various items. Strewn about on the workbench sat all the tools of an ambitious handyman. One who always had a project in his or her sites, but never finished them. A pair of home built sawhorses sat in the far corner.

"Here it is," Jerry said. "In all of its glory. I had so many ideas and projects I was going to accomplish in this basement. I was so ambitious. But you know how it goes. Life just always seems to have other plans in store."

"Right," Charlie said. "This is a great space. I love it."

"It has potential," Jerry agreed, hands on his hips, looking around the room. His eyes looked as though he was running an internal slideshow of all the what-ifs he could have accomplished. "What are some ideas of yours? Why is a basement so important to you?"

"I like to stay in shape," Charlie replied without hesitation. "It's nice and cool, I can lift weights down here and be comfortable. I may hang a TV on the wall to make a nice hang out spot."

"The possibilities are endless," Jerry said, swatting Charlie on the shoulder as though they were old friends.

Jerry stood in the same spot for an uncomfortable amount of time, hands on his hips, just staring at all of his unused tools, scraps of wood and other miscellaneous materials. It was clear he had some regret over time that had slipped by and wasn't happy to leave this house or his toys behind. Just then, he clapped his hands together loudly, startling Charlie.

"Ready to head upstairs and have that drink?"

"After you," Charlie said, maneuvering forward with his left hand.

Jerry took a few steps, then stopped suddenly, looking over his left shoulder to Charlie. His eyes screamed of confusion.

"Did you hear something?" Jerry asked with concern in his voice.

"I don't think so?" Charlie replied.

"Huh," Jerry went on. "Must have been my imagination. This old house has all kinds of creaks and cracks and sounds. You would think I would be used to it by now, but it still catches me by surprise."

Jerry led the way back up the narrow, creaky staircase. He walked into the main entryway first, and turned to wait for Charlie to emerge from the dark room.

"I'm going to run upstairs real quick and change out of this dirty shirt. Go ahead, take a seat, Margaret and I have some questions for you, and we can discuss if you're a good fit to rent the home," Jerry instructed.

"Sounds great," Charlie said. "Thank you for showing me around."

"No problem," Jerry said as he turned and made his way up the stairs. "I'll be right back," He shouted down at him.

Margaret sat at the head seat, her back facing Charlie. On the dining table sat 3 cans of ice cold diet soda and she had an envelope filled with miscellaneous papers regarding their home.

"Come on over, Charlie," Margaret said without turning around. "Let's have a cold drink and discuss the house."

Charlie slowly walked towards her and didn't say a word. She was unable to see him as he approached.

"We won't really be ready to leave for a couple of months, we just wanted to get the ball rolling. I am sure you understa—"

Her sentence ended abruptly. Her words had been replaced by a sharp gasp and a loud exhale, as the air from her lungs expelled from her body like a car tire that had run over a nail. Charlie had taken a hammer from Jerry's workbench, and without hesitation, wound back and swung the blunt end of the hammer around the front of his body, smashing Margaret in the right temple. She went quiet and fell out of the chair. The force from the hammer was so strong, she flipped and landed on her head on the hardwood floor. Her petite body curled into itself as she winced in pain, trying with all of her might and every tiny burst of oxygen she had left in her lungs to call out to her husband for help. Charlie watched in admiration for a moment as she writhed in agony with a large smile on his face. He let out a giggle as though nothing in the world made him happier than what he was witnessing. Blood poured from her temple, filling the whites of her eyes and flowed into her mouth, transforming her gasps to gurgling sounds like air pressure shooting through sitting water. Charlie knew Jerry would be downstairs at any moment and spun the hammer around, switching from the blunt end to the sharp. He grasped the handle with both hands, lifted it high over his head and blow after blow, caved Margaret's skull in, almost flattening it into the hardwood. With each hit, blood, bone and brain fragments burst into the air, splattering Charlie head to toe. Charlie stood straight up, breathing heavily with painful grunts coming from his throat like a wild animal. With his left hand, he wiped his face, smearing Margaret's blood across his mouth, lips and across his left cheek.

He stepped over Margaret's lifeless body and rushed to the kitchen. On the counter, he saw a large chef's knife. He picked it up, jumped over Margaret again and ran past the staircase that led to the upper level of the home. Just past the staircase was the living room. A large brown leather couch sat against the far wall with a rustic coffee table set in the middle of the room. A matching brown leather recliner sat to the left of the couch, and the entire room had a very odd Western style motif. Charlie hid around the corner and waited for Jerry to come downstairs, and prepared for what would be a fight to the death. He heard loud stomps above him headed towards the center of the home. Jerry was now at the top of the steps. Then one by one, he heard each stair as it was hit by Jerry's work boots. Stomp, stomp, stomp as Jerry moved. Jerry emerged from the staircase and burst into screams.

"Margaret!" He shouted.

He tried to run to Margaret's aide, but before he got far, he was stifled as Charlie thrust the chef's knife into his upper back, slicing through his abdomen. He held Jerry by the left shoulder as he continued to plunge the blade into his back over and over. Charlie was certain he punctured his right lung, as Jerry let out a horrific gasp of air as he fell to his knees. Jerry fell to all fours on the hardwood and began crawling towards his wife with all the power and strength he had left in his trembling body. Charlie could hear him fighting for air as the blood rushed to fill his lungs. His blood strangled him, as it now poured from his mouth, dripping off his bottom lip onto the once clean wood panels. He allowed Jerry to crawl to Margaret, slowly walking behind him as he went. Jerry collapsed upon Margaret's lifeless body as his last breaths were escaping his own. Charlie reached down and grabbed him by the forehead, lifted his head far back into his own chest and slid the sharp edge of the knife clean across his throat. Cutting so deep, Charlie almost cut his head clean off his shoulders. He held his head in place for a moment to allow blood to pour out, his life flooding away like a breached dam. Charlie let go of his head as Jerry's body collapsed onto Margaret's. There were no words, no talking of any kind. Especially from Charlie. From Jerry and Margaret, there was no begging for life or pleading for mercy. None of any kind. They both knew it was a waste of what precious oxygen they may have had left in their withering bodies. The only thing left to say was goodbye.

He took the knife in his left hand and pulled the hammer out of the back of his jeans again with his right. He stood over the two admiring his work. He then lifted the hammer up over his head, swinging down for one last hit to the back of Jerry's head, caving in his skull with the final blow. It wasn't necessary, but if nothing else, maybe it ended the suffering. Somehow Charlie felt good about that. Charlie stepped over the lifeless bodies of Margaret and Jerry and walked through the kitchen. The back door was still wide open, and he stopped at the top of the small staircase that led to the backyard and for a moment, closed his eyes and felt the breeze and sunshine hit his face. Just to the left of the stairs was some freshly dug soil from the garden. Across the backyard was a small wooden shed with barn style doors. It was painted a cute sky blue with white trim. He walked across the yard smiling as he went, soaking in the sites of the large, grassy yard. Inside the shed were gardening and yard maintenance tools where he found a spade end shovel. He picked it up, admired it for a moment and made his way to the garden.

He sank the shovel into the loose dirt, pushing it deep with his right foot one after another, and another, digging up the garden they had been so proud of. He continued to dig and dig, about 4 feet into the earth. A large pile of soil sat next to this newly dug hole, and he lifted the shovel over his head and plunged it into the pile. Charlie reentered the home and first, grabbed Jerry by the wrists and pulled him off of Margaret and dragged him across the hardwood floor through the kitchen, leaving thick, smeared blood in his wake. He dragged him down the stairs, across the grass and then turned his body over dropping him into the hole. He then went back inside and dragged Margaret the same way, by her limp, now cold wrists down the steps and tossed her lifeless body on top of Jerry's. He then backfilled the hole with the soil. Once the hole was filled, he stomped over it to pack the dirt in tightly over them. He leaned the shovel up against the back of the home, wiped the sweat from his brow and walked back inside the dead quiet house.

He promptly scrubbed the hardwood floors with soap and water, mopping the blood that had pooled up. As one towel became saturated, he packed it into a large black trash bag before grabbing a fresh one to continue. It took hours for him to clean the walls, floors and table from the blood splatter. When finished, or what he decided was good enough, he made his way up stairs. The stairs emptied out into a long hallway with doors running the length of the home. On the right was a guest room with a neatly put together bed set, matching dresser and tacky framed art on the walls you might see in a Motel 6. Across the hall sat a bathroom. Blue tiles wrapped the bathroom and shower area, with a matching blue fuzzy floor mat and toilet seat cover. At the end of the hall was the master bedroom. The master bedroom was large and decorated in a similar tacky style. A king sized bed sat in the middle of the room that was neatly made. A framed photo of Margaret and Jerry hung above positioned perfectly between two of the bed posts. To the right of the bed was a large closet. When opened he found a collection of designer clothing; Pants, fitted t-shirts, sports jackets and shiny dress shoes and boots.

To the left of the bedroom was the master bath. Charlie jumped into the shower and washed the dried blood off of his body. The blood had dried all over his face, arms and in his hair, and had mixed in with the soil from becoming an amateur gravedigger. He smelled the expensive body wash and shampoos, all from brands he had never heard of and could never afford. He scrubbed his hair over and over before washing his body clean and stood with the warm water pouring over his body, as though the Seattle water could cleanse him of his recent sins.

After his shower, he wrapped himself in a white monogrammed robe that hung in the bathroom. Before laying down in the king sized bed, he retrieved his ratty old hooded sweater and dug inside, pulling out a small, framed photograph. He walked across the bedroom and placed the frame on the dresser that sat in front of the foot of the bed. Inside the frame was a printed photograph of Emma. He opened all the windows and as the sun set, he laid in his new robe, stretched out on his new bed staring at the photograph. After a few moments, he closed his eyes as the Seattle evening set in and the cold breeze brushed over his body. He knew, he was home.

35

Charlie emerged from the home early, dressed head to toe in the best clothes he had ever worn. Tight fitting black designer jeans hugged the ankles of his new expensive black boots and a soft, bright white t-shirt underneath his new favorite black tailored jacket. His hair perfectly styled and slicked back, designer sunglasses hiding his eyes and intentions from society. He walked towards his new black BMW that was clean as a whistle, the black paint shimmering in the morning sunlight. As he walked, he tossed the car keys into the air, catching them in his right hand. *"That Jerry sure had good taste,"* he thought to himself. He clicked the keyless entry, climbed in and kicked the engine over. Music began screaming from the stereo. Charlie ejected the CD, stopping it as fast as he could. As the CD ejected, Charlie ripped it violently from the console. He held it up to see it was a Dave Matthew's Band album. Charlie rolled down the window and tossed the CD like a frisbee, as the shiny disc whipped through the air and landed on the front lawn. *"Good taste, aside from music,"* Charlie thought.

The street was one long road that wasn't maintained. On one side of the road sat a long line of old-fashioned, two-story homes, each one painted a different mix of colors. Many of the homes on the street were well kept with nicely manicured yards. Different flowers, trees and large shrubs graced the expensively maintained yards, making the homes that had not been cared for stick out like bad teeth. Across the street, the road was lined with thick trees. Charlie drove across town and finally pulled the car over next to a large community park. He sat parked against the curb, allowing the engine to idle. He rolled down the driver's side window to allow fresh air to pour in over him. The park stretched deep with beautiful green grass and gorgeous trees that went as far as he could see. Two basketball courts were nestled close to the sidewalk, and just past the courts was a clubhouse for community events. Behind the building was a large swimming pool. Through the open window, he could hear instructions being shouted in the distance. An early morning water aerobics class was in full force, with a large crowd of older women dancing out of sync in the shallow water as though a loose electrical wire had snapped and fallen in.

Down aways, the road hit an intersection cut off by a 4-way stop. Charlie watched the intersection, waiting patiently. He took a deep breath and rubbed his hands through his hair, as a blue Toyota Prius stopped at the intersection, it's right blinker flashing. Charlie's heart began skipping along with the blinker and they danced together to a silent love song. He watched as the Prius turned right and began driving directly towards him. He straightened up in his seat, took the car from park and as the Prius sped by, Charlie kicked it into drive, pulled a quick u-turn and began following behind, far enough not to be suspicious, close enough to keep up. The Prius drove erratically, just enough to imagine the driver was rushing, not thinking or paying attention to the road. Traffic had built within the city streets, as men and women made their way to their respective destinations. After a right turn here, a left turn there, running through a stale yellow light or two, the Prius started to slow. It eventually pulled into a wide open spot along the main road and parked in front of a trendy coffee shop. Charlie drove a few more car lengths before pulling around with another u-turn. A move most wouldn't dare to pull, let alone while driving a stolen car belonging to a dead man. Charlie pulled over on the side of the road and parked across the street. The driver's side door of the Toyota opened and out stepped a beautiful, young woman. She had dirty blonde hair pulled back into a messy ponytail, and black leggings stretched down her thin legs, tucked into a pair of worn out Doc Marten boots. A light washed denim jacket wrapped her body and a handbag was tossed without care over her right shoulder. She opened the back door and went through the process of unlatching a young child from a booster seat. A young girl who couldn't be more than 6, Charlie imagined, jumped out onto the sidewalk. She had bright blonde, almost golden hair in pigtails, pink and purple galoshes and a raincoat resembling a bumble bee. Hand in hand they entered the coffee shop.

"There you are, Emma," Charlie said out loud to himself as he watched every move the two made.

They had disappeared into Automatic Coffee, a popular morning stop, if the packed crowd was any indication. Charlie sat, keeping an eagle eye on the front door of the coffee shop until Emma emerged. She held a large, clear cup filled with some type of coffee. In the young girl's left hand was a small, child's sized white cup. Emma set her clear cup on top of the car as she opened the back seat and proceeded to lift the small child into the booster seat in the back. Emma then grabbed her coffee and walked around the back of the car. Without skipping a beat, the Toyota Prius was away from the curb, and speeding down the road yet again. Charlie put his car in drive and sped around with an illegal u-turn to follow.

Next stop was a school campus. Emma pulled into the parking lot at the front of the school, where many parents and students had amassed, all walking with a fun pep in their step. *"Oh, to be young and carefree again,"* Charlie thought. He parked across the street from the school entrance and watched from afar as Emma and the child walked hand in hand through the wide open iron gates, disappearing deep into the school out of sight. He continued to wait until Emma emerged, this time alone. She walked back to her car, got in and sped off, but not before Charlie could catch up and continue his surveillance. She drove through town, unknowingly with Charlie following her every move. Soon, Emma and Charlie in their separate cars passed by the park again, approaching the 4-way stop. She turned on her left blinker, and Charlie followed. A few blocks up, Emma took another left turn and drove into a nice neighborhood. At the end of the long street was a cul-de-sac. Before reaching the end, Emma pulled into the driveway on the third to last house on the block. Charlie continued past, not wanting to be seen. Little did Emma know, she had strayed in the sights of a mad dog. A predator lying in wait, a tiger in the weeds with his eyes locked in on an innocent bunny rabbit.

36

Before the birds had awakened Charlie had arrived at Emma's. He sat low in his seat, hoping not to alarm any early rising commuters or pesky neighbors who might monitor the neighborhood. This position allowed him a perfect view of her front door. If there was any movement, he wouldn't miss a thing. He was patient, calm, yet somehow sharp and ready to pounce even at this early hour, almost like this was second nature to him. Just as the sun rose over the horizon, breaking through the puffy clouds, Charlie was alerted by motion from the front door. The vintage wooden door opened as a man walked out, checking the locks behind him. A rather large man - tall, athletic build with a neatly trimmed beard over his good-looking face. He wore dark blue jeans and a trendy cold weather jacket zipped up to his throat. North Face, Patagonia or something else people gladly throw money at.

The man took off in a newer looking Silver Toyota. Charlie was torn whether he should continue watching the house to follow Emma, or follow this unknown man to get a feel for him. See what he is about, what he does and most importantly, who he was. After a few moments of contemplation, Charlie turned the key in his car, kicked the engine into gear and began following. Charlie followed him through town, turn after turn, stop light after stop light, keeping his eyes locked on his every move. The Toyota slowed and pulled into a 4-story parking garage in the downtown area of the city, and Charlie soon followed. The Toyota pulled into a marked spot on the first level of the garage. A few cars down on the left side of the aisle was another open spot, which Charlie took. He looked over his left shoulder to see the man had already exited and opened the trunk. Charlie looked ahead, seeing a large concrete pillar directly in front of him, a metal sign attached that read -

PARKING PASS REQUIRED
ALL OTHERS WILL BE TOWED

Charlie gave a flash look back at the man as he threw a backpack over his shoulders before turning to walk back towards the entrance of the garage.

"Fuck it," Charlie said out loud, turning off the car, getting out and walking quickly towards the exit.

Charlie watched from a distance as the man walked to the corner and took a left on the sidewalk. Once out of sight, Charlie picked up the pace to reach the corner himself. On the corner sat a bank, with large glass windows stretching 12 feet into the air. He pressed his back against the window and shot a glance over his left shoulder to see the man open the door to a coffee shop next door.

"Jackpot," Charlie said out loud to himself.

He reached the coffee shop, pulled the heavy glass door and walked inside. A different coffee shop than where he had seen Emma go the day before, but similar in too many ways. Stark white with gold tiled patterns stretched the room, with wooden shelves hanging all around loaded with bags of coffee beans, take away plastic cups and glass mugs. Just past the door sat a counter, reclaimed wood adorned the face of the short wall, with a marble counter sitting on top. The room was filled with people who looked way too busy to be sitting in their caffeinated dazes, too stressed out for espresso. Yet here they sat, living zombies in a world brimming with life. Charlie couldn't understand why they chose to live this way. Standing in line was the mystery man, as zombified and glazed over as the next guest. Charlie took up the space in line behind him. He was overcome with a nervous feeling. *"How do I get his attention? How can I find out who this guy is?"* He thought. Different ideas raced through his head as he began to sweat, and before he knew it, Charlie involuntarily bumped into the man from behind. Hard enough for him to lose his footing, hitting the person in front of him.

"Oh, shit," Charlie said, reaching out to grab the man's shoulders. "I'm so sorry."

"What the hell, man?" He asked, turning back to look at Charlie with complete and utter disdain.

"Sorry about that," Charlie said, taking a few steps back. "Are you OK?"

"Yeah, yeah. I'm fine," The man said.

"You know how it is, I'm just not myself before my morning cup," Charlie said nervously, letting out a friendly, yet somehow creepy, giggle.

"Just watch where you are going," The man said as he turned away. "Just take it easy."

"Hey, I'm sorry again," Charlie said, this time raising his voice slightly to get his attention.

"It's fine," The man said without turning around.

"You come in here often?" Charlie asked. The man didn't respond. "I love this place, I come here all the time. I really love their," Charlie said, looking up at the menu. He scanned it in a panic, hoping his eyes would land on a specific drink to sound like he knew what he was talking about. "Uh, the Hammerhead," He blurted out.

"Yeah, this place is good," The man said, again not turning around.

"What's your drink of choice?" Charlie asked, a sense of urgency in his voice, sounding almost maniacal.

"Uh," The man said, looking over his right shoulder. "I just get, uhm, just iced coffee with milk."

"That sounds great," Charlie said with excitement. "Maybe I should try that."

"Sure, man. Sure," The man said.

Charlie noticed him reach back with his left arm, removing a brown leather wallet from his back pocket. He noticed a bright yellow gold wedding band on his ring finger.

"You a married man?" Charlie blurted out.

"Why do you want to know?" The man asked, now half turned around to his right, glaring back at Charlie.

"I don't mean to be weird. It's just, well I am getting married soon. Tying the ol' knot. Hitching a ball and chain," Charlie said, nudging the man with a wink.

"Sure, whatever you say," The man replied.

"What's your name?" Charlie asked, reaching out his right hand. "I'm Charlie."

"Uh, Eddie," The man returned his hand and they shook.

"Good to meet you, Eddie," Charlie said with a big, stupid grin.

"You too," Eddie said, visibly uncomfortable with the interaction in which he had been forced to deal with.

A young man with clean cut hair parted on the left side and combed down his forehead approached the register.

"Next guest," he shouted.

"Look," Eddie said, turning around one last time. "I need to get to work, so have a good day, alright?"

"Where do you work?" Charlie asked, a tone of anger in his voice.

"Across the road, Paramount," Eddie said.

Charlie turned to look out the windows, noticing a big, old world theater across the street taking up most of the city block.

"No way," Charlie said, pretending to care. "That's a cool spot."

"Whatever you say man," Eddie said. "Can I get an iced coffee, splash of milk please?" Eddie said, placing his order.

"That will be 5.75," The clerk said back.

"This guy says you make the best coffee in the city," Charlie said, leaning over Eddie, speaking loudly.

"That's very nice of him," The clerk responded.

"Hey, man," Eddie said, his voice now filling with anger. "I am just trying to buy coffee and get on with my day, alright?"

"Sure, sure," Charlie said, backing off while lifting his hands up to his chest, showing his palms towards Eddie. "Just trying to be friendly."

Eddie pulled 8 dollars out of his wallet and handed it across the counter.

"That's fine, just, relax," Eddie said. He turned back to the clerk. "Keep the change."

"Thank you, sir. Your coffee will be right up," The clerk said.

Eddie had to bend towards the counter to walk past Charlie, who had crowded way too close for any reasonable person's comfort.

"Nice meeting you, Eddie," Charlie said, in a low, solemn voice. His eyes stared sharply, cutting through Eddie like a razor blade dancing across a wrist.

"Uh, you too, buddy," Eddie said, moving to the furthest corner in the coffee shop as he could to get away from Charlie.

Charlie stared at him, with just the slightest grin as he moved across the coffee shop. Eddie's skin was crawling.

"Excuse me, sir?" The clerk asked, getting Charlie's attention.

Charlie slowly turned his head towards the clerk, eyes wide open, as though he was staring directly through the young man, a creepy, ghoulish grin remained on his face. He stared quietly, blinked a few times before his face turned back to what people might consider normal. He began patting his back pockets frantically.

"You know what," Charlie said, setting his head backwards looking at the ceiling. "I forgot my wallet. Stupid me. This always happens. I guess I'll have to come back later."

"No problem sir," the clerk replied.

Charlie walked to the front, turned his back to the door and stared back at Eddie. He slowly pressed his weight backwards, opening the door, not breaking eye contact for even a split second. Once the door opened, he stepped backwards and walked out of the coffee shop onto the sidewalk. As Charlie walked around the bank, he stopped to watch the Paramount Theater. Soon, he saw Eddie running across the street towards the building, a large plastic cup of iced coffee in his right hand. He watched as Eddie jumped the curb and made his way down the alleyway, which sat to the right of the theater. Eddie soon was out of sight. Charlie nodded to himself and smiled.

37

Charlie continued stalking his prey, step by step, as they went about their every day, mundane lives. And now, the time had come to make his move. The point of no return. He found himself oddly calm, knowing what lay ahead as though he had done this before. For weeks he had watched the family as they went to work, participated in drop-off and pick-up routines and every other boring errand they took part in each and every long, drawn out day. He didn't live that way. What he was doing was his job. And he was damn good at it. He pulled up and parked across the street from Automatic Coffee. His hair slicked back cleanly, with slim black jeans cuffed at the ankle exposing a nice pair of designer black boots. A white plain t-shirt peaked through the unzipped designer jacket wrapping his slender body. He entered the coffee shop, where he stood for an awkwardly long time, allowing multiple guests to go ahead of him as he loitered by the front door. Charlie could feel the eyes of the employees and customers watching him, and he was growing uneasy. He was sweating. He looked out through the sprawling windows, then back at the clerk, let out a smile, and continued this charade for some time. Aware but without care that he was sketching out the other clientele. Just as he began thinking it was time to abort, he saw the familiar Prius come screaming down the road and pull over into a spot that was much too small, but somehow, like days before, she made it work.

"There you are," Charlie muttered, as he gathered himself and walked up to the counter.

"Are you ready to order, sir?" asked the clerk. A tattooed young man with the sides of his head shaved real close to the scalp with a big poofy mohawk.

"Yeah," Charlie said in contemplation of the scarce but cautiously curated menu.

As Charlie placed his order, he heard the glass door push open, and in walked Emma. *"Right on schedule,"* Charlie thought, forgetting he had just been sweating bullets.

"Can I get your name?" The Clerk asked.

"My name is Charlie."

Then, a voice rang out like the heavens opening above, as though a chorus of Angels had come out to play in the sunlight.

"Charlie!?" The voice shouted.

"Gotcha," Charlie thought, a sly smile washing over his face as he turned, pretending he didn't know who it could be. Little did she know, this was all orchestrated by Charlie - the Maestro of Evil.

• • •

The first acts of his sinister plot had played out perfectly, just as Charlie had planned them. Now it was on to the next chapter, the hardest one, but for his nefarious plan, it was crucial. Friday crept up like a fever. Today he had taken a cab downtown as he planned to stay in the area most of the day to ensure he was prepared. All day he paced the street in a one block radius, back and forth carrying a black duffle bag. To him, it seemed the more mindless he wandered, the more he fit in. After a few rounds, he went to the coffee shop and sipped tea. All afternoon he watched and sipped, and sipped and watched. The sun had begun to set and Charlie knew it was almost showtime. The grand finale was approaching, the big crescendo. He walked nonchalantly back to the parking garage and found a dark corner to hide. He dropped the bag to the ground and removed a black baseball cap and a black hooded sweatshirt. He tossed the ball cap over his neatly combed hair, pushed one arm after the other into the sweatshirt and zipped it up nice and tight. He then removed a crumbled up grocery bag before he made the slow walk back to the street.

The sun had finally retired for the day as darkness filled the streets. Any moment, Eddie would walk out the side door and head to the Elbow Room. He stood and watched from across the street as right on cue, the side door shot open, and Eddie emerged, turned left down the alley and walked into the darkness. When Eddie was out of sight, Charlie rushed across the street into the alley. The alley was dark, disgusting and reeked of urine and wet garbage thanks to three dumpsters that sat pushed against the theater's brick wall. Each dumpster was positioned about 4 feet from one another, taking up a large portion of the alley. Charlie darted towards the dumpsters and ducked in between two of the containers. He crouched down and sat back on his heels, leaning up against the wall. He tore apart the grocery bag, removing a rusty old hammer and a syringe. He leaned to his right slightly, allowing him clearance to place the capped syringe into his left pants pocket. He then reached up above his head and tossed the garbage back into one of the open dumpsters. He held the hammer in his left hand and with his right, pulled the hood of the sweater up over the top of his head, covering the ball cap. Wrapped around his neck was a black cloth, which he pulled up above his nose. Partially to hide himself, also to block the wretched smell from the alley. Here, he would wait.

Charlie checked his watch, noticing almost 3 hours had passed and he knew Eddie should be arriving soon. *"But what if he got a ride home tonight? What if it was Emma who picked him up?"* None of this mattered, he was locked in. There was no turning back. Through the street noise of locals looking for a night on the town, cars buzzing and music filling the air, he saw a shadow approaching. As the shadow materialized into a body, he knew it was Eddie. He positioned himself, hammer in hand, left finger tips barely clinging to the edge of the receptacle. As Eddie drew closer, Charlie peered over the trash bin watching him step by step. Eddie giggled to himself as he stumbled towards him, unaware anyone was watching his every move, ready to pounce. Eddie walked, flicking through his cell phone as he went, stumbling right past Charlie. Time felt as though it had halted into slow motion. It was now or never.

Charlie jumped to his feet, spun to his right and stood behind Eddie. He cocked his right arm high over his head, and in one motion WHACK. The round end of the hammer crashed into the top of his skull. Eddie let out a loud gasp, followed by a sickening whimper as he folded into himself, landing hard onto the pavement. The impact of his body hitting the ground sent his cell phone skipping along the damp asphalt. Charlie stood over Eddie, removed the syringe from his pants pocket and stuck it into his right arm, injecting a large dose of Midazolam into his body. This way Charlie could keep him unconscious for a long time for any other sinister idea that may tickle his fancy. The torturous possibilities were endless.

He searched Eddie's body and retrieved his car keys before dragging his limp, bleeding body between two trash bins. He ran to the parking garage to pick up Eddie's car. He pulled the car up to the trash bins, clicked open the trunk, and muscled Eddie's body up and in. He drove slowly home, following all local road laws in hopes of not being pulled over. He needed to stay calm, collected and patient. When he arrived home, he backed Eddie's car up the driveway, walked to the back and stuck the key into the trunk. He opened the hatch slowly, in case an alert, pissed off Eddie awaited him.

"Thank god. Still out," Charlie muttered to himself. "How you feeling in there, buddy?" He said, slapping Eddie's body a couple of times like they were old pals.

Charlie grabbed Eddie underneath his arms and began dragging him out of the trunk. He dragged his lifeless body up the steps and through the front door and continued dragging him, his feet scraping, across the threshold and directly through the front room to the stairs that led to the basement. His feet bumped and banged every stair on the way down, like a pile of bricks falling from the clouds. Charlie continued dragging him across the room to an old, rusty chair. *Should do the trick,"* he thought. He wrestled Eddie's body upright in the chair and began wrapping him with thick chains. First the feet, then his torso up to his chest, slapping a padlock on both ends of the chain. He then wrapped more chains around his hands one by one to the arms of the chair. Once Eddie was properly secured, Charlie took a step back and knelt over with his hands on his knees. He was rightfully winded, and as he tried to catch his breath, he stared deep into Eddie's lifeless eyes and said aloud, "Welcome home."

38

Charlie needed a shower that evening more than ever before in his life. He stood dripping wet with a soft white towel wrapped around his waist as he vigorously rubbed his wet hair with a hand towel. All the while, he stared intently at the framed photo of Emma on the dresser. He threw on another all black outfit. Black jeans, hooded sweater and a black cap. As he was digging through the closet, he noticed something on the top shelf. He reached up and grabbed a cloth item that was shoved between a couple of old shoe boxes. It was a black ski mask. *"Where were you a few hours ago?"* He thought. He shoved the mask into the pocket of his hooded sweater and ran down stairs. Before going out the front door, he stopped to check the doorway leading to the basement. Charlie had attached a steel latch with a thick padlock that hung like a Christmas ornament. He pulled on the padlock to ensure it wouldn't budge.

As Charlie drove Eddie's car across town, no chances were taken. No running stale yellow lights, full stops at stop signs. Almost *suspiciously* safe. As Charlie pulled up to the park on Pine Avenue, he pulled the black ski mask over his head. He parked the car against the curb and dropped Eddie's keys and cell phone on the floor on the passenger side. It was then he noticed Eddie's parking pass dangling from the rear-view mirror. He ripped it down and put it in his pocket. He then made the short walk around the block where he had parked his car, just up the street from the VanSant home. When he got to his car, he clicked the key entry to unlock the vehicle, opened the back door and ripped off the ski mask, tossing it carelessly in the backseat. Just then he looked up at the house beyond where his car was parked, and his eyes locked on the front window. Staring out at him was a woman in her late 60s. Their eyes remained locked, as Charlie tried to pretend his heart was not beating out of his chest, like a cartoon wolf about to devour a freshly cooked rabbit. After a few moments, the woman smiled and gave a friendly wave. Charlie nodded back. *"Well, that could be a problem,"* Charlie thought.

• • •

Mary Hart was a sweet woman at the tail end of her 60s. She worked to finish up some dishes late one Friday night. A rerun of Dateline played on the television in her living room, with the volume up curiously loud. Maybe to break through the noise of the running water, or maybe her hearing had diminished. As she finished the dishes and set the final plate on the rack to dry, she reached for the towel hanging on the handle of her stove. She dried her hands and replaced the towel in place precisely. Everything was in order in Mary's home, a woman of extreme discipline and cleanliness. The house was dark, but the darkness had never scared Mary. As far as she could remember her home had always been free of demons and devils, and the only bump in the night might come from a stubbed toe. The neighborhood had always been a safe one, and her two sons had moved out long ago. She filled a glass with water from the refrigerator and walked into her living room, flicking off the kitchen lights as she went. The living room was dark, illuminated only by the eternal glow of the television which shot scenes of crimes yet to be solved over the walls. She reached down to her coffee table and clicked the remote control, turning off the television. She took another sip of water as she turned to leave the room. To the left of her living room was a hallway that led through the interior of the home. Three doorways graced the hallway, 2 bedrooms and a guest bathroom. At the end of the hallway was the doorway to Mary's room. Like every night, she made the short trek down the dark hallway to bed. She felt safe, secure and protected in her home.

She entered the bedroom and promptly shut the door. Her bedroom was decently sized. Her bed sat in the middle of the room butted up against the wall, a night stand on either side. The one on the left, adorned with an old-fashioned lamp and a small decorative chair sat in the corner beside it. The other night stand was loaded with picture frames set upright showcasing photos of her son's and their respective families, along with her husband, Roy, who had passed away years prior. The wall opposite of the bed had a large dresser set against it, with a large flatscreen television on top. A doorway leading to a master bath was just left of the dresser.

She walked to the left side of her bed and took another sip of water before setting the glass on her nightstand. She untied her robe and folded it neatly over the chair before turning down the sheets and crawling into bed. She pulled the covers up to her chin and rolled over onto her left side, closed her eyes and began the long journey to sleep. Just as she drifted off, her eyes shot open to a sound coming from the bathroom. It wasn't a loud sound, just enough to alert her. She shook it off, pulled the covers even tighter and closed her eyes yet again. For a few short moments, Mary was at peace as she drifted to sleep, but those peaceful moments didn't last long. Again, she heard a noise, followed by another. It sounded like a slight squeal, like pressure being applied to fresh, glossy leather. Again, she heard the squeal, followed by another. An ominous feeling rushed over her like a wave crashing into the sand. The uneasy feeling flowing through her bones became impossible to ignore, and as she rolled onto her back, she saw a dark figure looming over her, the figure's arms stretched far above their head. She rolled to her left, as the figure's arms crashed down onto her pillow, swinging a hammer as they dropped.

Mary rolled so hard, she fell off the opposite side of the bed. Her heart pumping with adrenaline and fear, she jumped to her feet and stared directly into the eyes of evil. There, the dark figure stood, breathing heavily across the bed. They stood, locked in on one another for a moment before the intruder jumped up onto the bed, both feet landing in perfect sync. The intruder moved across the bed with precision speed. With one decent leap the stranger was at Mary. She reached for the night stand and picked up a picture frame. She cocked her arm back and swung it as hard as she could, shattering it over the intruder's left shoulder. The intruder let out a loud grunt. Mary ran around the front of the bed towards the door but it was no use. Before she knew it, the man had leapt over the bed with ease and as Mary's hand grasped the door knob, one turn away from safety, the man grabbed her by the back of the head with a hand full of hair, and in one motion, smashed her face into the closed door. Mary let out a loud yelp as blood poured down her face. Dazed, in agonizing pain and in absolute terror, she fell backwards into the man, who promptly shoved her with all of his might against the door. Somehow, she twisted her body, landing against the door with her back. She held her face with both her palms, opening her eyes the best she could to see the man's arm shoot forward with another swing of the hammer. She unlocked her knees and fell hard to the ground as the hammer smashed through the door, sending splinters of wood all around the room.

As the man fought to remove the hammer, which stuck in the door, Mary on all fours crawled as fast as she could through the pain. She stood up and ran to the bathroom, slammed the door shut and locked it. The man gave up on the hammer and chased her, but the door had been locked before he could make his way in after her. Feverishly, he turned the door knob only to find she had locked herself in. He began pounding on the door as Mary settled, back against the wall at the far end of the bathroom. Soon, the pounding stopped, and the house fell dead silent. The only things Mary could hear were the pounding of her heart and her lungs gasping for air. She sat for a moment, trembling with fear, blood continuously pouring down her face from what she only assumed was a broken nose. She wouldn't take a chance and open the bathroom door to check if he had left. She looked up above the sink to see one of the two windows was wide open, and the screen had been removed. She jumped to her feet and rushed to the window. If she could just yell for help, maybe a neighbor would hear her cries and come to her rescue. She placed her bloody hands on the counter, leaned forward and as she opened her mouth to scream for help, in an instant, everything went black. Reaching through the window with a massive blow, the attacker swung that hammer and smashed it into her forehead. Blood burst out from her head as she fell backwards, crashing through the glass shower doors behind her and landing on her back on the shower floor. The glass shards poured down over her body, cutting ribbons of her flesh.

She tried to stand up, but her body was shutting down from the blood loss. The cold feeling of death had set in, and just when she was finally able to open her eyes, she looked up to see the man standing over her. He stared down, breathing in and out rapidly. She shut her eyes, as the man reached the hammer above his head and continued with one blow after another to her head, face and shoulders. With each blow blood splattered the walls, the ceiling, *everything*. The man stood there for a moment to admire his horrific act as though it was some sort of macabre art piece, then walked to the sink and climbed up and out the window. When his feet hit the earth below, he lifted the screen, reattached it and like a burst of smoke from a snuffed out campfire, he disappeared into the night.

39

Present

Angus, disheveled and exhausted, sat deep in his office chair, hunched over his desk like an old towel left out on a clothes hanger in the rain. He held a yellow highlighter in his right hand as he looked over documents from Eddie's file, combing through every word, every syllable, trying to find something he may have missed. He had become locked on those pieces of paper like the meaning of life was hidden somewhere within, and he would stop at nothing until he cracked the code. He was startled back to reality when his desk phone rang. Like a bolt of lightning had struck him in the spine, he straightened up in his chair and raised the receiver to his ear.

"Detective Pratt," he said, sullen, resting his forehead in his free palm.

"Don't sound too excited," Frank said on the other end.

"Sorry," He replied, running his free hand over the top of his head. "I'm racking my brain down here trying to find anything we may have missed. There has to be something in here—"

"Listen Angus," Frank cut him off. "The Captain wants a meeting. You're going to want to come up here right away."

"What's this all about?" Angus asked.

After a long pause on the other end of the phone, Frank finally chimed in. "Just, head up here as soon as you can."

Frank abruptly hung up leaving Angus holding the receiver confused and unsure.

"What now?" Angus asked out loud as he put the receiver down, and ran both his hands over his tired face.

Angus exited the elevator on the top floor of the police station and sauntered down the hallway towards the Captain's office. Captain Maya Stewart was a no nonsense woman, and an absolutely stellar cop throughout her career. Her office was large and the decor was scarce yet well curated and decked out in dark stained hardwoods. An executive desk sat in the middle of the room and the entire wall behind her was made of built-in shelves, covered in old books and awards she had received. Two windows graced the wall to the right of the office overlooking a large courtyard below. Two big leather chairs sat just in front of her desk for meetings. She sat, hair pulled back tightly wearing a dark gray women's suit with her hands folded on the desk in front of her. Angus approached the office where the door had been left open. As he entered the doorway, he knocked lightly on the door frame. He noticed Frank sitting there, hands folded in his lap.

"Come in," Maya said, waving him inside. "Have a seat."

A wave of confusion washed over Angus' tired face as he walked across the office and took the chair next to Frank.

"Please tell me this report I got about you isn't true," Maya said, holding up a single sheet of paper.

"I don't know what you're referring to, Captain," Angus replied.

"Well, let's see, shall we?" Maya said, her voice raising slightly and slamming the sheet of paper onto her desk. "Detective Pratt forced his way into my home and proceeded to search without a warrant in an attempt to get me to confess to a crime of which I HAD NO PART!" Maya shouted, slamming her right palm onto the desk. "What the hell were you thinking?" She asked.

"I can explain everything," Angus said, both hands in the air in front of him as though he could somehow deflect the invisible daggers being shot.

"I don't want to hear your explanation. I don't want any excuses and I definitely don't need reports like this coming across my desk," Maya said.

"But, Maya," Angus said softly.

"Captain Stewart," she corrected. "This isn't a god damned joke."

"OK, Captain Stewart," Angus said with caution. "I know there's more to his story. You have to trust me."

"Angus, you're off the case," she shot back.

"What do you mean I'm off the case? You can't—" Angus tried to blurt out before he was shut down.

"I can, and I am," Maya said, her index finger pointed at him. "You're off the case. You're not thinking rationally and you're going to get yourself into serious trouble, or someone could get hurt. You're too emotionally invested."

"Come on, Captain," Angus pleaded.

"It's final," she shot back. "Look at you! You're exhausted and burnt out. Have you even been home to seen your wife and kids or slept?"

"With all due respect, I don't see how that is relevant to solving this case," Angus said.

"I can't have an exhausted, angry cop in the field going off the rails."

"That won't happen," He shot out, frustrated.

"It already has," she shot back, lifting the report in the air, and letting it go. The single sheet of paper flapped in the air and landed upon her desk.

"You knew about this?" Angus asked Frank.

"I just found out," Frank said.

"Frank will be taking over as lead on this case. You will turn over any and all notes or evidence you have collected directly to him," Maya instructed.

"And I assume this isn't a suggestion?" He asked.

"It's an order," she said, calming her voice slightly. "Take a break, Angus. Go home, see your family, sleep in. You need it. When you're ready to come back, we will get you on another case. One where you aren't so emotionally charged up."

"You know I can't do that," He said, shaking his head, breaking into a disagreeable giggle.

"You can, and you will," she said, staring into his eyes as though she could see his soul.

"And you *will* stay the fuck away from Charlie Claymore, you got it?" She added, pointing at him. "If you've ever listened to an order from me, let it be this one. I am dead serious, Angus. Stay away from him."

"Frank, come on," Angus tried pleading his case one last time.

"It's out of my hands," Frank said, shrugging him off.

"I can't believe this. You're making a big mistake."

"Well, believe it," Maya said, closing the door on his arguments and pleading. "Angus, what is it about this case in particular? You've been looking for lost husbands, wives and murderers for years. What is it about this specific case that has you so worked up? I've never received a report like this about you."

Angus ran his hands over his face while letting out a sigh so deep, it seemed to come all the way from his feet.

"I don't know, Captain," Angus said, unable to make eye contact. "I can't explain it. There's something *different* about this case. I *know* there is more to this story. I've seen people like Charlie before. They're bad news. I *know* I can figure this out, if you just give me more time."

"I'm sorry, Angus," Maya said softly. "Go home and get some rest. The case is in good hands, right Frank?"

"Absolutely," Frank said, nodding in approval.

"I guess I'll gather my things and leave them on my desk. Frank can come get them whenever he has time," Angus said, rising to his feet, defeated.

Angus turned and walked towards the door, opening it and heading out into the hallway.

"Shut the door behind you, please," Maya shouted.

"You got it," Angus said, a blatant level of disapproval in his voice. "—Captain," he said snarkily as he shut the door.

Angus entered his office like a tornado, grabbing a box from the corner and slamming it onto the desk. He began shuffling through paperwork, evidence and other files all relating to the VanSant and Hart cases, stuffing them with very little care into the box. Not long after his tantrum, Frank entered the office.

"Come on, Angus," Frank said, leaning against the doorframe. "You know what you did was out of protocol. We can't have that."

"This is bullshit and you know it," Angus said, his voice shattering.

"Be that as it may, you fucked up," Frank said matter-of-factly. "You know that was out of line, and you should have expected this to come down on you. What were you thinking?"

"I *know* Charlie is involved in this. I haven't been able to pinpoint exactly how, but I know he is."

"And if that turns out to be true, we'll catch him. But we still have to handle things by the book. We have to work according to the law. I know, it *is* bullshit, but there's nothing we can do about it."

"I don't know how you expect me to walk from this," Angus said, shaking his head.

"You heard the Captain. This isn't a suggestion. Go home, spend some time with Laura, take the kids on a vacation.

Whatever you want. Just get your mind off of this. When you feel refreshed, everything will go back to normal and you can find another case to fuck up."

"Thanks, Frank."

Angus walked around his desk towards the door, reaching his right hand out to Frank. Frank returned his and they shook.

"Get his ass, Frank," Angus said. "I know he's involved. I *fucking* know it. Get him."

"You got it," Frank assured. "That's everything?" He said, pointing at the box.

"That's everything. If you have any questions, I'm only a phone call away."

"Don't bet on it," Frank said. "Get outta here."

Angus nodded his head without saying another word. He walked slowly to the elevator and as he entered, he turned to look down the hallway. Frank stood in the doorway, watching as his partner left. *"Looks like I am on my own,"* Angus thought to himself as the elevator doors shut in front of him. *"I will catch you, Charlie Claymore,"* he thought. *"I will catch you."*

His body shook the entire drive home. He was drunk on a cocktail of emotions; Rage, anxiety, disappointment in himself and his department, all topped off with a strange dash of excitement. Excitement because regardless of what the Captain said, he had a plan. He gripped the steering wheel until his knuckles ached and turned pale white, all the while a strange and eerie smile washed across his tired face. He walked into his home with his head hanging low. He shut the door softly, though he wanted nothing more than to slam the door so hard it might have popped off the hinges and land on the front lawn. He walked into his living room where Laura was sitting with her legs curled up on the couch as she watched television and enjoyed a generously poured glass of red wine.

"Hey, honey," Laura said, noticing the gloomy expression on her husband's face. "What's wrong?"

"Ahh," Angus said, running his hand over the top of his head and staring at his feet. "I've got some bad news."

"What's wrong?" She asked, her feet now on the floor as she leaned forward.

"I just got the call. I need to go out of town," He said.

"Oh?" She said surprised. "What for?"

"Homicide in Spokane," He said, lying through his teeth. "Details are oddly close to the Hart case. The Captain asked me to head out immediately to look into it. I'm flying out in an hour."

"They think it was the same person?" She asked.

"We don't know. But I need to pack right away," he said as he turned his back to his wife, smiling to himself because she had bought the story.

"OK honey," she said. "When will you be back?"

"Not sure. Could be a couple of days."

He retreated to the bedroom and he reached to the top of the closet, pulling down a navy blue duffle bag lined with white trim and laid it onto the bed. He began packing his essentials - underwear, socks and a couple of white undershirts. He pulled the sock drawer out and began frantically rummaging through all the socks tied into nice little bundles. From the back of the drawer he lifted out a .357 revolver, admiring it for a moment and kicking out the cylinder to count 8 bullet casings locked and loaded. Just then, he heard footsteps coming down the hall and he turned, falling over the duffle bag as though his knees had given out. As he fell, he shoved the revolver deep into the bag so Laura wouldn't know he had taken it.

"Honey!" Laura yelped as she rushed to his side. "Are you OK?"

"Yeah, yeah," Angus said as he stood up, rubbing his face with his palms. "I'm just so tired. Hey, have we got any extra tubes of toothpaste? You know how much I hate hotel toothpaste," He said, letting out a nervous giggle.

"Of course. Anything else you need? Can I help you pack?"

"No, thank you. I already have everything," he assured.

He kept a close eye as she left the room to get toothpaste, and as soon as she walked out of sight, he rushed back to the closet. On the floor was a worn out box that once had housed a pair of work boots. He removed the lid to expose various boxes of ammunition inside. He grabbed the box for his .357 revolver, then pushed the box back into place as though it was never touched. He buried the box of bullets deep into the duffle bag.

"Here you go, honey," Laura said as she walked back into the room.

"What would I ever do without you?" Angus asked, leaning down to kiss her forehead. "I'll call you as soon as I get settled."

"You'd better," she insisted.

Angus lifted the duffle bag over his broad shoulder and made his way back to the car, the engine still warm from when he arrived. And as quick as he had come, he was gone again. But he wasn't going to Spokane. No, there was no dead body he was aware of, no copycat or serial killer to the best of his knowledge. It was all a smoke screen, a diversion for his real plan. He drove for 15 minutes before he pulled into the parking lot of the Ponderosa Motel. A small, two-story roadside motel that always had plenty of vacancies for drug addicts or folks attracted to hourly rates. It was equipped with a small parking lot where the fender's of the parked cars butted up so close to the motel room doors, it was shocking guests could even enter. A bright sign stretched high up into the sky, screaming with busted neon tubes of pink, green and electric blue with a gigantic neon Ponderosa Pine tree flickering in the darkness. He parked his car towards the back of the hotel, hoping it wouldn't be seen by anyone who might unfortunately travel to this part of town.

He entered the lobby of the motel and was hit by the smell of decades old filthy carpet, graced by stains that since occurring had now picked up their own stains. A stench of old cigarettes and dank, damp old cloth paired well with the overall thickness of garbage from the dumpsters just outside. On one side of the room sat two recliners decorated in what once was a bright yellow floral pattern. On the other side, a deteriorating wooden counter. Behind it sat a porky pig looking man wearing a white tank top and flannel pajama pants. He was licking his fingers unashamed while he enjoyed a plate of chicken wings.

"Excuse me, sir?" Angus asked as he approached the counter.

"Yeah?" The man asked back, not one bit interested that a customer had entered.

"I need uh, a room. At the far end of the building, if that's OK?"

"Sure", the man said. He lifted another chicken wing to his cracked lips, taking a large and sloppy bite of the drumstick before getting up from his stool.

The man turned to a corkboard behind him with 4 rows of gold hanging hooks, a set of keys dangling freely from each. He wiped his hands on his pajama pants before grabbing a set. He then dropped the keys onto the counter and slid them across to Angus, leaving a trail of sauce and saliva behind his sausage-like fingers.

"Here ya go," the man said, before taking another bite of a drumstick, smacking his lips as he went. He spoke to Angus while chewing, "How many nights you gonna need?"

"How about I pay for two now, then see how it goes?"

"Sure, whatever. That'll be fifty dollars for the two nights." The man said as he swallowed down the saucy chicken.

Angus pulled out his wallet and dropped a clean $50 bill onto the counter.

"Thanks for coming in. You're in room 12, it's all the way at the end." the man said as he clunked back down onto his stool without looking at Angus.

"Thanks. I assume I can't book a massage day at the ol' Ponderosa," Angus joked.

The man took another savage bite from a chicken wing, never acknowledging the sarcastic question.

Angus walked from the filthy lobby down to Room 12. He stuck the key in and jiggled it to open the door. Inside was a small bed with an ancient looking floral quilt stretched over and two pillows sat at the headboard. To the left of the bed was a small nightstand with a lamp on top and an old rotary phone. There was a window just to the left of the door with stained curtains and a wooden table sat underneath with one wobbly chair. On the table was a half empty beer bottle the cleaners must have missed. In front of the bed was a wooden stand with a television Angus imagined must have been purchased before he and Laura had got married. Past the bed was the bathroom, a stained white counter sat below a mirror covered in water spots. Luckily for Angus, the bathroom appeared to be the cleanest part of the room. He dropped his duffle bag at the foot of the bed and sat down hard next to it. He unzipped the bag, reached in and pulled out the loaded revolver. He sat there for a while, holding the handgun on his lap. He could only think about one thing; Charlie was living rent free in his head.

40

The next morning Charlie rose with the sun, decked out head to toe in running attire. He sat on the end of the bed as he slipped black Nike running shoes onto his feet and laced them up nice and tight. The bedroom windows behind the king sized bed sat wide open, allowing the chilly morning air to pour in and fill the room with beautiful smells of the trees and earth. Charlie loved the cold morning air as it cleaned the room. It was Mother Nature refreshing the space. He jogged downstairs to the main floor of the house and with a nice pep in his step, turned and entered the kitchen. He reached the cabinet above the sink, pulling out a small bowl. On the counter sat a box of instant oatmeal packets. He pulled two of them out and dumped the contents into the bowl. Oats poured from the brown, wax coated bags, sending a plume of oat dust up into the air. He then filled the bowl halfway with cold water before setting it inside the microwave. He set the time for 2 and a half minutes and leaned his lower back into the counter. He pointed his nose to the ceiling, closed his eyes and lost himself for a short time as the microwave hummed. He felt so relaxed at that moment he could have dozed off, but just as he drifted off, the screech of the microwave shot him back into reality. He pulled open the drawer that sat to the left of him, removed a spoon and retrieved the now steaming bowl of oatmeal. He walked out of the kitchen and across the house to the doorway leading to the basement. With a quick turn of the key, he removed the padlock and jogged down the stairs.

It was pitch black in the basement. When he reached the bottom of the stairs, he flicked the light switch and the exhausted lightbulb flickered a few times before stabilizing and lighting the space. Across the room sat Eddie, head slumping downward with his chin pressed against his chest, asleep. Blood had dried on the side of his head, face, his shoulders and down the front of the ratty t-shirt he had worn since the night he was kidnapped.

"Hey," Charlie said, before raising his voice even louder. "Hey!"

Eddie showed small signs of life as his head slowly rose from his chest, the agonizing pain making it difficult to move. His eyes were swollen and his head was throbbing like a 30 car pile up had happened inside his skull. He began twisting his head around in a circle motion trying anything to shake the pain in his neck and back.

"Ah, God," Eddie muttered to himself, drool spilling from his bottom lip down to the collar of his filthy shirt. "What *now*?" He shouted, as he came to life and started shaking with any strength he had in his burning joints.

"Whoa there, tiger," Charlie said with a slight giggle. "Slow down, boy. I brought you some breakfast."

"Fuck, you," Eddie spoke through whispers, as a deep breath filled his lungs.

"That's no way to talk to someone who brought you breakfast," Charlie said as he stirred the steaming oatmeal. "Now come on, open wide. Here comes the airplane."

Eddie kept his lips shut and only glared at Charlie. If looks could kill, it would have been curtains for Charlie, as those eyes shot daggers, bullets, *missiles*.

"Come on, you know this game. I'm sure you *must* have played it with Sophie a time or two," Charlie said as he held out the spoon.

"Don't you ever say her name, mother fucker!" Eddie shouted. He then cleared his throat from deep within, and spit at Charlie, hitting him in the left shoulder.

"You piece of *shit*," Charlie shouted, now enraged, his teeth clenched tightly.

Charlie poured the bowl of steaming hot oatmeal over Eddie's head. The hot, chunky liquid coated the top of his head and began dripping down his face, over his eyes, nose and coating both of his ears. It was so piping hot, Eddie could only let out loud screams as it began burning his skin.

"I bring you breakfast and *this* is the thanks I get? You're *spitting* at me?" Charlie screamed in such a rage, it could have shaken the foundation of the house.

Charlie cocked his right hand back far behind his body, and in one quick motion swung his open hand through the air, connecting perfectly with Eddie's left cheek. He smacked him so hard, oatmeal droplets splattered against the far wall. He took a few steps away from Eddie and rubbed his face with his right hand, unconcerned about the oatmeal that had coated his hand and now smeared across his face. He wore it like a badge of honor.

"You son of a bitch, why don't you just *kill me*?" Eddie shouted.

Charlie stutter stepped a second, looking over his right shoulder at him.

"Kill you?" Charlie asked, surprised, as he turned around.

"Yes," Eddie shouted. "Why are you doing this to me? Keeping me chained up like an animal? You won't *ever* let me go. So just kill me already, you fucking coward."

He leaned in real close to Eddie, so close the tips of their noses touched. He stared deep into his eyes, as Eddie stared back, he felt a chill of terror cover his body like a blanket in the winter. He could see every ounce of evil living within Charlie's possessed eyes. So close he could smell the rot emanating from his soul.

"*Kill* you," Charlie whispered. "No, I'm not going to kill you. Not yet. There's still so much fun to be had. Don't you want to have some more fun?"

"This. This isn't, f-fun," Eddie choked out.

"Oh, but it is *so* much fun," Charlie said, his face covered with a devilish smile. "And we're just getting started."

Charlie took his right index finger and ran it through Eddie's oatmeal soaked hair as though he was a child sneaking a taste of frosting from a birthday cake. He shoved the entire finger into his mouth, sucking all the wet, mushy oats off and swallowing it. He then ran his saliva soaked finger across Eddie's cheek.

"P-please, PLEASE, let me go!" Eddie screamed.

Charlie leaned back and let out a laugh from deep within his guts.

"Please, I-I, I promised my daughter I would t-take her to a Daddy Daughter dance. Please, I-I can't let her down. I-I won't say a w-word about where I was. I swear," Eddie pleaded for his release. "P-please. I c-can't let her down."

"Daddy Daughter dance, huh?" Charlie asked as he walked to the workbench.

He picked up a hammer and admired it for a moment. He spun the handle around in his palm until the claw faced towards Eddie.

"I don't think you will be making it to the dance," Charlie said quietly as he approached.

Charlie grabbed the hair on the back of Eddie's head, cocking it backwards with so much force Eddie feared he might snap his neck. Charlie shoved the claw of the hammer into Eddie's mouth and pressed it with immense pressure against the back of Eddie's two front teeth. He began pulling back on the handle, forcing the claw into the roof of his mouth. Eddie began shaking violently in the chair, screaming and shrieking with the claw pressed against the top of his mouth. Just as Eddie shut his eyes, fearing for what was to come, Charlie pulled the hammer out of his mouth, and fell laughing, placing his hands on his knees.

"Come on," Charlie said through his laughter. "You think I would do that? I don't have the stomach for anything *that* gruesome."

Eddie continued to breathe deep and fast as though he had just run a marathon. Charlie walked across the room and walked up the stairs. He stopped after a few steps and bent around the unfinished wall.

"You see how much fun we can have together?" Charlie said with a terrifying smile.

Charlie got to the top of the stairs and reattached the lock to the door. He walked to the dining room and dropped the hammer on the table before heading out the front door into the fresh, delicious morning air. After all this excitement, Charlie needed a run through the trees. As he began down the driveway at a slow pace, he continued to giggle to himself. At the bottom of the driveway he took a right and headed towards the end of the street to run through the dense forest. At the end of the street just before the gravel became dirt, sat an old car. As he ran past, he glanced over and saw the car was empty. Unconcerned he continued his jog and disappeared through the trees.

After a few moments, the driver's seat lifted from a flat position and sitting there was Angus. He reached up and grabbed the rear-view mirror, moving it to see if Charlie was out of sight. As soon as Charlie was nowhere to be seen, he reached into the glove box and pulled out his revolver. He held it in his lap and stared at Charlie's home.

"I got you now, you son of a bitch," Angus whispered to himself.

41

Angus sat in his car for a few minutes, and once he felt it was safe, he jogged across the street. He reached the porch and grabbed the door handle, but it was locked. With his back facing the wall, he maneuvered swiftly around the right side of the house and made his way to the backyard. At the back of the house Angus noticed the windows on the second floor were wide open. It wasn't going to be easy, but it was a way in. Shooting up the side of the wall was a metal trellis. As quick as his large, older body could, he scaled the trellis and made his way onto the roof. He stayed in a kneeling position and slowly moved towards the open windows, removing the screen and stepping inside. He now stood in the master bedroom of Charlie's home. Knowing he had very little time he began searching every inch of the space. He opened the closet and looked around, then the dresser drawers and found nothing but clothing, underwear, socks. It was then he noticed the framed photo of Emma on top of the dresser. He picked it up and admired it for a moment.

Angus dropped to the floor and began looking underneath the bed. He noticed two frames with photos mounted inside that had been shoved underneath. He pulled them from under the bed and held them up into the air one after the other. The frames held photos of the previous owners of the home. Angus' cop senses began firing on all cylinders, wondering who these people could be. For all he knew, it was Charlie's family. But he wasn't sold on that theory. Angus knew he wasn't breaking into Charlie's home to find some old frames underneath a bed. He knew what he needed to do. He knew the vault he needed to crack. Holding his revolver up in his right hand, he moved slowly and quietly across the bedroom and out into the hallway. The house was silent and every step Angus took made the floorboards creak and cry under his weight. He moved as gently as he could until he got to the stairway. He grabbed the gun with both hands and aimed it towards the bottom of the stairs. Each step creaked and groaned as he walked. He leaned against the wall inside the stairwell and glanced around the corner towards the dining room. *"Coast is clear,"* He thought. Angus reached the door that led to the basement, grabbed the lock and pulled on it with all of his might.

"Dammit," He said out loud, smacking the lock into the door resulting in a loud clanging noise.

Just then, he heard a screech come from the basement, like metal being dragged across concrete. In the silent house, it rang out like a siren.

"Hello," Angus shouted. "Is someone down there?" He pressed his ear against the door, waiting for any reply, a sound, *anything*.

The house remained silent for a moment until Angus heard something that made his heart drop into his shoes.

"H-Hello?" A voice called out from behind the door. "Is someone there?"

Angus' eyes shot open wider than a full moon hanging in the night's sky. He began pulling on the lock with every bit of his strength, but it wouldn't budge. He looked around the house until his eyes landed on the dining room table. To his pleasant surprise, he noticed a hammer had been left there. He slid his gun into the back of his pants and grabbed the hammer, rushed back to the basement door and began pummeling the lock with all he had. The sound echoed throughout the house like gunfire, and after four heavy hits, the latch gave way and snapped out of the wood. Angus grabbed the knob and threw the door open. He dropped the hammer on the ground and reached into the back of his pants for his gun. He held it out in front of him ready to fire as he began carefully down the staircase. All he could see was darkness below him.

"Seattle Police," Angus shouted. "Is anyone down here?"

"Help me!" Eddie shouted. "P-please help me!"

Angus rushed down, his big feet clobbering the wooden steps as he went. He landed hard on the cement floor, jolting forward and hitting the cinder block wall. He reached out and flicked the light switch making the light bulb flicker and flash for a moment before the room came to life. Sitting there, chained up, covered in blood was Eddie.

"Oh my God," Angus shouted as he put the gun back in his belt and rushed to his side. "You're Eddie VanSant!"

"Yes I am," Eddie shouted back. "Get me out of here. Oh my god, how did you find me?"

Angus began pulling at the chains trying to find any way to loosen their grip on Eddie's body, but they were locked in so tight he couldn't get them to move.

"Don't worry about how I found you, let's just get you the hell out of here," Angus said through a shaking breath.

"Thank you God," Eddie shouted as he looked up towards the ceiling.

"God dammit," Angus shouted as he pulled on the chains. "He has these too damn tight, I can't get them off."

"Over there," Eddie shouted, motioning towards the workbench with his head. "T-tools. H-he has tools. Maybe you can find s-something to cut these off."

Angus looked at the workbench where many tools were scattered about. Past the workbench was a small closet with the door halfway open. He began rummaging through the miscellaneous tools on top of the bench.

"There's nothing here!" Angus shouted.

"The closet," Eddie yelled, motioning with his head.

Angus kicked the closet door open the rest of the way. It housed many big tools for gardening, home demolition and other various items set upon heavy, steel shelves. In the back of the closet Angus began moving items out of the way trying to find something, *anything*, that could be used to break those chains. Between two of the steel shelf units sat a big bucket and inside Angus found a pair of bolt cutters.

"Got it!" Angus shouted, as he ran back into the room holding the key to Eddie's freedom.

"I need to spin you around, I can't get behind you to cut the locks," Angus explained, his voice shaking like an earth shattering quake.

He grabbed the chair and turned Eddie around, the feet of the chair scraping and scratching as it went. Angus crouched behind him and began clutching the bolt cutters, pressing all of his weight onto them trying to get the padlock to snap free.

"I just, can't get it to *break*," Angus said as he clenched his teeth, eyes shut, trying to cut the lock.

Angus pressed so hard, he thought his muscles might snap. His entire body trembled as he pressed on the cutters, but the thick steel wouldn't give. The bolt cutters finally slipped, sending Angus crashing to all fours onto the cold cement floor.

"Son of a bitch!" Angus shouted, as he gathered himself and got back to his feet. "Let me try again."

"Hurry up," Eddie begged. "He can't find you here."

"Don't worry," Angus tried to assure Eddie. "I watched him run into the woods. He won't be back anytime soon."

Angus positioned the cutters on the lock and again applied pressure, but the padlock didn't wouldn't give. He began grunting and shouting, hoping his primal noises would boost his muscular ability by just the right amount and allow him to cut the hardened steel. Through the grunting and screaming, neither Eddie nor Angus could hear the soft, faint footsteps of Charlie sneaking his way down the stairs. Angus and Eddie were now facing the opposite direction, giving Charlie a clear path to sneak his way across the basement ever so quietly. Slowly, he took one soft step, followed by another, until he stood over Angus. Charlie slowly lifted the hammer up over his head and in one swoop, smashed Angus in the back of the head with the blunt end. Angus let out a loud gasp, as the oxygen in his lungs exploded out of his mouth and he fell flat onto the cold floor. Blood splatter sprayed Eddie on the back of his head, and burst into the air spattering Charlie's face with droplets. He stood over Angus' body, staring down at him with his familiar devilish grin.

"No, no, no!" Eddie screamed in horror, his head now turned as far as his neck would allow to see what was happening.

Angus had blacked out momentarily, and Charlie was shocked to see him come out of his daze so soon after the vicious hit. Angus reached his left arm out as far as he could, planting it onto the concrete floor and tried to pull all of his weight away from Charlie. With no strength to muster and no fight left, he pulled his body the best he could, but it was all for nothing. As he reached for the tail of his shirt, he exposed the handgun he had stashed in his belt. Charlie reached down and pulled it from the back of his pants and in one quick motion swung it down as hard as he could, pistol whipping Angus with the butt end of his own gun. Angus' body went limp instantly from the second blow. Charlie straightened up, took a couple of deep breaths and wiped his mouth with his right hand, now dripping in blood. A red smear now graced his mouth.

"You wanted me to kill you, right?" Charlie asked through labored breath.

"No, I-I, Wait," Eddie pleaded.

Charlie stretched his arm and pressed the revolver into the back of Eddie's head so hard, it pushed his chin into his chest. He held the gun there, not only wanting, but hoping, for Eddie to crack from the stress, from the fear, from the unknown. Charlie pulled the gun away and shoved it into the front of his jogging pants. He rushed to the utility closet and began rummaging through the scattered items. All Eddie could hear were the crashes and clanking of metal as he tore the closet apart, before emerging with a large mess of chains. He tossed the chains against the wall beside Eddie, grabbed Angus by his limp hands and dragged his heavy body across the concrete. Running along the wall the length of the room was a thick cast iron pipe. On the far end of the basement the pipe ran against the wall and took a turn, running up to the main floor of the home. Charlie released Angus' hands allowing his arms and face to crash to the ground. He began wrapping the chain around the cast iron pipe. Over and over he twisted the chain, wrapping Angus' body from his ankles up to his chest. When the chain length ran out, he clasped the two ends together with a padlock. From Angus' left pocket he removed a pair of handcuffs and slapped them onto his wrists.

"There we go," Charlie said as he stood up straight, breathing hard. "Look at that. Now you have a roommate."

"W-Wait," Eddie muttered as he cried softly. "W-Why are you d-doing this? P-please. Have some fucking mercy!"

"You want to know my big master plan?" Charlie asked through laughter. "Why not. I did promise we would have some fun didn't I? We can play the game your way."

Charlie knelt down in front of Eddie, pulled the revolver from the front of his pants and jammed it hard underneath Eddie's chin.

"I'm going to keep you here as long as I want. I'm going to torture you, and fuck with you, and make every minute of your life a hell so unimaginable you will beg for death to come and take you away. And then, just then, the real fun will begin," he said, staring deep into Eddie's eyes as they filled with tears.

"I'm going to take Emma from you. I'm going to take Sophie from you. I won't replace you. No, not replace you," Charlie said as he ran the barrel of the revolver up Eddie's cheek to the top of his head, and turned it in circles against his left temple.

"I'm going to provide Emma an *upgrade* from you," Charlie said as he stood up straight, pulling the gun from Eddie's head. "How's that for a big plan? Sound like fun to you?"

"You're a fucking monster," Eddie said as tears poured down his cheeks.

Charlie giggled to himself as he looked Eddie in the eyes, "You have no idea how much of a monster I can become."

Charlie turned and walked across the room, stopping at the bottom of the staircase. He reached his hand out to the light switch and turned back to Eddie.

"Once Emma forgets about you, that's when I will allow you to die. And not a single second sooner."

He flicked the light switch and the basement went pitch black.

"Have a great day, fellas," Charlie said as he walked up the stairs, slamming the door to the basement shut behind him.

42

Charlie knew his plan had strayed off course and had become much more complicated. So many thoughts raced through his mind as he worked to replace the latch and padlock Angus had smashed off. He knew he couldn't risk someone else coming into his house and getting downstairs. He had realized two things. One, it wasn't time to allow this evil plot of his to spiral any more out of control so he could stay the course with Emma. Second, he needed a nap. Once the latch had been replaced and a padlock had been clicked into place, he went upstairs and fell into bed. Before he drifted off, the words from Eddie rang through his mind. *"You're a monster."* He halfway laughed it off, but couldn't help but think to himself, *"Could only a monster take a nap at a time like this?"* The truth was, he didn't care. He laid there and let the fresh air wash over his body, shut his eyes, took a few deep breaths and drifted off into a refreshing sleep. The struggle from that morning clearly took more out of Charlie than he had realized, as he slept the entire day away. He finally woke up as the sun began to set, and the cool night air set in and he started to shiver from the chill. He reached over to the side table and picked up his cell phone to check the time and saw he had missed a text message from Emma. She was asking when he would be coming over for dinner and to watch the Mariners vs Yankees game. First pitch was scheduled for 7:10 that evening, and the hour hand had just clicked past 5:00pm. So he got out of bed and jumped into the shower.

At the top of the closet he was ecstatic to find an old Seattle Mariners ball cap. He tossed it on his head before he ran down stairs and out the front door. Before heading to the car, he locked the front door and checked both the knob and deadbolt twice. He was growing paranoid after that morning's encounter, and he knew he could not afford another run in with any intruder.

On the drive to Emma's, Charlie stopped into a local pizza joint to surprise her with dinner. A hipster pizza spot had caught his eye in town. He got lucky and found a parking spot on the street right in front of Piebrid Moments. A punk rock themed restaurant serving pizza by the slice and full pies. Charlie walked in through a wide open glass door, and was greeted by the smell of warm, delicious crust and toppings baking away in the giant, beat up silver pizza oven that sat far behind the main counter.

Loud punk music blared throughout the air and intertwined with the delicious scent creating a counter culture heaven. Punk inspired posters and art covered the crimson walls, from the Ramones, Rancid, NOFX and of course the Misfits, who had clearly inspired the name of the restaurant. Just inside the doors sat a worn out counter with a register on top. To the left was a display case with pre-cooked pizzas where guests could walk in and order by the slice. Charlie admired the pizzas inside and giggled at the names as his eyes danced around the display. Each specialty pizza was named after a well known song from a punk band. For a second he considered bringing one of the specialty pies for dinner. There were so many to choose from and they all looked and smelled incredible. From the Stickin In My Pie named after NOFX with pepperoni, sausage, green peppers, red onions and topped with ricotta cheese, to the Hungry and

Miserable, a reference to Black Flag loaded up heavily with salami, house meatballs, mushrooms and more fresh ricotta. But Charlie knew what he was there for, and he wouldn't be swayed by these majestic looking gut bombs.

"Hey, man," the clerk shouted. "What can I get for you?"

It was impossible to tell the employees from the customers. No uniforms, no name tags, not even branded shirts. This clerk wore a faded Motorhead shirt, black denim cut-off shorts and checkerboard slip-on shoes. Tattoos were scattered over his arms and a mop of hair struggled to free itself from underneath a flour covered trucker hat.

"Can I get a large plain cheese to go?" Charlie asked.

"We only serve one size man," The clerk said back. "It's a 16 inch pie."

"How many slices is that?"

"We cut our pies into 12 slices," He assured.

"That sounds perfect," Charlie said as he reached for his phone and money case.

"You want to add any of our noose knots to your order?" The clerk asked in the typical upsell tone.

"What the hell is a noose knot?" Charlie asked.

"Noose knots are our house garlic knots. Our pizza dough is twisted up like a rope and we brush them with clarified garlic butter and sprinkle them with fresh garlic. Served with our house ranch dip," The clerk explained.

"Sure, throw in an order of little nooses," Charlie agreed.

"You got it, one cheese pie and an order of noose knots. That will be 27 dollar straight up."

"27 dollars, huh?" Charlie asked with a hint of dissatisfaction. "Here you go. Keep the change," Charlie said, as he handed over 30 dollars total.

Charlie leaned against the faded crimson wall in the far corner of the pizza place as he waited for his order. He watched as different groups of people chowed down on those hearty, gut busting pizzas. People from all walks of life gathered together in Piebrid Moments. It fascinated Charlie. No matter where you go in the world, no matter who you are, pizza can bring everyone together. Having a bad day? Order a pizza. Celebrating an accomplishment or a birthday? Pizza party.

"Charlie!" A voice shouted from behind the counter. "Cheese pie and noose knots ready to rock!"

Charlie picked up the pizza box, which had another smaller box on top holding the garlic knots and a bag with ranch dip. He dropped the pizza and other items onto the front seat and was finally on his way. He arrived just in time for the first pitch. He made his way up the walkway and knocked on the door. It took no time at all for Emma to swing that door wide open. When her eyes met Charlie's they shined like the morning sun reflecting off of the top of a calm, beautiful lake. Charlie was lost in the sparkle.

"Well, well," Emma said. "Did you bring me dinner, Mr. Claymore? What a sweet guy."

"You can't watch a baseball game without a fresh pizza. I don't know if you know the rules or not. But I'm here to show you the ropes," Charlie said.

"I appreciate that, sir," Emma said with an awkward giggle.

"Should I put it on the coffee table? We can eat right out of the box. Unless you are too high brow for that," Charlie joked.

"Watch your tongue if you know what's good for you," Emma replied as she reached out and softly punched Charlie in his right bicep.

Charlie dropped the pizza and other items onto the table. He took a seat in the middle of the couch, not only for a good viewing location for the ballgame, but he hoped Emma would sit close to him if he were in the dead center. A solid plan, he imagined.

"Stay put, I'll grab us a couple plates and some napkins," Emma shouted from the kitchen.

"Hey, look at that, perfect timing. I didn't miss the first pitch," Charlie said.

The pregame show was wrapping up as two older men sat in suits at a high tech looking desk, spewing their opinions and what they considered expertise.

"What do we have here?" Emma asked as she entered, two plates in hand and a stack of napkins.

"Did someone say cheese?" Charlie said, as he lifted the flap to the box, showcasing the all cheese pizza inside.

Steam and a delicious, intoxicating scent of sauce, melted cheese and perfectly baked dough filled the air.

"Charlie!" Emma shouted as a smile filled her face and she put her hand on her heart. "You remembered!"

"Of course I remembered," Charlie assured. "How could I possibly forget?"

"We haven't eaten a pizza together since, what? High school? And somehow you remembered I only enjoy plain cheese."

"It's my specialty. I have a memory like a vault."

"But why would you ever *need* to remember that I only love plain cheese pizza?" Emma asked.

"For this exact moment, of course," Charlie said with a friendly smile.

"Well," Emma said while looking away coyly, "You've blown me away yet again."

"That was the plan," Charlie said, shooting Emma a wide, flirty smile. "Where's my little buddy?" Charlie asked, looking over his shoulder towards the hallway.

"She's staying the night with a friend," Emma said as she lifted a steamy, melting slice of cheese pizza to her lips. "I sent her away. I thought it would be nice if, I don't know," Emma stopped.

"What?" Charlie asked stupidly. He knew where this was leading, but like a shy teenager he wanted Emma to say it.

Emma took a bite and stared at the television as though she didn't hear him. It was almost like when Charlie and Emma were together, they couldn't help but somehow revert to their teenage ways. Butterflies fluttering in their guts, nerves on edge, sweating palms. The entire rollercoaster of young adolescent emotions were firing on all cylinders. Anything else in the world became secondary somehow. It was like nothing else mattered when their eyes met and the energy between them erased their memories of the lives they had created outside of each other. There was something intoxicating about Charlie that she couldn't resist.

"Emma," Charlie said with a slight, playful giggle. "What is it?"

"Oh," Emma bounced on the couch as though she had felt a slight electrical shock under her legs. "I thought it would be nice if we had a night alone. Just the two of us. You know?" She took another bite of her pizza slice, eyes opened wide and sparkling, she never broke eye contact with Charlie.

"I think that sounds fantastic," Charlie said. "Now let me get a slice of this delicious pizza."

Charlie lifted a slice in his left hand and sat back on the sofa, and with what seemed like natural movement, Emma fell back and landed perfectly under his right arm.

"Good pizza, huh?"

"*Very* good," Emma said, taking another bite and staring forward at the television.

Charlie's heart raced, like a thousand angry birds trying to escape a cage that was on fire. He knew Emma must have noticed it, hell, he could almost see the beats pushing his shirt out with every pump. After a few moments holding Emma, with his heart struggling to keep pace in an unwinnable race, he finally broke the silence.

"Do you remember back when we were kids?" Charlie asked. "Well, not *kids*. But, I mean, teenagers."

"Are you nervous around me, Charlie Claymore?" Emma asked, staring up at him with the cutest little smile, both adorable and mocking.

"Well no, I mean," Charlie said, stuttering. "I'm not nervous. I'm just thinking back to when we were younger. When we were so close."

"Yeah, I remember," Emma said, not looking away from the baseball game.

The pitcher from the Mariners had taken the mound in the top of the first inning and promptly allowed a base hit to the first Yankee hitter. After a couple throws over to first, checking the runner, he threw a low breaking ball to the hitter. The hitter squared up, sending the baseball up the middle of the diamond and the ball was picked up by the second baseman who tossed it to the shortstop for one out. The shortstop fired the ball to first, but the runner was called safe.

"Out!" Emma shouted, sitting up on the edge of the couch away from Charlie's outstretched arm. "He was out. All day out. Come on, blue!" Emma yelled.

"He looked out to me," Charlie said. "We'll have to check the replay."

"Check the replay!" Emma shouted at the TV. "I've got out. He *has* to be out."

The umpires all crowded around home plate for an official review. After a long review period, the umpires admitted to getting the call wrong, and called the player out at first base. So much for speeding up the game, right MLB?

"Out! I knew it!" Emma shouted, both arms raised.

With her arms above her head, she twisted her body towards Charlie and fell into him so they were chest to chest. She wrapped her arms around his neck and hugged him with ferocious intensity, as though her life had depended on keeping a grasp on him. Charlie wrapped his arms around her waist and fell back into the couch. Emma's body followed, as she nestled up into his chest, and found a comfortable place under his right arm yet again. This time, she rested her head on his chest, along with her open right hand. The butterflies began fighting with one another inside Charlie's belly, and for a moment, he thought he felt the same chaotic beauty arise within Emma. They sat silent, embracing one another and he had reserved himself to soak in every second of it. If she didn't want to rehash the past, he felt he could at least foster the present and future with her. He was right about the butterflies and birds as they were fighting within her, too.

As they sat cuddled in each other's arms, Emma's cell began ringing from the pocket of her robe. She let out a short sigh, shifted her position enough to reach inside and pull it out. She glanced at the screen momentarily before rolling her eyes and declining the call. She then tossed the cell onto the coffee table.

"What uh, what was that all about?" Charlie asked.

"Oh, nothing," Emma said, returning to her position under Charlie's right arm. "It's my brother, Billy. Probably calling to check on me, *again*."

"You don't want to talk to Billy? He's probably worried about you."

"He knows Sophie and I are fine. Besides, I have *you* to keep me company," She said in a sweet, friendly tone.

They sat for a moment in silence, as Charlie could feel her staring through him. As the feeling grew too strong to ignore, he looked down at her.

"I always thought I was going to marry you," Emma said quietly.

The sparkle in her eyes cut through him like a laser shaping a diamond. Those birds were no longer fluttering inside him - They were at war.

"I-I, uh, I always thought so, too," Charlie muttered nervously. "I always had such a crush on you."

"I know," Emma said, staring deep into his eyes.

"Oh, r-really?"

"It was pretty obvious. I was a teenaged girl, I wasn't stupid," Emma said with a smile.

"I probably wasn't very slick back in those days, was I?"

"No," Emma said with a short, shy giggle. "But that's OK. That's what teenage love is all about. Being nervous, unsure of yourself. All those emotions and hormones are pumping through us. My God, it's a wonder we all survived those days."

"I sometimes wonder why we didn't get married," Charlie said.

"Yeah," Emma said, her face washed over by a contemplative look. "I sometimes wonder about that, too. Where we would be, had we given it a real shot. But, that isn't how the cards were dealt."

Emma pushed on Charlie's body and sat up on the couch, leaning away from him. *"Had I said too much?"* Charlie wondered. *"Did I fuck all this up? What was I thinking?"*

"What's wrong?" Charlie asked, with his hands stretched out as though she was falling and needed to be caught.

"Nothing, it's nothing," Emma said, crossing her arms against her body.

"Did I say something wrong?"

"No, it's not that," Emma assured. "It's just. That isn't how life worked out. For either of us. I have Eddie and Sophie. You have Gwen and you're *so* happy. And I know Eddie will be found. I know Eddie will come home and I-I'm in *love* with him. I just feel, I'm just so lost right now. And having you around has been such a godsend for us. I'm just, I can't explain it, Charlie. I'm confused and sad, and unsure of myself lately. I'm sorry."

"Oh Emma," Charlie said with as much compassion as he could muster. "Don't ever apologize. I should apologize if I made you uncomfortable. I didn't mean anything by what I said. I was just remembering our past. Reminiscing, you know?"

"Don't be sorry. There was a time I thought we could have had something between us. Unfortunately, that time passed. But you mean the world to me and your friendship means the world to me. You aren't going to leave are you?"

"I would never leave you," Charlie said, reaching for her hand and lifting it to his mouth. He kissed the top of her hand and squeezed it.

Emma smiled at Charlie then leaned over to him, grabbed the side of his head and kissed his cheek.

They continued to watch the Yankees play the Mariners, as friends. They laughed and joked and screamed at the television together. In the end, the Yankees beat the Mariners 6-2, and after the game had wrapped up Charlie excused himself for the night. Emma walked him to the door, they embraced each other for a hug and Emma kissed him again on the cheek, thanking him for a much needed evening. As Charlie drove home, his rage grew like a wildfire. He couldn't have unleashed his intense anger on Emma. In the end, he knew exactly who to take his rage out on, and he knew exactly where to find them.

43

Charlie's anger poured out of him like a flood. He blamed Eddie for everything that had happened. In fact, he blamed Eddie for everything in his life. He was approaching the final spiral staircase of his sanity, and he no longer cared where it led. He was out for blood, and he would stop at nothing to get what he wanted. He slammed his front door so hard, a framed photo fell off the wall and shattered on the hardwood floor. He ran upstairs to the master bedroom. Under the bed he removed a small duffle bag. From inside he pulled out a Yankees baseball jersey, a Yankees baseball cap and a team foam finger. He threw the items on and rushed back downstairs, removing the lock from the basement door and pulling it open with immense force. He marched down the stairs like the GrandMaster in a World Series parade. He was so proud of himself, showboating down the stairs, hoping his childish mockery of Eddie's favorite team would shatter his spirit, just like Emma's words had shattered his own. He marched proudly to Eddie and stood over him.

"Let's go Yankees!" Charlie shouted as he paraded around. "Yankees beat the slimy Mariners, Eddie! What have you got to say about that?" He yelled and rubbed Eddie's face, still caked in dried blood, with the foam finger.

"Do you think I give a *shit* about that? Fuck you," Eddie shouted.

"Some fan you are," Charlie chastised. "I would be *pretty bummed* if my team lost."

Charlie began dancing around in front of Eddie, mocking him and hitting him repeatedly with that soft, foam finger.

"That's because you're a psycho," Eddie shouted with a courageous laugh.

"What did you fucking say?" All fun and games had stopped.

"Charlie," Angus said from across the room. "Please stop all of this. It has gone way too far."

"You shut the fuck up," Charlie shouted, pointing at him with the end of the foam finger.

"You're in such deep shit for all of this. Don't let it spiral any further," Angus pleaded.

Charlie picked up a roll of silver duct tape from the bench before he removed the foam finger and tossed it at Eddie's head. It was soft, and it bounced off of the top of his head and fell to the cold hard ground. He crouched down and began pulling long strands from the roll.

"I'm sick and fucking tired of you talking. All you do is fucking talk," Charlie said through clenched teeth.

He began wrapping tape around Angus' head. One turn, followed by another, until most of his face was covered by the silver tape. He then reached in and pulled the tape down from Angus' eyes so he could see what was to come. He stood up straight and approached Eddie, bending down in front of him so they were eye to eye.

"How would you feel about the fact I watched tonight's game with a very special someone?"

"Fuck you," Eddie said, his teeth clenched even harder. "Stay away from my *wife*!"

"*Your* wife?" Charlie shouted. "She won't be *your* wife for much longer. That I can promise you. As a matter of fact," Charlie rubbed his chin for a second as a demonic smile washed over his face.

Just behind him sat an old sawhorse. He pulled it across the floor so it sat in front of Eddie. He reached through the chains and yanked his left wrist a couple of times, freeing it slightly. Eddie screamed in pain as he pulled and twisted his arm.

"What the FUCK," Eddie screamed. "Please stop this! What do you *want*?"

"You're going to find out what I want, and you're going to find out right now!" Charlie screamed in his face.

He entered the utility closet and came out with a long extension cord, bent down under the workbench and plugged it in. He stood up holding the other end of the power cord and quickly plugged something into it. The room filled with the sound of a motor whirring out of control. He turned and slowly approached Eddie, his right hand over his head holding an electric bonesaw. He continued to turn it on and off repeatedly, as he moved slowly across the room. The scream of the motor shot chills down Angus and Eddie's spines. Angus shook violently on the floor, screaming through the duct tape.

"No, no," Eddie begged. "Please, whatever you're about to do—"

"You have something I want. Something I have *always* wanted. And it's about time I take it from you," Charlie said as he stood over him.

He reached down and grabbed Eddie's left wrist, slapping his hand down on the edge of the sawhorse. He bent all of his fingers so they were facing downward, so only his left ring finger rested upon the flat surface. On his left ring finger was a yellow gold wedding band. He grabbed the tip of his ring finger, held it in place on the sawhorse and placed the blade of the bonesaw at the base of his hand. He turned on the bonesaw, pressing it deep into Eddie's skin. The motor changed from a high-pitched whine to a low pitched moan as it sliced through the skin, the muscle and then the bone.

Eddie screamed harder, louder and more ferocious than he ever had. He could feel every layer of his hand being pulverized. Angus' eyes were as wide as they ever had been, as he tried to scream for help to no avail. Blood, muscle tissue and bone fragments shot around the room, splashing both Eddie and Charlie in the face, and coating their bodies with spatter. Charlie's face was inches from Eddie's as he laughed. The bonesaw ripped through his finger until it had been cut completely from his hand. The bonesaw motor slowed to a stop as he dropped it to the ground. Blood dripped from each of their faces, bodies, and drenched their clothes. Eddie's screams had fallen to a breathy howl and moan as the blood rushed out of his body. Charlie walked back to the workbench and picked up another torture device that was once your ordinary tool. This time, he approached Eddie with a welding torch. He clicked it on and the end of the torch glowed bright white and hissed.

"I would close my eyes if I were you," Charlie said, winking at Angus.

He pressed the hot torch to Eddie's hand, cauterizing the bloody wound and just when Charlie thought he had heard the worst scream possible from a human being, he heard one he never imagined come from deep within Eddie. He convulsed in the chair, shaking violently as the welding torch seared his skin. He removed the torch, shut it off and let it drop to the floor. Eddie had now passed out from the pain and shock. A human being can only take so much torture before they shut down. Eddie had surpassed that by a good measure, but even as strong as he thought he was, he was no match for this level of sickening torture. On top of the sawhorse sat Eddie's ring finger. Charlie picked it up, removed the gold wedding band and placed it on his own ring finger. He then tossed the dismembered finger on Eddie's lap.

"I'll take Emma's ring. You can keep your shitty finger," Charlie said.

He bent over, picked up the bonesaw and began dancing around the room, humming an unknown tune to himself. Angus watched in horror, as Charlie sang and danced in celebration. His own sickening bonesaw serenade. Charlie's descent into madness was complete. He danced and danced to a song no one else could hear. And then, out of nowhere he dropped the bonesaw to the floor, and without saying a word walked to the stairs. He got to the top and shut the door behind him, replacing the padlock on the latch. He then walked slowly up stairs to his bedroom soaked head to toe in blood, all the while admiring the gold wedding band on his finger. He entered the master bedroom a possessed man as he fell backwards onto the bed. He continued to admire his left hand before bringing it to his chest and resting it over his heart.

"I do," He said out loud. "I do."

44

Many Years Ago.

"Charlie, let's go! You'll be late for school," Jane Claymore yelled up the stairs. Jane was in her mid 40s and a stay at home mom to the Claymore family. She was tall, slender and attractive. A tight tank top hugged her thin body and a pair of athletic pants stretched down her long legs. A signature early morning ponytail bounced back and forth on the back of her head.

Charlie, at age 15, stood in the upstairs bathroom as he ran product through his dense hair. With a couple of passes through, he styled his hair just offset to the right with a slight wave in the front. He wore blue jeans and his favorite hooded sweater - A Blink 182 pullover. It was dark blue and had a printed picture of a dancing rabbit on the front. When his hair was perfect, he rushed out of the bathroom and bolted down the stairs. The Claymore house was a decent sized home in your typical 1990s suburban neighborhood. It sat at the top of a cul-de-sac amidst 300 other homes that looked identical. Peach tiled roof, green grass out front with a fruit tree planted in the middle of the lawn.

At the bottom of the staircase sat a large family room with a dining room table right in the middle. On the opposite end was the modest kitchen. Sitting at the dining room table were

Charlie's siblings, his younger brother of 9 years old, Samuel, and his younger sister of 12, Sarah. Samuel, with his dark brown hair resembling a large mess on the top of his round head and Sarah, a spitting image of their mother with pretty blond hair pulled back into a matching ponytail. They sat across from one another as they plowed through their bowls of cereal and a side of buttered toast. Charlie burst into the dining room like a firestorm, ripping his backpack out of the head seat of the table like he was extracting Excalibur from a stone.

"Hey, slow down there, cowboy," Jane shouted. "Sit down and have some breakfast."

"I'll be OK," Charlie assured her. "I'm meeting the guys to walk to school."

"What will you eat?" She asked.

"I don't know," Charlie said, surveying the dining room table in front of him. "How about I eat Sammy's *toast*!"

Charlie reached across the table faster than a cobra's strike, taking two slices of buttered white bread that sat on a small plate in front of his brother. Sammy reached out to block the steal, but was unsuccessful in his attempt.

"Hey!" Sammy shouted across the table. "Give those back, shithead!"

"Sammy!" Jane screamed from the kitchen. "Watch your language."

"Yeah, Sammy," Charlie replied. "Where did you even learn that? Who speaks that way?"

"You. I heard you on the phone and you called Ethan a shithead."

"That's because Ethan *can* be a shithead," Charlie confirmed.

"Mom," Sarah chimed in. "Can you tell these idiots to stop cursing at the table?"

"She's right," Jane agreed. "Quit cursing at the dining table. Or cursing *anywhere*, really. I don't like to hear that kind of language."

"I only said what I heard my big brother say!" Sammy said, throwing Charlie under a very large, speeding bus.

"You need to be a better influence on your siblings," Jane said, pointing across the room at him. "You shouldn't be speaking that way in front of them."

"Busted!" Sarah shouted in a mocking tone.

"You're right, I'm sorry," Charlie said.

"Thank you," Jane said as she turned her back to the kids, and began placing some clean cups into an overhead cabinet.

Charlie noticed she had turned her back, when he squished his face to mock his brother and sister, flipping them both off. One middle finger for each of them.

"Mom, he just flipped us *both* off!" Sarah shouted.

"Charlie!" Jane shouted, turning around and shooting daggers in Charlie's direction.

"I did not!" Charlie said, lying through his teeth.

"What did I *just* say to you? You need to be a better example."

"And you're right! I wish I could stay for this enlightening conversation, but, I gotta go," Charlie said, taking a big bite from one of the buttered pieces of toast.

"We're going to talk about this later!" Jane shouted to Charlie as he rushed out the door.

"I can't wait," Charlie shouted back.

He pushed the screen door that led from the kitchen to the garage. The garage door was wide open to the street, and Charlie picked up his pace, ran down the driveway and turned right at the sidewalk.

On the sidewalk next to a busy two lane road, walked Ethan and Ben as they made their way towards Lehner High School. Ethan and Ben were his two best friends. Ethan, a lanky kid who was abnormally tall for a 15-year-old, wore light wash blue jeans, Converse All Star sneakers and a pull over hooded sweatshirt decorated with characters from a cartoon show. His messy, unkempt hair looked as though it was fighting their own roots to escape. Ben, a short teenager with long blonde hair reaching his shoulders, wore a pair of wire-framed glasses, baggy blue jeans and a Nirvana t-shirt which was too big for him. Ethan held a magazine in his hands as Ben attempted to look around him to catch a peek. Charlie came up from behind at a full sprint.

"Hey, you assholes," Charlie shouted as he ran. "Wait up!"

"Damn, *there* you are!" Ethan yelled over his shoulder. "What took you so long?"

"I was getting ready," Charlie said as he caught up to the other boys. He huffed a bit, catching his breath.

"Dude, if we had waited any longer we would have been late," said Ben.

"Oh, bullshit," Charlie muttered through his short breaths.

"Says the guy who's out of breath from running," Ben joked.

"Whatever," Charlie said, waving his hand through the air as though he could block Ben's words like they were physical objects. "What the hell are you guys looking at?"

"Check it out!" Ben said, pointing at the magazine spread open in Ethan's hands.

"My idiot neighbor threw out the latest Playboy, and look who is on the cover!" Ethan said, closing the magazine.

"Holy shit," Charlie said, eyes wide. "The new Pamela Anderson issue? Let me see that!"

Charlie reached for the magazine, but before he could get his hands on this teenage grail, Ethan snapped it right out of his grasp.

"Keep your grubby hands off of it. You know how valuable this is? It's not everyday you find nudie mags just lying around the street. This is more valuable than *gold*!"

"Get outta here," Charlie said, waving Ethan off. "At least hold it where we can all see it."

"That's what I've been saying this whole time. He won't even let me look at it," Ben said.

"Bullshit, I said look with your eyes, not your hands," Ethan snapped back.

"Open it up then, let's see!" Ben pleaded.

"Alright. Just calm down," Ethan said.

Ethan flipped through the magazine to just the right section and there she was, Pamela Anderson. Every teenage boy's wet dream in the 90s, and every grown man's secret crush.

"Holy *shit*, dude," Ben said in shock. "I can't believe we're getting to see this! You need to protect this thing. Hide it in a *very* safe place."

"What do you think, Charlie?" Ethan asked, holding the magazine open in Charlie's direction. "I bet you didn't think your Thursday morning would start *this* exciting."

"The most excitement I get is hearing my brother and sister fight over Lucky Charms or Cheerios," Charlie said.

"Those are some lucky charms right there," Ben joked.

"No shit," Ethan agreed.

"Put that thing away before someone sees us," Charlie said.

"Who's going to see us?" Ethan asked.

"Don't be such a wuss," Ben said, equally, if not even more annoyed than Ethan.

"You idiot, Mr. Harrison is *right* there," Charlie said, pointing at the corner of the sidewalk.

Ethan and Ben looked up simultaneously as their eyes met with Mr. Harrison. Ethan slammed the magazine shut, dropped his backpack to the ground, and turned his back to the crossing guard.

"Oh shit, oh shit," Ethan said, nervousness growing in his voice.

"I told you, dumbass," Charlie said.

"I didn't realize how close we were," Ethan barked.

Ethan unzipped his backpack and savagely shoved the magazine deep inside the largest compartment, zipping it as fast as his hands could. He stood and threw his backpack over his right shoulder just as Mr. Harrison approached. Mr. Harrison was not only the morning crossing guard, but he was also the boys stickler PE Teacher. He was young and resembled a villain you might see on a ski slope in an 80s movie bullying nerds and chasing girls. He had muscles that ripped through his tight Lehner High t-shirt, high shorts, long flowing brown hair and wore those brightly colored neon Oakleys teenagers in the 90s assumed only Dads and weird Uncles bought.

"Good Morning, boys," Mr. Harrison said. "Everything OK?"

"Yes, Mr. Harrison," All three boys said together.

"What have you got there, Ethan?" Mr. Harrison asked.

"Huh? Nothing. Just some homework."

"Uh huh," Mr. Harrison said, clearly not buying his story. "I don't need to check your backpack, do I?"

"No!" Ethan shouted. "It was, uh, just some, uh, you know,"

"Take it easy, son," Mr. Harrison said, with a loud belly laugh. "You're all good. Now go on, get to class before I confiscate whatever it is."

"Yes sir," The boys said together.

Lehner High was a gigantic campus that had been built as most of the students would say, "Forever ago." Most students who had been born and raised in town had parents who had attended and graduated from Lehner. Right in the front of the school was the main office that sat on top of a small staircase. To the right of the main office was a vast grassy area where students ate lunch and congregated. Cutting through the middle of the grass was a concrete walkway stretching deep into the heart of the school. The walkway splintered out into different corridors which led to the many classroom buildings scattered throughout campus. Next to the grass opposite the main office was a gymnasium where the Lehner High Bobcats basketball, volleyball and other teams played.

"Hey, so are we all hanging out at your house this weekend?" Ethan asked.

"That's the plan," Charlie said. "That is, if you both want to get your asses beat at Goldeneye."

"Yeah right! I ran a train on your asses last weekend," Ben shouted with a sense of pride.

"That's because you cheat and only use the Golden gun, you wuss," Ethan barked back.

"If it's a part of the game, it isn't cheating," Ben said with a sly smile.

"OK, look. Whatever," Charlie said. "I'm going to science class."

"Class doesn't start for like, 10 minutes, dude," Ben said.

"He wants to run into Emma," Ethan said as he laughed.

"What the hell is so funny about that?" Charlie barked.

"How long have you been chasing her? Since like, 7th grade? Give it a rest," Ben said.

"Isn't she seeing that Chris dude?" Ethan asked.

"Supposedly," Charlie said, rubbing the back of his head and looking at the ground nervously.

"Give it up, dude," Ethan said.

"She's still my friend. She's a better friend than either of you ding-a-lings."

Ethan pulled his backpack around to his chest, unzipping it just enough to reach in and bring the Playboy out into the light of day.

"Is she a better friend than, say, Pamela?" Ethan asked.

"Put that away, you are going to get us all suspended," Charlie barked, putting his hands over the magazine.

"Chill out," Ethan barked back as he shoved the nudie mag back into the backpack. "Run along, little boy. Your *real* friend is waiting for you."

"You're right!" Charlie barked. "She won't call me names like you two. I'll see you guys after school."

"If you make us wait too long, we will leave without you!" Ben yelled as Charlie turned and walked down the concrete path. "And tell her boyfriend we said hi!"

Charlie lifted his right hand up shooting them a proud middle finger behind his back. At the end of the path, he turned left and headed down into the depths of the campus. On either side of the walkway sat long rows of classrooms. After passing two rows, he turned right into the third corridor. Each building stretched deep with three classrooms per building, all of which had sets of massive windows allowing one to see inside or out. Charlie walked about halfway down, before leaning against the peach colored stucco wall. He knew Emma walked this same way for her first period class, and as usual, he would wait for her to say good morning, talk, flirt. Whatever was in the cards. After waiting a short time, Emma appeared and walked towards Charlie. She had on tight, light washed jeans tucked into a pair of bright red suede shoes and a dark blue zip up hooded sweater. Her dirty blonde hair pulled into a neat ponytail at the back of her head, her big, bright eyes sparkling as the morning sun hit them. She noticed Charlie leaning against the wall and waved as a big, friendly smile washed over her face.

"Charlie!" She shouted, picking up her pace. "Good Morning, good sir."

"Hey, Emma, how's it going?" Charlie said back, acting as cool as he could.

"I'm OK. Another day at Lehner High. Boring as usual." She said as they shared a laugh.

"Can I walk you to your first period?"

"Of course," Emma agreed. "I would be offended if you didn't."

Charlie extended his left arm and Emma locked her right arm into his and they continued to walk together in that classic way.

"So," Charlie started in, nervousness peeking out of his throat. "Where's Chris this morning?" He asked to be nice, even though he didn't want to know, or didn't care. He was just happy he wasn't *there*.

"Who knows," Emma said, rolling her eyes. "I would rather hang out with you."

A smile grew on Charlie's face which he couldn't contain. He looked at the floor in an attempt to hide his clear joy.

"I prefer it this way, too," Charlie said, finally picking his eyes up from the floor.

"I figured you did," she said with a smile, hugging his left arm tightly. "Hey, this hoodie is soft. It feels like it would be *super* comfortable. Here, trade me."

"Trade you?" Charlie asked surprised. "I can't trade you hoodies."

"Come on," she said, her big, bright and sparkly eyes staring through Charlie, cutting his heart to ribbons. "You won't share your big, comfortable hoodie? Even with me?"

Charlie stared at the sky for a moment, almost as though he was fighting a gravitational pull from her eyes. He knew he wasn't strong enough to fight it. His stomach was fluttering as their eyes locked.

"I don't think yours will even fit me. It's tiny," he argued.

"Stop it," Emma said as she began unzipping her sweatshirt. "Don't be so pedestrian. Come on. Give it over, Mr. Claymore."

Emma pushed her small sweatshirt against Charlie's chest. Charlie rolled his eyes and began removing his own. Charlie's hoodie swallowed Emma's petite body as she slipped it over her head and slipped her arms through. The elastic bottom stretched down past her thighs, and the cuffs on the arms fell well past her fingertips. Charlie wrestled with Emma's hoodie for a moment before getting his arms through the sleeves, pulled it around his waist and zipped it up. Surprisingly he got it around his body, but the elastic bottom pulled way up above his belt, and the sleeves stopped somewhere above his wrists.

"See? It fits you like a glove. You look great!" She said as a smile stretched ear to ear.

"Clearly," He said sarcastically, lifting his arms up showcasing the sleeves stuck at his forearms.

"I think you look good. How do I look?" She asked as she swung around cutely like a ballerina.

"It's a little big, but I imagine that's what you had hoped for?"

"Now you get it," she said with a wink. "It's so comfy. I could fall asleep in it."

"Well don't get used to it," Charlie said. "We can swap back after school."

"I do not *think* so, sir," Emma said with a big belly laugh. "I think I might just keep it."

"What? Get outta here!"

"You agreed to trade. We can't turn back time. Don't tell me you want to go back on our deal," she said, punching him softly in the shoulder.

"OK, OK," Charlie finally agreed. "If it makes you happy, I'm happy."

"That's the spirit," she said.

Emma threw her arms around Charlie's shoulders, giving him a hug. Charlie wrapped his arms around her waist and held her for a moment.

"I need to get to class," Emma said. "See you after school?"

"Sure thing," Charlie agreed.

Emma turned from him and walked towards the end of the building where her first period class would take place.

"Emma! Wait up," Charlie shouted at her. "My friends are coming over this weekend to hang out. Would you want to, I don't know, come along?"

Emma turned to face Charlie, but continued walking backwards.

"Count on it, Mr. Claymore," she said, fixing her right hand into a gun, firing it with a wink.

She blew him a kiss, turned away and soon was out of sight as she entered the classroom. Charlie sat and smoldered for a moment, waiting for that blown kiss to land. He walked to his classroom with a mile wide smile. In his first period class, he could barely pay attention to the lesson occurring right in front of him. All he could focus on was Emma. He couldn't help it, as his body was wrapped by Emma's essence which haunted the hooded sweater. He breathed deeply, taking in the smells left within the threads. An intoxicating blend of sweet raspberry and watermelon emanated from every stitch. He wondered what body spray she must use to create that aroma. Whatever it was, he was happy it existed, and even happier she did.

45

Charlie had set up his Nintendo 64 in the family living room for a full day of Goldeneye on Saturday. At the time, Goldeneye was the most epic video game anyone could imagine. 4 vs 4 head-to-head death matches all based around James Bond.

"Ok Charlie," Jane said as she entered the room. "Don't disappoint us today. We're leaving you alone and letting your friends come over. I don't want to find the house trashed when we come back."

"Don't worry, everything is under control. I won't let those idiots ruin the house."

"Your father and I are trusting you today. I left some money on the kitchen counter so you and the guys can order a couple pizzas. You sure you don't want to come?"

"Sea World with my family? Or pizza and Goldeneye with my friends," Charlie said sarcastically, lifting and dropping his hands as though he was weighing his options. "I think I'll stay here. But thank you."

"Stay out of trouble. We'll see you tonight. Love you."

"Love you too, Mom. Have fun."

Charlie sat on the floor of the living room as he listened for the door to shut that led to the garage, as soon as he heard the family car kick into gear and pull out of the driveway, *"Freedom,"* he thought.

It wasn't long before he heard a knock at the door. He jumped up from the floor and pulled the door open to find Ethan and Ben. Ben wore a backpack draped over his right shoulder and Ethan was carrying a 12 pack of Cherry Pepsi.

"Let's get this show on the road, dorks," Ben shouted as he entered. "You nerds ready to get your asses beat?"

"Bullshit, Ben," Ethan said, handing the 12 pack of soda to Charlie.

"Cherry Pepsi. Great call," Charlie said.

Sitting on the carpet of the living room was a blue cooler filled with ice. Inside there was already plenty of soda, enough to keep three teenage boys wired for a week.

"So, are we going to get this bloodbath going or what?" Ben asked as he sat down in front of the tv, picking up a controller.

"Yeah, yeah, uh, absolutely," Charlie said, sounding nervous.

"What's wrong, dude?" Ethan asked.

"Nothing, no, nothing," Charlie continued.

"Alright dude, what's with you today? You can't be a weirdo on Goldeneye day," Ethan urged.

Just then, there was another knock at the door. Charlie rushed over as Ethan pulled back the blinds to see who was outside.

"Dude, you invited *Emma*?" Ethan asked.

"What the hell, man? Why did you invite her?" Ben asked, equally surprised. "You *know* she has a boyfriend, right?"

"Yes Ben, *I know* she has a boyfriend. What the hell does that matter?"

"I mean, it doesn't, really," Ben said, confused by his own worry. "I just don't want to see my friend bummed out."

"Don't worry about me. I want her here," Charlie said. "And you idiots like her. She's *your* friend, too."

"But we haven't been not so secretly in love with her since middle school, dude," Ethan said.

"Are you going to open the door or make her wait outside all day?" Ben asked. "Come on already, it's Goldeneye time. Quit prolonging your punishment."

"Shut the hell up," Charlie said as he reached for the doorknob.

He opened the door and couldn't hide his happiness, even if his life depended on it. Emma stood in the doorway glowing.

"Hey, you made it," Charlie said. "Come on in."

"So I *can* come in?" Emma asked sarcastically. "I thought you might make me stay outside."

Charlie moved out of the doorway, motioning with his arm for her to come inside. She stepped in and began looking all around, soaking in the decor and layout.

"Hey, guys," she said with a nervous wave.

They simultaneously said hello with a friendly wave.

"So what are you three troublemakers up to today?" She asked.

"Goldeneye tournament!" Ben shouted with excitement. "Are you in?"

"I'm here, aren't I? I'm so *in*," She said. "That is, if all three of you are looking to lose."

"Oh *shit*," Ethan said, covering his mouth. "Those are fighting words to Ben."

"Hey, hey," Ben said, dropping the controller to the ground. "I hope you are ready to put your money where your mouth is,"

"You guys bet on video games?" She asked.

"No, it's just a figure of speech," Charlie said. "Ben is an idiot, don't pay him any attention."

"I'll keep that in mind," she said.

"Where's Chris today?" Ben asked.

"See what I mean?" Charlie cut in. "He is an idiot."

"What did I say?" Ben asked, arms outstretched, confused.

"Don't pay him any attention, Emma," Charlie said under his breath.

"No," Ben said. "Pay attention to me."

"It's fine," Emma said. "I don't know, I haven't spoken to him."

"Really? You don't think he cares if you are hanging out with three other dudes?" Ethan asked.

"I'm not too worried about it," Emma assured. "I'm a big girl."

Charlie couldn't help but smile at the words coming from Emma's mouth. Chris may have been her boyfriend, but she chose to spend the day with Charlie. That fact was not lost on him.

"Are we going to get into Goldeneye anytime this *century*?" Ben asked, his patience wearing thin. "I know a couple people who like to talk *a lot* of shit, and not one of them has picked up a controller."

"I'm ready," Emma said as she turned to Charlie. "But first, a tour? I've never been to your house. I want to see the place."

"Oh, absolutely," Charlie said.

"*Come on* Charlie," Ben pushed.

"Take it easy, Ben," Ethan said as he sat on the floor. "You and I will play for now. Let them do their thing."

"Alright, I'll warm up by kicking *your* ass."

"Shall we?" Charlie asked, motioning with his arm behind Emma.

Charlie led Emma through his house, showing it off like he had built it. He could hardly hide how excited he was. They made their way upstairs and she began looking into each doorway curiously as though she was trying to find something. At the top of the stairs were four doorways. One leading to the upstairs restroom, the Master Bedroom and two smaller bedrooms. Down the hall to the left of the staircase was

Charlie's. It became clear what she was looking for was behind that door.

"Which one is *your* room?" Emma asked, an adorable smile gracing her pretty face.

"Oh, uh," Charlie stuttered nervously. "It's uh, t-that one right here. D-do you want to s-see it?"

"Of course I do," she said with a sneaky smile as she pushed the door open. "What did you think this tour was all about?"

Emma walked into his bedroom and began admiring the posters, trinkets and other items strewn about. The room was a decent size, equipped with a bed to the far left against the wall. Just past the doorway against the wall sat an old wooden credenza that was worn out from many years of use. On top sat a CD player with detachable speakers that resembled a spaceship with its shiny silver plastic casing and flashing lights. Next to the stereo sat 3 rows of CD cases that had been stacked without care. At the foot of the bed was a laundry hamper with clothes that appeared to be trying to escape to a cleaner, happier room. Next to the bed sat a small wooden night stand, on top of it sat a 90s era clear plastic wired telephone.

"So this is Charlie's bedroom, huh?" Emma asked.

"What do you think? Sorry I didn't really do much cleaning. I didn't, uh, well I didn't think you would see this." Charlie said with a nervous laugh.

"Don't even worry about it," Emma assured. "Trust me, my room is *much* worse."

"Really? Well, I-I would l-love to see that sometime."

Charlie immediately began rubbing the back of his head and staring at his feet. His face went bright red from his admission of wanting to visit her bedroom.

"I, I'm so sorry," Charlie could barely speak. Sweat began forming on his forehead. "I, I didn't mean it like that."

"It's ok," Emma said with a friendly smile.

Their eyes met and for a moment they both stayed silent, as the tension within those four walls grew stronger. Emma sat on the edge of the bed and set her hands on her thighs. After a moment in silence, she pushed herself so she landed on her back softly and began scooting herself closer to the wall. She laid on her side with her elbow resting on one of Charlie's pillows, using her palm to hold her head up.

"*Very* comfy, Charlie," she said, her eyes flirting more and more.

"Yeah, you know."

Charlie found it increasingly difficult to speak, as his nerves were firing off like the grand finale of a fireworks show. "It, uh. It does the trick."

Emma continued to gaze into Charlie's eyes from her lying position and with her right hand began patting on the bed, motioning for him to come closer. He nervously walked to the bed and sat. He looked back over his right shoulder so he could see Emma in his peripheral vision.

"What's wrong buddy? Come on, talk to me."

"Nothing at all. I'm uh. I-I'm just glad you're here," Charlie said nervously as he rubbed his sweaty palms on his jeans.

Charlie continued to pat his knees and let out a long, drawn out breath. Emma's eyes were fixed on him, accompanied by a permanent smile that washed over her pretty face.

"Calm down," she urged. "What's the problem?"

"N-no problem. Just, you know, make yourself at home."

Emma took in a deep breath and released it loudly as she reached for Charlie. She grabbed him by the right shoulder and pulled him towards her until he finally gave out and laid next to her. She continued to gaze down at him as his nervousness reached peak levels.

"See, that wasn't so painful, was it?" She asked with a sweet smile and a flutter of her eyelashes.

Emma took in another deep breath and as she released, she dropped her head gently, laying it upon Charlie's chest. She then let out yet another sweet sigh, as though she was relieved, comfortable, safe. She reached across his body with her right arm and wrapped it under his waist.

"Why have we never done this before?" She whispered.

"I-I, don't know," his heart was fighting his ribcage to free itself. "Not that I haven't wanted to."

"Same here," she confirmed.

Charlie couldn't believe his eyes or ears. He felt like he was dreaming. Emma lifted her head and rested her chin on his chest and stared directly into his eyes.

"You know, I could just take you right now. You know that right? Just," she stopped herself and looked around the room nervously. "Just make out with you."

"You don't want to do that, do you?" He asked with a stupid giggle.

"I don't know," she said. "Do you?"

So many thoughts, words and emotions raced through Charlie's brain. He had a Formula 1 race occurring just behind his eyes. Just as the words found the escape from his throat, they were interrupted as Ben rushed up the stairs, bursting into the room.

"Hey, Charlie," He shouted as he approached. "You have a couple boxes of pizza rolls. Can I heat them up?"

He was stopped dead in his tracks as he rushed into the bedroom to find Emma snuggled up with Charlie.

"Whoa," He shouted, as he dropped the box of pepperoni pizza rolls onto the carpet. "Oh, uh, shit. I'm sorry. Uh, I'll leave you guys alone."

"No, hey, Ben," Charlie shouted, as he jumped up out of bed to his feet. "It's cool, dude. It's cool. We were uh, we were just about to head back down. Right Emma?"

"We sure were," Emma said, still laying on the bed staring at Charlie.

"Alright, then," Ben said as he reached for the box of snacks. "So, about those pizza rolls?"

"Take whatever you want. I don't care," Charlie said, his frustration beyond apparent.

Charlie imagined Ben probably didn't care about what he had just seen, so long as pizza rolls were involved. Like many situations in life, he thought to himself, *"Thank God for pizza rolls."*

"Ok then," Charlie said as he rubbed the back of his head. "Shall we get going?"

"To be continued?" She asked.

"Of course. Uhm, absolutely," Charlie blurted out, blushing more than he ever had.

Charlie moved back to the side of the bed and sat down on the edge. He took a deep breath, held it for a moment before releasing it loudly. Emma jumped up to her knees and hugged him from behind. She gave him one, long kiss on his right cheek and whispered into his ear.

"I am going to marry you one day, Charlie Claymore," she whispered. "It is written in the stars. It is our destiny."

And in a flash, Emma jumped off the bed to her feet and was gone. Charlie was in shock, feeling like he had just witnessed a car crash.

"Come on," she urged. "Let's go get some of those pizza rolls before Ben eats them all."

46

Present.

Charlie woke the next morning to the sound of his cell chiming over and over on the table next to his bed. He pushed himself up, sat with his back against the wall and lifted his hands to rub the sleep from his eyes when he noticed his hands were still caked in blood. He hadn't washed up or changed clothes before falling asleep. It was then he remembered he was covered in Eddie's blood, leaving dried, cracking stains all over his body. He still had Eddie's wedding band on his ring finger. It, like the rest of his body, was doused in dark, thick, dried blood. He reached for his cell phone and flicked the touchscreen. He had a few messages from Emma. They read as follows -

"You know, Charlie. Every time we get together it's at my house. I don't think that's fair."

"Next time, I want to come see YOUR house, Mr. Claymore. And I won't take NO for an answer."

"How about tonight? Consider it a date. AND YOU'RE COOKING! Reply with your answer below. YES or YES."

"Well, this just got interesting," He thought to himself.

Many thoughts began racing through his head about Emma visiting. *"They're locked up,"* He thought. *"What's the harm?"* He rose out of bed and made his way to the bathroom, vigorously washing his hands and face. Dark crimson liquid filled the sink, splattering the counter and the mirror. After a long period of scrubbing, he reached for the towel, ran it under the hot water and began scrubbing the bathroom. If Emma came over, he couldn't have blood spatter all over his bedroom. He pulled his t-shirt carelessly over his head and removed his pants, shoving them deep into a hamper. As he walked across the room to the closest for a fresh set of clothes, he stopped and looked over to the dresser, the framed photo of Emma still propped up. He snatched it, opened the top drawer, and tossed it in. Once he was dressed in fresh clothes unsoiled by a literal bloodbath, he rushed downstairs and into the kitchen. Again, he emptied 2 packets of dried oatmeal each into 2 separate bowls before filling them with piping hot water. He set the bowls down on the floor, unlocked the padlock and removed it from the steel latch. He then retrieved the steaming bowls and made his way down stairs.

"Rise and shine, boys," He shouted as he stomped loudly down the stairs. "It's chow time."

Eddie could barely lift his head, his chin buried deep into the middle of his chest. Angus glared at him in agonizing pain through the silver duct tape still wrapped around his head, face and mouth. First, he knelt down in front of Eddie. He scooped up a big helping of the instant oatmeal and pushed the spoon towards his mouth. Eddie painfully lifted his blood soaked head as high as he could, clinging to what life he still had left. He glared into Charlie's eyes with so much hate that had Charlie's frozen heart not been surrounded by cement, the stare alone would have melted him.

"Come on, you need to eat," Charlie said, pushing the spoon again towards Eddie's mouth. "Don't be proud. Just eat the damn oatmeal."

Reluctantly, Eddie opened his mouth and accepted the food. He slowly chewed the mushy grains and swallowed. Charlie then scooped another generous portion and gently put the spoon back into his mouth.

"See," Charlie said as though he was feeding a toddler mushy peas. "Not so hard, now is it?"

Charlie dropped the bowl onto the concrete floor, looked Eddie in the eye with a smile and leaned in real close. He pressed his mouth against Eddie's left ear.

"Don't worry," He whispered. "All of this will end soon enough." He tapped his open palm on Eddie's right thigh like a coach pepping up a nervous player.

Charlie turned to look at Angus and let out a frustrated sigh. Charlie knew if Angus got his hands on him, he could kill him.

"Now to you," Charlie said. "I don't even know if I want to feed you. But, I can't have you dying of starvation."

Charlie approached, knelt down real low and leaned in so their faces touched.

"When you die. I want to make that shit count," He whispered. "When that day comes I am going to get a serious workout, won't I buddy? I will probably need to cut you into pieces to even drag your big ass out of here."

He pulled the duct tape without care. He scooped up a spoonful of the mushy oatmeal and pushed the spoon to his face.

"I don't want that shit," Angus barked.

"You're going to eat one way or another. Even if I have to rip your mouth wide open and pour it down your *fucking* throat," Charlie barked.

Angus obliged, fearing what Charlie was capable of. After the show he had put on the night before, he figured he was capable of the unimaginable. He opened his mouth just wide enough for the spoon to fit inside, as oatmeal smeared over his lips. He chewed slowly and swallowed them down.

"They will get you for this. For *all* of this," He stopped himself, and attempted to adjust his position, letting out awfully painful grunts with every move.

"No," Charlie said, shaking his head and smiling. "They won't."

"Eventually you will slip up. They all do. Smarter people than you have done worse, and they have all been caught. It's when they get cocky, they slip. And you are one of the most cocky mother fucking pieces of trash I have ever witnessed," He said. "It's only a matter of time."

"Is that so," Charlie said, biting his bottom lip. His rage began to boil up once again.

"That *is* so. You think you have this all figured out. But we can both see it in your eyes. We can smell the fear on you. You're scared. You're in too deep and you don't know how to dig yourself out. Let us go before this goes any further. It doesn't have to be this way."

"No, it does have to be this way," Charlie told him. "You see, tonight everything falls into place."

"What do you mean? What exactly is your plan?"

"You would love all the gritty details, wouldn't you?"

"Call it the cop in me."

"Ok," Charlie said, dropping the spoon into the bowl and setting them both down onto the floor. "Let's try this on for size. You think *I'm* scared? In over my head? That you and your cop buddies will *get me*? Please. I know you and your partner investigated that murder in Eddie boys neighborhood. I saw you there. I talked to you outside her house. And look at me? Still a free man."

"Wait, what are you? No. How could you? Why?" Angus asked as his brain spun out of control, realizing Charlie had in fact murdered Mary Hart.

"That's right," Charlie said, nodding his head. "I killed that bitch. And you didn't *get me*. And how scared I must have been, standing outside the crime scene. You think I am scared? I'm made of fucking stone. It's *you* who is scared. You have been scared all your life. And right now, you're terrified, and that's how I like you."

Charlie reached for the roll of duct tape, picked it up and tore off a long piece. He reached out for Angus and slapped it across his jaw, pressing it tightly over his mouth.

"Let's take the same precautions with you, huh Eddie? I am going to need you both to be especially quiet this evening," Charlie said, as he let out a deep belly laugh.

He stood and tore off another long strip, stretching the tape out and slapping it over his mouth and pressing it on tightly. Angus had twisted and turned in his tied up position, forcing the chains to smack into the iron pipe continuously. It sent a high pitched pinging sound echoing through the home.

"I had a bad feeling about you," Charlie said as he reached into the back pocket of his jeans. He removed a syringe and held it up into the air. "That is why I was prepared with a fail safe. I knew I couldn't trust you."

He bit the end of the syringe and removed the orange cap, spitting it onto the floor. He then shoved the needle into Angus' left arm before doing the same to Eddie.

"There," He said, with a terribly creepy smile. "Now we can have a nice, quiet evening. Feel free to sleep the day away boys."

He turned and walked towards the staircase with extra confidence in each step. When he reached the base of the stairs, he turned back to Eddie.

"I don't want either of you making much noise tonight. Emma wouldn't like knowing you two are down here chained up. So," He said, lifting his finger to his lips, letting out a soft shushing noise.

Eddie sprang to life and began rocking the chair back and forth violently, thinking maybe he could escape somehow. Charlie watched and laughed as he rocked back and forth and calmly walked up the stairs, leaving them darkness. When he reached the top of the stairs, like so many times before, he shut the door and replaced the latch. In one quick motion, he snapped the padlock shut and turned away. Though this time, somehow, Charlie didn't notice that the lock didn't engage. The padlock hung there, wide open, for anyone to walk right into his basement of horrors.

47

Charlie spent most of the day shopping. He hoped tonight could be the night Emma finally slipped away from Eddie and when she did, he would be there to catch her. He had planned out what promised to be an incredible meal; Roast chicken in a red wine sauce on top of creamy, cheesy polenta. On the side, a beautiful summer salad with fresh cut vegetables and a homemade vinaigrette. He was ecstatic, as the tomatoes for the evening's salad had come directly from the garden out back. *"Margaret and Jerry made great fertilizer,"* He thought to himself. The tomatoes were big, vibrant and exploded with flavor. *"What Emma doesn't know won't kill her,"* He thought. This was all new to him, but he planned on pulling out all the punches this evening. He would make it perfect. He had ransacked the home and found some candle holders and some beautiful white candles for ambiance. He began preparations, following the recipe carefully. Everything had to be perfect. Any hiccup threatened his final act. He stood over the stove as a cast iron skillet heated up with a drizzle of olive oil. He dropped bone-in chicken thighs onto a cutting board and gently sprinkled salt and pepper onto the skin side. He picked up one, followed by the second dropping them into the piping hot cast iron and the chicken screamed and sizzled in the hot oil. Just then, he heard a knock at the door. He grabbed a hand towel, rubbed his hands clean, swung the towel over his right shoulder and opened the door. Emma stood on the stoop holding a bottle of red wine. She was wearing a white and blue striped button up collared shirt tucked into skin tight, lighter wash jeans. Her hair was done up in her cute, signature ponytail.

"Well, well, well," Charlie said with a smile. "If it isn't Emma. Come on in."

"Thank you, kind sir," Emma said as she entered. "I brought this for you. Well, for *us*."

"Oooo," Charlie said as he admired the bottle. "What have we got here?"

"Just a little something, nothing fancy. I thought it would be nice to have a little red with dinner. Or maybe an after dinner drink. Maybe *both*."

"I like the way you think," Charlie said. "Sheridan Cellars Pinot? I have never heard of this one. Is it any good?"

"Absolutely," she assured. "It isn't expensive or anything so don't get too excited."

"Good is good if you ask me," He told her. "I don't care what the price is."

"Smells good in here," Emma said, her nose wrinkling as she sniffed the deliciousness twirling throughout the air.

"Oh shit," Charlie shouted as he turned and burst back into the kitchen. "The chicken!"

"Don't ruin dinner!" She shouted.

Charlie got back just in time to reach into the cast iron skillet with a pair of metal tongs and flip the chicken. He sprinkled again with a light dusting of salt and pepper, grabbed the towel from his shoulder and wiped his forehead.

"Are you going to show me around?" Emma shouted from the hallway.

She walked around the home soaking everything in. Now that she was finally inside, she wanted to see it all.

"Absolutely," Charlie shouted from the kitchen. "Just give me one second. I don't want to mess this up and end up having to order Chinese."

"Can I show myself around?"

"Be my guest," Charlie shouted as he lifted the chicken with the tongs, checking to ensure it was transforming to a perfect, golden brown.

"There we go," Charlie said out loud, proud of himself.

He lifted each piece of chicken from the skillet and placed them onto a baking sheet. He squeezed half a lemon over each before placing the baking sheet into the oven. He then grabbed a bunch of green onion and over a plate, took a pair of kitchen shears and began cutting the strands into small pieces as a garnish.

"How was your day? Anything eventful?" He shouted.

"Not really," she said as she walked through the living room.

"Same here," He shouted to her. "Spent most of the day shopping. Otherwise, I just relaxed. Sometimes it's nice to have a do nothing day."

"I'm with you. That's all I do these days. Nothing. Well, of course I take care of Sophie but, you get my point."

Emma stepped back into the hallway when she noticed the latch on the door that led to the basement. She reached out and flicked the padlock. She stared at it, confused, and then peaked towards the kitchen. Charlie was out of sight, so she twisted the padlock and lifted it out of the latch. She wrapped her hand around the knob and began turning it slowly. All the while, a playful mask appeared on her face.

"I hope you're hungry," Charlie shouted.

"I'm starving," She answered, removing her hand from the knob, like a child who had been caught with her hand in a cookie jar.

She waited a moment, and slowly reached for the door knob yet again and turned it, pulling the door wide open. She looked down and saw a staircase leading to infinite darkness. She stuck her head in, trying to get an idea of what might be at the bottom of those stairs. She looked towards the kitchen again noticing Charlie was still out of sight. She took a soft step inside, then a second. Quietly she began the descent into the basement.

"This recipe was a little more advanced than I was prepared for, but for you, it's worth it," Charlie shouted. He got no answer. "Emma? You there?" He shouted.

No answer.

He grabbed the towel from his shoulder, wiped his hands and walked into the hallway. He noticed the basement door was wide open, and Emma was nowhere to be seen. Like a bolt of lightning he rushed to the doorway, tossing the kitchen shears onto the dining room table as he went. There he saw Emma halfway down the stairs.

"NO!" Charlie screamed. "Don't go down there!"

Emma was startled by the intensity of his scream and stopped dead in her tracks. She turned around slowly, cowering.

"*What the fuck*?" She shouted.

"You don't want to go down there," He pleaded.

"Why not?" She asked, as her face and tone grew concerned.

"Trust me," He said, both of his hands up, motioning for her to stop.

"You don't think I've never seen a creepy basement before?"

"It's not that," He said, searching the deepest parts of his mind for any excuse that could be even remotely believable. "It's a gigantic mess down there. I'm incredibly embarrassed."

"What do you mean?" She asked, her face squished in confusion.

"Just, please?" He begged. "Come back up the stairs, please? Do me this *one* favor."

She turned and looked back towards the bottom of the staircase. She could see the concrete floor only a few steps away. Charlie felt like his heart was about to burst inside of his chest. Sweat poured from his forehead as his outstretched hands trembled. Just then, Emma took a deep breath, let out an annoyed sigh, turned back around and began walking up the stairs.

"Geez," she said as she passed him in the hallway. "No reason to freak the fuck out."

"I'm sorry," He said. "It's just such a mess. I wouldn't want you to judge me."

"I wouldn't judge you by a messy basement," she said. "Basements are supposed to be messy. That's why they're underground. That's where everyone puts the shit they don't want to deal with."

"I'm sorry I shouted at you," He said.

Charlie let out a nervous laugh and wiped his forehead. Feverishly, he reached for the padlock and locked it in place.

"Would you mind helping me finish dinner?" He asked.

"I thought you were cooking *me* dinner?" She asked, with her hands on her hips like an attitude filled child.

"I *am* cooking for you," He said. "But it could be fun. Cooking together."

She stared at him for a moment with an annoyed look on her face. Soon, she broke character and smiled.

"That does sound like fun. Let's get cooking."

48

Frank knocked on the door to Captain Maya's office, opening the door as he did so. She had called Frank in, as her patience was growing thin with the VanSant case.

"You wanted to see me, Captain?" Frank asked.

"Yes, come inside. Take a seat."

Frank came in and let out a deep sigh as he sat. It was almost never good to be called into the Captain's office.

"Where do we stand with this Eddie VanSant situation?" She asked.

"We're still working on it, Ma'am. But I assure you, we're being vigilant."

"Have you found *anything* new and relevant to this case? What about this Charlie Claymore Angus was so obsessed with?"

"We've got nothing on him," Frank said. "All signs pointed to a dead end. Turns out he's just a good friend of the wife."

"We need to get somewhere on this case, Frank. We can't have this looming over us any longer."

"I completely agree. In fact, I'm heading down to the garage shortly to meet with someone named Patrick Miller. He reached out to us. Apparently, he had car pooled with Eddie a couple days prior to his disappearance."

"You think he might know something?"

"Possibly. I want him to look at the car."

"Why the car?" She asked.

"I know it's a little out of the box, but I feel like that might be just what we need. If he rode in the car often, maybe he would notice something we missed. A snag, a tear, a stain that wasn't there before. It's definitely a Hail Mary, but it might be all we have left."

"Let me know if you find or hear anything. They want this case figured out. We need to pick up the pace."

"You got it, Captain," Frank said. "I'm on it."

Frank stood up and turned to leave the room. Before he could leave, Maya got his attention.

"Have you heard from Angus? How's he doing?" She asked.

"No, I don't know," Frank said. "I just hope he's taking a mental break from everything. He needed it."

"He sure did," Maya agreed. "If you hear from him, tell him we're all thinking of him and look forward to him returning."

"Will do, Captain," Frank said. "I'll let you know what we find with the car. We really could use a break."

• • •

Frank waited patiently for Patrick Miller in the underground garage. He knew meeting with Patrick was nothing short of a long shot, but he hoped maybe he might get lucky and Patrick would notice something the investigators hadn't. The elevator doors to the underground garage opened, and out walked the guest of honor. Patrick Miller was a co-worker of Eddie's at the Paramount Theater. He was short and upon first sight, Frank assumed he was older than Eddie. Salt and pepper hair rested on the sides of his head, the top thin and wispy. A plain white tee sat over his belly and tan slacks stretched down his legs to a pair of old boots. He approached Frank who stood next to Eddie's car. All the doors, the hood and the trunk had been opened prior to his arrival.

"You must be Patrick. I'm Detective Frank McKenna. Thank you for coming down. We could really use some help, if you can tell us anything it would be greatly appreciated."

"Not a problem," Patrick said, extending his hand and returning the handshake. "What is it you want to know?"

"You worked with Eddie, correct? What was the work relationship like exactly?" Frank asked, pulling a notepad and pen from inside his sport coat.

"We work together quite a bit," Patrick corrected him. "I work in the maintenance department doing set building, lighting, setting up and tearing down for events."

"How did you know Eddie? From both of your time at the Paramount?"

"I work with his department," Patrick said. "When they book an event, they come to us with the details and we make them happen."

"And recently Eddie began giving you a ride to work?"

"He heard my wife's car was having some issues and I was letting her use mine. So, he offered to pick me up now and then. He's a nice guy."

"How often did you get a ride to work with Eddie?"

"Not every day," Patrick confirmed. "A couple times a week."

"Did you ride with him the day of his disappearance?"

"Not that day, no," Patrick said. "Unfortunately."

"Why unfortunately?"

"I can't help but think maybe if I was there this wouldn't have happened. Maybe I could have helped."

"Well, we wanted you to come down and look through the car and see if you noticed something that maybe we hadn't.

Stains, tears in fabric or anything out of the ordinary. Can you do that for us?"

"Sure," He confirmed. "I would be happy to help. I just hope you find Eddie and bring him home safe."

"That's our hope as well," Frank confirmed.

Patrick was given latex gloves and covers for his boots. He started in the back seat looking over the fabric on the seats, the roof, and console. After checking, he looked at Frank and shot him a shrug. He then got in the front seat and looked over the dash, the chair, looked over the passenger seat, checked the dials behind the steering wheel. Again, he shot Frank a shrug.

"I don't know what to tell you, Detective," Patrick said. "It all looks normal to me. Nothing really jumps out as any different than the last time I was in the car."

"Damn," Frank said. "Thank you for your time. We're exhausting all of our resources to bring Eddie home."

"I hope you guys find him soon," Patrick said. "Actually, there is one thing I noticed."

"What's that?" Frank asked, staring at his notebook, almost disinterested.

"His parking pass is gone," Patrick said.

Frank's eyes shot open like they had springs attached.

"What did you just say? Something about a parking pass?" Frank asked.

"He had a parking pass hanging from the mirror. We all got one for the garage. But Eddie's is gone," Patrick said nonchalantly.

Frank began frantically flipping through his notebook. He remembered Angus telling him about the parking pass in Charlie's car. His fingers couldn't move fast enough to flip back through the pages to that day.

"The parking passes they give you," Frank said, his voice trembling. "Would those be City Star Parking permits?"

"Yeah," Patrick confirmed, a confused look washed over his face. "How'd you know?"

"Oh, fuck," Frank muttered. "Thank you, you've helped more than you will ever understand."

"What exactly did you just find out?" Patrick shouted.

"I think I know where Eddie is." Frank said, as he turned and ran towards a service elevator.

Frank began smashing the buttons of the elevator as if his life depended on it. The elevator doors swung open, and he rushed in, pressing the button for the first floor. He pulled his cell phone out and began dialing.

"911 Emergency," The voice said.

"This is Detective Frank McKenna," Frank shouted, flipping frantically through his notebook. "I need all units dispatched *now* to 825 Lochwood. I know where Eddie VanSant is."

49

Charlie stood above the counter as he chopped up brightly colored fresh greens and tossed them into a large bowl before slicing the tomatoes from the garden. Emma sat at the dining room table admiring him as he worked. He glowed as he looked over at her staring in adoration of him. It made him go crazy, and for the first time, he felt like he had what he always wanted. It felt like Emma and him were a couple, living a beautiful life in a nice home, preparing a home-cooked meal. For these moments he lived the perfect lie. The dining room table had been set in preparation for dinner with two settings placed perfectly with silverware wrapped in white linen. A white table cloth had been placed and four candles stretched high into the air. Emma lit each candle and the flames flickered and danced off the walls.

"I hope you're hungry," Charlie said, a proud smile on his face. "You're going to lose your mind over this food, I guarantee it."

"Oh you guarantee it?" Emma asked.

"Count on it. You're going to love this meal so much that you might ask to move in here."

This comment threw her off, and it was clear by the look on her face. It was clear, they may not be on the same page about where this evening was headed.

"Move in here? With you?" She asked. "Why would I move in *here*?"

Charlie had to think quickly to throw her off the scent. He could never let on to Emma. So he shifted gears as fast as his brain would allow.

"I was just playing," He said with a giggle. "Don't be silly. I-I was just making a stupid joke."

He wanted to preserve the lie as long as he could while he broke her down, made her comfortable, weaseled into her heart and made himself a home. But the lie didn't last long, as Emma shifted the conversation, unknowing that Charlie would do anything he could to prevent it.

"Eddie was a pretty good cook," she said, "I've missed his home-cooked meals. Having to do it all myself lately has been, *blah*."

"Is that so?" Charlie responded.

"He did a lot of things around the house. Good husband, good *friend*. *Great* father to Sophie."

"Good to hear," Charlie said, frustration growing inside of him.

"I haven't heard from those detectives in awhile. I can't believe they haven't found him yet. It's killing us not knowing if he is alive or dead or if he's ever coming home," Emma said, dropping her head and becoming increasingly emotional.

"I'm sure they are doing everything they can," Charlie said.

"I need to call them," Emma said, as she reached for her purse. "Maybe I should call now. I can't think of anything else."

"No," Charlie shouted. "I-I mean, it's getting late. Maybe you should call first thing in the morning. Y-You don't want to bother them at home."

"I don't really care," she said.

She found Angus' number, pressed "call" and the other end began ringing. Charlie stood in the kitchen, eyes wide as a planet as his heart pounded. *"Did I take his cell phone?"* He thought. *"What the fuck did I do with it?"* He wondered. The other end rang and rang until it landed upon voicemail.

"Ah, voicemail, " Emma said.

"What did I tell you?" Charlie said, pointing the end of a large chef's knife in her direction. "Call in the morning."

"You're probably right," she said, nodding her head and setting her phone down on the table. "That chicken really does smell fantastic. It reminds me of a dish Eddie used to make. You know how smells can take you back to certain places and times? Man, he was great in the kitchen. Not to mention being great in *other* rooms as well, if you know what I mean. I *definitely* miss that."

"Right, look," Charlie said, turning to Emma, holding the sharp knife up in the air. "Is there any way we can talk about something else?"

"I guess," Emma said. "Is it a problem that I'm talking about my husband? I thought you wanted to be there for me? I'm sorry to inform you that listening to someone vent is a part of being there for them."

"No, I mean, yeah," Charlie said, reaching deep into his soul to find the last bits of friendship he had left. "I was just hoping to, you know, help ease your mind a bit tonight with dinner and a good time."

"It's been hard to ease my mind lately," she admitted. "I'm going to have to break some sad news to Sophie soon and I am *really* not looking forward to it. She's going to take it so hard."

"What news is that?" Charlie asked.

"There's an event coming up, and with Eddie still missing, I don't think it will be possible to attend. It's going to break her heart."

"Oh right, that daddy daughter dance," Charlie said, not looking up from chopping vegetables.

Emma's heart sank like an elevator whose wires had snapped, her eyes open wide with fear.

"W-wait," Emma said, "How do you know about the daddy daughter dance?"

Charlie stopped mid slice, as every muscle in his body froze. *"Think fast, think fast,"* he thought.

"Y-you mentioned it to me. When we went to Sophie's recital. Remember? You told me all about it."

"No I *definitely* didn't," Emma said, slowly standing up. "I know I didn't mention it, because I couldn't even *think* about it. It broke my heart to admit he can't take his daughter to this. How could I have told *you* about it, if I haven't been able to vocalize my feelings until this *very moment*?"

Charlie, shaking and sweating, began staring at the ceiling. He knew his lie was paper thin and Emma could see right through.

"No, No," He said, his voice trembling. "I know you told me about it. How else could I know?" He laughed, shook his head and went back to slicing with that razor-sharp knife.

"Charlie," Emma said, slowly backing away from the kitchen. "How did you know about this? There's only *two* people who could have told you. Who...Who told you about that dance?"

"What do you mean?" He asked, his voice trembling with a nervous laugh. He was now sweating bullets.

"Charlie," she whispered, as tears welled up in her eyes. She took another step away from him. "What have you done? How did you know about the dance?"

Charlie's nervousness was transforming into rage. He set his palms onto the counter top, hung his head and began clenching his teeth.

"What is going on? *How* did you know?" Her voice raised as the fear inside her grew.

The rage in his body was so strong now, he couldn't say a word. He just continued breathing loudly. So loud, Emma could hear him panting like a rabid dog.

"Say something. *Anything*," Emma pleaded.

Charlie lifted his hands off the counter and slammed them back down. Vegetables flew into the air, and other food items spilled onto the floor.

"You fucking *promised* me," Charlie screamed.

"I promised you *what*?" Emma shouted back.

"Don't you remember?" Charlie shouted, turning just his head to look at Emma.

Emma's fear reached new heights which she never thought she would experience. From the look on Charlie's face, she knew she was no longer in the presence of her childhood friend. This was no friend. This was a monster, and she was deep within his grasp.

"You promised me you would fucking marry *me*? Remember? I sure fucking do!"

Charlie stood up straight and turned towards Emma, holding the chef's knife so tightly in his right hand, his knuckles were white.

"Oh my god," Emma whispered. "You're insane."

"Am I?" He said with a terrifying laugh. "*You* fucking said it. That day in my bedroom," He shouted, pointing the end of the razor-sharp knife at her.

"No I don't fucking remember!" Emma shouted. "We were kids, Charlie! How can you hold one thing I *might have* said over my head? We were fucking teenagers!"

"We were meant to be, Emma," He said matter-of-factly, with a shrug. "It's time you understood that."

Emma looked over her left shoulder as her eyes locked on the doorway leading to the basement. She looked back at Charlie, her mouth and eyes wide open. She lifted her right hand over her mouth and let out a loud gasp. As she stared at Charlie, she noticed his eyes shift towards the dining room table, and she looked to see what he had seen. Still sitting on top of the dining room table were the kitchen shears. They looked at each other again, and they were off to the races. Emma pounced at the table as Charlie rushed from the kitchen to intercept her. Emma beat him to the table, picked up the shears, pushed her body off of the table and began running. Charlie got to the table but couldn't stop his momentum. He hit the table with all of his weight, and fell face first over, landing so he was sprawled out on his chest. When he did this, all four candles toppled over, one of them to the ground, landing just underneath the low hanging linen curtains. The flame from the candle danced upwards as the curtains ignited.

Emma shoved the shears into her back pocket as she bolted towards the basement door. She grabbed the padlock and began tugging on it with all of her strength. She looked to see Charlie back on his feet, coming right at her. She turned to the front door, whipped it open, and took off running down the front steps, turning once she hit the grass towards the forest. Charlie stopped at the front door, watching as Emma ran at a full sprint into the dead of night. He looked back at the dining room curtains which were now engulfed in flames. He watched them ignite and turned to look at the basement door that was padlocked shut. He smiled to himself and stepped onto the porch. He walked down the front steps and ran towards the forest after Emma. Just then, on the dining room table, Emma's phone rang. It was Frank McKenna.

50

Emma ran through the dense trees, shrubs and muddy ground. Leaves crunched and twigs snapped under her feet with every labored step. Her breath was giving out, but she reached down into the depths of her being to continue running, and she had hoped she could run long enough she might find help. Charlie ran behind her through the forest, picking up his pace as he made his way through thick tree stumps and brush, knowing sooner than later, Emma would hit the deep ravine that cut through the trees. She continued running as she was more terrified now than she had ever been. Soon, she noticed something illuminated by the moonlight cutting through the forest. A drop off was ahead of her and she dug her feet deep into the wet soil, stopping herself before she ran off the cliff to the rocky riverbed below. She stood, looking down at the sharp rocks and running water as options raced through her head. She looked to her right, to her left, but didn't see a clear path out.

"It's a big drop, isn't it," Charlie shouted as he emerged from behind a tree. "Go ahead, make the jump. It'll make quite the mess, but the water should wash you away."

"Where the fuck is Eddie?" Emma shouted.

"He's safe," He said, with a devilish laugh. "For now." He slowly walked towards her with that chef's knife in hand.

"Why are you doing this?" Emma screamed, tears pouring down her face as she cried in terror. "You're supposed to be my *friend*."

"I *am* your friend, Emma. That's *why* I did this. That's why I did *all* of this," He said proudly. "I had followed you both for weeks, learning your routines, learning your lives so I could remove Eddie from this soiled picture of *your* life, and I could get you *back*."

"Get me back?" She asked. "I was never yours. I was never going to *be* yours."

"Be that as it may," Charlie said, scratching underneath his chin with the pointy end of the large knife, moonlight shimmering off the blade. "Eddie will be gone soon. But you've still got me, Emma. I'm right here."

"I'm married to Eddie," She screamed with all her might. "I was never going to marry you. I never want anything to do with you ever again, you fucking monster!"

"*Monster*?" He said with a laugh. "You have no idea what kind of monster I can be. Emma, we are *just* getting started."

"What the *fuck* does that mean?" She screamed.

Emma looked over Charlie's head, noticing in the distance, the sky glowed a bright yellow and orange as flames swallowed Charlie's house. Flames and smoke filled the night sky, as ash rained down.

"Ah," Charlie said, with a loud exaggerated sniff of the air. "Do you smell that? Doesn't it smell great?"

"Smell what?" She asked, as she slowly began stepping to her left, with hopes of running past Charlie. She knew she had to take a chance. "Your piece of shit house burning down?"

"Not the house," He said with a laugh. "That smell is Eddie and Angus as they burn alive. You see, they're chained in the basement. They're both in there *right now*. I assume they're probably smelling the smoke themselves. And soon, it's going to get *real hot* in there."

Emma covered her mouth with both of her hands, and without thinking took off in a full sprint towards the burning home. Charlie reached out with both arms, grabbing her and pulling her towards him as they both fell to the muddy ground.

"No, No!" She screamed as she fought with Charlie. "Fuck you, let me go! Eddie! *Eddie! No!*" She continued to scream until her voice cracked.

Charlie wrestled her to the ground, twisted her body, pushing her from behind with enough force to slam her face into the mud. He knelt down behind her, grabbed her by the hair pulling her head back and knocking her onto all fours as he straddled her from behind. He held on to her hair tightly and wrapped his other hand under her chin, forcing her to look up at the flames.

"Look at it," He grunted. "Quit fighting me. We can watch Eddie burn *together*. And when he's gone, we can start our lives, a *new* life. You, me and Sophie. Doesn't that sound great? It's what we've always wanted. I've lived my entire life haunted by the stench of your rotting promises. They've crushed me, sent me spiraling out of control. It's OK, kiddo. Shush, just calm down. When the unforgiving sun peaks through the burned cracks of that house, he will be gone. Transformed to nothing more than dust. A memory we can *both* erase. And you and I can disappear together and leave these cursed lives we've been stuck with behind. Isn't it just beautiful? As the flames grow, the smoke of Eddie's burning body will cleanse us both. Look at it. Look at it!"

They could hear sirens screaming towards the house as it became engulfed in flames which danced high into the night sky. Many emergency vehicles were storming the location, but Charlie didn't care. It didn't stop him. Emma grabbed his hand that was around her throat, pulling it as much as she could, but it was no use. He was too strong, and she was in a position which made it impossible to get any leverage. She was outmatched. He pulled her hair even tighter, tearing strands out as he went. Just then, she remembered something. With her left hand she reached behind her body as far as her shoulder would allow. She pushed and pushed until the muscles in her left shoulder felt like they would snap. Finally, she was able to reach the kitchen shears she had in her back pocket. She held them and swung upwards over her head with her left hand, but Charlie saw the feeble attempt coming and grabbed her by the wrist. Emma dropped her right hand deep into the wet soil for any small amount of leverage she could find and continued pushing the shears against all of Charlie's strength.

"It's no fucking use," Charlie shouted. "Stop *fighting* me!"

She looked down at her right hand and glanced back at the shears she held on to tightly in her left. Without thinking, Emma let out a loud scream that echoed throughout the forest. She let go of the kitchen shears and they began their slow descent to the wet dirt. In a last chance moment, with all her strength, she twisted her right shoulder and swung her body underneath Charlie. She then lifted her right hand out of the mud and swung it upwards, catching the shears in her right palm. As she fell to her back, in one quick motion she thrust them upwards stabbing Charlie in the left eye, leaving the scissors protruding from his skull. He recoiled, jumped to his feet and stumbled from the pain as he took a few large, labored steps backwards. Both of his hands reached for his left eye, when he felt the shears pointing out of his face, stuck deeply into his eye socket.

"You fucking bitch!" He screamed, trembling and shaking in horrific pain. "I will fucking *kill you*!"

Charlie wrapped his hands around the end of the shears and ripped them slowly from his eye socket. Blood began shooting out of the wound, covering his face as it poured. He screamed and shouted from the horrific pain, but as a man possessed, it wasn't enough to stop him.

"Nothing lasts forever, Emma. Not even us. No, nothing but death," He said through whimpers, his left hand holding his eye socket, as blood trickled through his fingers. "You leave me no choice. I'm going to kill us *both*. Then, in death, we can be together forever. And if that doesn't work, at least you won't exist. And you can't haunt me any longer."

"Bring it on, you mother fucker," she shouted, breathing so deep that her chest puffed.

He dug his feet into the dirt, and charged directly at Emma, but this time she was ready for him and she jumped into the air, landing a kick directly to his chest. As he stumbled backwards, Emma landed in a superhero-style power stance that would make Scarlett Johansson proud. Her face was washed over by a mask of pure rage. Next to her right hand sat a thick branch, heavy and dense. She wrapped both of her hands around it, hoisted it up with a loud grunt, spun around and tossed it at Charlie with everything she had. The branch connected with his chest landing a heavy blow. The force of the trunk was enough to make him lose his footing and stumble backwards, so much so he had to dig his heèls deep into the ground to not fall into the ravine. He cowered over, pressing his open, trembling palms into his knees as blood continued to pour down his face, soaking his shirt in crimson liquid. He slowly lifted his head to look towards Emma, his mouth wide open.

"Emma," Charlie whispered. "You can't stop this. He's gone. I'm all you have left."

"Then I would rather die alone," she grunted.

She took off into a full sprint, jumped into the air and landed one last blow to Charlie's head with both of her feet. As she fell to the cold, wet ground, Charlie dropped into the ravine, falling backwards to the sharp rocks below. Emma stood, gathered herself and rushed to the edge. She leaned over to see Charlie's lifeless body, bloody and mangled, on the rocks below, as a steady stream of water flowed over him. She spit off of the cliff in his direction before looking over her right shoulder at the flames. She shot off like a bolt of lightning towards the house.

51

As Emma emerged from the forest, she was met by the entire cavalry of police officers and fire rescue. Frank McKenna noticed her, covered head to toe in dirt and drenched in blood and took off running towards her.

"Emma, over here!" He shouted.

He opened his outstretched arms as she crashed into his chest. He pulled her in and held her tightly. She was inconsolable and couldn't get any words out.

"Where is he?" He asked. "Where's Charlie?"

"No, no, no," Emma shouted. She then pointed at the house as the flames raged.

"Eddie and Angus are in there!" She finally shouted. "They're in the basement!"

"Oh *fuck!*" Frank screamed. "Someone take her, now!"

He turned, ran a couple of steps and began waving down the firemen who had arrived on scene.

"We've got two people in there! In the basement! One of them is Detective Pratt, the other is Eddie VanSant!"

The fire and rescue team began throwing their gear on, but weren't quick enough. Frank looked at the house, and without a second thought he ran towards the front door. As he ran, he ripped his jacket off and wrapped it over his face. In no time, he was up those front steps and kicked in the front door. A group of six firemen began running towards the home after him, but he had already rushed inside. The fire truck out front began dousing the house with water, as the flames stretched stories high. A paramedic ran to Emma and wrapped her in a blanket, pulling her away from the fire. As they moved, she screamed out, fighting him every step of the way. She couldn't stand outside and watch as her husband burned to death inside Charlie's house of horror and madness.

"Let me go!" She screamed. "Please! My husband is inside!"

The paramedic fought with Emma and finally got her to the street, forcing her to sit down in the back of an ambulance. She held the blanket tightly around her body as the roof of the home started to collapse, shooting thick embers high up into the sky that began raining down.

"Holy shit!" A firefighter screamed from down the road. "Look at that! Go, go! Get them!"

A group of firefighters in protective gear ran towards the front door of the house as Frank emerged, his suit had been completely burned off of his body. In his arms, he had Eddie, and he continued to drag him from under his arms out of the house and onto the front lawn. Behind him, a firefighter rushed out, arm in arm with Angus. The fire crew ran to the porch and snatched up Eddie, Frank and Angus, and moved them away from the flames. Just then, a horrible sound filled the air. The entire wood structure of the house finally collapsed into itself. As the firefighters, Frank, Angus and Eddie raced to safety, the flames swallowed the home as it collapsed into a giant pile of flaming rubble, sending a plume of smoke, ash and glowing embers high into the night sky. Emma jumped up from out of the ambulance as she saw Eddie lying on the front lawn, almost lifeless and barely moving.

"Eddie!" She shouted as she tried to run to him.

"It isn't safe," The paramedic shouted, holding her by the shoulder. "Let us take it from here!"

Paramedics rushed to the yard and promptly lifted Eddie, Angus and Frank each onto their own stretchers. Emma stood by the ambulance as she watched in slow motion. After everything, Eddie was alive and coming right towards her. When the stretcher reached Emma, Eddie turned his head, smiled and outstretched his left hand.

"Hey, sweetheart," He said lightly. "I missed you."

Emma continued crying and held his hand with both of hers tighter than she had ever held anything in her life. She pulled his hand to her mouth and began kissing it over and over.

"I didn't think I would ever see you again," she said through tears.

"I wasn't going anywhere. I love you," he said.

"Come on, we need to get you both to the hospital," Another paramedic told Emma.

They pushed Eddie's stretcher into the back of an ambulance and Emma climbed in with him. Just then she looked out and saw Angus was being loaded into a separate ambulance.

"Can you give me one second?" Emma asked.

"Sure," The paramedic said. "But make it quick, we need to get him in for treatment."

Emma jumped out of the ambulance, pulled the blanket tightly around her body and walked to Angus as he laid out in the chilly, evening air.

"Are you going to be OK, Detective?" She asked.

"Oh, yeah," He said, hiding the pain he was in.

"Thank you, Angus," she said, grabbing his hand and squeezing it.

"I'm just glad Eddie and Frank are OK. And of course, you as well," he said with a smile.

"Only thanks to you," Emma said, tears rolling down her cheeks.

"Where's Charlie?" Angus whispered.

"Send the cops through the trees to the cliff. They'll find him at the bottom of the ravine."

"Is he alive?"

"No," Emma said.

Angus squeezed her hand tight, shut his eyes and smiled. A single tear raced down his left cheek. But he wasn't sad. He was ecstatic.

"Take care of that guy, alright? He's one of the good ones."

"He is," she smiled back. "Thank you. For everything."

Emma let go of Angus's hand and walked back to the ambulance to Eddie. She climbed in, sat on the bench and grabbed his right hand with both of hers and pulled it to her chest. A paramedic walked behind, slammed the doors and smacked the back two times, and with the lights flashing the ambulance pulled away from the burning house. Emma stared out the back window and watched as the crumbled mess of rubble that was once Charlie's torture chamber was reduced to nothing more than ash.

Soon, a team of police officers made their way through the dense forest towards the ravine. Flashlight beams shot every which way through the branches until they reached the cliff.

"She said he should be right down here," One officer shouted.

The officers crowded around each other at the edge of the cliff, shining their lights down to the bottom to find Charlie's body was gone.

"Where is he?" One officer asked.

"I don't know, I can't see anything," Another responded.

"Didn't she say he was right here?" The first officer asked.

"Yes, but I don't see him," The officer replied.

"Call it in right away. We need to find this son of a bitch before he gets too far," The first officer ordered.

52

Emma knocked three times on the open hospital room door, looking in at Frank as he laid in his bed.

"Hey, are you alive in there?".

"Barely," Frank said as he tried to sit up.

"No, don't move. You're in pain," she urged.

She walked across the hospital room, grabbed a chair and pulled it to the side of the bed.

"I want to thank you," she said, reaching out to grab his right hand.

"You don't have to thank me," He said. "Just doing my job."

"If it wasn't for you, Eddie and Angus both may have died in that fire. You're our hero," she said.

Frank smiled at her and squeezed her hand.

"I'm glad everyone is going to be OK," he said. "Is Charlie—" He stopped himself.

"Dead," she said matter-of-factly.

"Good," He said.

"So, when do you get out of here?" She asked. "Are you going to be OK, all things considered?"

"A few scrapes and a few burns," He said. "Nothing that a little bed rest and a few rounds of golf won't heal," He smiled up at her. "How's Eddie?"

"Resting," she said, letting out a deep sigh. "That monster beat him pretty badly, and he hasn't eaten or drank much of anything for weeks. So he is going to stay here until he gets his strength back."

"You should go home, get some rest. You've been through a lot yourself," He urged.

"No," she said, shaking her head and smiling. "I'm going to stay with him. Hell, I don't think I can let him out of my sight ever again."

They both shared a laugh. It felt good to laugh. She squeezed Frank's hand again before standing up.

"You take care of yourself," she said, "I'll come check on you from time to time. We won't be going home anytime soon. Besides, I think we're linked for life."

"Sounds good," Frank said. "You take care of yourself and that guy of yours."

"Thank you, Frank," she said. "Dinner at our place when you're all healed up. It will be nice to see you and Angus on good terms for a change and put all of this behind us. We owe you both so much."

"No. You owe us nothing," He said, shaking his head. "But I *will* take you up on dinner."

"You got it," she said smiling.

She turned and walked to the door, turning back before she exited.

"Get well soon, Frank," she said with a smile. "Thank you."

53

One Year Later.

Angus pulled up to the VanSant home with his wife and two kids in the car and parked against the curb. They each got out, and in his wife's hands she held a large plastic bowl with tin foil over the top.

"You got the potato salad?" Angus asked.

"Sure do," His wife Laura said. "Are you sure this is enough to bring for a BBQ?"

"That's all Emma asked for," He confirmed. "I offered more, but who am I to argue with the woman of the house?"

"Smart man," she said.

Angus, Laura and their children Junior and Karen marched up the concrete walkway, knocked, and Eddie promptly opened the front door.

"Come on in, everyone," Eddie shouted.

"Good to see you, Eddie," Angus said, extending his hand for a hand shake.

"Laura, thank you for coming," Eddie said, wrapping his right arm around her shoulders for a gentle hug. "Oh is this for us?"

"My famous potato salad. I hope it's enough for everyone."

"It's perfect, thank you," Eddie said.

"Where's that amazing wife of yours?" Angus asked.

"She'll be out soon. She moves a little slower these days," Eddie said with a joking roll of the eyes.

"No rush," Angus said. "We've got all the time in the world."

Eddie led the way through the kitchen and out to the back yard. The VanSant backyard was as beautiful as the rest of the home. Lush landscaping, perfectly manicured green grass with a picnic table positioned close to the house and a large umbrella shooting up from the middle stretching into the sky. The table was set up with all the picnic food you could imagine - Bowls of different types of potato chips, fresh green salad, bowls of fresh fruit, appetizers from the grill including bacon wrapped grilled jalapeno poppers, different dips and of course, the Pratt family potato salad. Sitting at the table was Frank. next to him sat his wife, Lillian. Lillian, in her mid 40s, had curly dark brown hair and was tall and slender. She wore a beautiful sundress which paired perfectly with Frank's bright red floral Hawaiian shirt.

"I should have known if food was involved, you'd be here early," Angus remarked.

"You know me too well," Frank said, standing up and shaking his hand. "Good to see you Laura."

"Oh Frank," she said, followed by a friendly hug.

Lillian gave Angus a hug, then one to Laura.

"Cheese burgers for everyone?" Eddie shouted, standing by the hot grill.

"Double cheese for me," Angus said.

"Double cheese, hun?" Laura asked.

"OK, OK," Angus caved. "Make it a single."

"Good man," Eddie said, clicking a pair of tongs in his direction.

Emma emerged from the back door wearing a beautiful yellow sundress stretching all the way to her feet printed with different Hawaiian flowers and thin straps gracing her shoulders. The midsection of the sundress stretched outward showing Emma was indeed pregnant with her and Eddie's second child.

"Hello, everyone," Emma said loudly with a boisterous wave.

Everyone shouted out different greetings at their hostess as she walked into the sunshine. She walked over to Eddie and gave him a long kiss. She then said hello and received a deep, long hug from each guest.

"How are you feeling?" Angus asked.

"Feeling good," she said happily with a smile. "The second time around so far isn't as bad. I don't know how it was for other mothers. But I feel good."

"Great to hear," Laura chimed in. "Junior was a nightmare pregnancy for me."

"He still can be a nightmare," Angus said under his breath.

"Oh you," Laura said. "Do you want to know if it will be a boy or girl? Or do you want to be surprised?"

"Well," Emma said, looking at Eddie with a nervous smile. "We already know. We just told Sophie last night that she is going to have a little brother."

Everyone joined together with a nice hoot and holler at the news of a little boy joining the VanSant family.

"Have you picked any names yet?" Lillian asked.

"Do you want to tell them, honey?" Emma asked Eddie.

"I would *love* to," Eddie obliged. "We were thinking," Eddie paused for effect.

"Well don't keep us waiting all day, Edward," Angus shouted.

"Soon you will meet Angus Franklin VanSant," Eddie said. "Named after two of our own, personal heroes."

The entire group applauded, as Angus and Frank stood up from the picnic table to shake Eddie's hand and they both gave Emma a hug and a kiss on the cheek.

"It's truly an honor," Angus said.

"Sure is," Frank agreed. "Although. Frank as the *first* name, not a bad choice."

"Don't you start," Emma said, as everyone joined together for a laugh.

54

Hannah Reed, a beautiful woman in her late 20s with olive skin, long flowing black hair and big brown eyes, walked down the sidewalk in a hipster neighborhood of Denver, Colorado. The street was lined by small pizza joints, donut shops, coffee shops and more craft beer bars than one could ever visit. She wore a black zip up hooded sweatshirt, a pair of short, yellow, cloth shorts and a pair of yellow flip-flops matching perfectly. Like most people in this neighborhood, she walked with her head buried into her cell phone, checking various apps for the latest pictures that had been posted online. It was early Wednesday morning, just a little after 9:00am and like most mornings, Hannah stopped into her favorite locally owned coffee bar to get an iced coffee and a muffin.

Sitting on the corner of the street was the Lazy Bean Coffee Collective. Black and white checkerboard tiles stretched from the floor up the walls to the ceiling. Edison style bulbs were strung corner to corner, and the ceiling was painted matte black. Perfectly curated plants hung over the walls, and against the furthest wall to the right was gold neon signage in cursive font that read "Drink Coffee Every Day". The front of the building was equipped with a roll up set of windows, opening the shop to the outside world for gorgeous natural light and a neighborhood breeze. Black and gold tables lined the wall under the neon sign, and a wooden bar stretched the front of the space that was left open from the roll up doors.

Hannah entered, her face still buried in her phone as she stood in a line. The man who was at the front of the line finished his order, and immediately stepped to the right of the counter. As the line moved forward, Hannah glanced up, took a step forward, and went back to her phone. She then did a double take and stared intently at the man who had just ordered. She stared for a second, cocked her head to one side, squinted her eyes, and was overtaken by happiness.

"Charles?" She asked. "Is that *you*?"

The man slowly turned his head to his left, looking over his shoulder at Hannah. The man wore slim fit black jeans with a black bomber jacket wrapping his body, showing off a plain white shirt. Around his neck was a thin gold chain, with a man's gold wedding band hanging down to the middle of his chest. His hair was slicked back neatly, and he wore a black patch over his left eye. He stared back at Hannah for a second with a concerned, almost angry look on his face. That look turned from hatred to friendly as his one, good, visible eye opened wide and he shot Hannah a big, stupid, yet friendly smile.

"Hannah," He shouted back to her with a big, dumb grin. "What are *you* doing here?"

The End. For Now.

ACKNOWLEDGEMENTS

Thank You to Tabitha for always supporting whatever wild idea I may come up with and always being my number one fan, regardless of how outlandish those ideas may be. Thanks for always pushing me to keep working no matter how beat down I may feel. Thank You to Wilma, Rufus and Sidney for being the sweetest support babies that have ever graced this planet. Thank You to my Mom, Lohn, Dad and Janien for always being there for me, no matter how hard I have made it at times. Same goes for Audra, Chet, Rebekah, Delilah and Ephraim. Thank You for being you, and for loving me for me, always.

Thank you to my Beer Night in San Diego crew Thomas, Mike and Noah for always having my back like I promise I will always have yours. Thank you to the Burgeon Beer crew for keeping me "hydrated" and for the years of support. Thanks to Rex Pickett, Chris DeMakes, Miguel Chen and Ryan Woldt for years of inspiration and their time in reviewing this book early. It means the world to me.

A huge Thank You and High Fives to - The tremendous, lifelong friendship of JulieAnne, Matthew and Stormy. The Scoville Family, the Zirpolo Family, the Van Sickles, The Servis and Gelsomino families, Raylee for the laughs and believing in me and everyone who has listened to and supported BNISD, I owe each of you a beer. Duddy, Steve, Bill and (evil) Matt for being true brothers through it all. Kevin Smith for more inspiration than he will ever know. And to all friends and family that believed in, supported or at least tolerated me over the years. Thank You from the bottom of my heart. Also, The Golden State Warriors and San Diego Padres. Get those rings.

Last but certainly not least, Thank You to Reagan and the Black Rose Family for taking a chance on an unknown writer and truly, 100% truly, making his dream a reality. I will forever be indebted to your trust and confidence. And to anyone who bought, found, borrowed and read this book. Thank You, Thank You, THANK YOU. You have contributed, knowingly or not, in making a dream come true. And for that, I will be forever thankful.

To anyone and everyone out there with a dream - Get out and make it happen. Don't ever let anyone tell you what you can or can not do. If you have a dream, make it happen. Do the work and make that dream a reality. The only one stopping you, is you. I know this, because I was once the same way. Let nothing stand in your way. The book you are currently holding in your hands is proof that dreams can come true. Now, go make yours happen.

If you read this story - Thank You. Much Love, Always.

ABOUT THE AUTHOR

Cody James Thompson is a writer from San Diego, California. He has been writing for many years and is finally diving into the world of novels and storytelling. Previously, he wrote as a columnist with his work featured in *San Diego CityBeat*, *San Diego Weekly Reader*, *The Westcoaster Magazine*, *San Diego Downtown News* and he was the staff columnist for *San Diego Uptown News* writing about the beverage industry. With storytelling, he focuses mainly on thriller inspired work. When he is not writing or reading he spends time with his wife and their two pit bulls, cheers on his Golden State Warriors and San Diego Padres and can be found writing, producing and hosting the first and longest running beer podcast in San Diego - Beer Night in San Diego.

NOTE FROM THE AUTHOR

Word-of-mouth is crucial for any author to succeed. If you enjoyed *Bone Saw Serenade*, please leave a review online—anywhere you are able. Even if it's just a sentence or two. It would make all the difference and would be very much appreciated.

Thanks!
Cody J. Thompson

We hope you enjoyed reading this title from:

BLACK ROSE
writing™

www.blackrosewriting.com

Subscribe to our mailing list – *The Rosevine* – and receive **FREE** books, daily deals, and stay current with news about upcoming releases and our hottest authors.
Scan the QR code below to sign up.

Already a subscriber? Please accept a sincere thank you for being a fan of Black Rose Writing authors.

View other Black Rose Writing titles at
www.blackrosewriting.com/books and use promo code
PRINT to receive a **20% discount** when purchasing.

CPSIA information can be obtained
at www.ICGtesting.com
Printed in the USA
LVHW091407261022
731628LV00016B/734

9 781685 130541